PRAISE FOR LAIRD BARRON

THE IMAGO SEQUENCE AND OTHER STORIES:
"[Barron's] successfully transposed the oddly yoked pleasure and dread of Lovecraft's work to a modern and more complex idiom with skillful craftsmanship, intelligence, and a fertile, detailed imagination."
— William Mingin, *Strange Horizons*

"When a horror story really works for me, I throw the book against the wall with a shriek and hide behind the sofa. Then, trembling, and in tears I crawl across the floor in supplication and pick up where I left off. Laird Barron does this to me."
—Christopher Hsiang, *io9.com*

OCCULTATION AND OTHER STORIES:
"With sharp prose and wise, original stories, Barron has repeatedly proven himself one of the strongest voices in the field. This collection is a must read."
—Sarah Langan, author of *Audrey's Door* and *The Keeper*

"Laird Barron is one of those writers who makes other writers want to break their pencils. I'm serious. His work is that good. Worse than that, he's an original (damn him!), and the finest writer to join the ranks of the dark fantastic in a long, long time."
—Norman Partridge, author of *Dark Harvest* and *Lesser Demons*

"For my money, Laird Barron is far and away the best of the new generation of horror writers."
—Michael Shea, World Fantasy Award-winning author of *Polyphemus*

"…one senses that he has the potential to change the expectations of the next generation of readers by elevating the genre to a new standard of excellence."
—Lucius Shepard, author of *Trujillo*

"If you think there aren't any new Richard Mathesons or Harlan Ellisons out there, you need to read Laird Barron."
—Stewart O'Nan, bestselling author of *A Prayer for the Dying*

"Another brilliant engagement with weird fiction from a writer fast becoming a modern master."
—Jeff VanderMeer, author of *Annihilation* and *Finch*

THE CRONING:
"Powerfully written and imaginative, I literally couldn't put it down!"
—Joseph S. Pulver, Sr., author of *The Orphan Palace*

"Already a master of the horror short story, he shows himself equally skilled at novel-length work."
—*Publishers Weekly*, starred review

"*The Croning* deserves a place in the bookcase next to T.E.D. Klein's *The Ceremonies*, Ira Levin's *Rosemary's Baby* and Fritz Leiber's *Our Lady Of Darkness* and that is the highest recommendation that I can give."
—*CrowsNBones.com*

THE BEAUTIFUL THING THAT AWAITS US ALL:
"Tremendous ... Particularly affecting and effective is the constant sense of an occult force that swells behind the action of the stories."
—Adam Nevill, author of *The Ritual*

"Relentlessly readable, highly atmospheric, sharply and often arrestingly written—Barron's prose style resembles, by turns, a high-flown Jim Thompson mixed with a pulp Barry Hannah."
—*Slate*

"The scariest writer on the planet has to be Laird Barron."
—Paul Goat Allen, *The Barnes & Noble Book Blog*

"Laird Barron has, in a remarkably short period of time, emerged as one of the leading writers of contemporary weird fiction."
—S. T. Joshi

"You could say these stories are what happens when Jack London and Zane Grey go drinking with William Hope Hodgson and Algernon Blackwood. But what they really are is Laird Barron, and they are terrifying and awe-inspiring. If you haven't yet tried his work, this is a great place to start."
—Brian Keene, author of *The Rising*

OCCULTATION

Other books by Laird Barron:

The Imago Sequence and Other Stories
The Light is the Darkness
The Croning
The Beautiful Thing That Awaits Us All

OCCULTATION

AND OTHER STORIES

LAIRD BARRON

NIGHT SHADE BOOKS
New York

"The Forest," first published in *Inferno: New Tales of Terror and the Supernatural,* edited by Ellen Datlow, Tor Books, 2007.
"Occultation," first published as "The Occultation" in *Clockwork Phoenix: Tales of Beauty and Strangeness,* edited by Mike Allen, Norilana Books, 2008.
"The Lagerstätte," first published in *The Del Rey Book of Science Fiction and Fantasy,* edited by Ellen Datlow, Del Rey Books, 2008.
"Mysterium Tremendum" is original to this volume.
"Catch Hell," first published in *Lovecraft Unbound,* edited by Ellen Datlow, Dark Horse Comics, 2009.
"Strappado," first published in *Poe: 19 New Tales Inspired by Edgar Allan Poe,* Solaris Books, 2009.
"The Broadsword," first published in *Black Wings: New Tales of Lovecraftian Horror,* edited by S. T. Joshi, PS Publishing, 2010.
"--30--" is original to this volume.
"Six Six Six" is original to this volume.

Night Shade books may be purchased in bulk at special discounts for sales promotion, corporate gifts, fund-raising, or educational purposes. Special editions can also be created to specifications. For details, contact the Special Sales Department, Night Shade Books, 307 West 36th Street, 11th Floor, New York, NY 10018 or info@skyhorsepublishing.com.

Night Shade Books® is a registered trademark of Skyhorse Publishing, Inc. ®, a Delaware corporation.

Visit our website at www.nightshadebooks.com.

10 9 8 7 6

Library of Congress Cataloging-in-Publication Data is available on file.

Cover art by Matthew Jaffe
Cover design by Claudia Noble
Interior layout and design by Ross E. Lockhart

ISBN: 978-1-59780-514-8

Printed in the United States of America

Acknowledgments:
My agents, Brendan Deneen and Colleen Lindsay.

Barbara Baar; Andrew Migliore; JD Busch; Dexter Morgan; Jeff Ford; Charles Tan; Chris Perridas; Tom Tyson; John, Fiona, and David Langan; Stewart O'Nan; Paul Witcover; Terry Weyna; John Pelan; Sarah Langan; Gavin Grant; Wilum Pugmire; Richard Gavin; Ian Rogers; Steve Berman; Simon Strantzas; Marc Laidlaw; Norm Partridge; Lee Thomas; Gene O'Neill; Livia Llewellyn; Nick Kaufmann; Nick Gevers; Paul Tremblay; Rick Bowes; Jack Haringa; John Skipp; Cody Goodfellow; Kelly Link; Lucius Shepard; Elizabeth Hand; ST Joshi; Jerad Walters; Nick Mamatas; David Hartwell and Kathryn Cramer; Mike Allen; Vera Nazarian; Peter Crowther; Ann VanderMeer; Jeff VanderMeer; Gordon Van Gelder; Ellen Datlow.

Thank you to my stalwart companions Athena, Horatio, Ulysses, and Persephone: ever loyal, ever true.

Thanks to the readers: you're what it's all about.

Thank you to Jeremy Lassen, Jason Williams, John Joseph Adams, Ross Lockhart, Marty Halpern, Claudia Noble, Matthew Jaffe, and all the gang at Night Shade Books.

Special thanks to Michael and Linda Shea, two of the kindest hearts I know.

For Jody Rose. A rock in the storm

CONTENTS

Introduction by Michael Shea............. 1

The Forest 5

Occultation 33

The Lagerstätte 45

Mysterium Tremendum 73

Catch Hell 121

Strappado 149

The Broadsword 163

--30-- 197

Six Six Six 231

INTRODUCTION BY MICHAEL SHEA

Laird Barron's carnivorous cosmos… Or perhaps it's more a *conspiracy* his cosmos draws you into than a digesting maw.

And rather than being absorbed as a nutrient, you may be absorbed into an older and more potent Form—your limbs and neck may grow rubbery and rather more elongate, and your new tree-toad fingers might enable you to crawl across ceilings, thence to peer down on old, still-mortal friends and acquaintances, studying them from many angles with your new stalked eyes.

Barron's cosmos is an omni-morph that can dragoon you whenever/wherever it wants into its swarming, pullulating fabric. This, of course, is a simple Axiom of the reality we all share, every second of our lives, with our Universe: in that great Starry Engine, we all end as mulch, and then, as Other Things….

But, wonderfully, this radiant, hair-raising Truth is the very engine of Barron's imagination.

As often with craftsmen who are blazing the path of a new form, his imagery flows like music. (Like Jack Vance's, his prose too is a pumpin' Baroque, though of a more democratic shade.) And what a pleasure it is, the easily unspooling sensory mosaic of Barron's prose! It limns and kindles equally his characters' thoughts in their stream, and the stream of their actions evoked to our eyes. He moves ghostly from the innards of his characters out into their cosmoi, with a largesse of language where there's yet not a single wasted syllable.

Here's Partridge, automotive passenger in the opening scene of "The Forest." To his dreaming mind's eye, a phantasmic woman, who was just now offering Partridge a large tarantula,

"…offered him a black phone. The woman said 'Come say

goodbye and good luck! Come quick!' Except the woman did not speak. Toshi's breathless voice bled through the receiver. The woman in the cold white mask brightened then dimmed like a dying coal or a piece of metal coiling into itself.

Partridge opened his eyes and rested his brow against window glass. He was alone with the driver. The bus trawled through a night forest. Black trees dripped with fog. The narrow black road crumbled from decades of neglect. Sometimes poor houses and fences stood among the weeds and the ferns and mutely suggested many more were lost in the dark…."

Beautiful! What a sure touch! And we may seize entirely at random amidst Barron's pages, and display this faceted fullness in every paragraph.

Barron's verbal surfaces are like anaconda-skins. Jeweled they are, with bright crystals of sense and sensation, and his sinuous narrative line slides a smooth constrictor's grip around the rapt reader's sensibilities.

Meanwhile, on the macro level of his stories' structures, Barron weaves his fabric by means of a kind of assonance or resonance, a powerfully reverberant imagery.

For instance, we enter "The Lagerstätte" through the mind of a suicidal woman newly widowed and orphaned of her child. Her errant dreams, cancered with loss, lead her into a kind of Necro-Mundus that is haunted, even paved with the self-slain. We move with her through death after death of her own, and also—via her empathic heart—through the death-after-death of her suicidal encounter-group friends—all dying and dying with a dying fall. It's a metaphysical assonance, if you will, the echo of an archetypal human fate, image after image of self-slaughter in surreal reverberation. The Jackpot of Barron's work—and every single story of his I've read *is* a jackpot—is the durably architected visions he constructs. In this tale he has *built* before our eyes a Lagerstätte. A kind of Burgess Shale wherein self-killed women agelessly sink or hurtle to their deaths, stratum on eon-sunk stratum of their dying falls….

This reverberatory technique is wonderfully various: the approaching horror strikes a note now here, now there—a face, an utterance, a slant of light, a half-glimpsed shape evoking a half-obliterated memory…. Barron's polyhedral style is perfect for *haunting* places. The narrative eye, as jeweled as a bug's, draws utterance from everything, both above and below. In "The Broadsword," our Protag's very Past becomes transformed. Oviposited in his youth by the Other-Worldly, his Age is gravid with those Aliens' growth. Half of his Past is revised before his staring eyes and quaking heart, half his years respooled onto a transcosmic spindle of alien consciousness.

This is a marvelous Haunted House story without any build-up or ground-laying. We sip Barron's sentences, and the apparitions come prickling up right through our scalps. The Protag's Alien-infested Past twines its luridly beautiful branchings through the big old hulk of the Hotel Broadsword, and Other Worlds hiss and mutter at the tenants from its closets and corners and ceilings, and finally....

That big old hotel is a kind of epitome of what every one of these stories, in its essence, does. Our earthly architecture is full of coigns and corners, crevices and crevasses, where the Cosmos peeks through. Consider our title story, "Occultation." Our Protags, back in their desert motel after partying in a roadside bar, have done some fucking, and now lie smoking cigarettes. And up in one corner of the ceiling, notice…is it a stain, or a shadow, or a shape…? Hypotheses lead to divagations… lead to more haunting hypotheses… lead to fear, and at length, to an actual attempt to turn on the light… which doesn't work. Though a desert tortoise the size of an automobile appears outside soon after, it is not that which brings… death?

Or consider "Strappado," where a small swarm of sophisticated Internationals—on plump expense accounts of various provenance—get whispered word of a creative presence in the neighborhood (a slummish exurb not far downcoast from Mumbai)—a Name for creative anarchy, a Dark Genius, *avant de l'avant-garde.* The rumor of his doings carries a cachet of thrilling scandal, and now these chance-met lucky few can be in his next film.... Barrels of bones figure in our denouement and, for the living, nightmare metamorphoses of their former selves.

Simply put, the Universe aggressively surrounds Barron's characters. They may be touring or picnicking or camping or fucking or just fucking around…whatever their fears and their lusts and their searching, *all* their energies are like little wriggling lures to the Benthic, the *Hadal* giants hanging near them on every side.

But understand. This *Occultation*, this ground-breaking book, is not a feast of mere annihilations. These fates are—every one of them—*Transformations.* And to be transformed, to be Remade, is not a passive exercise. It is an excruciating eclosion, a branching, fracturing emergence into a much bigger, hungrier universe. I think only Laird Barron could convincingly create a scene in which his Protag porks Satan Himself, grows gravid with, and then delivers to our staring eyes *the seething offspring of that unholy coitus.*

I won't even glance at the other wonders collected in *Occultation.* If you haven't heard me yet, you won't. The best way to sum up this fresh, abounding talent is to note that Barron has that key spark of the greatest horrific writers—a truly metaphysical heart. He has knelt in the Chapel where we all worship, or fail to—has knelt in the Chapel, and truly *heard* the echoes of its vastness....

—Michael Shea, author of
The Autopsy & Other Tales, September 2009

THE FOREST

After the drive had grown long and monotonous, Partridge shut his eyes and the woman was waiting. She wore a cold white mask similar to the mask Bengali woodcutters donned when they ventured into the mangrove forests along the coast. The tigers of the forest were stealthy. The tigers hated to be watched; they preferred to sneak up on prey from behind, so natives wore the masks on the backs of their heads as they gathered wood. Sometimes this kept the tigers from dragging them away.

The woman in the cold white mask reached into a wooden box. She lifted a tarantula from the box and held it to her breast like a black carnation. The contrast was as magnificent as a stark Monet if Monet had painted watercolors of emaciated patricians and their pet spiders.

Partridge sat on his high, wooden chair and whimpered in animal terror. In the daydream, he was always very young and powerless. The woman tilted her head. She came near and extended the tarantula in her long, gray hand. "For you," she said. Sometimes she carried herself more like Father and said in a voice of gravel, "Here is the end of fear." Sometimes the tarantula was a hissing cockroach of prehistoric girth, or a horned beetle. Sometimes it was a strange, dark flower. Sometimes it was an embryo uncurling to form a miniature adult human that grinned a monkey's hateful grin.

The woman offered him a black phone. The woman said, "Come say goodbye and good luck. Come quick!" Except the woman did not speak. Toshi's breathless voice bled through the receiver. The woman in the cold white mask brightened then dimmed like a dying coal or a piece of metal coiling into itself.

Partridge opened his eyes and rested his brow against window glass. He was alone with the driver. The bus trawled through a night forest. Black trees dripped with fog. The narrow black road crumbled from decades

5

of neglect. Sometimes poor houses and fences stood among the weeds and the ferns and mutely suggested many more were lost in the dark. Wilderness had arisen to reclaim its possessions.

Royals hunted in woods like these. He snapped on the overhead lamp and then opened his briefcase. *Stags, wild boar, witches. Convicts.* The briefcase was nearly empty. He had tossed in some traveler's checks, a paperback novel and his address book. No cell phone, although he left a note for his lawyer and a recorded message at Kyla's place in Malibu warning them it might be a few days, perhaps a week, that there probably was not even phone service where he was going. Carry on, carry on. He had hopped a redeye jet to Boston and once there eschewed the convenience of renting a car or hiring a chauffeur and limo. He chose instead the relative anonymity of mass transit. The appeal of traveling incognito overwhelmed his normally staid sensibilities. Here was the first adventure he had undertaken in ages. The solitude presented an opportunity to compose his thoughts—his excuses, more likely.

He'd cheerfully abandoned the usual host of unresolved items and potential brushfires that went with the territory—a possible trip to the Andes if a certain Famous Director's film got green-lighted and if the Famous Director's drunken assertion to assorted executive producers and hangers-on over barbecued ribs and flaming daiquiris at the Monarch Grille that Richard Jefferson Partridge was the only man for the job meant a blessed thing. There were several smaller opportunities, namely an L.A. documentary about a powerhouse high school basketball team that recently graced the cover of *Sports Illustrated*, unless the documentary guy, a Cannes Film Festival sweetheart, decided to try to bring down the governor of California instead, as he had threatened to do time and again, a pet crusade of his with the elections coming that fall, and then the director would surely use his politically savvy compatriot, the cinematographer from France. He'd also been approached regarding a proposed documentary about prisoners and guards at San Quentin. Certainly there were other, lesser engagements he'd lost track of, these doubtless scribbled on memo pads in his home office.

He knew he should hire a reliable secretary. He promised himself to do just that every year. It was hard. He missed Jean. She'd had a lazy eye and a droll wit; made bad coffee and kept sand-filled frogs and fake petunias on her desk. Jean left him for Universal Studios and then slammed into a reef in Maui learning to surf with her new boss. The idea of writing the want-ad, of sorting the applications and conducting the interviews and finally letting the new person, the stranger, sit where Jean had sat and handle his papers, summoned a mosquito's thrum in the bones behind Partridge's ear.

These details would surely keep despite what hysterics might come in the meanwhile. Better, much better, not to endure the buzzing and whining and the imprecations and demands that he return at once on pain of immediate career death, over a dicey relay. He had not packed a camera, either. He was on vacation. His mind would store what his eye could catch and that was all.

The light was poor. Partridge held the address book close to his face. He had scribbled the directions from margin to margin and drawn a crude map with arrows and lopsided boxes and jotted the initials of the principles: Dr. Toshi Ryoko; Dr. Howard Campbell; Beasley; and Nadine. Of course, Nadine—she snapped her fingers and here he came at a loyal trot. There were no mileposts on the road to confirm the impression that his destination was near. The weight in his belly sufficed. It was a fat stone grown from a pebble.

Partridge's instincts did not fail him. A few minutes before dawn, the forest receded and they entered Warrenburgh. Warrenburgh was a loveless hamlet of crabbed New England shop fronts and angular plank and shingle houses with tall, thin doors and oily windows. Streetlights glowed along Main Street with black gaps like a broken pearl necklace. The street itself was buckled and rutted by poorly tarred cracks that caused sections to cohere uneasily as interleaved ice floes. The sea loomed near and heavy and palpable beneath a layer of rolling gloom.

Partridge did not like what little he glimpsed of the surroundings. Long ago, his friend Toshi had resided in New Mexico and Southern California, did his best work in Polynesia and the jungles of Central America. The doctor was a creature of warmth and light. *Rolling Stone* had characterized him as "a rock star among zoologists" and as the "Jacques Cousteau of the jungle," the kind of man who hired mercenaries to guard him, performers to entertain his sun drenched villa, and filmmakers to document his exploits. This temperate landscape, so cool and provincial, so removed from Partridge's experience of all things Toshi, seemed to herald a host of unwelcome revelations.

Beasley, longstanding attendant of the eccentric researcher, waited at the station. "Rich! At least you don't look like the big asshole *Variety* says you are." He nodded soberly and scooped Partridge up for a brief hug in his powerful arms. This was like being embraced by an earth mover. Beasley had played Australian rules football for a while after he left the Army and before he came to work for Toshi. His nose was squashed and his ears were cauliflowers. He was magnetic and striking as any character actor, nonetheless. "Hey, let me get that." He set Partridge aside and grabbed the luggage the driver had dragged from the innards of the bus. He hoisted the suitcases into the bed of a '56 Ford farm truck. The truck was museum quality. It was fire engine red with a dinky American flag on the antenna.

They rumbled inland. Rusty light gradually exposed counterchange shelves of empty fields and canted telephone poles strung together with thick, dipping old-fashioned cables. Ducks pelted from a hollow in the road. The ducks spread themselves in a wavering pattern against the sky.

"Been shooting?" Partridge indicated the .20 gauge softly clattering in the rack behind their heads.

"When T isn't looking. Yeah, I roam the marshes a bit. You?"

"No."

"Yah?"

"Not in ages. Things get in the way. Life, you know?"

"Oh, well, we'll go out one day this week. Bag a mallard or two. Raise the dust."

Partridge stared at the moving scenery. Toshi was uninterested in hunting and thought it generally a waste of energy. Nadine detested the sport without reserve. He tasted brackish water, metallic from the canteen. The odor of gun oil and cigarette smoke was strong in the cab. The smell reminded him of hip waders, muddy clay banks and gnats in their biting millions among the reeds. "Okay. Thanks."

"Forget it, man."

They drove in silence until Beasley hooked left onto a dirt road that followed a ridge of brambles and oak trees. On the passenger side overgrown pastures dwindled into moiling vapors. The road was secured by a heavy iron gate with the usual complement of grimy warning signs. Beasley climbed out and unlocked the gate and swung it aside. Partridge realized that somehow this was the same ruggedly charismatic Beasley, plus a streak of gray in the beard and minus the spring-loaded tension and the whiskey musk. Beasley at peace was an enigma. Maybe he had quit the bottle for good this time around. The thought was not as comforting as it should have been. If this elemental truth—Beasley the chronic drunk, the lovable, but damaged brute—had ceased to hold, then what else lurked in the wings?

When they had begun to jounce along the washboard lane, Partridge said, "Did T get sick? Somebody—I think Frank Ledbetter—told me T had some heart problems. Angina."

"Frankie... I haven't seen him since forever. He still working for Boeing?"

"Lockheed-Martin."

"Yah? Good ol' L&M. Well, no business like war business," Beasley said. "The old boy's fine. Sure, things were in the shitter for a bit after New Guinea, but we all got over it. Water down the sluice." Again, the knowing, sidelong glance. "Don't worry so much. He misses you. Everybody does, man."

Toshi's farm was more of a compound lumped in the torso of a great, irregular field. The road terminated in a hard pack lot bordered by a sprawl of sheds and shacks, gutted chicken coops and labyrinthine hog pens fallen to ruin. The main house, a Queen Anne, dominated. The house was a full three stories of spires, gables, spinning iron weathercocks and acres of slate tiles. A monster of a house, yet somehow hunched upon itself. It was brooding and squat and low as a brick and timber mausoleum. The detached garage seemed new. So too the tarp and plastic-sheeted nurseries, the electric fence that partitioned the back forty into quadrants and the military drab shortwave antenna array crowning the A-frame barn. No private security forces were in evidence, no British mercenaries with submachine guns on shoulder slings, nor packs of sleek, bullet-headed attack dogs cruising the property. The golden age had obviously passed into twilight.

"Behold the Moorehead Estate," Beasley said as he parked by slamming the brakes so the truck skidded sideways and its tires sent up a geyser of dirt. "Howard and Toshi bought it from the county about fifteen years ago—guess the original family died out, changed their names, whatever. Been here in one form or another since 1762. The original burned to the foundation in 1886, which is roughly when the town—Orren Towne, 'bout two miles west of here—dried up and blew away. As you can see, they made some progress fixing this place since then."

Partridge whistled as he eyed the setup. "Really, ah, cozy."

There were other cars scattered in the lot: a Bentley; a Nixon-era Cadillac; an archaic Land Rover that might have done a tour in the Sahara; a couple of battered pickup trucks and an Army surplus jeep. These told Partridge a thing or two, but not enough to surmise the number of guests or the nature of Toshi's interest in them. He had spotted the tail rotor of a helicopter poking from behind the barn.

Partridge did not recognize any of the half-a-dozen grizzled men loitering near the bunkhouse. Those would be the roustabouts and the techs. The men passed around steaming thermoses of coffee. They pretended not to watch him and Beasley unload the luggage.

"For God's sake, boy, why didn't you catch a plane?" Toshi called down from a perilously decrepit veranda. He was wiry and sallow and vitally ancient. He dressed in a bland short sleeve button-up shirt a couple of neck sizes too large and his ever present gypsy kerchief. He leaned way over the precarious railing and smoked a cigarette. His cigarettes were invariably Russian and came in tin boxes blazoned with hyperbolic full-color logos and garbled English mottos and blurbs such as "Prince of Peace!" and "Yankee Flavor!"

"The Lear's in the shop." Partridge waved and headed for the porch.

"You don't drive, either, eh?" Toshi flicked his hand impatiently. "Come on, then. Beasley—the Garden Room, please."

Beasley escorted Partridge through the gloomy maze of cramped halls and groaning stairs. Everything was dark: from the cryptic hangings and oil paintings of Mooreheads long returned to dust, to the shiny walnut planks that squeaked and shifted everywhere underfoot.

Partridge was presented a key by the new housekeeper, Mrs. Grant. She was a brusque woman of formidable brawn and comport; perhaps Beasley's mother in another life. Beasley informed him that "new" was a relative term as she had been in Campbell's employ for the better portion of a decade. She had made the voyage from Orange County and brought along three maids and a gardener/handyman who was also her current lover.

The Garden Room was on the second floor of the east wing and carefully isolated from the more heavily trafficked byways. It was a modest, L-shaped room with a low, harshly textured ceiling, a coffin wardrobe carved from the heart of some extinct tree, a matching dresser and a diminutive brass bed that sagged ominously. The portrait of a solemn girl in a garden hat was centered amidst otherwise negative space across from the bed. Vases of fresh cut flowers were arranged on the windowsills. Someone had plugged in a rose-scented air freshener to subdue the abiding taint of wet plaster and rotting wood; mostly in vain. French doors let out to a balcony overlooking tumbledown stone walls of a lost garden and then a plain of waist-high grass gone the shade of wicker. The grass flowed into foothills. The foothills formed an indistinct line in the blue mist.

"Home away from home, eh?" Beasley said. He wrung his hands, out of place as a bear in the confined quarters. "Let's see if those bastards left us any crumbs."

Howard Campbell and Toshi were standing around the bottom of the stairs with a couple of other elder statesmen types—one, a bluff, aristocratic fellow with handlebar mustaches and fat hands, reclined in a hydraulic wheelchair. The second man was also a specimen of genteel extract, but clean-shaven and decked in a linen suit that had doubtless been the height of ballroom fashion during Truman's watch. This fellow leaned heavily upon an ornate blackthorn cane. He occasionally pressed an oxygen mask over his mouth and nose and snuffled deeply. Both men stank of medicinal alcohol and shoe polish. A pair of bodyguards hovered nearby. The guards were physically powerful men in tight suit-jackets. Their nicked-up faces wore the perpetual scowls of peasant trustees.

Toshi lectured about a so-called supercolony of ants that stretched six thousand kilometers from the mountains of Northern Italy down along the coasts of France and into Spain. According to the reports, this was the largest ant colony on record; a piece of entomological history in the making. He halted his oration to lackadaisically introduce the Eastern gentlemen as Mr. Jackson Phillips and Mr. Carrey Montague and then jabbed Campbell in the ribs, saying, "What'd I tell you? Rich is as suave as an Italian prince. Thank God I don't have a daughter for him to knock up." To Partridge he said, "Now go eat before cook throws it to the pigs. Go, go!" Campbell, the tallest and gravest of the congregation, gave Partridge a subtle wink. Meanwhile, the man in the wheelchair raised his voice to demand an explanation for why his valuable time was being wasted on an ant seminar. He had not come to listen to a dissertation and Toshi damned-well knew better…Partridge did not catch the rest because Beasley ushered him into the kitchen whilst surreptitiously flicking Mr. Jackson Phillips the bird.

The cook was an impeccable Hungarian named Gertz, whom Campbell had lured, or possibly blackmailed, away from a popular restaurant in Santa Monica. In any event, Gertz knew his business.

Partridge slumped on a wooden stool at the kitchen counter. He worked his way through what Gertz apologetically called "leftovers." These included sourdough waffles and strawberries, whipped eggs, biscuits, sliced apples, honey dew melon and chilled milk. The coffee was a hand-ground Columbian blend strong enough to peel paint. Beasley slapped him on the shoulder and said something about chores.

Partridge was sipping his second mug of coffee, liberally dosed with cream and sugar, when Nadine sat down close to him. Nadine shone darkly and smelled of fresh cut hayricks and sweet, highly polished leather. She leaned in tight and plucked the teaspoon from his abruptly nerveless fingers. She licked the teaspoon and dropped it on the saucer and she did not smile at all. She looked at him with metallic eyes that held nothing but a prediction of snow.

"And…action," Nadine said in a soft, yet resonant voice that could have placed her center stage on Broadway had she ever desired to dwell in the Apple and ride her soap and water sex appeal to the bank and back. She spoke without a trace of humor, which was a worthless gauge to ascertain her mood anyhow, she being a classical Stoic. Her mouth was full and lovely and inches from Partridge's own. She did not wear lipstick.

"You're pissed," Partridge said. He felt slightly dizzy. He was conscious of his sticky fingers and the seeds in his teeth.

"Lucky guess."

"I'm a Scientologist, Grade Two. We get ESP at G-2. No luck involved."

"Oh, they got you, too. Pity. Inevitable, but still a pity."

"I'm kidding."

"What… even the cultists don't want you?"

"I'm sure they want my money."

Nadine tilted her head slightly. "I owe the Beez twenty bucks, speaking of. Know why?"

"No," Partridge said. "Wait. You said I wouldn't show—"

"—because you're a busy man—"

"That's the absolute truth. I'm busier than a one-armed paper hanger."

"I'm sure. Anyway, I said you'd duck us once again. A big movie deal, fucking a B-list starlet in the South of France. It'd be something."

"—and then Beasley said something on the order of—"

"Hell yeah, my boy will be here!—"

"—come hell or high water!"

"Pretty much, yeah. He believes in you."

Partridge tried not to squirm even as her pitiless gaze bore into him. "Well, it was close. I cancelled some things. Broke an engagement or two."

"Mmm. It's okay, Rich. You've been promising yourself a vacation, haven't you? This makes a handy excuse; do a little R&R, get some *you* time in for a change. It's for your mental health. Bet you can write it off."

"Since this is going so well… How's Coop?" He had noticed she was not wearing the ring. Handsome hubby Dan Cooper was doubtless a sore subject, he being the hapless CEO of an obscure defense contractor that got caught up in a Federal dragnet. He would not be racing his classic Jaguar along hairpin coastal highways for the next five to seven years, even assuming time off for good behavior. Poor Coop was another victim of Nadine's gothic curse. "Condolences, naturally. If I didn't send a card…"

"He *loves* Federal prison. It's a country club, really. How's that bitch you introduced me to? I forget her name."

"Rachel."

"Yep, that's it. The makeup lady. She pancaked Thurman like a corpse on that flick you shot for Coppola."

"Ha, yeah. She's around. We're friends."

"Always nice to have friends."

Partridge forced a smile. "I'm seeing someone else."

"Kyla Sherwood—the Peroxide Puppet. Tabloids know all, my dear."

"But it's not serious."

"News to her, hey?"

He was boiling alive in his Aspen-chic sweater and charcoal slacks. Sweat trickled down his neck and the hairs on his thighs prickled and chorused their disquiet. He wondered if that was a massive pimple pinching the flesh between his eyes. That was where he had always gotten the worst of them in high school. His face swelled so majestically people thought he had broken his nose playing softball. What could he say with this unbearable pressure building in his lungs? Their history had grown to epic dimensions. The kitchen was too small to contain such a thing. He said, "Toshi said it was important. That I come to this…what? Party? Reunion? Whatever it is. God knows I love a mystery."

Nadine stared the stare that gave away nothing. She finally glanced at her watch and stood. She leaned over him so that her hot breath brushed his ear. "Mmm. Look at the time. Lovely seeing you, Rich. Maybe later we can do lunch."

He watched her walk away. As his pulse slowed and his breathing loosened, he waited for his erection to subside and tried to pinpoint what it was that nagged him, what it was that tripped the machinery beneath the liquid surface of his guilt-crazed, testosterone-glutted brain. Nadine had always reminded him of a duskier, more ferocious Bettie Page. She was thinner now; her prominent cheekbones, the fragile symmetry of her scapulae through the open-back blouse, registered with him as he sat recovering his wits with the numb intensity of a soldier who had just clambered from a trench following a mortar barrage.

Gertz slunk out of hiding and poured more coffee into Partridge's cup. He dumped in some Schnapps from a hip flask. "Hang in there, my friend," he said drolly.

"I just got my head beaten in," Partridge said.

"Round one," Gertz said. He took a hefty pull from the flask. "Pace yourself, champ."

Partridge wandered the grounds until he found Toshi in D-Lab. Toshi was surveying a breeding colony of cockroaches: *Pariplenata americana*, he proclaimed them with a mixture of pride and annoyance. The lab was actually a big tool shed with the windows painted over. Industrial-sized aquariums occupied most of the floor space. The air had acquired a peculiar, spicy odor reminiscent of hazelnuts and fermented bananas. The chamber was illuminated by infrared lamps. Partridge could not observe much activity within the aquariums unless he stood next to the glass. That was not going to happen. He contented himself to lurk at Toshi's elbow while a pair of men in coveralls and rubber gloves performed maintenance on an empty pen. The men scraped substrate into garbage bags and hosed the container and applied copious swathes of petroleum jelly to the rim where the mesh lid attached. Cockroaches were escape artists extraordinaire, according to Toshi.

"Most folks are trying to figure the best pesticide to squirt on these little fellas. Here you are a cockroach rancher," Partridge said.

"Cockroaches…I care nothing for cockroaches. This is scarcely more than a side effect, the obligatory nod to cladistics, if you will. Cockroaches…beetles…there are superficial similarities. These animals crawl and burrow, they predate us humans by hundreds of millions of years. But…beetles are infinitely more interesting. The naturalist's best friend. Museums and taxidermists love them, you see. Great for cleaning skeletal structures, antlers and the like."

"Nature's efficiency experts. What's the latest venture?"

"A-Lab—I will show you." Toshi became slightly animated. He straightened his crunched shoulders to gesticulate. His hand glimmered like a glow tube at a rock concert. "I keep a dozen colonies of dermestid beetles in operation. Have to house them in glass or stainless steel—they nibble through anything."

This house of creepy-crawlies was not good for Partridge's nerves. He thought of the chair and the woman and her tarantula. He was sickly aware that if he closed his eyes at that very moment the stranger would remove the mask and reveal Nadine's face. Thinking of Nadine's face and its feverish luminescence, he said, "She's dying."

Toshi shrugged. "Johns Hopkins…my friends at Fred Hutch…nobody can do anything. This is the very bad stuff; very quick."

"How long has she got." The floor threatened to slide from under Partridge's feet. Cockroaches milled in their shavings and hidey holes; their tick-tack impacts burrowed under his skin.

"Not long. Probably three or four months."

"Okay." Partridge tasted breakfast returned as acid in his mouth.

The technicians finished their task and began sweeping. Toshi gave some orders. He said to Partridge, "Let's go see the beetles."

A-Lab was identical to D-Lab except for the wave of charnel rot that met Partridge as he entered. The dermestid colonies were housed in corrugated metal canisters. Toshi raised the lid to show Partridge how industriously a particular group of larvae were stripping the greasy flesh of a small mixed-breed dog. Clean white bone peeked through coagulated muscle fibers and patches of coarse, blond fur.

Partridge managed to stagger the fifteen or so feet and vomit into a plastic sink. Toshi shut the lid and nodded wisely. "Some fresh air, then."

Toshi conducted a perfunctory tour, complete with a wheezing narrative regarding matters coleopteran and teuthological, the latter being one of his comrade Howard Campbell's manifold specialties. Campbell had held since the early '70s that One Day Soon the snail cone or some species of jellyfish was going to revolutionize neurology. Partridge nodded politely and dwelt on his erupting misery. His stomach felt as if a brawler had used it for a speed bag. He trembled and dripped with cold sweats.

Then, as they ambled along a fence holding back the wasteland beyond the barn, he spotted a cluster of three satellite dishes. The dishes' antennas were angled downward at a sizable oblong depression like aardvark snouts poised to siphon musty earth. These were lightweight models, each no more than four meters across and positioned as to be hidden from casual view from the main house. Their trapezoidal shapes didn't jibe with photos Partridge had seen of similar devices. These objects gleamed the yellow-gray gleam of rotting teeth. His skin crawled as he studied them and the area of crushed soil. The depression was over a foot deep and shaped not unlike a kiddy wading pool. This presence in the field was incongruous and somehow sinister. He immediately regretted discarding his trusty Canon. He stopped and pointed. "What are those?"

"Radio telescopes, obviously."

"Yeah, what kind of metal is that? Don't they work better if you point them at the sky?"

"The sky. Ah, well, perhaps later. You note the unique design, eh? Campbell and I...invented them. Basically."

"Really? Interesting segue from entomological investigation, doc."

"See what happens when you roll in the mud with NASA? The notion of first contact is so glamorous, it begins to rub off. Worse than drugs. I'm in recovery."

Partridge stared at the radio dishes. "UFOs and whatnot, huh. You stargazer, you. When did you get into that field?" It bemused him how Toshi Ryoko hopscotched from discipline to discipline with a breezy facility that unnerved even the mavericks among his colleagues.

"I most assuredly haven't migrated to that field—however, I will admit to grazing as the occasion warrants. The dishes are a link in the chain. We've got miles of conductive coil buried around here. All part of a comprehensive surveillance plexus. We monitor everything that crawls, swims or flies. Howard and I have become enamored of astrobiology, crypto zoology, the occulted world. Do you recall when we closed shop in California? That was roughly concomitant with our lamentably over-publicized misadventures in New Guinea."

"Umm." Partridge had heard that Campbell and Toshi disappeared into the back country for three weeks after they lost a dozen porters and two graduate students in a river accident. Maybe alcohol and drugs were involved. There was an investigation and all charges were waived. The students' families had sued and sued, of course. Partridge knew he should have called to offer moral support. Unfortunately, associating with Toshi in that time of crisis might have been an unwise career move and he let it slide. *But nothing slides forever, does it?*

"New Guinea wasn't really a disaster. Indeed, it served to crystallize the focus of our research, to open new doors…"

Partridge was not thrilled to discuss New Guinea. "Intriguing. I'm glad you're going great guns. It's over my head, but I'm glad. Sincerely." Several crows described broad, looping circles near the unwholesome machines. Near, but not too near.

"Ah, but that's not important. I imagine I shall die before any of this work comes to fruition." Toshi smiled fondly and evasively. He gave Partridge an avuncular pat on the arm. "You're here for Nadine's grand farewell. She will leave the farm after the weekend. Everything is settled. You see now why I called. "

Partridge was not convinced. Nadine seemed to resent his presence—she'd always been hot and cold when it came to him. What did Toshi want him to do? "Absolutely," he said.

They walked back to the house and sat on the porch in rocking chairs. Gertz brought them a pitcher of iced tea and frosted glasses on trays. Campbell emerged in his trademark double-breasted steel-blue suit and horn-rimmed glasses. For the better part of three decades he had played the mild, urbane foil to Toshi's megalomaniacal iconoclast. In private, Campbell was easily the dominant of the pair. He leaned against a post and held out his hand until Toshi passed him a smoldering cigarette. "I'm glad you know," he said, fastening his murky eyes on Partridge. "I didn't have the nerve to tell you myself."

Partridge felt raw, exhausted and bruised. He changed the subject. "So…those guys in the suits. Montague and Phillips. How do you know them? Financiers, I presume?"

"Patrons," Campbell said. "As you can see, we've scaled back the operation. It's difficult to run things off the cuff." Lolling against the post, a peculiar hybrid of William Burroughs and Walter Cronkite, he radiated folksy charm that mostly diluted underlying hints of decadence. This charm often won the hearts of flabby dilettante crones looking for a cause to champion. "Fortunately, there are always interested parties with deep pockets."

Partridge chuckled to cover his unease. His stomach was getting worse. "Toshi promised to get me up to speed on your latest and greatest contribution to the world of science. Or do I want to know?"

"You showed him the telescopes? Anything else?" Campbell glanced at Toshi and arched his brow.

Toshi's grin was equal portions condescension and mania. He rubbed his spindly hands together like a spider combing its pedipalps. "Howard…I haven't, he hasn't been to the site. He has visited with our pets, however. Mind your shoes if you fancy them, by the way."

"Toshi has developed a knack for beetles," Campbell said. "I don't know what he sees in them, frankly. Boring, boring. Pardon the pun—I'm stone knackered on Dewar's. My bloody joints are positively gigantic in this climate. Oh—have you seen reports of the impending Yellow Disaster? China will have the whole of Asia Minor deforested in the next decade. I imagine you haven't—you don't film horror movies, right? At least not reality horror." He laughed as if to say, *You realize I'm kidding, don't you, lad? We're all friends here.* "Mankind is definitely eating himself out of house and home. The beetles and cockroaches are in the direct line of succession."

"Scary," Partridge said. He waited doggedly for the punch line. Although, free association was another grace note of Campbell's and Toshi's. The punch line might not even exist. Give them thirty seconds and they would be nattering about engineering *E. coli* to perform microscopic stupid pet tricks or how much they missed those good old Bangkok whores.

Toshi lighted another cigarette and waved it carelessly. "The boy probably hasn't the foggiest notion as to the utility of our naturalistic endeavors. Look, after dinner, we'll give a demonstration. We'll hold a séance."

"Oh, horseshit, Toshi!" Campbell scowled fearsomely. This was always a remarkable transformation for those not accustomed to his moods. "Considering the circumstances, that's extremely tasteless."

"Not to mention premature," Partridge said through a grim smile. He rose, upsetting his drink in a clatter of softened ice cubes and limpid orange rinds and strode from the porch. He averted his face. He was not certain if Campbell called after him because of the blood beating in his ears. Toshi did clearly say, "Let him go, let him be, Howard... She'll talk to him..."

He stumbled to his room and crashed into his too-short bed and fell unconscious.

Partridge owed much of his success to Toshi. Even that debt might not have been sufficient to justify the New England odyssey. The real reason, the motive force under the hood of Partridge's lamentable midlife crisis, and the magnetic compulsion to heed that bizarre late-night call, was certainly his sense of unfinished business with Nadine. Arguably, he had Toshi to thank for that, too.

Toshi Ryoko immigrated to Britain, and later the U.S., from Okinawa in the latter '60s. This occurred a few years after he had begun to attract attention from the international scientific community for his brilliant work in behavioral ecology and prior to his stratospheric rise to popular fame due to daredevil eccentricities and an Academy Award-nominated documentary of his harrowing expedition into the depths of a Bengali wildlife preserve. The name of the preserve loosely translated into English as "The Forest that Eats Men." Partridge had been the twenty-three-year-old cinematographer brought aboard at the last possible moment to photograph the expedition. No more qualified person could be found on the ridiculously short notice that Toshi announced for departure. The director/producer was none other than Toshi himself. It was his first and last film. There were, of course, myriad subsequent independent features, newspaper and radio accounts—the major slicks covered Toshi's controversial exploits, but he lost interest in filmmaking after the initial hubbub and eventually faded from the public eye. Possibly his increasing affiliation with clandestine U.S. government projects was to blame. The cause was immaterial. Toshi's fascinations were mercurial and stardom proved incidental to his mission of untangling the enigmas of evolutionary origins and ultimate destination.

Partridge profited greatly from that tumultuous voyage into the watery hell of man-eating tigers and killer bees. He emerged from the crucible as a legend fully formed. His genesis was as Minerva's, that warrior-daughter sprung whole from Jupiter's aching skull. All the great directors wanted him. His name was gold—it was nothing but Beluga caviar and box seats at the Rose Bowl, a string of "where are they now" actresses on his arm, an executive membership in the Ferrari Club and posh homes in Malibu and Ireland. Someday they would hang his portrait in the American Society of Cinematography archives and blazon his star on Hollywood Boulevard.

There was just one glitch in his happily-ever-after: Nadine. Nadine Thompson was the whip-smart Stanford physiologist who had gone along for the ride to Bangladesh as Toshi's chief disciple. She was not Hollywood sultry, yet the camera found her to be eerily riveting in a way that was simultaneously erotic and repellant. The audience never saw a *scientist* when the camera tracked Nadine across the rancid deck of that river barge. They saw a woman-child—ripe, lithe and lethally carnal.

She was doomed. Jobs came and went. Some were comparative plums, yes. None of them led to prominence indicative of her formal education and nascent talent. None of them opened the way to the marquee projects, postings or commissions. She eventually settled for a staff position at a museum in Buffalo. An eighty-seven-minute film shot on super-sixteen millimeter consigned her to professional purgatory. Maybe a touch of that taint had rubbed off on Partridge. Nadine was the youthful excess that Hollywood could not supply, despite its excess of youth, the one he still longed for during the long, blank Malibu nights. He carried a load of guilt about the whole affair as well.

Occasionally, in the strange, hollow years after the hoopla, the ground-swell of acclaim and infamy, she would corner Partridge in a remote getaway bungalow, or a honeymoon seaside cottage, for a weekend of gin and bitters and savage lovemaking. In the languorous aftermath, she often confided how his magic Panaflex had destroyed her career. She would forever be "the woman in that movie." She was branded a real-life scream queen and the sex pot with the so-so face and magnificent ass.

Nadine was right, as usual. "The Forest that Eats Men" never let go once it sank its teeth.

He dreamed of poling a raft on a warm, muddy river. Mangroves hemmed them in corridors of convoluted blacks and greens. Creepers and vines strung the winding waterway. Pale sunlight sifted down through the screen of vegetation; a dim, smoky light full of shadows and shift-ing clouds of gnats and mosquitoes. Birds warbled and screeched. He crouched in the stern of the raft and stared at the person directly before him. That person's wooden mask with its dead eyes and wooden smile gaped at him, fitted as it was to the back of the man's head. The wooden mouth whispered, "You forgot your mask." Partridge reached back and found, with burgeoning horror, that his skull was indeed naked and defenseless.

"They're coming. They're coming." The mask grinned soullessly.

He inhaled to scream and jerked awake, twisted in the sheets and sweat-ing. Red light poured through the thin curtains. Nadine sat in the shadows at the foot of his bed. Her hair was loose and her skin reflected the ruddy light. He thought of the goddess Kali shrunk to mortal dimensions.

"You don't sleep well either, huh," she said.

"Nope. Not since Bangladesh."

"That long. Huh."

He propped himself on his elbow and studied her. "I've been considering my options lately. I'm thinking it might be time to hang up my spurs. Go live in the Bahamas."

She said, "You're too young to go." That was her mocking tone.

"You too."

She didn't say anything for a while. Then, "Rich, you ever get the feeling you're being watched?"

"Like when you snuck in here while I was sleeping? Funny you should mention it..."

"Rich."

He saw that she was serious. "Sometimes, yeah."

"Well you are. Always. I want you to keep that in mind."

"Okay. Will it help?"

"Good question."

The room darkened, bit by bit. He said, "You think you would've made it back to the barge?" He couldn't distance himself from her cry as she flailed overboard and hit the water like a stone. There were crocodiles everywhere. No one moved. The whole crew was frozen in that moment between disbelief and action. He had shoved the camera at, who? Beasley. He had done that and then gone in and gotten her. Blood-warm water, brown with mud. He did not remember much of the rest. The camera caught it all.

"No," she said. "Not even close."

He climbed over the bed and hugged her. She was warm. He pressed his face into her hair. Her hair trapped the faint, cloying odor of sickness. "I'm so fucking sorry," he said.

She didn't say anything. She rubbed his shoulder.

That night was quiet at the Moorehead Estate. There was a subdued dinner and afterward some drinks. Everybody chatted about the good old days. The real ones and the imaginary ones too. Phillips and Montague disappeared early on and took their men-at-arms with them. Nadine sat aloof. She held onto a hardback—one of Toshi's long out of print treatises on insect behavior and ecological patterns. Partridge could tell she was only pretending to look at it.

Later, after lights out, Partridge roused from a dream of drowning in something that wasn't quite water. His name was whispered from the foot of the bed. He fumbled upright in the smothering dark. "Nadine?" He clicked on the lamp and saw he was alone.

It rained in the morning. Toshi was undeterred. He put on a slicker and took a drive in the Land Rover to move the radio telescopes and other equipment into more remote fields. A truckload of the burly, grim laborers followed. The technicians trudged about their daily routine, indifferent to the weather. Campbell disappeared with Phillips and Montague. Nadine remained in her room. Partridge spent the morning playing poker with Beasley and Gertz on the rear porch. They drank whiskey—coffee for Beasley—and watched water drip from the eaves and thunderheads roll across the horizon trailing occasional whip-cracks of lightning. Then it stopped raining and the sun transformed the landscape into a mass of illuminated rust and glass.

Partridge went for a long walk around the property to clear his head and savor the clean air. The sun was melting toward the horizon when Beasley found him dozing in the shade of an oak. It was a huge tree with yellowing leaves and exposed roots. The roots crawled with pill bugs. Between yawns Partridge observed the insects go about their tiny business.

"C'mon. You gotta see the ghost town before it gets dark," Beasley said. Partridge didn't bother to protest. Nadine waited in the jeep. She wore tortoise shell sunglasses and a red scarf in her hair. He decided she looked better in a scarf than Toshi ever had, no question. Partridge opened his mouth and Beasley gave him a friendly shove into the front passenger seat.

"Sulk, sulk, sulk!" Nadine laughed at him. "In the garden, eating worms?"

"Close enough," Partridge said, and hung on as Beasley gunned the jeep through a break in the fence line and zoomed along an overgrown track that was invisible until they were right on top of it. The farm became a picture on a stamp and then they passed through a belt of paper birches and red maples. They crossed a ramshackle bridge that spanned an ebon stream and drove into a clearing. Beasley ground gears until they gained the crown of a long, tabletop hill. He killed the engine and coasted to a halt amid tangled grass and wildflowers and said, "Orren Towne. Died circa 1890s."

Below their vantage, remnants of a village occupied the banks of a shallow valley. If Orren Towne was dead its death was the living kind. A score of saltbox houses and the brooding hulk of a Second Empire church waited somberly. Petrified roofs were dappled by the shadows of moving clouds. Facades were brim with the ephemeral light of the magic hour.

Beasley's walkie-talkie crackled and he stepped aside to answer the call.

Nadine walked partway down the slope and stretched her arms. Her muscles stood forth in cords of sinew and gristle. She looked over her shoulder at Partridge. Her smile was alien. "Don't you wish you'd brought your camera?"

The brain is a camera. What Partridge really wished was that he had gone to his room and slept. His emotions were on the verge of running amok. The animal fear from his daydreams had sneaked up again. He smelled the musk of his own adrenaline and sweat. *The brain is a camera and once it sees what it sees there's no taking it back.* He noticed another of Toshi's bizarre radio dishes perched on a bluff. The antenna was focused upon the deserted buildings. "I don't like this place," he said. But she kept walking and he trailed along. It was cooler among the houses. The earth was trampled into concrete and veined with minerals. Nothing organic grew and no birds sang. The subtly deformed structures were encased in a transparent resin that lent the town the aspect of a waxworks. He thought it might be shellac.

Shadows fell across Partridge's path. Open doorways and sugar-spun windows fronted darkness. These doors and windows were as unwelcoming as the throats of ancient wells, the mouths of caves. He breathed heavily. "How did Toshi do this? *Why* did he do this?"

Nadine laughed and took his hand playfully. Hers was dry and too-warm, like a leather wallet left in direct sunlight. "Toshi only discovered it. Do you seriously think he and Howard are capable of devising something this extraordinary?"

"No."

"Quite a few people spent their lives in this valley. Decent farming and hunting in these parts. The Mooreheads owned about everything. They owned a brewery and a mill down the road, near their estate. All those busy little worker bees going about their jobs, going to church on Sunday. I'm sure it was a classic Hallmark. Then it got cold. One of those long winters that never ends. Nothing wanted to grow and the game disappeared. The house burned. Sad for the Mooreheads. Sadder for the people who depended on them. The family circled its wagons to rebuild the mansion, but the community never fully recovered. Orren Towne was here today, gone tomorrow. At least that's the story we hear told by the old-timers at the Mad Rooster over cribbage and a pint of stout." Nadine stood in the shade of the church, gazing up, up at the crucifix. "This is how it will all be someday. Empty buildings. Empty skies. The grass will come and eat everything we ever made. The waters will swallow it. It puts my situation into perspective, lemme tell you."

"These buildings should've fallen down. Somebody's gone through a lot of trouble to keep this like—"

"A museum. Yeah, somebody has. This isn't the only place it's been done, either."

"Places like this? Where?" Partridge said. He edged closer to the bright center of the village square.

"I don't know. They're all over if you know what to look for."

"Nadine, maybe…Jesus!" He jerked his head to peer at a doorway. The darkness inside the house seemed fuller and more complete. "Are there people here?" His mind jumped to an image of the masks that the natives wore to ward off tigers. He swallowed hard.

"Just us chickens, love."

A stiff breeze rushed from the northwest and whipped the outlying grass. Early autumn leaves skated across the glassy rooftops and swirled in barren yards. Leaves fell dead and dry. Night was coming hard.

"I'm twitchy—jet lag, probably. What do those weird-looking rigs do?" He pointed at the dish on the hill. "Toshi said they're radio telescopes he invented."

"He said he invented them? Oh my. I dearly love that man, but sometimes he's such an asshole."

"Yeah. How do they work?"

Nadine shrugged. "They read frequencies on the electromagnetic spectrum."

"Radio signals from underground. Why does that sound totally backwards to me?"

"I didn't say anything about radio signals."

"Then what did you say?"

"When we get back, ask Toshi about the node."

"What are you talking about?" Partridge's attention was divided between her and the beautifully grotesque houses and the blackness inside them.

"You'll see. Get him to show you the node. That'll clear some of this stuff up, pronto."

Beasley called to them. He and the jeep were a merged silhouette against the failing sky. He swung his arm overhead until Nadine yelled that they would start back in a minute. She removed her shades and met Partridge's eyes. "You okay, Rich?" She refused to relinquish her grip on his hand.

"You're asking *me*?"

She gave him another of her inscrutable looks. She reached up and pushed an unkempt lock from his forehead. "I'm not mad, in case you're still wondering. I wanted you to see me off. Not like there're any more weekend rendezvous in the stars for us."

"That's no way to talk," he said.

"Just sayin'." She dropped his hand and walked away. In a moment he followed. By the time they made the summit, darkness had covered the valley. Beasley had to use the headlights to find the way home.

Gertz served prawns for dinner. They ate at the long mahogany table in the formal dining room. Jackson Phillips begged off due to an urgent matter in the city. Beasley packed him and one of the muscle-bound bodyguards into the helicopter and flew away. That left six: Toshi; Campbell; Nadine; Carrey Montague and the other bodyguard; and Partridge. The men wore suits and ties. Nadine wore a cream-colored silk chiffon evening gown. There were candles and elaborate floral arrangements and dusty bottles of wine from the Moorehead cellar and magnums of top-dollar French champagne from a Boston importer who catered to those with exclusive tastes and affiliations. Toshi proposed a toast and said a few words in Japanese and then the assembly began to eat and drink.

Somewhere in the middle of the third or fourth course, Partridge realized he was cataclysmically drunk. They kept setting them up and he kept knocking them down. Toshi or Campbell frequently clapped his back and clinked his glass and shouted "*Sic itur ad astra!*" and another round would magically appear. His head was swollen and empty as an echo chamber. The winking silverware and sloshing wineglasses, the bared teeth and hearty laughter came to him from a sea shell. He caught Nadine watching him from across the table, her eyes cool, her mouth set inscrutably. He poured more liquor down his throat to break their moment of recognition, and when he checked again she'd left the table, her untouched meal, and sailed from the room.

Dinner blurred into a collage of sense and chaos, of light and dark, and he gripped his glass and blinked dumbly against the shattering flare of the low-slung chandelier and laughed uproariously. Without transition, dinner was concluded and the men had repaired to the den to relax over snifters of Hennessy. They lounged in wing-backed leather chairs and upon opulent leather divans. Partridge admired the vaulted ceiling, the library of towering lacquered oak bookcases and the impressive collection of antique British rifles and British cavalry sabers cached in rearing cabinets of chocolate wood and softly warped glass. Everything was so huge and shiny and far away. When the cigar and pipe smoke hung thick and the men's cheeks were glazed and rosy as the cheeks of Russian dolls, he managed, "I'm supposed to ask you about the node."

Campbell smiled a broad and genial smile. "The node, yes. The node, of course, is the very reason Mr. Phillips and Mr. Montague have come to pay their respects. They hope to buy their way into Heaven."

"He's right, he's right," Mr. Carrey Montague said with an air of merry indulgence. "Jack had his shot. Didn't he though. Couldn't hack it and off he flew."

"I was getting to this," Toshi said. "In a roundabout fashion."

"Exceedingly so," Campbell said.

"Didn't want to frighten him. It's a delicate matter."

"Yes," Campbell said dryly. He puffed on his pipe and his eyes were red around the edges and in the center of his pupils.

"Shall I. Or do you want a go?" Toshi shrugged his indifference.

"The node is a communication device," Campbell said through a mouthful of smoke. "Crude, really. Danforth Moorehead, the Moorehead patriarch, developed the current model. Ahem, the schematic was delivered to him and he effected the necessary modifications, at any rate. Admittedly, it's superior to the primitive methods—scrying, séances, psychedelic drugs, that nonsense. Not to mention some of the more gruesome customs we've observed in the provincial regions. Compared to that, the node is state of the art. It is a reservoir that filters and translates frequency imaging captured by our clever, clever radio telescopes. It permits us to exchange information with our…neighbors."

Partridge dimly perceived that the others were watching him with something like fascination. Their eyes glittered through the haze. "With who? I don't—"

"Our neighbors," Campbell said.

"Oh, the things they show you." Carrey Montague sucked on his oxygen mask until he resembled a ghoul.

Partridge swung his head to look from face to face. The men were drunk. The men seethed with restrained glee. No one appeared to be joking. "Well, go on then," he said dreamily. His face was made of plaster. Black spots revolved before him like ashen snowflakes.

"I told you, Richard. Mankind can't go on like this."

"Like what?"

Toshi chuckled. "Assuming we don't obliterate ourselves, or that a meteorite doesn't smack us back to the Cambrian, if not the Cryptozoic, this planet will succumb to the exhaustion of Sol. First the mammals, then the reptiles, right down the line until all that's left of any complexity are the arthropods: beetles and cockroaches and their oceanic cousins, practically speaking. Evolution is a circle—we're sliding back to that endless sea of protoplasmic goop."

"I'm betting on the nuclear holocaust," Campbell said.

Partridge slopped more brandy into his mouth. He was far beyond tasting it. "Mmm hmm," he said intelligently and cast about for a place to inconspicuously ditch his glass.

"NASA and its holy grail—First Contact, the quest for intelligent life in the universe…all hogwash, all lies." Toshi gently took the snifter away and handed him a fresh drink in a ceramic mug. This was not brandy; it was rich and dark as honey in moonlight. "Private stock, my boy. Drink up!" Partridge drank and his eyes flooded and he choked a little. Toshi nodded in satisfaction. "We know now what we've always suspected. Man is completely and utterly alone in a sea of dust and smoke. Alone and inevitably slipping into extinction."

"Not quite alone," Campbell said. "There are an estimated five to eight million species of insects as of yet unknown and unclassified. Hell of a lot of insects, hmm? But why stop at bugs? Only a damned fool would suppose that was anything but the tip of the iceberg. When the time of Man comes to an end *their* time will begin. And be certain this is not an invasion or a hostile occupation. We'll be dead as Dodos a goodly period before they emerge to claim the surface. They won't rule forever. The planet will eventually become cold and inhospitable to any mortal organism. But trust that their rule will make the reign of the terrible lizards seem a flicker of an eyelash."

"You're talking about cockroaches," Partridge said in triumph. "Fucking cockroaches." That was too amusing and so he snorted on his pungent liquor and had a coughing fit.

"No, we are not," Campbell said.

"We aren't talking about spiders or beetles, either," Toshi said. He gave Partridge's knee an earnest squeeze. "To even compare them with the citizens of the *Great Kingdom*…I shudder. However, if I *were* to make that comparison, I'd say this intelligence is the Ur-progenitor of those insects scrabbling in the muck. The mother race of idiot stepchildren."

Campbell knelt before him so they were eye to eye. The older man's face was radiant and distant as the moon. "This is a momentous discovery. We've established contact. Not us, actually. It's been going on forever. We are the latest…emissaries, if you will. Trustees to the grandest secret of them all."

"Hoo boy. You guys. You fucking guys. Is Nadine in on this?"

"Best that you see firsthand. Would you like that, Rich?"

"Uhmm-wha?" Partridge did not know what he wanted except that he wanted the carousel to stop.

Campbell and Toshi stood. They took his arms and the next thing he knew they were outside in the humid country night with darkness all around. He tried to walk, but his legs wouldn't cooperate much. They half dragged him to a dim metal door and there was a lamp bulb spinning in space and then steep, winding concrete stairs and cracked concrete walls ribbed with mold. They went down and down and a strong, earthy smell overcame Partridge's senses. People spoke to him in rumbling nonsense phrases. Someone ruffled his hair and laughed. His vision fractured. He glimpsed hands and feet, a piece of jaw illumed by a quivering fluorescent glow. When the hands stopped supporting him, he slid to his knees. He had the impression of kneeling in a cellar. Water dripped and a pale overhead lamp hummed like a wasp in a jar. From the corner of his eye he got the sense of table legs and cables and he smelled an acrid smell like cleaning solvents. He thought it might be a laboratory.

—Crawl forward just a bit.

It was strange whatever lay before him. Something curved, spiral-shaped and darkly wet. A horn, a giant conch shell, it was impossible to be certain. There was an opening, as the *external os* of a cervix, large enough to accommodate him in all his lanky height. Inside it was moist and muffled and black.

—There's a lad. Curl up inside. Don't fight. There, there. That's my boy. Won't be long. Not long. Don't be afraid. This is only a window, not a doorway.

Then nothing and nothing and nothing; only his heart, his breathing and a whispery static thrum that might've been the electromagnetic current tracing its circuit through his nerves.

Nothingness grew very dense.

Partridge tried to shriek when water, or something thicker than water, flowed over his head and into his sinuses and throat. Low static built in his ears and the abject blackness was replaced by flashes of white imagery. He fell from an impossible height. He saw only high-velocity jump-cuts of the world and each caromed from him and into the gulf almost instantly. Fire and blood and moving tides of unleashed water. Bones of men and women and cities. Dead, mummified cities gone so long without inhabitants they had become cold and brittle and smooth as mighty forests of stone. There loomed over everything a silence that held to its sterile bosom countless screams and the sibilant chafe of swirling dust. Nadine stood naked as ebony in the heart of a ruined square. She wore a white mask, but he knew her with the immediacy of a nightmare. She lifted her mask and looked at him. She smiled and raised her hand. Men and women emerged from the broken skyscrapers and collapsed bunkers. They were naked and pallid and smiling. In the distance the sun heaved up, slow and red. Its deathly light cascaded upon the lines and curves of cyclopean structures. These were colossal, inhuman edifices of fossil bone and obsidian and anthracite that glittered not unlike behemoth carapaces. He thrashed and fell and fell and drowned.

Nadine said in his ear, *Come down. We love you.*

The cellar floor was cool upon his cheek. He was paralyzed and choking. The men spoke to him in soothing voices. Someone pressed a damp cloth to his brow.

—Take it easy, son. The first ride or two is a bitch and a half. Get his head.

Partridge groaned as gravity crushed him into the moldy concrete.

Someone murmured to him.

—They are interested in preserving aspects of our culture. Thus Orren Towne and places, hidden places most white men will never tread. Of course, it's a multifaceted project. Preserving artifacts, buildings, that's hardly enough to satisfy such an advanced intellect…

Partridge tired to speak. His jaw worked spastically. No sound emerged. The concrete went soft and everyone fell silent at once.

Partridge stirred and sat up. He tried to piece together how he ended up on the back porch sprawled in a wooden folding chair. He was still in his suit and it was damp and clung to him the way clothes do after they have been slept in. The world teetered on the cusp of night. Parts of the sky were orange as fire and other parts were covered by purple-tinted rain clouds like a pall of cannon smoke. Partridge's hair stood in gummy spikes. His mouth was swollen and cottony. He had drooled in his long sleep. His body was stiff as an old plank.

Beasley came out of the house and handed him a glass of seltzer water. "Can't hold your liquor anymore?"

Partridge took the glass in both hands and drank greedily. "Oh, you're back. Must've been a hell of a party," he said at last. He had slept for at least sixteen hours according to his watch. His memory was a smooth and frictionless void.

"Yeah," Beasley said. "You okay?"

Partridge was not sure. "Uh," he said. He rolled his head to survey the twilight vista. "Beasley."

"Yeah?"

"All this." Partridge swept his hand to encompass the swamped gardens and the decrepit outbuildings. "They're letting it fall down. Nobody left from the old days."

"You and me. And Nadine."

"And when we're gone?"

"We're all gonna be gone sooner or later. The docs…they just do what they can. There's nothing else, pal." Beasley gave him a searching look. He shook his shaggy head and chuckled. "Don't get morbid on me, Hollywood. Been a good run if you ask me. Hell, we may get a few more years before the plug gets pulled."

"Is Montague still here?"

"Why do you ask?"

"I heard someone yelling, cursing. Earlier, while I slept."

"Huh. Yeah, there was a little fight. The old fella didn't get his golden ticket. He wasn't wanted. Few are. He shipped out. Won't be coming back."

"I guess not. What was he after?"

"Same thing as everybody else, I suppose. People think Toshi is the Devil, that he can give them their heart's desire if they sign on the dotted line. It ain't so simple."

Partridge had a wry chuckle at that. "Damned right it's not simple, partner. I'm still selling my soul to Tinsel Town. No such luck as to unload the whole shebang at once." Partridge shook with a sudden chill. His memory shucked and jittered; it spun off the reel in his brain and he could not gather it fast enough to make sense of what he had seen in the disjointed frames. "Lord, I hate the country. Always have. I really should get out of here, soon."

"My advice—when you get on that bus, don't look back," Beasley said. "And keep your light on at night. You done with that?"

"Um-hmm." He could not summon the energy to say more right then. The strength and the will had run out of him. He put his hand over his eyes and tried to concentrate.

Beasley took the empty glass and went back into the house. Darkness came and the yard lamps sizzled to life. Moths fluttered near his face, battered at the windows and Partridge wondered why that panicked him, why his heart surged and his fingernails dug into the arm rests. In the misty fields the drone of night insects began.

He eventually heaved to his feet and went inside and walked the dim, ugly corridors for an interminable period. He stumbled aimlessly as if he were yet drunk. His thoughts buzzed and muttered and were incoherent. He found Toshi and Campbell crouched in the den like grave robbers over a stack of shrunken, musty ledgers with hand-sewn covers and other stacks of photographic plates like the kind shot from the air or a doctor's X-ray machine. The den was tomb-dark except for a single flimsy desk lamp. He swayed in the doorway, clinging to the jam as if he were in a cabin on a ship. He said, "Where is Nadine?"

The old men glanced up from their documents and squinted at him. Toshi shook his head and sucked his teeth. Campbell pointed at the ceiling. "She's in her room. Packing. It's Sunday night," he said. "You should go see her."

"She has to leave," Toshi said.

Partridge turned and left. He made his way up the great central staircase and tried a number of doors that let into dusty rooms with painters cloths draping the furniture. Light leaked from the jamb of one door and he went in without knocking.

"I've been waiting," Nadine said. Her room was smaller and more feminine than the Garden Room. She sat lotus on a poster bed. She wore a simple yellow sun dress and her hair in a knot. Her face was dented with exhaustion. "I got scared you might not come to say goodbye."

Partridge did not see any suitcases. A mostly empty bottle of pain medication sat on the night stand beside her wedding ring and a silver locket she had inherited from her great grandmother. He picked up the locket and let it spill through his fingers, back and forth between his hands.

"It's very late," she said. Her voice was not tired like her face. Her voice was steady and full of conviction. "Take me for a walk."

"Where?" He said.

"In the fields. One more walk in the fields."

He was afraid as he had been afraid when the moths came over him and against the windows. He was afraid as he had been when he pulled her from the water all those years ago and then lay in his hammock bunk dreaming and dreaming of the crocodiles and the bottomless depths warm as the recesses of his own body and she had shuddered against him, entwined with him and inextricably linked with him. He did not wish to leave the house, not at night. He said, "Sure. If you want to."

She climbed from the bed and took his hand. They walked down the stairs and through the quiet house. They left the house and the spectral yard and walked through a gate into the field and then farther into heavier and heavier shadows.

Partridge let Nadine lead. He stepped gingerly. He was mostly night blind and his head ached. Wet grass rubbed his thighs. He was soaked right away. A chipped edge of the ivory moon bit through the moving clouds. There were a few stars. They came to a shallow depression where the grass had been trampled or had sunk beneath the surface. Something in his memory twitched and a terrible cold knot formed in his stomach. He whined in his throat, uncomprehendingly, like a dog.

She hesitated in the depression and pulled her pale dress over her head. She tossed the dress away and stood naked and half-hidden in the fog and darkness. He did not need to see her, he had memorized everything. She slipped into the circle of his arms and he embraced her without thinking. She leaned up and kissed him. Her mouth was dry and hot. "Come on," she muttered against his lips. "Come on." Her hands were sinewy as talons and very strong. She grasped his hair and drew him against her and they slowly folded into the moist earth. The soft earth was disfigured with their writhing and a deep, resonant vibration traveled through it and into them where it yammered through their blood and bones. She kissed him fiercely, viciously, and locked her thighs over his hips and squeezed until he gasped and kissed her back. She did not relinquish her fistful of his hair and she did not close her eyes. He stared into them and saw a ghost of a girl he knew and his own gaunt reflection which he did not know at all. They were sinking.

Nadine stopped sucking at him and turned her head against the black dirt and toward the high, shivering grass. There was no breeze and the night lay dead and still. The grass sighed and muffled an approaching sound that struck Partridge as the thrum of fluorescent lights or high-voltage current through a wire or, as it came swiftly closer, the clatter of pebbles rolling over slate. Nadine tightened her grip and looked at him with a sublime combination of glassy terror and exultation. She said, "Rich—"

The grass shook violently beneath a vast, invisible hand and a tide of chirring and burring and click-clacking blackness poured into the depression from far-flung expanses of lost pasture and haunted wilderness, from the moist abyssal womb that opens beneath everything, everywhere. The cacophony was a murderous tectonic snarl out of Pandemonium, Gehenna and Hell; the slaughterhouse gnash and whicker and serrated wail of legion bloodthirsty drills and meat-hungry saw teeth. The ebony breaker crashed over them and buried them and swallowed their screams before their screams began.

After the blackness ebbed and receded and was finally gone, it became quiet. At last the frogs tentatively groaned and the crickets warmed by degrees to their songs of loneliness and sorrow. The moon slipped into the moat around the Earth.

He rose alone, black on black, from the muck and walked back in shambling steps to the house.

Partridge sat rigid and upright at the scarred table in the blue-gray gloom of the kitchen. Through the one grimy window above the sink, the predawn sky glowed the hue of gun metal. His eyes glistened and caught that feeble light and held it fast like the eyes of a carp in its market bed of ice. His black face dripped onto his white shirt which was also black. His black hands lay motionless on the table. He stank of copper and urine and shit. Water leaked in fat drops from the stainless steel gooseneck tap. A grandfather clock ticked and tocked from the hall and counted down the seconds of the revolutions of the Earth. The house settled and groaned fitfully, a guilty pensioner caught fast in dreams.

Toshi materialized in the crooked shadows near the stove. His face was masked by the shadows. He said in a low, hoarse voice that suggested a quantity of alcohol and tears, "Occasionally one of us, a volunteer, is permitted to cross over, to relinquish his or her flesh to the appetites of the colony and exist among them in a state of pure consciousness. That's how it's always been. These volunteers become the interpreters, the facilitators of communication between our species. They become undying repositories of our civilization…a civilization that shall become ancient history one day very soon."

Partridge said nothing.

Toshi said in his hoarse, mournful voice, "She'll never truly die. She'll be with them until this place is a frozen graveyard orbiting a cinder. It is an honor. Yet she waited. She wanted to say goodbye in person."

Partridge said nothing. The sun floated to the black rim of the horizon. The sun hung crimson and boiling and a shaft of bloody light passed through the window and bathed his hand.

"Oh!" Toshi said and his mouth was invisible, but his eyes were bright and wet in the gathering light. "Can you *imagine* gazing upon constellations a hundred million years from this dawn? Can you imagine the wonder of gazing upon those constellations from a hundred million eyes? Oh, imagine it, my boy…"

Partridge stood and went wordlessly, ponderously, to the window and lingered there a moment, his mud-caked face afire with the bloody radiance of a dying star. He drank in the slumbering fields, the distant fog-wreathed forests, as if he might never look upon any of it again. He reached up and pulled the shade down tight against the sill and it was dark.

OCCULTATION

In the middle of playing a round of *Something Scary* they got sidetracked and fucked for a while. After they were done fucking, they lighted cigarettes. Then, they started drinking. Again.

—My God. Look at that, she said.

He grunted like he did when he wasn't listening.

—Hey! I'm creeped out, she said.

—By what? He balanced two shot glasses on his lap and tried to avoid spilling tequila all over the blankets. He'd swiped the tumblers from the honky-tonk across the highway where he'd also scored the X that was currently softening their skulls. The motel room was dark, the bed lumpy, and she kept kicking restlessly, and he spilled a bit regardless. He cursed and downed his in one gulp and handed her the other glass, managing not to burn her with the cigarette smoldering between his fingers.

She accepted her drink, took a deep sip and then held the glass loosely so the edge cast a faint, metallic light across her breasts. She exhaled and pointed beyond the foot of the bed to a spot on the wall above the dead television. —That, she said.

—What?

—That! Right there!

—Shit. Okay. He dragged on his cigarette, then poured another shot and strained it through his teeth, stalling. —Pretty weird.

—Yep, pretty weird is right. What *is* it?

He made a show of squinting into the gloom. —Nothing, probably. You trying to torch the place?

Ashes crumbled from her cigarette and glowed like fallen stars against the sheets. She swept them into her palm, then into the now empty glass. —It just freaks me out.

—You're easily freaked, then.

—No, I'm not. I'm the only girl in my family who watches horror movies. I don't even cover my eyes for the scary parts.

—Yeah?

—Hell yeah. I don't spook. I don't.

—After some consideration I think it's a shadow.

—That's *not* a shadow. It came out when you were doing the story thing.

—See how a little bit of light from the highway comes in under the blinds? Shadows all over the place.

—Nope. I'm telling you, it came out while you were talking.

—Oh, then it's gotta be a ghost. No other sane explanation. Wooooo-hooooo!

—Shaddup. I need another shot.

—Want this? Couple swallows at the bottom. He sloshed the bottle back and forth.

—Gimme. She snapped her fingers, then grabbed the bottle when he swung it close.

—Wait a sec, we'll solve this right now. He leaned against her, reaching across their bodies for the bedside lamp.

—No!

—Huh? What's the matter?

—Don't do it.

—I'm trying to turn on the light, not cop a feel.

—Go ahead and cop a feel, but leave the light alone, 'kay? She thumped the bottle against his arm until he retreated.

—Whatever. Jesus. Got any more cigs?

She fumbled a pack of cigarettes from the nightstand, lighted one from hers and handed it to him. —Last one, she said, crumpling the pack for emphasis.

He slid toward his edge of the bed and slumped against the headboard and smoked in silence. A semi rumbled past on the interstate and the blinds quivered against the window frame. Outside was scrub and desert. The motel lay embedded in the implacable waste like a lunar module stranded between moon craters.

—Don't sulk, she said.

—I'm not.

—Like hell.

—I'm not sulking.

—Then what?

—I'm looking at the wall. Maybe you're right. Maybe it's something else. Why can't we turn on the light? A coyote howled somewhere not too far off. Its cry was answered and redoubled until it finally swelled into a frantic, barking cacophony that moved like a cloud across the black desert.

—Holy shit, what's that? he said.

—Coyotes, she said. Scavenging for damned souls.

—Sounds fucking grandiose for coyotes.

—And what do you know? They're the favored children of the carrion gods. Grandiosity is their gig.

He laughed, a little strange, a little wild, as if echoing the animal harmony. —So, what are they doing around here? Going through a landfill?

—Maybe you drew them in earlier with your howling.

—Bullshit. They can't hear that. All the way out in the tumbleweeds?

—Sure they can. Howl again. I dare you.

—If coyotes sound this bad, I'd hate listening to jackals. Or dingoes. Remember that news story, years ago, about the woman on the picnic with her family?

—'A dingo ate my baby!' God, that's awful. But comical in a horrible way.

—It isn't comical in any way, honey. You're scaring the children.

—Please. Nobody really knows what happened. The kid's mom probably offed her, you ask me.

—There's a great relief. Why do so many parents kill their kids, you think?

—Lots of reasons. Don't you want to strangle the little fuckers sometimes? Like those shits on the flight when we went to see your parents? What a mistake that was, by the way. That one girl kept kicking my seat so hard my head was bouncing. And her mom....

—Ha! It was fun watching you get so mad, though.

She didn't answer, but sat rigidly upright. She trembled.

—Honey? He rubbed her back. —What's the matter?

—Go ahead, she said. Her voice was small.

—Go ahead and what?

—Turn on the light, she said in that small voice. Her cigarette was out and the darkness gathered around them, oily and deep. Faint illumination came through the blinds like light bleeding toward the bottom of a well, a dungeon.

—*You* turn it on, he said. —You're right there.

—I can't move.

—What the hell are you talking about?

—Please. I'm too scared to move, all right? She was whining, borderline hysterical. She enjoyed being frightened, savored the visceral thrill of modulated terror, thus Something Scary, and thus the What If Game

(What if a carload of rednecks started following us on a lonely road? What if somebody was sneaking around the house at night? What if I got pregnant?), and thus her compulsion to build the shadow, the discolored blotch of wallpaper, into something sinister. As was often the case with her, a mule's dose of alcohol combined with sleep deprivation rapidly contributed to the situation getting out of hand.

—Fine. He flopped across her lap and found the lamp chain with his fingertips and yanked. The chain clicked and nothing happened. He tried several times and finally gave up in disgust. Meanwhile, her left hand dug into his shoulder. Her skin was icy.

—Owww, he said, pushing toward his side, happy to get away.

—I knew it. She turned her head so her mouth was closer to his ear and she could kind of whisper. —I knew the light was going to crap out on us. We're alone in here.

—Well, I hope so. I wouldn't like to think some big hairy ax murderer was hiding under the bed.

—I already checked. She chuckled weakly and her icy talon found his bicep now, though somewhat less violently. She was almost calm again. —I looked for Anthony Perkins hiding in the bathroom, too.

—Good! Did you scout around for a peephole? The night clerk could be in the next room winding up his camera. Next thing you know, we're internet porn stars.

—That'd suck. She'd begun to slur. —Man, I hate the desert.

—You also hated Costa Rica, if I recall. Who hates Costa Rica?

—Tarantulas. Centipedes. I hate creepy crawlies.

—Who doesn't?

—Exactly! Thank you! There's a species of centipede, Venezuela, somewhere in South America, anyway; it's as long as your forearm. Eats bats. Knocks them outta the air with its venom-dripping mandibles, and bang! Bat Surprise for dinner.

—You're super drunk. I thought I had most of the tequila.

—Yep, I'm off my ass. Some cowboy bought me like eight shooters while you were in the bathroom. You were in there forever.

—Come again? he said, scandalized.

—Down, boy. He didn't grope me. He just plied me with booze on the off chance I'd let him grope me later. No biggie.

—No biggie? No biggie? Was it that stupid-looking sonofabitch in the Stetson? The guy who couldn't stop ogling your tits?

—You're describing half the bar. Who cares? I gave baby Travolta the slip and ran off with you!

—Awesome.

They lay there for a time, she playing with her lighter, grinding short, weak sparks from the wheel; he listening for the coyote chorus and keeping one eye on the weird blotch of shadow on the wall. Both of them were thinking about the story he'd half told earlier about his uncle Mo who'd done a stint with the Marines and had a weird experience during shore leave in the Philippines; the Something Scary tale that had been so sublimely interrupted.

She said, —Maybe I'm a little intimidated about the Filipino strippers. I can't pick up a pop bottle with my pussy. Or shoot ping pong balls outta there, either.

—Those girls come highly recommended, he said. —Years of specialized training.

—Sounds like your uncle sure knew his way around Filipino whorehouses.

—Wasn't just the whorehouses. Those old boys went crazy on shore leave 'cause that far-out shit was front and center in just about every bar in town. They were dumbass kids—pretty fortunate nobody got his throat slit. According to Mo, a bunch of the taxi drivers belonged to gangs and they'd cart drunk soldiers into the jungle and rob them.

—Enough about the whores and thieving taxi drivers. Get to the scary part. If there's anything more disturbing than Marines slobbering on bottles some whore has been waving around with her cooch, I wanna hear it.

—More disturbing? Uncle Mo told me one about these three guys in Nam who snuck into a leper colony to get some ass. Back then, I guess the locals put the immediate family in the colony whether they were infected or not, so the fellows figured there had to be some prime tail up for grabs.

—Ick! Moving on….

—Okay, R&R in Manila. Mo, and Lurch, a corpsman from his platoon, were whooping it up big time; they'd been drinking three days straight. Barhopping, y'know, and eventually a couple party girls latched onto them and they all headed back to this shack by the docks the guys were renting. A rickety sonofagun, third floor, sorta hanging out over the water. Long story short, Mo's in the bedroom and the girl is smoking his pole. His mind wanders and he happens to look out the window. Across the way, through the window of this other crappy house, there's a naked Filipino broad getting her muffin dusted by some GI. Talk about symmetry, eh? It's raining like a cow pissing on a flat rock and a sash is whacking around in the wind, cutting off the view every few seconds. The broad grins over at Uncle Mo and she reaches up and covers her ears. Then she just lifts her head off her shoulders. Mo's standing there, straddle-legged and slack-jawed and the woman's head keeps on grinning at him and her lips start moving. She's laughing at him. He notices there's something coming out of her neck, like a beak, or who the fuck knows what, 'cause the shade is flapping, see. Meanwhile the other grunt is going to town on her pussy, oblivious to the fact this freak is tucking her head under her arm like a bowling ball.

—And then?

—Then nothing. End of story. Mo and the stripper went back to the main room and drank some more and blazed the night away. He came to forty-eight hours later when his platoon sergeant dumped a bucket of water on his head and kicked his ass back to the ship for the clap inspection.

—Clap inspection?

—After shore leave all the grunts had to drop their pants so an NCO could check them for VD. Heh-heh.

—What a crock of shit, she said. —That's not even scary.

—Sorry. I made the last part up. The part about Mo getting a BJ while the hooker and the other dude were getting busy across the way was true. I think. Uncle Mo lies about stuff, so you never really know.

She groaned in disgust. —Where'd you even get the idea?

—I dunno. Popped into my head while I was lying there. Figured it would get a rise outta you. He laughed and poked her arm, dropped his hand to her leg.

She pushed his hand aside. —Now that that's over. Check this out: I found something odd earlier, she said. —A bible.

—Lots of motels have bibles lying around, he said. —And Jack Chick tracts. He was studying the shadow again. —You know, that thing *does* resemble an insect. Thought it had wings earlier, but I dunno. Can't see shit in here. Wait a minute… It's a water stain. This rat hole leaks like a sieve, betcha anything.

—The bathroom wall is rotten. I was sitting on the toilet and felt a cool breeze. I could stick my fingers outside. Freezing out there.

—Peephole, he said. —For the desert cannibals. There's an abandoned atomic testing range a few dunes over. History Channel did a documentary on them. So I hear.

—I dunno about that, but what I do know is something poisonous could a crawled in any old time and made a nest, could be waiting to lay eggs in our ears when we fall asleep. If that's the case, I gotta tell you, twenty bucks a night seems like a rip-off.

He chuckled.

—Why are you laughing? she said.

—Earlier, I was pissing and noticed something a bit fucked up.

—I think you might have an enlarged prostate.

—The hell are you going on about?

—Frequent urination is a sign of an enlarged prostate. Don't you watch infomercials? They could save your life.

—Anyway. I'm taking one of my apparently frequent pisses, when I notice there's no toilet paper. Like the gentleman I am, I find another roll in the cabinet and get ready to put it on the hanger rod. All for you, snookums.

—You *are* a gentleman, she said.

—Yeah, I raised the seat and everything. I pulled the rod out and set it aside. Unfortunately, I dropped the toilet paper and it went flying out the door and I had to chase it down, wadding the unspooled paper as I went. Man, you could trace pictures with that stuff. It's like one-ply.

—The moral of the story is, shut the door when taking a piss.

—No, that's not the moral of the story. There's more. I go back just in time to watch a big-ass spider squeeze itself out of the rod and scurry into the sink. Thing had a body maybe the size of a jawbreaker; red and yellow, and fleshy, like a plum. It was so damned hefty I could see light reflecting in its eyes. Then it took off down the drain. I think it was irate I screwed with its cozy little home. He had a laugh over the scenario.

—For real? she said.

—Oh, yeah.

She thought things over for a bit. —No way in hell I'm going back in there. I'll pee behind a cactus. A jawbreaker?

—Hand to a stack of bibles, he said, wiping his eyes and visibly working to appear more solemn.

—The bible! She half climbed from bed, groped for the dresser, and after a few anxious moments came back with something heavy and black. She snicked the lighter until its flame revealed the pebbled hide of a small, thick book.

—What kind of bible is that? he said.

—Greek. Byzantine. I dunno, she said. Gilt symbols caught the flame and glistened in convoluted whorls and angular slashes; golden reflections played over the blankets, rippled across the couple's flesh. The pages were thin as white leaves and covered in script to match the cover design. Many of the pages were defiled by chocolaty fingerprints. The book smelled of cigarette musk and mothballs. It was quite patently old.

—This has got to be a collector's item. Some poor schlep forgot it here. He turned the book over in his hands, riffling the pages. No name on it… Finders-keepers.

—Hmm, I dunno....

—Dunno what?

—Whether that's a good idea.

—Billy will go apeshit over this thing. Besides, I owe him a hundred bucks.

—I don't care if Billy goes apeshit over antiquarian crap. That's what antiquarians do, right? You owe me the hundred bucks, anyway, motherfucker.

—Don't you want to know what it is?

—I already know what it is; it's a bible.

He shrugged and handed the book over. —Whatever. Do what you want. I don't care.

—Great! She tossed the book over her shoulder in the general direction of the dresser.

—Man, you really are so wasted.

—Gettin' my second wind, boy. I'm bored.

—Go to sleep. Then you won't be bored.

—Can't sleep. I'm preoccupied with that spider. She's in those rusty pipes, rubbing her claws together and plotting vengeance. Go kill her, would ya?

—You kiddin'? It's pitch dark in there—she'd get the drop on me.

—Hmp. I'm chilly. Let's screw.

—No thanks. I'd just whiskey dick you for half an hour and pass out.

—I see. You won't kill a predatory bug, but you'll club our romance like a baby seal. Swell.

—Wah, wah, he said.

It had grown steadily chillier in the room. She idly thumbed the lighter wheel and watched their breath coalesce by intermittent licks of flame. The shadow above the television had become oblong and black as the cranium of a squid. She raised her arm and the shadow seemed to bleed upward and sideways, as if avoiding the feeble nimbus of fire. —Man, why would that thing appear during your story. Maybe I only noticed it then. Right...?

—I called the shadow forth. And summoned the coyotes. Go to sleep. He rolled over and faced the opposite wall.

—Hell with this. I need a cig. Honey.

—Don't honey me. I'm bushed. He pulled a pillow over his head.

—Fine. She flounced from the bed and promptly smacked her shin on the chair that had toppled over from the weight of her jeans and purse. —Ahh! She hopped around, cursing and fuming and finally yanked on her pants and blouse, snatched up her purse and blundered through the door into the night.

It was cold, all right. The stars were out, fierce and prehistoric. The dark matter between them seemed blacker than usual and thick as tar. She hugged herself and clattered along the boardwalk past the blank windows and the cheap doors with descending numbers to the pop and cigarette machines by the manager's office. No bulbs glowed along the walkway, the office was a deep, dark pit; the neon vacancy sign reared blind and black. Luckily, the vending panels oozed blurry, greenish light to guide her way. Probably the only light for miles. She disliked that thought.

She dug whiskey-soaked dollar bills and a few coins from her purse, started plugging them into the cigarette machine until it clanked and dispensed a pack of Camels. The cold almost drove her scurrying back to the room where her husband doubtless slumbered with dreams of unfiltered cigarettes dancing in his head, but not quite. She cracked the pack and got one going, determined to satisfy her craving and then hide the rest where he'd never find them. Lazy, unchivalrous bastard! Let him forage for his own smokes.

Smoke boiled in her lungs; she leaned against a post and exhaled with beatific self-satisfaction, momentarily immune to the chill. The radiance of the vending machines seeped a few yards across the gravel lot, illuminating the hood of her Volkswagen Beetle and a beat-to-hell pickup she presumed belonged to the night clerk. She was halfway through her second cigarette when she finally detected a foreign shape between the Volkswagen and the pickup. Though mostly cloaked in shadow and impossibly huge, she recognized it as a tortoise. It squatted there, the crown of its shell even with the car window. Its beak and monstrously clawed forepaws were bisected by the wavering edge of illumination. There was a blob of skull perhaps the diameter of a melon, and a moist eye that glimmered yellow.

—Wow, she said. She finished her cigarette. Afraid to move, she lighted another, and that was tricky with her hands shaking so terribly, then she smoked that one too and stared at the giant tortoise staring back at her. She thought, for a moment, she saw its shell rhythmically dilate and contract in time with her own surging heart.

The night remained preternaturally quiet there on the edge of the highway, absent the burr of distant engines or blatting horns, or the stark sweep of rushing headlights. The world had descended into a primeval well while she'd been partying in their motel room; it had slipped backward and now the desert truly was an ancient and haunted place. What else would shamble from the wastes of rock and scrub and the far-off dunes?

She finished the third cigarette and stuffed the pack in her jeans pocket, and with a great act of will sidled the way she'd come; not turning her back, oh no, simply crabbing sideways, hips brushing doorknobs as she went. The tortoise remained in place, immobile as a boulder. The cosmic black tar began eating a few handfuls of stars here and there, like peanuts.

Once at what she prayed was a safe distance, she moved faster, counting doors, terrified of tripping in the dark, of sprawling on her face, and thus helpless, hearing the sibilant shift and crunch of a massive body sliding across gravel. But she made it to the room without occurrence and locked the door and pressed against it, sobbing and blubbering with exhaustion.

He lay face down in the middle of the crummy bed, his naked body a pale gray smear in the gloom. She went to him and shook him. He raised his head at a drunken pitch and mumbled incoherencies. He didn't react to her frantic account of the giant tortoise, her speculation that it might be even now bearing down upon them for a late-night snack, that the world might be coming to an end.

—Goddamn it, wake up! she said and smacked his shoulder, hard. Then, as her eyes adjusted, she saw tears on his cheeks, the unnatural luster of his eyes. Not tears; sweat poured from him, smoked from him, it saturated the sheets until they resembled a sloughed cocoon. The muscles of his shoulder flexed and bunched in agonized knots beneath her hand.

—There's been an incident, he whispered.

She wrapped her arms around her knees and bit her thumb and began to rock ever so slightly. —Baby, I just saw a goddamned turtle the size of a car in the parking lot. What incident are *you* talking about?

—It wasn't a water stain. You were right. It's a worm, like a kind that lived in the Paleozoic. The worm slithered off the wall when you left, made a beeline right over here.... He pushed his face into the sheets and uttered a bark. —Look at the wall.

She looked at the wall. The ominous shadow was gone, melted away, if it had ever been. —What happened? she said.

—The worm crawled up my ass and there it waits. It's gonna rule the world.

She didn't know what to say. She cried softly, and bit her thumb, and rocked.

—I'm high, he said. His entire body relaxed and he began to snore.

—Oh, you jerk, she said, and cried shamelessly, this time in relief. No more pills with tequila chasers for her. She wiped her nose and curled into a ball against his clammy flank and fell unconscious as if she'd been chloroformed.

When she awakened it was still very dark. They lay spine to spine, her leg draped over his, her arm trailing over the edge and near the carpet.

His body twitched against hers the way a person does when they dream of running, flying, being pursued through vast, sunless spaces. She closed her eyes.

He shuddered.

Something hit the floor on the opposite side of the bed with a fleshy thud, like a coconut dropping from a tree into wet sand. Her breath caught and her eyes bulged as she listened to the object slowly roll across the floorboards in a bumpy, lopsided fashion. This was a purposeful, animated movement that bristled every hair on her body. She reached over her shoulder and gripped his arm. —Psst! Honey! It was like shaking a corpse.

Quietly, muffled by the mattresses, someone under the bed began to laugh.

THE LAGERSTÄTTE

October 2004

   Virgil acquired the cute little blue-and-white-pinstriped Cessna at an auction; this over Danni's strenuous objections. There were financial issues; Virgil's salary as department head at his software development company wasn't scheduled to increase for another eighteen months and they'd recently enrolled their son Keith in an exclusive grammar school. Ten grand a year was a serious hit on their rainy-day fund. Also, Danni didn't like planes, especially small ones, which she asserted were scarcely more than tin, plastic, and balsawood. She even avoided traveling by commercial airliner if it was possible to drive or take a train. But she couldn't compete with love at first sight. Virgil took one look at the four-seater and practically swooned, and Danni knew she'd had it before the argument even started. Keith begged to fly and Virgil promised to teach him, teased that he might be the only kid to get his pilot's license before he learned to drive.

   Because Danni detested flying so much, when their assiduously planned weeklong vacation rolled around, she decided to boycott the flight and meet her husband and son at the in-laws place on Cape Cod a day late, after wrapping up business in the city. The drive was only a couple of hours—she'd be at the house in time for Friday supper. She saw them off from a small airport in the suburbs, and returned home to pack and go over last minute adjustments to her evening lecture at the museum.

   How many times did the plane crash between waking and sleeping? There was no way to measure that; during the first weeks the accident cycled through a continuous playback loop, cheap and grainy and soundless like a closed circuit security feed. They'd recovered pieces of fuselage from the water, bobbing like cork—she caught a few moments of news footage before someone, probably Dad, killed the television.

They threw the most beautiful double funeral courtesy of Virgil's parents, followed by a reception in his family's summer home. She recalled wavering shadowbox lights and the muted hum of voices, men in black hats clasping cocktails to the breasts of their black suits, and severe women gathered near the sharper, astral glow of the kitchen, faces gaunt and cold as porcelain, their dresses black, their children underfoot and dressed as adults in miniature; and afterward, a smooth descent into darkness like a bullet reversing its trajectory and dropping into the barrel of a gun.

Later, in the hospital, she chuckled when she read the police report. It claimed she'd eaten a bottle of pills she'd found in her mother-in-law's dresser and curled up to die in her husband's closet among his little league uniforms and boxes of trophies. That was simply hilarious because anyone who knew her would know the notion was just too goddamned melodramatic for words.

March 2005

About four months after she lost her husband and son, Danni transplanted to the West Coast, taken in by a childhood friend named Merrill Thurman, and cut all ties with extended family, peers, and associates from before the accident. She eventually lost interest in grieving just as she lost interest in her former career as an entomologist; both were exercises of excruciating tediousness and ultimately pointless in the face of her brand new, freewheeling course. All those years of college and marriage were abruptly and irrevocably reduced to the fond memories of another life, a chapter in a closed book.

Danni was satisfied with the status quo of patchwork memory and aching numbness. At her best, there were no highs, no lows, just a seamless thrum as one day rolled into the next. She took to perusing self-help pamphlets and treatises on Eastern philosophy, and trendy art magazines; she piled them in her room until they wedged the door open. She studied Tai Chi during an eight-week course in the decrepit gym of the crosstown YMCA. She toyed with an easel and paints, attended a class at the community college. She'd taken some drafting as an undergrad. This was helpful for the technical aspects, the geometry of line and space; the actual artistic part proved more difficult. Maybe she needed to steep herself in the bohemian culture—a coldwater flat in Paris, or an artist commune, or a sea shanty on the coast of Barbados.

Oh, but she'd never live alone, would she?

Amidst this reevaluation and reordering, came the fugue, a lunatic element that found genesis in the void between melancholy and nightmare. The fugue made familiar places strange; it wiped away friendly faces and replaced them with beekeeper masks and reduced English to the low growl of the swarm. It was a disorder of trauma and shock, a hybrid of temporary dementia and selective amnesia. It battened to her with the mindless tenacity of a leech.

She tried not to think about its origins, because when she did she was carried back to the twilight land of her subconscious; to Keith's fifth birthday party; her wedding day with the thousand-dollar cake, and the honeymoon in Niagara Falls; the Cessna spinning against the sun, streaking downward to slam into the Atlantic; and the lush corruption of a green-black jungle and its hidden cairns—the bones of giants slowly sinking into the always hungry earth.

The palace of cries where the doors are opened with blood and sorrow. The secret graveyard of the elephants. The bones of elephants made a forest of ribcages and tusks, dry riverbeds of skulls. Red ants crawled in trains along the petrified spines of behemoths and trailed into the black caverns of empty sockets. Oh, what the lost expeditions might've told the world!

She'd dreamt of the Elephants' Graveyard off and on since the funeral and wasn't certain why she had grown so morbidly preoccupied with the legend. Bleak mythology had interested her when she was young and vital and untouched by the twin melanomas of wisdom and grief. Now, such morose contemplation invoked a primordial dread and answered nothing. The central mystery of her was impenetrable to casual methods. Delving beneath the surface smacked of finality, of doom.

Danni chose to endure the fugue, to welcome it as a reliable adversary. The state seldom lasted more than a few minutes, and admittedly it was frightening, certainly dangerous; nonetheless, she was never one to live in a cage. In many ways the dementia and its umbra of pure terror, its visceral chaos, provided the masochistic rush she craved these days—a badge of courage, the martyr's brand. The fugue hid her in its shadow, like a sheltering wing.

May 6, 2006
(D. L. Session 33)

Danni stared at the table while Dr. Green pressed a button and the wheels of the recorder began to turn. His chair creaked as he leaned back. He stated his name, Danni's name, the date and location.

—How are things this week? He said.

Danni set a slim metal tin on the table and flicked it open with her left hand. She removed a cigarette and lighted it. She used matches because she'd lost the fancy lighter Merrill got her as a birthday gift. She exhaled, shook the match dead.

—For a while, I thought I was getting better, she said in a raw voice.

—You don't think you're improving? Dr. Green said.

—Sometimes I wake up and nothing seems real; it's all a movie set, a humdrum version of *This Is Your Life!* I stare at the ceiling and can't shake this sense I'm an imposter.

—Everybody feels that way, Dr. Green said. His dark hands rested on a clipboard. His hands were creased and notched with the onset of middle age; the cuffs of his starched lab coat had gone yellow at the seams. He was married; he wore a simple ring and he never stared at her breasts. Happily married, or a consummate professional, or she was nothing special. A frosted window rose high and narrow over his shoulder like the painted window of a monastery. Pallid light shone at the corners of his angular glasses, the shiny edges of the clipboard, a piece of the bare plastic table, the sunken tiles of the floor. The tiles were dented and scratched and bumpy. Fine cracks spread like tendrils. Against the far walls were cabinets and shelves and several rickety beds with thin rails and large, black wheels.

The hospital was an ancient place and smelled of mold and sickness beneath the buckets of bleach she knew the custodians poured forth every evening. This had been a sanitarium. People with tuberculosis had gathered here to die in the long, shabby wards. Workers loaded the bodies into furnaces and burned them. There were chutes for the corpses on all of the upper floors. The doors of the chutes were made of dull, gray metal with big handles that reminded her of the handles on the flour and sugar bins in her mother's pantry.

Danni smoked and stared at the ceramic ashtray centered exactly between them, inches from a box of tissues. The ashtray was black. Cinders smoldered in its belly. The hospital was "no smoking," but that never came up during their weekly conversations. After the first session of him watching her drop the ashes into her coat pocket, the ashtray had appeared. Occasionally she tapped her cigarette against the rim of the ashtray and watched the smoke coil tighter and tighter until it imploded the way a demolished building collapses into itself after the charges go off.

Dr. Green said, —Did you take the bus or did you walk?

—Today? I walked.

Dr. Green wrote something on the clipboard with a heavy golden pen. —Good. You stopped to visit your friend at the market, I see.

Danni glanced at her cigarette where it fumed between her second and third fingers.

—Did I mention that? My Friday rounds?

—Yes. When we first met. He tapped a thick, manila folder bound in a heavy-duty rubber band. The folder contained Danni's records and transfer papers from the original admitting institute on the East Coast. Additionally, there was a collection of nearly unrecognizable photos of her in hospital gowns and bathrobes. In several shots an anonymous attendant pushed her in a wheelchair against a blurry backdrop of trees and concrete walls.

—Oh.

—You mentioned going back to work. Any progress?

—No. Merrill wants me to. She thinks I need to reintegrate professionally, that it might fix my problem, Danni said, smiling slightly as she pictured her friend's well-meaning harangues. Merrill spoke quickly, in the cadence of a native Bostonian who would always be a Bostonian no matter where she might find herself. A lit major, she'd also gone through an art-junkie phase during grad school, which had wrecked her first marriage and introduced her to many a disreputable character as could be found haunting the finer galleries and museums. One of said characters became ex-husband the second and engendered a profound and abiding disillusionment with the fine-arts scene entirely. Currently, she made an exemplary copy editor at a rather important monthly journal.

—What do you think?

—I liked being a scientist. I liked to study insects, liked tracking their brief, frenetic little lives. I know how important they are, how integral, essential to the ecosystem. Hell, they outnumber humans trillions to one. But, oh my, it's so damned easy to feel like a god when you've got an ant twitching in your forceps. You think that's how God feels when He's got one of us under His thumb?

—I couldn't say.

—Me neither. Danni dragged heavily and squinted. —Maybe I'll sell Bibles door to door. My uncle sold encyclopedias when I was a little girl.

Dr. Green picked up the clipboard. —Well. Any episodes—fainting, dizziness, disorientation? Anything of that nature?

She smoked in silence for nearly half a minute. —I got confused about where I was the other day. She closed her eyes. The recollection of those bad moments threatened her equilibrium. —I was walking to Yang's grocery. It's about three blocks from the apartments. I got lost for a few minutes.

—A few minutes.

—Yeah. I wasn't timing it, sorry.

—No, that's fine. Go on.

—It was like before. I didn't recognize any of the buildings. I was in a foreign city and couldn't remember what I was doing there. Someone tried to talk to me, to help me—an old lady. But, I ran from her instead. Danni swallowed the faint bitterness, the dumb memory of nausea and terror.

—Why? Why did you run?

—Because when the fugue comes, when I get confused and forget where I am, people frighten me. Their faces don't seem real. Their faces are rubbery and inhuman. I thought the old lady was wearing a mask, that she was hiding something. So I ran. By the time I regained my senses, I was near the park. Kids were staring at me.

—Then?

—Then what? I yelled at them for staring. They took off.

—What did you want at Yang's?

—What?

—You said you were shopping. For what?

—I don't recall. Beets. Grapes. A giant zucchini. I don't know.

—You've been taking your medication, I presume. Drugs, alcohol?

—No drugs. Okay, a joint occasionally. A few shots here and there. Merrill wants to unwind on the weekends. She drinks me under the table—Johnny Walkers and Manhattans. Tequila if she's seducing one of the rugged types. Depends where we are. She'd known Merrill since forever. Historically, Danni was the strong one, the one who saw Merrill through two bad marriages, a career collapse and bouts of deep clinical depression. Funny how life tended to put the shoe on the other foot when one least expected.

—Do you visit many different places?

Danni shrugged. —I don't—oh, the Candy Apple. Harpo's. That hole-in-the-wall on Decker and Gedding, the Red Jack. All sorts of places. Merrill picks; says it's therapy.

—Sex?

Danni shook her head. —That doesn't mean I'm loyal.

—Loyal to whom?

—I've been noticing men and… I feel like I'm betraying Virgil. Soiling our memories. It's stupid, sure. Merrill thinks I'm crazy.

—What do you think?

—I try not to, Doc.

—Yet, the past is with you. You carry it everywhere. Like a millstone, if you'll pardon the cliché.

Danni frowned. —I'm not sure what you mean—

—Yes, you are.

She smoked and looked away from his eyes. She'd arranged a mini gallery of snapshots of Virgil and Keith on the bureau in her bedroom, stuffed more photos in her wallet and fixed one of Keith as a baby on a keychain. She'd built a modest shrine of baseball ticket stubs, Virgil's moldy fishing hat, his car keys, though the car was long gone, business cards, cancelled checks, and torn up Christmas wrapping. It was sick.

—Memories have their place, of course, Dr. Green said. —But you've got to be careful. Live in the past too long and it consumes you. You can't use fidelity as a crutch. Not forever.

—I'm not planning on forever, Danni said.

August 2, 2006

Color and symmetry were among Danni's current preoccupations. Yellow squash, orange baby carrots, an axis of green peas on a china plate; the alignment of complementary elements surgically precise upon the starched white table-cloth—cloth white and neat as the hard white fabric of a hospital sheet.

Their apartment was a narrow box stacked high in a cylinder of similar boxes. The window sashes were blue. All of them a filmy, ephemeral blue like the dust on the wings of a blue emperor butterfly; blue over every window in every cramped room. Blue as dead salmon, blue as ice. Blue shadows darkened the edge of the table, rippled over Danni's untouched meal, its meticulously arrayed components. The vegetables glowed with subdued radioactivity. Her fingers curled around the fork; the veins in her hand ran like blue-black tributaries to her fingertips, ran like cold iron wires. Balanced on a windowsill was her ant farm, its inhabitants scurrying about the business of industry in microcosm of the looming cityscape. Merrill hated the ants and Danni expected her friend to poison them in a fit of revulsion and pique. Merrill wasn't naturally maternal and her scant reservoir of kindly nurture was readily exhausted on her housemate.

Danni set the fork upon a napkin, red gone black as sackcloth in the beautiful gloom, and moved to the terrace door, reaching automatically for her cigarettes as she went. She kept them in the left breast pocket of her jacket alongside a pack of matches from the Candy Apple.

The light that came through the glass and blue gauze was muted and heavy even at midday. Outside the sliding door was a terrace and a rail; beyond the rail, a gulf. Damp breaths of air were coarse with smog, tar, and pigeon shit. Eight stories yawned below the wobbly terrace to the dark brick square. Ninety-six feet to the fountain, the flagpole, two rusty benches, and Piccolo Street where winos with homemade drums, harmonicas, and flutes composed their symphonies and dirges.

Danni smoked on the terrace to keep the peace with Merrill, straight-edge Merrill, whose poison of choice was Zinfandel and fast men in nice suits, rather than tobacco. Danni smoked Turkish cigarettes that came in a tin she bought at the wharf market from a Nepalese expat named Mahan. Mahan sold coffee too, in shiny black packages; and decorative knives with tassels depending from brass handles.

Danni leaned on the swaying rail and lighted the next to the last cigarette in her tin and smoked as the sky clotted between the gaps of rooftops, the copses of wires and antennas, the static snarl of uprooted birds like black bits of paper ash turning in the Pacific breeze. A man stopped in the middle of the crosswalk. He craned his neck to seek her out from amidst the jigsaw of fire escapes and balconies. He waved and then turned away and crossed the street with an unmistakably familiar stride, and was gone.

When her cigarette was done, she flicked the butt into the empty planter, one of several terra cotta pots piled around the corroding barbeque. She lighted her remaining cigarette and smoked it slowly, made it last until the sky went opaque and the city lights began to float here and there in the murk, bubbles of iridescent gas rising against the leaden tide of night. Then she went inside and sat very still while her colony of ants scrabbled in the dark.

May 6, 2006
(D. L. Session 33)

Danni's cigarette was out; the tin empty. She began to fidget. —Do you believe in ghosts, Doctor?

—Absolutely. Dr. Green knocked his ring on the table and gestured at the hoary walls. —Look around. Haunted, I'd say.

—Really?

Dr. Green seemed quite serious. He set aside the clipboard, distancing himself from the record. —Why not. My grandfather was a missionary. He lived in the Congo for several years, set up a clinic out there. Everybody believed in ghosts—including my grandfather. There was no choice.

Danni laughed. —Well, it's settled. I'm a faithless bitch. And I'm being haunted as just desserts.

—Why do you say that?

—I went home with this guy a few weeks ago. Nice guy, a graphic designer. I was pretty drunk and he was pretty persuasive.

Dr. Green plucked a pack of cigarettes from the inside pocket of his white coat, shook one loose and handed it to her. They leaned toward one another, across the table, and he lighted her cigarette with a silvery Zippo.

—Nothing happened, she said. —It was very innocent, actually.

But that was a lie by omission, was it not? What would the good doctor think of her if she confessed her impulses to grasp a man, any man, as a point of fact, and throw him down and fuck him senseless, and refrained only because she was too frightened of the possibilities? Her cheeks stung and she exhaled fiercely to conceal her shame.

—We had some drinks and called it a night. I still felt bad, dirty, somehow. Riding the bus home, I saw Virgil. It wasn't him; he had Virgil's build and kind of slouched, holding onto one of those straps. Didn't even come close once I got a decent look at him. But for a second, my heart froze. Danni lifted her gaze from the ashtray. —Time for more pills, huh?

—Well, a case of mistaken identity doesn't qualify as a delusion. Danni smiled darkly.

—You didn't get on the plane and you lived. Simple. Dr. Green spoke with supreme confidence.

—Is it? Simple, I mean.

—Have you experienced more of these episodes—mistaking strangers for Virgil? Or your son?

—Yeah. The man on the bus, that tepid phantom of her husband, had been the fifth incident of mistaken identity during the previous three weeks. The incidents were growing frequent; each apparition more convincing than the last. Then there were the items she'd occasionally found around the apartment—Virgil's lost wedding ring gleaming at the bottom of a pitcher of water; a trail of dried rose petals leading from the bathroom to her bed; one of Keith's crayon masterpieces fixed by magnet on the refrigerator; each of these artifacts ephemeral as dew, transitory as drifting spider thread; they dissolved and left no traces of their existence. That very morning she'd glimpsed Virgil's bomber jacket slung over the back of a chair. A sunbeam illuminated it momentarily, dispersed it amongst the moving shadows of clouds and undulating curtains.

—Why didn't you mention this sooner?

—It didn't scare me before.

—There are many possibilities. I hazard what we're dealing with is survivor's guilt, Dr. Green said. —This guilt is a perfectly normal aspect of the grieving process.

Dr. Green had never brought up the guilt association before, but she always knew it lurked in the wings, waiting to be sprung in the third act. The books all talked about it. Danni made a noise of disgust and rolled her eyes to hide the sudden urge to cry.

—Go on, Dr. Green said.

Danni pretended to rub smoke from her eye. —There isn't any more.

—Certainly there is. There's always another rock to look beneath. Why don't you tell me about the vineyards. Does this have anything to do with the *Lagerstätte*?

She opened her mouth and closed it. She stared, her fear and anger tightening screws within the pit of her stomach. —You've spoken to Merrill? Goddamn her.

—She hoped you'd get around to it, eventually. But you haven't and it seems important. Don't worry—she volunteered the information. Of course I would never reveal the nature of our conversations. Trust in that.

—It's not a good thing to talk about, Danni said. —I stopped thinking about it.

—Why?

She regarded her cigarette. Norma, poor departed Norma whispered in her ear, *Do you want to press your eye against the keyhole of a secret room? Do you want to see where the elephants have gone to die?*

—Because there are some things you can't take back. Shake hands with an ineffable enigma and it knows you. It has you, if it wants.

Dr. Green waited, his hand poised over a brown folder she hadn't noticed before. The folder was stamped in red block letters she couldn't quite read, although she suspected ASYLUM was at least a portion.

—I wish to understand, he said. —We're not going anywhere.

—Fuck it, she said. A sense of terrible satisfaction and relief caused her to smile again. —Confession is good for the soul, right?

August 9, 2006

In the middle of dressing to meet Merrill at the market by the wharf when she got off work, Danni opened the closet and inhaled a whiff of damp, moldering air and then screamed into her fist. Several withered corpses hung from the rack amid her cheery blouses and conservative suit jackets. They were scarcely more than yellowed sacks of skin. None of the desiccated, sagging faces were recognizable; the shade and texture of cured squash, each was further distorted by warps and wrinkles of dry-cleaning bags. She recoiled and sat on the bed and chewed her fingers until a passing cloud blocked the sun and the closet went dark.

Eventually she washed her hands and face in the bathroom sink, staring into the mirror at her pale, maniacal simulacrum. She skipped makeup and stumbled from the apartment to the cramped, dingy lift that dropped her into a shabby foyer with its rows of tarnished mailbox slots checkering the walls, its low, grubby light fixtures, a stained carpet, and the sweet-and-sour odor of sweat and stagnant air. She stumbled through the security doors into the brighter world.

The fugue descended.

Danni was walking from somewhere to somewhere else; she'd closed her eyes against the glare and her insides turned upside down. Her eyes flew open and she reeled, utterly lost. Shadow people moved around her, bumped her with their hard elbows and swinging hips; an angry man in brown tweed lectured his daughter and the girl protested. They buzzed like flies. Their miserable faces blurred together, lit by some internal phosphorous. Danni swallowed, crushed into herself with a force akin to claustrophobia, and focused on her watch, a cheap windup model that glowed in the dark. Its numerals meant nothing, but she tracked the needle as it swept a perfect circle while the world spun around her. The passage, an indoor-outdoor avenue of sorts. Market stalls flanked the causeway, shelves and timber beams twined with streamers and beads, hemp rope and tie-dye shirts and pennants. Light fell through cracks in the overhead pavilion. The enclosure reeked of fresh salmon, salt water, sawdust, and the compacted scent of perfumed flesh.

—*Danni.* Here was an intelligible voice amid the squeal and squelch. Danni lifted her head and tried to focus.

—*We miss you,* Virgil said. He stood several feet away, gleaming like polished ivory.

—What? Danni said, thinking his face was the only face not changing shape like the flowery crystals in a kaleidoscope. —What did you say?

—*Come home.* It was apparent that this man wasn't Virgil, although in this particular light the eyes were similar, and he drawled. Virgil grew up in South Carolina, spent his adult life trying to bury that drawl and eventually it only emerged when he was exhausted or angry. The stranger winked at her and continued along the boardwalk. Beneath an Egyptian cotton shirt, his back was almost as muscular as Virgil's. But, no.

Danni turned away into the bright, jostling throng. Someone took her elbow. She yelped and wrenched away and nearly fell.

—Honey, you okay? The jumble of insectoid eyes, lips, and bouffant hair coalesced into Merrill's stern face. Merrill wore white-rimmed sunglasses that complemented her vanilla dress with its wide shoulders and brass buttons, and her elegant vanilla gloves. Her thin nose peeled with sunburn. —Danni, are you all right?

—Yeah. Danni wiped her mouth.

—The hell you are. C'mon. Merrill led her away from the moving press to a small open square and seated her in a wooden chair in the shadow of a parasol. The square hosted a half-dozen vendors and several tables of squawking children, overheated parents with flushed cheeks, and senior citizens in pastel running suits. Merrill bought soft ice cream in tiny plastic dishes and they sat in the shade and ate the ice cream while the sun dipped below the rooflines. The vendors began taking down the signs and packing it in for the day.

—Okay, okay. I feel better. Danni's hands had stopped shaking.

—You do look a little better. Know where you are?

—The market. Danni wanted a cigarette. —Oh, damn it, she said.

—Here, sweetie. Merrill drew two containers of Mahan's foreign cigarettes from her purse and slid them across the table, mimicking a spy in one of those '70s thrillers.

—Thanks, Danni said as she got a cigarette burning. She dragged frantically, left hand cupped to her mouth so the escaping smoke boiled and foamed between her fingers like dry ice vapors. Nobody said anything despite the NO SMOKING signs posted on the gate.

—Hey, what kind of bug is that? Merrill intently regarded a beetle hugging the warmth of a wooden plank near their feet.

—It's a beetle.

—How observant. But what kind?

—I don't know.

—What? You don't know?

—I don't know. I don't really care, either.

—Oh, please.

—Fine. Danni leaned forward until her eyeballs were scant inches above the motionless insect. —Hmm. I'd say a *Spurious exoticus minor*, closely related to, but not to be confused with, the *Spurious eroticus major*. Yep.

Merrill stared at the beetle, then Danni. She took Danni's hand and gently squeezed. —You fucking fraud. Let's go get liquored up, hey?

—Hey-hey.

May 6, 2006
(D. L. Session 33)

Dr. Green's glasses were opaque as quartz.

—The *Lagerstätte*. Elucidate, if you will.

—A naturalist's wet dream. Ask Norma Fitzwater and Leslie Runyon, Danni said and chuckled wryly. —When Merrill originally brought me here to Cali, she made me join a support group. That was about, what? A year ago, give or take. Kind of a twelve-step program for wannabe suicides. I quit after a few visits. Group therapy isn't my style and the counselor was a royal prick. Before I left, I became friends with Norma, a drug addict and perennial house guest of the state penitentiary before she snagged a wealthy husband. Marrying rich wasn't a cure for everything, though. She claimed to have tried to off herself five or six times, made it sound like an extreme sport.

—A fascinating woman. She was pals with Leslie, a widow like me. Leslie's husband and brother fell off a glacier in Alaska. I didn't like her much. Too creepy for polite company. Unfortunately, Norma had a mother-hen complex, so there was no getting rid of her. Anyway, it wasn't much to write home about. We went to lunch once a week, watched a couple of films, commiserated about our shitty luck. Summer camp stuff.

—You speak of Norma in the past tense. I gather she eventually ended her life, Dr. Green said.

—Oh, yes. She made good on that. Jumped off a hotel roof in the Tenderloin. Left a note to the effect that she and Leslie couldn't face the music anymore. The cops, brilliant as they are, concluded Norma made a suicide pact with Leslie. Leslie's corpse hasn't surfaced yet. The cops figure she's at the bottom of the bay, or moldering in a wooded gully. I doubt that's what happened though.

—You suspect she's alive.

—No, Leslie's dead under mysterious and messy circumstances. It got leaked to the press that the cops found evidence of foul play at her home. There was blood or something on her sheets. They say it dried in the shape of a person curled in the fetal position. They compared it to the flash shadows of victims in Hiroshima. This was deeper, as if the body had been pressed hard into the mattress. The only remains were her watch, her diaphragm, her *fillings*, for Christ's sake, stuck to the coagulate that got left behind like afterbirth. Sure, it's bullshit, urban legend fodder. There were some photos in the *Gazette*, some speculation amongst our sorry little circle of neurotics and manic depressives.

—Very unpleasant, but, fortunately, equally improbable.

Danni shrugged. —Here's the thing, though. Norma predicted everything. A month before she killed herself, she let me in on a secret. Her friend Leslie, the creepy lady, had been seeing Bobby. He visited her nightly, begged her to come away with him. And Leslie planned to.

—Her husband, Dr. Green said. —The one who died in Alaska.

—The same. Trust me, I laughed, a little nervously, at this news. I wasn't sure whether to humor Norma or get the hell away from her. We were sitting in a classy restaurant, surrounded by execs in silk ties and Armani suits. Like I said, Norma was loaded. She married into a nice Sicilian family; her husband was in the import-export business, if you get my drift. Beat the hell out of her, though; definitely contributed to her low self-esteem. Right in the middle of our luncheon, between the lobster tails and the éclairs, she leaned over and confided this thing with Leslie and her deceased husband. The ghostly lover.

Dr. Green passed Danni another cigarette. He lighted one of his own and studied her through the blue exhaust. Danni wondered if he wanted a drink as badly as she did.

—How did you react to this information? Dr. Green said.

—I stayed cool, feigned indifference. It wasn't difficult; I was doped to the eyeballs most of the time. Norma claimed there exists a certain quality of grief, so utterly profound, so tragically pure, that it resounds and resonates above and below. A living, bleeding echo. It's the key to a kind of limbo.

—The *Lagerstätte*. Dr. Green licked his thumb and sorted through the papers in the brown folder. —As in the Burgess Shale, the La Brea Tar Pits. Were your friends amateur paleontologists?

—*Lagerstätten* are "resting places" in the Deutsch, and I think that's what the women meant.

—Fascinating choice of mythos.

—People do whatever it takes to cope. Drugs, kamikaze sex, religion, anything. In naming, we seek to order the incomprehensible, yes?

—True.

—Norma pulled this weird piece of jagged, gray rock from her purse. Not rock—a petrified bone shard. A fang or a long, wicked rib splinter. Supposedly human. I could tell it was *old*; it reminded me of all those fossils of trilobites I used to play with. It radiated an aura of antiquity, like it had survived a shift of deep geological time. Norma got it from Leslie and Leslie had gotten it from someone else; Norma claimed to have no idea who, although I suspect she was lying; there was definitely a certain slyness in her eyes. For all I know, it's osmosis. She pricked her finger on the shard and gestured at the blood that oozed on her plate. Danni shivered and clenched her left hand. —The scene was surreal. Norma said: *Grief is blood, Danni. Blood is the living path to everywhere. Blood opens the way.* She said if I offered myself to the *Lagerstätte,* Virgil would come to me and take me into the house of dreams. But I wanted to know whether it would really be him and not… an imitation. She said, *Does it matter?* My skin crawled as if I were waking from a long sleep to something awful, something my primal self recognized and feared. Like fire.

—You believe the bone was human.

—I don't know. Norma insisted I accept it as a gift from her and Leslie. I really didn't want to, but the look on her face, it was intense.

—Where did it come from? The bone.

—The *Lagerstätte*.

—Of course. What did you do?

Danni looked down at her hands, the left with its jagged white scar in the meat and muscle of her palm, and deeper into the darkness of the earth. —The same as Leslie. I called them.

—You called them. Virgil and Keith.

—Yes. I didn't plan to go through with it. I got drunk, and when I'm like that, my thoughts get kind of screwy. I don't act in character.

—Oh. Dr. Green thought that over. —When you say called, what exactly do you mean?

She shrugged and flicked ashes into the ashtray. Even though Dr. Green had been there the morning they stitched the wound, she guarded the secret of its origin with a zeal bordering on pathological.

Danni had brought the weird bone to the apartment. Once alone, she drank the better half of a bottle of Maker's Mark and then sliced her palm with the sharp edge of the bone and made a doorway in blood. She slathered a vertical seam, a demarcation between her existence and the abyss, in the plaster wall at the foot of her bed. She smeared Virgil and Keith's initials and sent a little prayer into the night. In a small clay pot she'd bought at a market, she shredded her identification, her (mostly defunct) credit cards, her social security card, a lock of her hair, and burned the works with the tallow of a lamb. Then, in the smoke and shadows, she finished getting drunk off her ass and promptly blacked out.

Merrill wasn't happy; Danni had bled like the proverbial stuck pig, soaked through the sheets into the mattress. Merrill decided her friend had horribly botched another run for the Pearly Gates. She had brought Danni to the hospital for a bunch of stitches and introduced her to Dr. Green. Of course Danni didn't admit another suicide attempt. She doubted her conducting a black-magic ritual would help matters either. She said nothing, simply agreed to return for sessions with the good doctor. He was blandly pleasant, eminently nonthreatening. She didn't think he could help, but that wasn't the point. The point was to please Merrill and Merrill insisted on the visits.

Back home, Merrill confiscated the bone, the ritual fetish, and threw it in the trash. Later, she tried like hell to scrub the stain. In the end she gave up and painted the whole room blue.

A couple days after that particular bit of excitement, Danni found the bone at the bottom of her sock drawer. It glistened with a cruel, lusterless intensity. Like the monkey's paw, it had returned and that didn't surprise her. She folded it into a kerchief and locked it in a jewelry box she'd kept since first grade.

All these months gone by, Danni remained silent on the subject.

Finally, Dr. Green sighed.—Is that when you began seeing Virgil in the faces of strangers? These doppelgängers? He smoked his cigarette with the joyless concentration of a prisoner facing a firing squad. It was obvious from his expression that the meter had rolled back to zero.

—No, not right away. Nothing happened, Danni said. —Nothing ever does, at first.

—No, I suppose not. Tell me about the vineyard. What happened there?

—I… I got lost.

—That's where all this really begins, isn't it? The fugue, perhaps other things.

Danni gritted her teeth. She thought of elephants and graveyards. Dr. Green was right, in his own smug way. Six weeks after Danni sliced her hand, Merrill took her for a daytrip to the beach. Merrill rented a convertible and made a picnic. It was nice; possibly the first time Danni felt human since the accident; the first time she'd wanted to do anything besides mope in the apartment and play depressing music.

After some discussion, they chose Bolton Park, a lovely stretch of coastline way out past Kingwood. The area was foreign to Danni, so she bought a road map pamphlet at a gas station. The brochure listed a bunch of touristy places. Windsurfers and birdwatchers favored the area, but the guide warned of dangerous riptides. The women had no intention of swimming; they stayed near a cluster of great big rocks at the north end of the beach—below the cliff with the steps that led up to the posh houses; the summer homes of movie stars and advertising executives; the beautiful people.

On the way home, Danni asked if they might stop at Kirkston Vineyards. It was a hole-in-the-wall, only briefly listed in the guidebook. There were no pictures. They drove in circles for an hour tracking the place down—Kirkston was off the beaten path; a village of sorts. There was a gift shop and an inn, and a few antique houses. The winery was fairly large and charming in a rustic fashion, and that essentially summed up the entire place.

Danni thought it was a cute setup; Merrill was bored stiff and did what she always did when she'd grown weary of a situation—she flirted like mad with one of the tour guides. Pretty soon, she disappeared with the guy on a private tour.

There were twenty or thirty people in the tour group—a bunch of elderly folks who'd arrived on a bus and a few couples pretending they were in Europe. After Danni lost Merrill in the crowd, she went outside to explore until her friend surfaced again.

Perhaps fifty yards from the winery steps, Virgil waited in the lengthening shadows of a cedar grove. That was the first of the phantoms. Too far away for positive identification, his face was a white smudge. He hesitated and regarded her over his shoulder before he ducked into the undergrowth. She knew it was impossible, knew that it was madness, or worse, and went after him, anyway.

Deeper into the grounds she encountered crumbled walls of a ruined garden hidden under a bower of willow trees and honeysuckle vines. She passed through a massive marble archway, so thick with sap it had blackened like a smoke stack. Inside was a sunken area and a clogged fountain decorated with cherubs and gargoyles. There were scattered benches made of stone slabs, and piles of rubble overrun by creepers and moss. Water pooled throughout the garden, mostly covered by algae and scum; mosquito larvae squirmed beneath drowned leaves. Ridges of broken stone and mortar petrified in the slop and slime of that boggy soil and made waist-high calculi amongst the freestanding masonry.

Her hand throbbed with a sudden, magnificent stab of pain. She hissed through her teeth. The freshly knitted, pink slash, her Freudian scar, had split and blood seeped so copiously her head swam. She ripped the sleeve off her blouse and made a hasty tourniquet. A grim, sullen quiet drifted in; a blizzard of silence. The bees weren't buzzing and the shadows in the trees waxed red and gold as the light decayed.

Virgil stepped from behind stalagmites of fallen stone, maybe thirty feet away. She knew with every fiber of her being that this was a fake, a body double, and yet she wanted nothing more than to hurl herself into his arms. Up until that moment, she didn't realize how much she'd missed him, how achingly final her loneliness had become.

Her glance fell upon a gleaming wedge of stone where it thrust from the water like a dinosaur's tooth, and as shapes within shapes became apparent, she understood this wasn't a garden. It was a graveyard.

Virgil opened his arms—

—I'm not comfortable talking about this, Danni said. —Let's move on.

August 9, 2006

Friday was karaoke night at the Candy Apple.

In the golden days of her previous life, Danni had a battalion of friends and colleagues with whom to attend the various academic functions and cocktail socials as required by her professional affiliation with a famous East Coast university. Barhopping had seldom been the excursion of choice.

Tonight, a continent and several light-years removed from such circumstances, she nursed an overly strong margarita, while up on the stage a couple of drunken women with big hair and smeared makeup stumbled through that old Kenny Rogers standby, "Ruby, Don't Take Your Love to Town." The fake redhead was a receptionist named Sheila, and her blonde partner, Delores, a vice president of human resources. Both of them worked at Merrill's literary magazine and they were partying off their second and third divorces respectively.

Danni wasn't drunk, although mixing her medication with alcohol wasn't helping matters; her nose had begun to tingle and her sensibilities were definitely sliding toward the nihilistic side. Also, she seemed to be hallucinating again. She'd spotted two Virgil look-alikes between walking through the door and her third margarita; that was a record, so far. She hadn't noticed either of the men enter the lounge, they simply appeared.

One of the mystery men sat amongst a group of happily chattering yuppie kids; he'd worn a sweater and parted his hair exactly like her husband used to before an important interview or presentation. The brow was wrong though, and the smile way off. He established eye contact and his gaze made her prickle all over because this simulacrum was so very authentic; if not for the plastic sheen and the unwholesome smile, he was the man she'd looked at across the breakfast table for a dozen years. Eventually he stood and wandered away from his friends and disappeared through the front door into the night. None of the kids seemed to miss him.

The second guy sat alone at the far end of the bar; he was much closer to the authentic thing; he had the nose, the jaw, even the loose way of draping his hands over his knees. However, this one was a bit too rawboned to pass as *her* Virgil; his teeth too large, his arms too long. He stared across the room, too-dark eyes fastened on her face and she looked away and by the time she glanced up again he was gone.

She checked to see if Merrill noticed the Virgil impersonators. Merrill blithely sipped her Corona and flirted with a couple lawyer types at the adjoining table. The suits kept company with a voluptuous woman who was growing long in the tooth and had piled on enough compensatory eye shadow and lipstick to host her own talk show. The woman sulked and shot dangerous glares at Merrill. Merrill smirked coyly and touched the closest suit on the arm.

Danni lighted a cigarette and tried to keep her expression neutral while her pulse fluttered and she scanned the room with the corners of her eyes like a trapped bird. Should she call Dr. Green in the morning? Was he even in the office on weekends? What color would the new pills be?

Presently, the late dinner and theater crowd arrived en masse and the lounge became packed. The temperature immediately shot up ten degrees and the resultant din of several dozen competing conversations drowned all but shouts. Merrill had recruited the lawyers (who turned out to be an insurance claims investigator and a CPA) Ned and Thomas, and their miffed associate Glenna (a court clerk), to join the group and migrate to another, hopefully more peaceful watering hole.

They shambled through neon-washed night, a noisy, truncated herd of quasi-strangers, arms locked for purchase against the mist-slick sidewalks. Danni found herself squashed between Glenna and Ned the Investigator. Ned grasped her waist in a slack, yet vaguely proprietary fashion; his hand was soft with sweat, his paunchy face made more uncomely with livid blotches and the avaricious expression of a drowsy predator. His shirt reeked so powerfully of whiskey it might've been doused in the stuff.

Merrill pulled them to a succession of bars and nightclubs and all-night bistros. Somebody handed Danni a beer as they milled in the vaulted entrance of an Irish pub and she drank it like tap water, not really tasting it, and her ears hurt and the evening rapidly devolved into a tangle of raucous music and smoke that reflected the fluorescent lights like coke-blacked miners lamps, and at last a cool, humid darkness shattered by headlights and the sulfurous orange glow of angry clouds.

By her haphazard count, she glimpsed in excess of fifty incarnations of Virgil. Several at the tavern, solitary men mostly submerged in the recessed booths, observing her with stony diffidence through beer steins and shot glasses; a dozen more scattered along the boulevard, listless no-mads whose eyes slid around, not quite touching anything. When a city bus grumbled past, every passenger's head swiveled in unison beneath the repeating flare of dome lights. Every face pressed against the dirty windows belonged to him. Their lifelike masks bulged and contorted with inconsolable longing.

Ned escorted her to his place, a warehouse apartment in a row of identical warehouses between the harbor and the railroad tracks. The building had been converted to a munitions factory during the Second World War, then housing in the latter '60s. It stood black and gritty; its greasy windows sucked in the feeble illumination of the lonely beacons of passing boats and the occasional car.

They took a clanking cargo elevator to the top, the penthouse, as Ned laughingly referred to his apartment. The elevator was a box encased in grates that exposed the inner organs of the shaft and the dark tunnels of passing floors. It could've easily hoisted a baby grand piano. Danni pressed her cheek to vibrating metal and shut her eyes tight against vertigo and the canteen-like slosh of too many beers in her stomach.

Ned's apartment was sparsely furnished and remained mostly in gloom even after he turned on the floor lamp and went to fix nightcaps. Danni collapsed onto the corner of a couch abridging the shallow nimbus of light and stared raptly at her bone-white hand curled into the black leather. Neil Diamond crooned from velvet speakers. Ned said something about his record collection and, faintly, ice cracked from its tray and clinked in glass with the resonance of a tuning fork.

Danni's hand shivered as if it might double and divide. She was cold now, in the sticky hot apartment, and her thighs trembled. Ned slipped a drink into her hand and placed his own hand on her shoulder, splayed his soft fingers on her collar, traced her collar bone with his moist fingertip. Danni flinched and poured gin down her throat until Ned took the glass and began to nuzzle her ear, his teeth clicking against the pearl stud, his overheated breath like smoldering creosote and kerosene, and as he tugged at her blouse strap, she began to cry. Ned lurched above her and his hands were busy with his belt and pants, and these fell around his ankles and his loafers. He made a fist in a mass of her hair and yanked her face against his groin; his linen shirttails fell across Danni's shoulders and he bulled himself into her gasping mouth. She gagged, overwhelmed by the ripeness of sweat and whiskey and urine, the rank humidity, the bruising insistence of him, and she convulsed, arms flailing in epileptic spasms, and vomited. Ned's hips pumped for several seconds and then his brain caught up with current events and he cried out in dismay and disgust and nearly capsized the couch as he scrambled away from her and a caramel gush of half-digested cocktail shrimp and alcohol.

Danni dragged herself from the couch and groped for the door. The door was locked with a bolt and chain and she battered at these, sobbing and choking. Ned's curses were muffled by a thin partition and the low thunder of water sluicing through corroded pipes. She flung open the door and was instantly lost in a cavernous hall that telescoped madly. The door behind her was a cave mouth, the windows were holes, were burrows. She toppled down a flight of stairs.

Danni lay crumpled, damp concrete wedged against the small of her back and pinching the back of her legs. Ghostly radiance cast shadows upon the piebald walls of the narrow staircase and rendered the scrawls of graffiti into fragmented hieroglyphics. Copper and salt filled her mouth. Her head was thick and spongy and when she moved it, little comets shot through her vision. A moth jerked in zigzags near her face, jittering upward at frantic angles toward a naked bulb. The bulb was brown and black with dust and cigarette smoke. A solid shadow detached from the gloom of the landing; a slight, pitchy silhouette that wavered at the edges like gasoline fumes.

Mommy? A small voice echoed, familiar and strange, the voice of a child or a castrato and it plucked at her insides, sent tremors through her.

—Oh, God, she said, and vomited again, spilling herself against the rough surface of the wall. The figure became two, then four and a pack of childlike shapes assembled on the landing. The pallid corona of the brown bulb dimmed. She rolled away, onto her belly, and began to crawl…

August 10, 2006

The police located Danni semiconscious in the alley behind the warehouse apartments. She didn't understand much of what they said and she couldn't muster the resolve to volunteer the details of her evening's escapades. Merrill rode with her in the ambulance to the emergency room where, following a two-hour wait, a haggard surgeon determined Danni suffered from a number of nasty contusions, minor lacerations, and a punctured tongue. No concussion, however. He punched ten staples into her scalp, handed over a prescription for painkillers, and sent her home with an admonishment to return in twelve hours for observation.

After they'd settled safe and sound at the apartment, Merrill wrapped Danni in a blanket and boiled a pot of green tea. Lately, Merrill was into feng shui and Chinese herbal remedies. It wasn't quite dawn and so they sat in the shadows in the living room. There were no recriminations, although Merrill lapsed into a palpable funk; hers was the grim expression of guilt and helplessness attendant to her perceived breach of guardianship. Danni patted her hand and drifted off to sleep.

When Danni came to again, it was early afternoon and Merrill was in the kitchen banging pots. Over bowls of hot noodle soup Merrill explained she'd called in sick for a couple days. She thought they should get Danni's skull checked for dents and rent some movies and lie around with a bowl of popcorn and do essentially nothing. Tomorrow might be a good day to go window shopping for an Asian print to mount in their pitifully barren entryway.

Merrill summoned a cab. The rain came in sheets against the windows of the moving car and Danni dozed to the thud of the wipers, trying to ignore the driver's eyes upon her from the rearview. He looked unlike the fuzzy headshot on his license fixed to the visor. In the photo his features were burnt teak and warped by the deformation of aging plastic.

They arrived at the hospital and signed in and went into the bowels of the grand old beast to radiology. A woman in a white jacket injected dye into Danni's leg and loaded her into a shiny, cold machine the girth of a bread truck and ordered her to keep her head still. The technician's voice buzzed through a hidden transmitter, repulsively intimate as if a fly had crawled into her ear canal. When the rubber jackhammers started in on the steel shell, she closed her eyes and saw Virgil and Keith waving to her from the convex windows of the plane. The propeller spun so slowly she could track its revolutions.

—The doctor says they're negative. The technician held photographic plates of Danni's brain against a softly flickering pane of light. —See? No problems at all.

The crimson seam dried black on the bedroom wall. The band of black acid eating plaster until the wall swung open on smooth, silent hinges. Red darkness pulsed in the rift. White leaves crumbled and sank, each one a lost face. A shadow slowly shaped itself into human form. The shadow man regarded her, his hand extended, approaching her without moving his shadow legs.

Merrill thanked the woman in the clipped manner she reserved for those who provoked her distaste, and put a protective arm over Danni's shoulders. Danni had taken an extra dose of tranquilizers to sand the rough edges. Reality was a taffy pull.

Pour out your blood and they'll come back to you, Norma said, and stuck her bleeding finger into her mouth. Her eyes were cold and dark as the eyes of a carrion bird. Bobby and Leslie coupled on a squeaking bed. Their frantic rhythm gradually slowed and they began to melt and merge until their flesh rendered to a sticky puddle of oil and fat and patches of hair. The forensics photographers came, clicking and whirring, eyes deader than the lenses of their cameras. They smoked cigarettes in the hallway and chatted with the plainclothes about baseball and who was getting pussy and who wasn't; everybody had sashimi for lunch, noodles for supper, and took work home and drank too much. Leslie curdled in the sheets and her parents were long gone, so she was already most of the way to being reduced to a serial number and forgotten in a cardboard box in a storeroom. Except, Leslie stood in a doorway in the grimy bulk of a nameless building. She stood, hip-shot and half-silhouetted, naked and lovely as a Botticelli nude. Disembodied arms circled her from behind, and large, muscular hands cupped her breasts. She nodded, expressionless as a wax death masque, and stepped back into the black. The iron door closed.

Danni's brain was fine. No problems at all.

Merrill took her home and made her supper. Fried chicken; Danni's favorite from a research stint studying the migration habits of three species of arachnids at a southern institute where grits did double duty as breakfast and lunch.

Danni dozed intermittently, lulled by the staccato flashes of the television. She stirred and wiped drool from her lips, thankfully too dopey to suffer much embarrassment. Merrill helped her to bed and tucked her in and kissed her goodnight on the mouth. Danni was surprised by the warmth of her breath, her tenderness; then she was heavily asleep, floating facedown in the red darkness, the amniotic wastes of a secret world.

August 11, 2006

Merrill cooked waffles for breakfast; she claimed to have been a "champeen" hash-slinger as an undergrad, albeit Danni couldn't recall that particular detail of their shared history. Although food crumbled like cardboard on her tongue, Danni smiled gamely and cleared her plate. The fresh orange juice in the frosted glass was a mouthful of lye. Merrill had apparently jogged over to Yang's and picked up a carton the exact instant the poor fellow rolled back the metal curtains from his shop front, and Danni swallowed it and hoped she didn't drop the glass because her hand was shaking so much. The pleasant euphoria of painkillers and sedatives had drained away, usurped by a gnawing, allusive dread, a swell of self-disgust and revulsion.

The night terrors tittered and scuffled in the cracks and crannies of the tiny kitchen, whistled at her in a pitch only she and dogs could hear. Any second now, the broom closet would creak open and a ghastly figure shamble forth, licking lips riven by worms. At any moment the building would shudder and topple in an avalanche of dust and glass and shearing girders. She slumped in her chair, fixated on the chipped vase, its cargo of wilted geraniums drooping over the rim. Merrill bustled around her, tidying up with what she dryly attributed as her latent German efficiency, although her mannerisms suggested a sense of profound anxiety. When the phone chirped and it was Sheila reporting some minor emergency at the office, her agitation multiplied as she scoured her little address book for someone to watch over Danni for a few hours.

Danni told her to go, she'd be okay—maybe watch a soap and take a nap. She promised to sit tight in the apartment, come what may. Appearing only slightly mollified, Merrill agreed to leave, vowing a speedy return.

Late afternoon slipped over the city, lackluster and overcast. Came the desultory honk and growl of traffic, the occasional shout, the off-tempo drumbeat from the square. Reflections of the skyline patterned a blank span of wall. Water gurgled, and the disjointed mumble of radio or television commentary came muffled from the neighboring apartments. Her eyes leaked and the shakes traveled from her hands into the large muscles of her shoulders. Her left hand ached.

A child murmured in the hallway, followed by scratching at the door. The bolt rattled. She stood and looked across the living area at the open door of the bedroom. The bedroom dilated. Piles of jagged rocks twined with coarse brown seaweed instead of the bed, the dresser, her unseemly stacks of magazines. A figure stirred amid the weird rocks and unfolded at the hips with the horrible alacrity of a tarantula. *You filthy whore.* She groaned and hooked the door with her ankle and kicked it shut.

Danni went to the kitchen and slid a carving knife from its wooden block. She walked to the bathroom and turned on the shower. Everything seemed too shiny, except the knife. The knife hung loosely in her fingers; its blade was dark and pitted. She stripped her robe and stepped into the shower and drew the curtain. Steam began to fill the room. Hot water beat against the back of her neck, her spine and buttocks as she rested her forehead against the tiles.

What have you done? You filthy bitch. She couldn't discern whether that accusing whisper had bubbled from her brain, or trickled in with the swirling steam. *What have you done?* It hardly mattered now that nothing was of any substance, of any importance besides the knife. Her hand throbbed as the scar separated along its seam. Blood and water swirled down the drain.

Danni. The floorboards settled and a tepid draft brushed her calves. She raised her head and a silhouette filled the narrow door, an incomprehensible blur through the shower curtain. Danni dropped the knife. She slid down the wall into a fetal position. Her teeth chattered, and her animal self took possession. She remembered the ocean, acres of driftwood littering a beach, Virgil's grin as he paid out the tether of a dragonhead kite they'd bought in Chinatown. She remembered the corpses hanging in her closet, and whimpered.

A hand pressed against the translucent fabric, dimpled it inward, fingers spread. The hand squelched on the curtain. Blood ran from its palm and slithered in descending ladders.

—Oh, Danni said. Blearily, through a haze of tears and steam, she reached up and pressed her bloody left hand against the curtain, locked palms with the apparition, giddily cognizant this was a gruesome parody of the star-crossed lovers who kiss through glass. —Virgil, she said, chest hitching with sobs.

—You don't have to go, Merrill said, and dragged the curtain aside. She too wept, and nearly fell into the tub as she embraced Danni and the water soaked her clothes, and quantities of blood spilled between them, and Danni saw her friend had found the fetish bone, because there it was, in a black slick on the floor, trailing a spray of droplets like a nosebleed.

—You can stay with me. Please stay, Merrill said. She stroked Danni's hair, hugged her as if to keep her from floating away with the steam as it condensed on the mirror, the small window, and slowly evaporated.

May 6, 2006
(D. L. Session 33)
   —Danni, do you read the newspapers? Watch the news? Dr. Green said this carefully, giving weight to the question.
   —Sure, sometimes.
   —The police recovered her body months ago. He removed a newspaper clipping from the folder and pushed it toward her.
   —Who? Danni did not look at the clipping.
   —Leslie Runyon. An anonymous tip led the police to a landfill. She'd been wrapped in a tarp and buried in a heap of trash. Death by suffocation, according to the coroner. You really don't remember.
   Danni shook her head. —No. I haven't heard anything like that.
   —Do you think I'm lying?
   —Do you think I'm a paranoid delusional?
   —Keep talking and I'll get back to you on that, he said, and smiled.
   —What happened at the vineyard, Danni? When they found you, you were quite a mess, according to the reports.
   —Yeah. Quite a mess, Danni said. She closed her eyes and fell back into herself, fell down the black mineshaft into the memory of the garden, the *Lagerstätte*.
   Virgil waited to embrace her.
   Only a graveyard, an open charnel, contained so much death. The rubble and masonry were actually layers of bones; a reef of calcified skeletons locked in heaps; and mummified corpses; enough withered faces to fill the backs of a thousand milk cartons, frozen twigs of arms and legs wrapped about their eternal partners. These masses of ossified humanity were cloaked in skeins of moss and hair and rotted leaves.
   Norma beckoned from the territory of waking dreams. She stood upon the precipice of a rooftop. She said, Welcome to the Lagerstätte. *Welcome to the secret graveyard of the despairing and the damned. She spread her arms and pitched backward.*
   Danni moaned and hugged her fist wrapped in its sopping rags. She had come unwitting, although utterly complicit in her devotion, and now stood before a terrible mystery of the world. Her knees trembled and folded.
   Virgil shuttered rapidly and shifted within arm's reach. He smelled of aftershave and clove, the old, poignantly familiar scents. He also smelled

of earthiness and mold, and his face began to destabilize, to buckle as packed dirt buckles under a deluge and becomes mud.

Come and sleep, he said in the rasp of leaves and dripping water. His hands bit into her shoulders and slowly, inexorably drew her against him. His chest was icy as the void, his hands and arms iron as they tightened around her and laid her down in the muck and the slime. His lips closed over hers. His tongue was pliant and fibrous and she thought of the stinking, brown rot that carpeted the deep forests. Other hands plucked at her clothes, her hair; other mouths suckled her neck, her breasts, and she thought of misshapen fungi and scurrying centipedes, the ever scrabbling ants, and how all things that squirmed in the sunless interstices crept and patiently fed.

Danni went blind, but images streamed through the snarling wires of her consciousness. *Virgil and Keith rocked in the swing on the porch of their New England home. They'd just finished playing catch in the backyard; Keith still wore his Red Sox jersey, and Virgil rolled a baseball in his fingers. The stars brightened in the lowering sky and the streetlights fizzed on, one by one. Her mother stood knee-deep in the surf, apron strings flapping in a rising wind. She held out her hands. Keith, pink and wrinkled, screamed in Danni's arms, his umbilical cord still wet. Virgil pressed his hand to a wall of glass. He mouthed, I love you, honey.*

I love you, Mommy, Keith said, his wizened infant's face tilted toward her own. Her father carefully laid out his clothes, his police uniform of twenty-six years, and climbed into the bathtub. We love you, girlie, Dad said, and stuck the barrel of his service revolver into his mouth. Oh, quitting had run in the family, was a genetic certainty given the proper set of circumstances. Mom had drowned herself in the sea, such was her grief. Her brother, he'd managed to kill himself in a police action in some foreign desert. This gravitation to self-destruction was ineluctable as her blood.

Danni thrashed upright. Dank mud sucked at her, plastered her hair and drooled from her mouth and nose. She choked for breath, hands clawing at an assailant who had vanished into the mist creeping upon the surface of the marsh. Her fingernails raked and broke against the glaciated cheek of a vaguely female corpse; a stranger made wholly inhuman by the slow, steady vise of gravity and time. Danni groaned. Somewhere, a whippoorwill began to sing.

Voices called for her through the trees; shrill and hoarse. Their shouts echoed weakly, as if from the depths of a well. These were unmistakably the voices of the living. Danni's heart thudded, galvanized by the adrenal response to her near-death experience, and, more subtly, an inchoate sense of guilt, as if she'd done something unutterably foul. She scrambled to her feet and fled.

Oily night flooded the forest. A boy cried, *Mommy, mommy!* Amid the plaintive notes of the whippoorwill. Danni floundered from the garden, scourged by terror and no small regret. By the time she found her way in the dark, came stumbling into the circle of rescue searchers and their flashlights, Danni had mostly forgotten where she'd come from or what she'd been doing there.

Danni opened her eyes to the hospital, the dour room, Dr. Green's implacable curiosity.

She said, —Can we leave it for now? Just for now. I'm tired. You have no idea.

Dr. Green removed his glasses. His eyes were bloodshot and hard, but human after all. —Danni, you're going to be fine, he said.

—Am I?

—Miles to go before we sleep, and all that jazz. But yes, I believe so. You want to open up, and that's very good. It's progress.

Danni smoked.

—Next week we can discuss further treatment options. There are several medicines we haven't looked at; maybe we can get you a dog. I know you live in an apartment, but service animals have been known to work miracles. Go home and get some rest. That's the best therapy I can recommend.

Danni inhaled the last of her cigarette and held the remnants of fire close to her heart. She ground the butt into the ashtray. She exhaled a stream of smoke and wondered if her soul, the souls of her beloved, looked anything like that. Uncertain of what to say, she said nothing. The wheels of the recorder stopped.

MYSTERIUM
TREMENDUM

1.

We bought supplies for our road trip at an obscure general goods store in Seattle—a multi-generational emporium where you could purchase anything from space-age tents to snowshoes once worn by Antarctic explorers. That's where we came across the guidebook.

Glenn found it on a low shelf in the rear of the shop, wedged between antique souvenir license plates and an out of print *Jenkins' Field Guide to Birds of Puget Sound*. Fate is a strange and wondrous force—the aisles were dim and narrow and a large, elderly couple in muumuus was browsing the very shelf and it was time for us to go, but as I opened my mouth to suggest we head for the bar down the street, one of them, the man I think, bumped a rack of postcards and several items splatted on the floor. The man didn't glance back as he walked away.

Glenn despised that sort of rudeness, although he contented himself to mutter and replace the fallen cards. So we poked at the shelves and there *it* was. He brushed off the cover, gave it a look, then passed it around to Victor, Dane, and myself. The book shone in the dusty gloom of that aisle, and it radiated an aura of antiquity and otherworldliness, like a blackened bone unearthed from the Burgess Shale. The book was pocket-sized and bound in dark leather. An embossment of a broken red ring was the only cover art. Its interior pages were of thin, brown paper crammed with articles and essays and route directions typed in a small, blurry font that gave you a migraine if you stared at it too long. The table of contents divided Washington State into regions and documented, in exhaustive detail, areas of interest to the prospective tourist. A series of appendices provided illustrations and reproductions of hand-drawn maps. The original copyright was 1909, and this seventh edition had been printed in 1986. On the title page: attributed to *Divers Hands* and no publisher; entitled *Moderor de Caliginis*.

"*Moderor de Caliginis!*" Victor said in a flawless imitation of Bruce Campbell in *Army of Darkness*. He punctuated each syllable with a stabbing flourish—a magician conjuring a rabbit, or vanishing his nubile assistant. Dane tilted his head so his temple touched Victor's. "But what does it mean?" he said in the stentorian tone of a 1950s broadcaster reporting a saucer landing. He'd done a bit of radio in college. "I flunked Latin," Glenn said, running his thumb across the book's spine. His expression was peculiar.

The proprietor didn't know anything either. He pawed through a stack of manifests without locating an entry or price for the book. He sold it to Glenn for five dollars. We took it home (along with two of the fancy tents) and I stuck it in the top drawer of my nightstand. Those crinkly, musty pages, their water stains and blemishes, fascinated me. The book smelled as if it had been fished from a stagnant well and left to dry on a rock. Its ambiguous pedigree and nebulous diction hinted at mysteries and wonders. I was the one who translated the title. *Moderor de Caliginis* means *The Black Guide*. Or close enough.

2.

I'd lived with Glenn for five years in a hilly Magnolia neighborhood. Our house was a brick two story built in the 1930s and lovingly restored by the previous owner. The street was quiet and crowded by huge, spreading shade trees. There was a sheer stone staircase walkup from the curb and a good-sized yard bordered by a wrought-iron fence and dense shrubbery. Glenn was junior partner at a software development firm that hadn't quite been obliterated by the dot-com implosion. His office was a nook across from the kitchen with a view of the garden and moldering greenhouse. I wrote articles for the culture sections of several newspapers and did free-lance appraisals for galleries and estates. Glenn got a kick out of showing my column photo around—I wore my hair shaggy, with thick sideburns and a thicker mustache, and everybody thought I looked like a 1970s pimp or an undercover vice cop. I moonlighted as an instructor at a dojo in the University District. We taught little old ladies to poke muggers and rapists in the eyes with car keys and hat pins. Good times.

Dane and Victor flew in from Denver for the long-planned and plotted sojourn through the hills and dales of our fair state. The plan included them spending a week or so doing the tourist bit in town before we lit out into the wilds. I knew the fellows through Glenn who'd attended college with them. Dane managed telecommunications and advertising for the

Denver Broncos. A rugged blond with a flattened nose and cauliflower ears from amateur boxing matches and tavern brawls. His partner Victor was stocky and bald and decidedly non-violent. He'd inherited a small fortune from his parents and devoted his time to editing an online poetry journal of repute. The journal was once mentioned by then U.S. poet laureate Billy Collins in his weekly column. Victor was a Charles Simic and Mark Strand man and I liked him from the start. Glenn referred to them as Ebony and Ivory on account of Victor's resemblance to a young Stevie Wonder and Dane's being as white as a bar of soap.

We threw a party and invited a few friends from Glenn's company and some writer and photographer colleagues of mine. Glenn barbequed steak on the back porch. I mixed a bunch of margaritas in pitchers and after dinner we sat around drinking as the sky darkened and the stars came out.

The big news was Dane and Victor had gotten hitched in California before Proposition Eight overturned the Ninth Circuit Court of Appeals. This was a year and a half gone by, so their visit was part vacation and part honeymoon. I confess to a flash of jealousy at the matching rings, the wallet of sepia tone wedding photos and the sea of family and friends in those photos. The permanence of their relationship galled me and I loathed myself for it. Glenn hadn't proposed and I was too stubborn, too afraid of rejection to propose to *him*. I slipped away while everybody was laughing about the wedding hijinks.

Glenn sauntered in as I was rinsing the dishes and put his arm around me and kissed my cheek. He was tall and lanky and had to lean over to do it. I'd drunk four or five margaritas in the meantime and my eyes were watery and doubtless red. He was oblivious, not that I held it against him. Glenn could be tender and thoughtful and wasn't so much indifferent as clueless. Despite his interest in classical music, literature and art, and a possibly less wholesome, but no less cerebral, fascination with the esoteric and the occult, he didn't like to think very deeply about certain things. His father was dead; a career railroad man, second generation Irish, he dropped in his traces from a heart attack when Glenn was fifteen. Glenn's parents had known he was gay since grade school and they accepted him. Everything came easy. He cheerfully took what we had for granted as he took everything else for granted. The guy read books and worked with strings of code, for Christ's sake. Truly a miracle he possessed any social graces whatsoever.

As for me, my father had been a white boy from the Bronx who served thirty years in the Army, the last decade of it as a colonel. My mother was a former Brazilian teen-queen bathing beauty who married Dad to get the hell out of her hometown. Dad passed away in his sleep from an overdose of pills a few weeks before I met Glenn. I sometimes wondered if it'd been accidental, or closer to the protagonist's opt-out in that famous little novel by Graham Greene. Mom pretended I'd court a fine young lady one day soon and sire a brood of kids. My three brothers were scattered across the world. The eldest kept in touch from India. Otherwise, I received birthday cards, the odd phone call or email, and that was that. Glenn kissed me again—hard and on the mouth, and he tasted sweetly of booze. I wiped my eyes and grinned and let it ago like I always did.

Gnats and mosquitoes descended. The guests retreated to the living room. Glenn put on music and began serving another round of drinks from the wet bar. I fetched *Moderor de Caliginis* and took it to my office. An examination of the book revealed phone numbers and mailing addresses amidst the other text, although considering the edition's publishing date, I assumed most were dead ends. In tiny print on the copyright page was a line that read SUBMISSIONS with a P.O. Box address in Walla Walla.

Meanwhile, the party was in full gear. Between songs, raucous laughter floated to me. My CDs—Glenn preferred classical music; Beethoven, Chopin, Gershwin, Sibelius. That wouldn't do at our casual get-togethers. Somebody sang along to the choruses of Neil Sedaka, Miles Davis, and Linda Ronstadt, a step behind and off-key. Daulton, our grizzled tomcat, jumped onto the easy chair near my desk and went to sleep. Old Daulton was a comforting soul.

I hunched over my computer monitor and ran searches of key phrases from the book. A guy in Germany claimed there were numerous versions of the *Black Guide*—he'd acquired editions for regions in France, Spain, Portugal, and South Africa. A college student in Pullman wrote of a friend of a friend who'd used the book to explore caves in Yakima. That struck me as odd—I wasn't familiar with any notable caves in Washington. Another man, an anthropologist named Berman, explained that several of the entries provided contact information for practitioners of the occult. During the late 1990s he'd visited some of these persons and joined them in séances, divinations, and fertility rituals. He was currently a professor at Central Washington University. On a lark, I sent him an email, noting I'd inherited a copy of the guide.

The most interesting item I retrieved during my three lonely hours at the keyboard was the journal of an individual from Ellensburg who went by the handle of Rose. Rose started her journal in April 2007. There were three entries—the first talked about not really wanting a journal at all, but keeping one on the advice of her therapist. The second was a twenty-five-hundred-word essay on her travels abroad and eventually finding the *Black Guide* at a gift shop in Ellensburg. Apparently Rose had sought the book for several years and was elated. The guide contained a listing of secret attractions, hidden places, and persons "in the know" regarding matters esoteric and arcane. In the final entry, she mentioned packing for a trip with three friends to the "tomb" on the Olympic Peninsula and would make a full report upon her return. The journal hadn't been updated since June 2007. Nonetheless, I left an anonymous message inquiring after her status. This satisfied me in a perverse way—it felt as if I'd thrown her a lifeline.

I signed off around three A.M. Glenn was already in bed and snoring. I lay beside him and stared at the pale reflection of streetlights on the ceiling. Who was Rose? Young, pretty, wounded. Or, maybe not. The kind of girl who took pictures of herself in period costumes. Pale, thick mascara, in her rhinestone purse a deck of tarot cards she'd inherited from an older woman, a long lost sweetheart. Rose was a girl with many friends and lovers, yet who was usually alone. I pressed the *Black Guide* against the breast of my pajamas and wondered where she was at that moment. I dreamed of her that night, but in the morning all I remembered was flying above an endless forest and the rocky bluff of a small mountain, and into a cave that swallowed me whole.

3.

"C'mon. Tell Willem a Tommy story." Glenn wore a loopy smirk. He'd done one too many shots of Cuervo. "Oh, yes!" Victor pounded his empty glass on the table. "Okay, okay. Here's one about Thomas-san," Dane said. His hair was tousled, his cheeks were flushed. He eyed me with an intensity that indicated such a story symbolized a great confidence, that I was on the verge of admittance to the inner circle.

This was in the early evening after hiking up and down Queen Anne Hill since breakfast, peeking into shops, trying the innumerable bistros and pubs on for size, and yelling raucous comments at the construction boys ripping apart the sidewalk in front of the Phoenician Theatre. Now we were just off campus at a corner booth in a dimly lighted hole-in-the-wall called The Angry Norseman. We'd drunk with the vigor of sailors on shore leave the entire day and were almost sober again. A gaggle of college students in University of Washington sweatshirts congregated at the bar and overflowed the tables. It was getting rowdy.

"Who the hell is Tommy?" I said.

"A short, stubby guy who took six years to graduate," Glenn said. "Older than us. Balding, but he had this Michael Bolton thing going on. Hair down to his bum. Managed a pizza parlor."

"Mean sonofabitch," Dane said. "He'd get drunked up and pick fights with the frat boys. One of 'em whacked him in the head with a golf club. Just pissed him off."

"I remember that." Glenn chuckled, and licked the salt from his wrist. He downed his tequila. His eyes were bright. "Cops locked him in the tank overnight and slapped him with disorderly conduct."

"A real loveable asshole," Dane said. Glenn said, "He got killed waterski-ing a couple years ago. First time out, too. Strapped on a pair of skis and got his neck broken fifteen minutes later. Tried to jump a ramp. Dunno who the hell was driving. All their fault, y'know."

"Holy shit," I said. Glenn patted my hand and shrugged. "Whole thing was moronic. Sorta fit, though. He was gonna go out from a rotten liver, a motorcycle accident, or a prison fight. That's just how it was with the crazy fool."

"Wait, that's—" Victor closed his mouth. Dane said, "Anyway. This isn't really a Tommy story per se. We had this other buddy named Max. Ol' Maximus was a real cocksman and he was cozy with this little rich girl who was going to an all-girl school on the other end of town. A real honey."

"Hear, hear," Glenn raised his glass. "Glittery green eye-shadow, Catholic schoolgirl skirts and thigh-high lace-up boots. Ruff!"

"Right, right. Becky Rimmer."

"You're kidding," I said.

"Her name *was* Rimmer. Kinda unfortunate. Her folks were out of town and she invited Max over for the weekend, and me, Glenn, Tommy and Vicky latched on. Becky didn't like it much, but what the hell was she gonna do? So we arrive at the house—and man, it's posh. A gaming room with a kickass sound system and a stocked bar. We were in seventh heaven. She laid down the ground rules—be careful with the new pool table and hands off Daddy's scotch. No problem! Max promised."

"Becky disappears with Max for some nooky. First thing—Tommy, who's already high as a kite, decides to shoot some pool. He misses the cue ball and digs a three inch groove in the felt."

"And the booze?" I said. Dane pantomimed guzzling from a bottle. "Heh, Thomas had her old man's supply of Dewar's in his guts in short order. Pretty quick, Danny boy gets bored and decides to check on Becky and Max who've locked themselves in Daddy's den and are making like wild animals. Tommy gets some tools from the garage and the next thing we know, he's standing on a stool and drilling a hole in the door to make a peephole. Laughing like a lunatic, sawdust piling on his shoes."

Victor said, "Me and Dane dragged him away from the door and gave him some more booze. Things are going okay until there's a crash from the den and Max starts hollering. Turns out, he was banging the girl on a glass coffee table and at the height of the rumpy pumpy it shattered and she dropped through. They were going at it doggy-style, so she sliced her arms and knees. Nothing serious, but it looked awful. Blood and jizz everywhere."

"Yeah," Dane said. "A scene from one of Takashi Miike's films. Naturally, we took her to the hospital. The docs gave her some sutures and bandaged her head to toe. Many awkward questions were asked. Max drives her home and the rest of us split. Mom and Dad get back early. Becky's lying in bed trying to think of a story when she hears her mom in the study go, "Oh. My. God. What is this *filth* —?" And, as Mommy dearest comes through the door waving her daughter's soiled undergarments, from downstairs her dad bellows, "WHO THE HELL DRANK MY DEWAR'S?"

I laughed so hard my side ached. "What did she do?"

"Girl was a soap opera junkie. She squinted and said in a pitiful whisper, 'Mommy? Mommy? Is that you?'"

Glenn bought us another round. Conversation turned to the impending trip. Victor unfolded a sheet of paper and showed us notes he'd made in heavy pencil. On the itinerary was a day hike on Mount Vernon, a tour of the Tacoma Museum of Glass, a leisurely day in the state capital of Olympia, then a blank slate. There'd definitely be a night or two camping on the Peninsula; *where* was yet to be settled. Victor said, "That leaves us some days to check out the sights. Maybe visit Port Angeles?"

After much noncommittal mumbling from the three of them, I took the *Black Guide* from my pocket and thumbed through the section on the Olympic Peninsula. "The Lavender Festival in Sequim is coming up. Port Angeles is close by, and Lake Crescent. Glenn and I stayed at the lodge a few years ago. Gorgeous scenery."

"Absolutely," Glenn said. Victor said, "I hear it's spooky. The Lady of the Lake murders…"

"Oh, that was ages ago," I said, albeit it made me uneasy that I'd recently read a passage in the guide documenting the scandalous tale. Too many coincidences were accumulating for my taste. Dane took the guide and turned it toward the dim lamp hanging above our table. He grinned. "Vicky, look at this!" Victor leaned in and scanned the page. Dane said, "This thing is a kick in the pants. Says there's a hotel in Centralia where they hold séances once a month. And a…dolmen up a trail on Mystery Mountain."

"See," I said, "we should put Sequim on the calendar. Go visit this dolmen after we see how the lavender jelly gets made."

"What's that, anyhow?" Dane said. "A prehistoric tomb," Glenn said. "There aren't any dolmens in this state. Maybe I'm wrong, but it sounds fishy." He spent an inordinate amount of time cruising Wikipedia. "Up a trail, eh?"

"About seventeen or eighteen miles up a crappy road, more like. The Kalamov Dolmen and Cavern. There are some campsites. It's on the edge of a preserve." Victor stroked his goatee. Dane said, "This is a seriously cool idea. I gotta see it. I gotta." He poked Victor in the ribs and laughed. "C'mon, baby. This sounds awesome, don't it?" Victor agreed that it indeed sounded awesome. Glenn promised to arrange for a bed and breakfast in Sequim and to make a few calls regarding the mysterious dolmen. If nothing else, the park seemed as decent a place as any to camp for a night or two. The guide mentioned trout in the mountain streams. I wasn't much for the sport, but Glenn and Dane had dabbled in fly fishing.

Once I got the guide back, I studied the entry on the Kalamov Dolmen and its attendant notes in the appendix, which included references to celestial phases and *occultation rites*. I didn't know what any of that stuff meant. Nonetheless, we'd have lively anecdotes for future vacation slide shows and a story to tell, I was certain.

4.

Glenn and I frequently made love the first year we were together. Not so much later. We were perpetually exhausted because of project deadlines, hostile takeovers at the workplace and, of late, the ever-shrinking newspaper circulation. Glenn had climbed the ladder by dint of overtime and weekends; I still received more commissions than I could shake a stick at. Familiarity took its toll as well.

Once Dane and Victor arrived, Glenn tried to fuck me every night. That hurt my feelings. I knew he was jealous of Victor—Victor was a flirt and he came on to me in a not too serious way. Glenn laughed it off; however, when the lights dimmed…. He was also a territorial sonofabitch and it aroused him that they were screwing like rabbits down the hall. I tried not to let it bother me too much, although I drew the line at him groping me while dead drunk. That night, after we piled into a cab and finally made it home from The Angry Norseman, I smacked his hands away as he kept grabbing at my zipper. He persisted. I lurched downstairs and crashed on the couch, a maneuver I hadn't resorted to since our last real argument the year prior.

There was a special on the History Channel. A crack team of geologists and a film crew were mucking about Spain, exploring caverns and whatnot. My eyelids drooped. I slowly emerged from a doze to hear a man discussing holy rites among the Klallam tribes and other ancient peoples of the Pacific Northwest. He described burial mounds along the

Klallam River and the locations of megaliths and dolmens throughout Western Washington. I was confused, second-guessing Glenn's assertions that no ancient megaliths or dolmens existed in our state, but the narrator continued: *Of particular interest is the Kalamov Cavern site near Mystery Mountain National Park. The Kalamov Dolmen, named after Dr. Boris Kalamov, who discovered it in 1849, is remarkable in its size and antiquity. A relic of the Neolithic Age...three thousand B.C. Perhaps older. A word of caution is in order. There is a dangerous...*The monologue faded and someone wailed in pain.

I lifted my head and the room was full of blue, unfocused light. The television screen skipped, and ghostly figures shifted between bars of static. Soundless because I'd hit the mute button prior to nodding off. Every channel was full of snow and shadow, except for the ones with the black bar saying NO SIGNAL. Unsettled without knowing precisely why, I rubbed my eyes and went to the window. The neighborhood was blanketed in darkness but for a scattering of porch lights. The cityscape was hidden by the canopy of the trees. I hugged myself against an inexplicable chill as I attempted to recall the odd commentary of the dream.

Turning, I saw a man sitting in the armchair in the corner near the pine shelf that housed a meager selection of my books. A burst of light from the TV screen revealed this wasn't Glenn or our guests. I was woozily drunk—the topknot, the surly, piggish features, the short, bulky frame, was precisely how I'd envisioned the inimitable Tommy of college lore. He reclined mostly concealed in shadow, but I saw he was naked, one thick leg folded across the other to artfully cover his manhood. His flesh was very pale; the flesh of a creature who'd dwelt in a sunless grotto for ages. He raised a finger to his lips. "I've just come to talk," he said, imparting menace with the over-enunciation of each syllable, hinting that on any other day I'd experience something other than conversation. "Scream, and our buddy Glenn is going to come running. He'll trip over Vicky's jacket on the top step and roll down the stairs. It'll be a mess, trust me."

I wiped drool from the corner of my mouth. The horrible vision of Glenn falling, shattering his spine, kept me from yelling. I said, "You're him."

"Call me Tom."

"Tom. Can't be."

"Didn't say I *was* Tom. I said, *call* me Tom. Got any hooch? That's a rhetorical question, by the way."

I shuffled to the kitchen and immediately noticed the cellar door ajar by several inches. The way down was via a narrow wooden staircase missing its railing. The cellar itself was small and cramped and mildewed and we never used it. I took a bottle of Stoli from the cupboard. I poured two tall water glasses a finger below the rims and carried them to the living room. In the back of my mind I'd hoped this would break the spell, that I'd snap out of this somnambulant state and find the visitor had evaporated. He hadn't. Tom accepted the glass and drank half of it in one long gulp. I sat on the couch, elbows on my knees, clasping my own drink with both shaky hands. "Why you? I don't get it. Why you and not my granny? Or my dad?" He shrugged. I said, "It's because of that story tonight."

"Real double-breasted asshole, wasn't I?" he said, and laughed. "Your granny and your old man don't have anything to say to you, I guess. You're making assumptions about where I come from, anyway. This ain't like that. See wings on me? Horns?"

"Maybe *An American Werewolf in London* made a bigger impression on me than I thought. Next time we meet, your face will be a melted pizza."

"Loved that fucking movie. Damn, that nurse was hot. For months I got a boner every time I heard a shower running."

"She didn't do much for me."

"I suppose not."

"What's going on here?"

"I could use a smog. Drinking and smoking go hand and hand. My old man was Black Irish. Like Glenn's. We Black Irish smoke and drink and beat our wives." Tommy laughed, grating and nasty.

"Glenn quit," I said. "I don't smoke, either. Sorry." Tom stared at me through the dark. His eyes glistened in the blue radiance of the TV, brightening, dimming, disappearing with each flicker of the screen. There was a hateful weight in that stare. "Dane smokes," he said. "So, go ask *him* for a *smog*," I said. He laughed again. "You wouldn't like what happens."

I had another vision, a confused, menacing premonition that sickened me even though I couldn't see anything but weird, jerky movement in the shadows, and a smash close-up of Dane's eyes growing too wide. I walked into the kitchen and rummaged in a drawer until I found a pack of Kools that had been squished under the silverware tray since forever. I lighted a cigarette on the burner, returned to Tom and handed it over. He said, "Tastes shitty like a cigarette should." I had set my glass on the arm of the couch. I drank the rest of the vodka while Tom smoked. A sulfurous stench filled the room. "You play with Ouija boards when you was a kid, Willem?" I nodded. "Sure, in high school. I bought one—Parker Brothers."

"Hell, all you need is a piece of construction paper and a glass. They work. Ouija boards. Other things too. Like that book you've been dicking with. It completes a circuit." I snapped my fingers. "I knew it. The book."

"Right on, Ace. The book. *The Black Guide.* You been fucking around with it, haven't you?"

"If by fucking around with it, you mean reading it, then yeah. I have."

"C'mon, those drawings in the back—you didn't copy some of them? Maybe scribbled a few of those weird doodads that look like hieroglyphics onto scratch paper. Tried to sound out some of those gobbledygook Latin phrases. You're a nerd. Course you did."

He was right. I'd copied a diagram of a solar eclipse and its related al-chemical symbols into my moleskin journal with the heavy enamel pen my younger brother bought me back when we were still talking. I'd also made dozens of curlicue doodles of the broken circle on the cover. There was something ominously compelling about that ring—it struck a chord on what I could only describe as an atavistic level. It spoke to my inner hominid and the hominid screeched and capered its distress. "What if I did? Did I do something wrong?" My voice was flat and metallic in my ears. I sounded strident and absurd. He said, "Remember the Golden Rules. Action equals reaction. The Crack that runs through everything stares into you. Big fish eats little fish. Night's agents watch you, ape."

"Yeah? Why are you here? Why are you warning me and not your chums. Their idea to use the book for sightseeing, not mine."

"I'm not here to warn anybody. I'm here to give you a good ol' mindfuck-ing, among other things. Think you found the book by accident? There are no accidents around here. Time is a ring. Everything and everyone gets squished under the wheel."

"I don't understand."

"Then you, my friend, are an idiot. And friend, keep going the way you're going and maybe a friend will slice your heart from your chest and take a bite out of it like a Washington's Best in the name of The First Power. That's how friends are."

"This is an *idiotic* imaginary conversation," I said. There wasn't anything imaginary, however, about the searing alcohol in my burps, or the fact my head was wobbling, nor the flutter-flutter of my heart. "Shoo, fly, shoo."

Tom didn't answer. The cherry of his cigarette dulled and blackened. A split second before his shape merged with the darkness, it changed. The room became cold. A woman said, *There are frightful things.* I couldn't tell where the whisper originated. I finally gathered the courage to switch on the lamp and I was alone.

Sleep was impossible. I made a cup of coffee and crept into my office and ran a search on the Kalamov Cavern, the Kalamov Dolmen, and Dr. Kalamov himself. There wasn't a record of a dolmen of any kind in Washington. Boris Kalamov turned out to be no doctor at all, but a rather smarmy eighteenth-century charlatan who faked his academic credentials in order to bolster extraordinary claims made in his series of faux scholarly books regarding naturalism and the occult. The good doctor's fraudulent escapades came to a sad end thanks to French justice—he was convicted of some cryptic act of pagan barbarism and confined to a Parisian asylum for the remainder of his years. As to whether any of Dr. Kalamov's treatises mentioned a cavern or dolmen on the Olympic Peninsula, I'd likely never know as all were long out of print. However, Mystery Mountain National Park was indeed where the *Black Guide* indicated, and open for business until mid October.

Glenn scrambled eggs for breakfast. He didn't comment on my absence from bed. I spent enough late nights at the computer he scarcely noticed anymore. He was hung over—all of us were. Pale sunlight streamed through the window and illuminated our chalky faces as we sat at the kitchen table and sipped orange juice and picked at scrambled eggs. The whiteness of Glenn's cheeks, the raccoon-dark circles of his blank eyes, startled me. My own hands shone, for a moment, gnarled, and black-veined, as if from tremendous age. I gulped a whole glass of juice, coughing a bit, and when I looked again I saw it was only an illusion. I'd seen it before, watching Glenn sleep with the light illuminating him in such a way that his future self, the wrinkled senior citizen, was forecast.

5.

Glenn's Land Rover was a rattletrap, sky-blue hulk. He'd driven the rig exactly four times since purchasing it at an estate sale in Wenatchee some years prior. Normally, we tooled around in his Saab or rode the bus. The Land Rover had bench seats wide enough to host a football team, a huge cargo bed, and smelled of mold, rust, and cigarette smoke. "Hurray," Victor said when Glenn backed it out of the garage. "Let's get this safari started!"

September was unseasonably warm. The Land Rover lacked modern amenities including a CD player and air conditioning. I sat in back with the window rolled down. Everybody wore off-the-rack Hawaiian shirts (a gag dreamed up by Dane) and sunglasses—designer shades for my companions; for me, a cheapo set I'd gotten at an airport gift shop. I also strapped on a pair of steel-toed boots as I usually did when away from home. One never knew when one might need to stomp a mugger or other nefarious type. Victor wore a digital camera on a strap around his neck. While drinking one night, he'd confided parlaying his access (through Dane's position) to the Broncos' sideline into almost twenty-five-hundred close-up pictures of the cheerleaders in action. He was toying with the notion of auctioning the album on the underground channels of the internet. I thought there were already plenty of candid cheerleader shots floating around the internet; then what did I know?

The voyage started well—Victor even pronounced a soothsaying to that effect: "Sun and moon augur a favorable and erotically charged escapade!" I said goodbye to the cat—a neighbor would pop in and feed him every day—and locked the doors. The hiking trip to Mount Vernon was a relaxed affair as none of us were hardcore outdoorsmen. We had a picnic in the foothills and returned to the lodge well before dark, where we played pinochle with some other tourists, and drank beer until it was time to turn in for the night. Glenn and I got into bed. He typed on his computer while I labored over *The Essential Victor Hugo*—the Blackmore translation. My problem was less with Hugo than the nagging urge to dig the *Black Guide* from my suitcase and have another go at the procession of peculiar diagrams in the appendices and to attempt to tease more meaning from the enigmatic entries and footnotes.

I'd told Glenn about my encounter with Tom, careful to frame it as a weird dream. Glenn frowned and asked for more details. He was intrigued by the occult, fascinated to learn of the secret lives of the famous artists I studied. His interest in such matters waxed stronger than mine—alas, his patience for wading through baroque texts wasn't equal to the task. Upon listening to the tale of Tom's apparition, he'd muttered, "What does it mean?" He was too calm, obviously throttling a much more visceral reaction. Whether this deeper emotion was one of sympathy for my strange encounter, or worry that my screws were loose, I couldn't tell. And I'd said, "I was drunk. It didn't mean anything," while thinking otherwise. Tom indeed referred to cigarettes as "smogs," a fact I'd been unaware, and thus a detail that lent creepy and disturbing authenticity to the encounter. Dream or not, I hadn't cracked the book for three days. I imagined it burning a hole in the case, a chunk of meteorite throbbing with sinister energy.

The next day we spent a few hours at the Tacoma Museum of Glass, then soldiered on to Olympia for a desultory afternoon of wandering the streets and poking around the cafes and boutiques. While my companions were sipping ice coffees, I stepped into a used bookstore and investigated the regional history and travel sections. I got into a conversation with the clerk on duty, a bored ex-librarian who stirred to life when I showed her the guide. She adjusted her glasses and made ticking noises with her tongue as she flipped pages. "I've heard of these. Farmers' Almanacs for pagans."

The ex-librarian was tall and thin and wore cat's-eye glasses with pearly frames. Her hair was black and straight and her hands were bigger than

Dane's. She asked where I'd gotten the book and seemed disappointed that I couldn't remember the name of the store in Seattle. I asked her what she made of the appendices, directing her to the drawings and arcane symbols. "Well, I'm sure I can't say." She shut the book with one hand in the resounding manner they must teach in Librarian School. She smiled obliquely. "Perhaps you should visit one of the individuals listed in *Moderor de Caliginis*. Such a person could doubtless tell you a few things."

Long shadows lay across the buildings when I rejoined everyone at the sidewalk table. My ice coffee had melted to a cup of slush. I envisioned the ex-librarian's hair swept in a raven's wing over her bony shoulder, her simple blouse and Capri pants transformed into an elegant evening dress some vamp in a Hammer film might toss on for a wild night at the castle. Her smile smoldered in my imagination. Clammy and unnerved, I suggested we repair to the hotel and change for dinner.

The Flintlock Hotel (est. 1895) was a brick and plaster building set back from Capitol Boulevard between a floral shop and an antique furniture store. The boulevard was lined with trees, and a mini U.S. flag rustled on every light pole between downtown and the Tumwater Bridge. Glenn had rented the McKinley Quarters. This was on the third floor, overlooking the street; a cozy number with a sitting room, bedroom and two baths. There were all kinds of frontier photographs in frames and the place smelled like roses and Douglas fir. Dane and Victor got the Monroe Suite down the hall. Same décor, same layout, but a view of the alley.

I told Glenn I had a migraine. Concerned, he volunteered to cancel our dinner plans and stay in to watch over me. I was having none of that—what I needed was a couple of hours rest, then, I'd join him and the boys for drinks and dancing at one of the clubs. He ordered warm milk and aspirin from room service and waited with me like a perfect dear until it arrived. He watched me take the aspirin and drink the milk. He felt my forehead then left with his jacket slung over his shoulder.

I waited five minutes, then dialed the anthropologist at his office. We'd arranged to talk a couple of days beforehand. Dr. Berman answered on the second ring. "Look, this guide. It's special." His voice was rough. I pictured him: alone in the wing of a large, decrepit campus museum, a disheveled academic wearing a tweed jacket and thick glasses, slouched in a chair at a desk cluttered with papers and a skull paperweight. His office was lighted by a single lamp. He was smoking a cigarette, a cheap bottle of whiskey in arm's reach. "Say, any notes in the margins? Pages eighty through one-ten. That'd be the chapters on the Juniper Dunes, Olympia, the Mima mounds..."

"Yeah," I said. "So that was you. I can't read your handwriting."

"Neither can I." His chair creaked in the background. I got the impression he was pouring from his bottle and congratulated myself on being so damned clever. I said, "Why'd you get rid of the book?"

"I didn't. My assistant accidentally put it in a box of materials the department donated to the University of Washington. It was some months before I discovered the mistake. The university had no record of its arrival. If I may ask, where did you find it?" I told him. He said, "Odd. Well, perhaps I could inveigle you to return it to me. To be honest, it might fetch a considerable sum on the collector market. Likely more than I can afford."

"I'm not interested in money. Sure, I'll send it back—after our vacation. Where did *you* come across the book?"

"In the foothills of the Cascades. I was backpacking with friends. They knew of this cabin near an abandoned mine. Supposedly a trapper dwelt there in the 1940s. The place was remarkably intact, albeit vermin-infested. The book lay at the bottom of a rusty footlocker, buried beneath newspaper clippings and magazines. Passing strange. A hiker must've hidden it. I often ponder the scenario that led to such an act." While he talked, I reflected that anthropologists and their ilk came by their reputations as tomb robbers honestly. He got cagey when I inquired after his experiences with the pagans mentioned in the book. "Ah, all I can say is some farmers here and there cleave to ancient customs. More country folk look to the sun, the moon, and the stars for succor than you might think. The nature spirits and the old gods. They don't advertise, what with Western culture and Christianity's persecution of such traditions." This latter comment struck an unpleasant chord. I said, "The good folk don't advertise, except in the little black book. You mean cults. Satanists?"

"Those too, I suppose. I don't know firsthand, but to my knowledge I never met any."

"My boyfriend tells me Washington State is a hotbed of satanic worship," I said. "By the way. Have you visited the Kalamov Dolmen?"

"The what?"

"Page, um, seventy-two. The Kalamov Dolmen on Mystery Mountain."

There was a long pause. "I don't recall reading that entry. A dolmen? Hard to believe I'd miss something so important. Well, the guide has a peculiar…effect. The font is so tiny." He hesitated and the bottle and glass clinked again. "This may sound, nutty, but be careful. As I said, I met decent folk on the main. User-generated content has its perils. There exists a certain potential for mischief on behalf of whoever anonymously recommends an attraction or service. Look sharp."

"Sure, Doc." We said goodbye, then I blurted, "Oh, wait. I meant to ask—you happen to meet any of the folks who've owned the book? There's a girl in your area…Rose. That's her online persona." I gave him the rundown of Rose's journal entries. "Hmm. Doesn't ring any bells," Dr. Berman said. "She found the book in Ellensburg? I taught there for a decade. I wonder if she was one of my students. A striking coincidence if so. Please, keep in touch." We said goodbye again, for real.

Tree branches scraped the window. A streetlamp illuminated the edges of the leaves. I checked my watch. The good doctor had seemed in a hurry to end the conversation. Maybe he knew more about the anonymous journalist than he admitted. I unzipped my suitcase and lifted *Moderor de Caliginis* in its swaddling cloth from amid my socks and underwear. I unwrapped the guide and set it on the table. "Boy, you do get around," I said. A shiny black beetle, easily the size of my thumbnail, crawled from the lumpy pages. It scuttled across the tabletop and fell to the carpet, shriveled in death.

6.

I went downstairs to the lounge and started a tab with a double vodka on the rocks. The place was small and half full of patrons, yet full of mirrors, thus it appeared busy. Behind the bar there was a big photograph of three loggers standing in the sawn wedge of a redwood. The trio had short hair and handlebar mustaches. Two of them leaned on double-headed axes. The third logger stood a Swede saw on end so it rested against his shoulder. The men wore dirty long johns and suspenders. I finished my drink and the bartender set me up with another without my asking.

A guy in a cream-colored suit sweated on the crescent dais under blue and gold lights, and crooned a Marty Robbins ballad about the life of a twentieth-century drifter. I loved Marty Robbins, but I always hated that song. "Hey there, stud." Victor squeezed my arm as he slid in next to me. He wore a cardigan that smelled of smoke and aftershave. The bartender brought him something pink with an umbrella floating in the middle.

"Where are the other Musketeers?" I said. Victor toyed with the umbrella. "Athos and Porthos are flirting with a bevy of cute tourista chicks at the Brotherhood Tavern down the street. Totally yanking the poor girls' chains. Too hilarious for me. I bailed." I laughed. "How cute are they?" He shrugged, sipped his drink and smiled back. "Not at all, really. Dane's hammered. I told him if he gets drunk and obnoxious I'm Audi 5000. Let Glenn drag his worthless carcass back to the hotel." I said, "Hear, hear," and drained my vodka. I crunched the ice and watched the door. The lobby was dim and the doorway hung in space, a black rectangle.

The singer finished his set with "Cool Water" and "Big Iron." He made his way from the dais and slumped farther down the bar. His toupee was bad and he'd pancaked his makeup far too heavily. His face seemed familiar, but I couldn't place it. Victor asked the bartender to put his drinks on our bill. The singer raised his glass and grinned at us and I saw that his dentures were as cheap and awful as everything else. "Poor bastard," I said, and went to work on my third double. I still smelled the acrid odor of the Kools I'd given the phantom visitor of a few nights prior. The memory of the scent made me ill. It also made me crave a cigarette. "I've got an odd question."

"Ya, okay. Shoot."

"That friend of yours who passed away. Tom. He into anything, I dunno, for want of a better term—weird? Such as fortune telling, magic…anything of that nature?"

Victor gave me a long, wondering look. He shook his head and laughed. "Oh, hells yeah. Didn't Glenn ever tell you? Man, we all got into that shit. Tarot cards, mainly. But, I really dug cultural anthropology. Those dudes get into spooky situations. And the poets of yore. Keats and company. Can't read the classical poets without coming across funky ideas. Anyhow, the whole point of college is to experiment. Did I ever!"

"Anything heavy?"

"Like black magic? Voodoo? We joked around, but no, nothing heavy. Tommy boy was extra flakey. Dane and I tried astral projection with him and this Deadhead girl. Lawanda. Tommy kept cutting up until we quit and Dane went and scored some weed to keep him quiet. What about you? Are you a true believer?"

"I'm a theorist. Thing is, I've been studying that guide book we got in Seattle."

"I seen that, girlfriend. A hoax, I'm sure. I bet you anything it's a novelty gag. Somebody printed a couple dozen of them, like pamphlets, and scattered them to the winds." I considered enumerating the reasons his theory didn't hold water. The book materials were too expensive to suggest a joke, its articles and essays were too complex. I refrained because my tongue was getting thick from the booze and also because I wanted him to be correct. He said, "What's Tommy got to do with the book?"

"Not a damned thing. Popped into my head for some reason. You didn't care for Tom much, huh?"

"He was cruel to me. Dane and Glenn were his boys. None of us called him Tom, by the way. In fact, saying it aloud gives me chills. His father called him Tom. Used to beat his ass, or something. Dude was touchy about that. He's in my dreams a lot since the accident."

"That's understandable. You should get some grief counseling if you haven't." Victor rubbed his bald head and gave me another look. "But I didn't like him." I said, "Doesn't matter. He's part of your life. In those dreams—what's he want?"

"He doesn't want anything. He moves in the background like a ghost. That makes total sense, though. The irony! I'm at a party with Dane. The party's in a posh Malibu house, one of those places that hangs over a cliff, and the host is my second grade teacher, except he's actually a cinematographer, or a screenwriter named Rick or Dick. He's got a star on the boulevard. I mingle with all sorts of people I've known. Weird combinations of grade school classmates and high school sweethearts, janitors, the chick who used to pour coffee at an all-night diner on the corner, a guy who dealt weed from the back of his El Camino when I lived in North Portland, some hookers who hung out near my friend's apartment, and famous dead people—Ginsberg and Kerouac; Johnny Cash and Natalie Wood. Lee Van fucking Cleef. Then I'll spot Tommy in a corner or on the deck, maybe lurking behind some bushes. Sometimes he's watching me and I'll try to go talk with him. He disappears before I get there." Victor's diamond ring sparked like fire.

I knew he was lying because of how he leaned away from me. Not wholesale lying; some of it was true. The ice had disappeared. I signaled for another drink. My lips were numb; always a bad sign. My forehead was cold and that meant I was afraid. I thought about Tom and the beetle and the pentagram in Appendix B of *Moderor de Caliginis*. I thought about the rough pentagram I'd carved into my desk with a penknife. I'd done it without thinking and covered it with the keyboard afterward, ashamed. This double shot didn't last long either.

"How'd he die? Really."

"Waterskiing."

"Come on, man."

Victor glanced toward the door before signaling the bartender. "I need another one." He waited until a fresh drink was in hand to continue. "Look, I wanted to let you in on this the other night. We invented the waterskiing story. *Dane* invented the story. I think he and Glenn have convinced themselves that's what actually happened. Ah, Dane's gonna wring my neck. We agreed to let it be. Tommy fell into a sinkhole. We'd camped in the hills—a couple of miles from here, in fact—and were hiking some trail. A lot of it blurs, you know? Traumatic stress syndrome, or whatever. One minute Tommy was behind me, the next he was gone. The hole wasn't much. I doubt he ever even saw it. Rescue teams came the next day, but the thing was too deep and too unstable. The proverbial bottomless pit. They didn't recover the body. I admit, me and Dane and Glenn freaked.

After we finally got our shit together, we didn't talk about it at all. First time somebody asked, Dane smiled and told them the skiing whopper. Couldn't believe my ears. I didn't argue, though. I went along with it. Except, when Glenn was telling you…frankly, that shocked the hell out of me. You two are serious. You're serious, aren't you?"

"That's the most horrible thing I've ever heard," I said. Victor nodded. "Pretty awful. Thomas didn't suffer, at least. Poor bastard."

"You didn't see him fall?" I don't know why it occurred to me to ask. "He fell. No other explanation. I doubt the guy slipped into the bushes and faked his own death. Living in Maui under an assumed name…nah."

"I'm kinda puzzled why you guys still want to go camping after an experience like that. Me, I'd burn my hiking boots and backpack in a nice bonfire."

"Don't be silly. We've gone camping a half-dozen times at least. Honestly, I see it your way. Dane and Glenn—those two are macho, macho, macho. What happened to Tommy just made them more bullheaded and foolhardy. Dane wants to go tramping the Indonesian backwoods next year, or the year after. Please, God, no. Snakes, spiders, diseases. I might take a pass."

"Uh-huh, and he'll wind up hitting on some eighteen-year-old studmuffin islander and blame it on the booze and loneliness."

"Ha, yeah. He'd actually blame it on me, if he cheated. Which he wouldn't. He's well aware I carry a switchblade."

"You carry a switchblade?"

"In my sock. Not that I'd use it. I'm too pretty to fight. Although, if D. decided to fuck around, I might make an exception for his balls."

I'd had enough. My body was Jell-O. Victor and I leaned on one another as we walked out of the bar and into the elevator. He gave me a sloppy goodnight kiss that landed on my ear as we parted ways. I crawled under the covers and slept, but not before I spent a few unhappy moments envisioning Tommy lying in subterranean darkness, his legs shattered. He screamed and screamed for help that wouldn't arrive. I said, *"Yes, for the love of God."*

7.

Sequim (pronounced *Skwim* by the locals) was lovely that summer. The town rested near the Dungeness River at the heart of a shallow basin of the Dungeness-Sequim Valley and not far from the bay. Fields of lavender and poppies and tulips dominated the countryside. There were farms and mills and old, dusty roads that wound between wooden fences and stands of oak and birch and poplar trees. Raymond Carver wrote a poem about Sequim. I'd never read that one.

Our merry band rolled into town after dark and, since Sequim was the kind of place that locked its doors at sundown, we proceeded directly to the bed and breakfast—a cute two-story farmhouse—where Glenn had rented our rooms. The proprietors were an elderly couple named Leland and Portia Teller. Mrs. Teller fixed us a nice dinner despite our being three hours late. Baked salmon, steamed carrots, sourdough bread, and ice cream and black coffee for dessert. After dinner, we sat on the front porch in a collection of rockers and a swing, and smoked cigarettes. Glenn shared one with Dane. They reclined on the swing and giggled like teenagers. The night was muggy and overcast. Lights were off all over town except for the neon flicker of a bar several blocks down and across the parking lot of a community baseball diamond.

It was a good thing I hadn't been drinking because watching Glenn casually indulge in a habit we'd mutually conquered at great physical and mental anguish ignited a slow burn in my chest. Were I drunk and vulnerable, God knows what I'd have done—wept, cursed him, slapped him, walked away into the night and disappeared. A half-dozen times I opened my mouth to say something sharp and ill-tempered. I mastered the impulse. I knew how Glenn would react if I confronted him. He'd laugh and play it as a joke. Then we wouldn't talk for the rest of the trip.

I bit my tongue and moved to the opposite end of the porch and counted lights. Small towns disquieted me with their clannishness, their secretiveness, how everybody interacted as an extended, dirt-beneath-the-fingernails family, how they scurried into their modernized huts as the sun set. A city boy was always a stranger, no matter how much money he spent, or how much he smiled. Being gay and from the wicked metropolis wasn't a winning combination with country folk.

Later, tucked as near the edge of the bed as possible, I studied the cover of the *Black Guide,* entranced by the broken ring. What was the significance? Its thickness, the suggestion of whorls, brought to mind images of the Ouroboros, the serpent eating its tail. This wasn't the Ouroboros. This was more wormlike, leechlike, and it disturbed me that it wasn't eating its tail. The jaws, the proboscis, the shearing appendage, were free to devour other, weaker delicacies.

8.

The next day marked the opening celebrations of the Lavender Festival, an event that included a downtown farmers' market and fair, and a bus tour of the seven major lavender farms in the area. None of us were lavender aficionados, yet we'd all enjoyed the film *Perfume: The Story of a Murderer,* while Victor and I had also read the novel by Süskind.

There were two buses ready to ferry us around the area. I was grateful for the tinted windows and air conditioning as the temperature had already climbed into the nineties by eleven A.M. The sun hung low and blazed hellishly, but, secure in our plush seats behind dim glass, we laughed. Glenn surprised me by holding my hand. The bus was crowded with senior citizens and a smattering of sunburned couples and their raucous children. Nobody paid us any mind, nor did I think they would; however, his lack of customary reserve took me off guard. I accepted his overture as further rapprochement for hurting my feelings by smoking with Dane. Obviously he wished to appease my jealousy by jumping at the idea of the farm tour.

The tour was organized in the manner of a wine-tasting. We spent the long, insufferably hot day visiting restaurants and observing demonstrations of lavender's multifarious uses in the culinary arts. The traveling show wound down late in the afternoon and we loaded into the Land Rover and sped off in search of booze. The Sarcobatus Tavern was closest, and not too crowded despite the numerous tourists wandering the streets.

A half-dozen college-aged guys occupied a table near the bar. Clean-shaven, muscular, decked in regulation fraternity field attire—baseball caps, sweaters, cargo pants, and athletic shoes. There were a lot of empty bottles on the table. Clearly out of their element and heat-maddened, a couple of the kids gave us hard, bleary stares. "Damn it," I said. "What?" Glenn said, although he apparently noticed them too because he squeezed my elbow, then stepped away from me. Dane actually said hello to the group in a loud, gregarious tone. A burly kid wearing a Washington State University Cougars cap said something unfriendly and his friends clapped and jeered. Dane winked and flipped the double bird to each of them ("—and you, and you, and you, and you too, cutie pie!") with exaggerated gusto, and while the college boys fumed and sulked, he ordered a round of beers that we carried to the opposite corner of the tavern near a pinball machine with its cord pulled out of the wall.

"Great Scott," Glenn said a few moments after picking up a stray newspaper and scanning the headlines. It still amazed me that my lover seldom actually swore by means of shit, or asshole, or that hoary crowd-pleaser, fuck. No, with Glenn it was always hell, damn, holy cow, and Great Scott, and, on special occasions, jeepers and Zounds. I wasn't fully privy to the origin of this eccentricity, except to note it had to do with a fondness of Golden Age comics and an aversion to his father's egregious addiction to cursing, which I gather had been a subject of lifelong embarrassment. "Ten shot dead at a cantina in Ciudad Juarez. Two guys in motorcycle helmets ran in and opened fire with submachine guns. No leads. Police suspect it's connected to drugs…" We all snorted derisive laughter at his humor. Dane said, "Man, I really liked vacationing in Mexico. No way, Jose. That isn't any place for a gringo these days."

"It's not any place for *Mexicans*," Glenn said. "Eleven thousand people killed since 2006 via drug violence. I think you might be safer signing up for Iraq."

"Nonsense— Cancun is safe as houses, as the Brits say," Victor said. "Um, sure, of course Cancun is safe," Glenn said, "but Cancun isn't Mexico. It's an American college resort. Home away from home of damn fool tourists and yon Neanderthals."

"The hell you say!"

"Cancun's *technically* Mexico, just not the *real* Mexico."

"What about Cabo?"

"Fake Mexico."

"I wanna Corona," Dane said. "Hey, barkeep, four Coronas. A ripe lemon wedge this time, for the love of Baby Jesus. Now, friends, let us weep for poor old May-he-co."

We drank our beers and decided the hour had come to mosey out of town. I went into the restroom and pissed and when I returned only three of the frat brothers were still hanging around the tavern. Music from outside throbbed through the window glass. I found everybody else in the parking lot, a fist-fight already in progress. Dane was on one knee, pressed against the wheel well of a truck tricked out with oversized tires and radio antenna. The truck's headlights were on, its door was open and radio speakers boomed "Four Kicks" by The Kings of Leon. Cougars-cap and two of the other guys stood in a semicircle and were punching him in the head. His scalp and nose ran with blood.

I lunged and Glenn caught my arm. "Don't get in his way, baby." Dane bellowed and surged to his feet, scattering his opponents. He slapped Cougars-cap on the ear. While the kid held his ear and shrieked, Dane snatched the antenna off the truck and began whipping all three of them. He grinned through a mask of gore, cocking his forearm behind his neck and then slashing in an elegant diamond pattern. The dying sun limned him in gold. He was a Viking god exacting retribution on his foes. The hair on my arms prickled and I gaped in awe. Then Glenn yelled and I turned and partially blocked a golf club swung at my head. The other three frat boys had followed us—Glenn rolled around on the ground with the guy who'd tackled him. Another went after Victor, who adroitly fled behind the Land Rover. I had a moment to admire at the lightness of his step. The golf club made a *thwock!* as it struck my upraised arm. The pain cranked a rotor in my brain and turned operation over to the lizard. I laughed with rage and joy and impending lunacy.

I caught the golf club as my attacker—a J. Crew pretty boy—readied for another crack at me, and wrenched him off balance. I kneed him in the balls. He vomited and slumped on all fours and I grabbed his hair and kneed him in the jaw, twice, with enthusiasm. His nose and jaw squished nicely. He crawled away spewing blood and teeth as he shrieked. The other punk sat astride Glenn's chest and they were choking one another. I drove the toe of my steel-toed boot into the frat boy's kidney and he recoiled like a worm zapped by an electrode. He went purple almost instantly as his throat shut, paralyzed. Glenn rolled him over and proceeded to smash his face. The notion that someone might actually die in the fracas flickered through my mind, but my will to put the brakes on melted fast as the ultra violence swept me along.

Pivoting again, I saw Victor had scooted up onto the windshield of the Land Rover, kicking wildly. His opponent belly-flopped across the hood, intent on clambering atop him. I grabbed the kid's ankles and jerked him backward, dragged him over the jaggedy hood ornament, hoisting his legs as in a game of wheelbarrow so his face slid down the grille, clunked off the bumper and slammed into the asphalt. I dropped his legs. He didn't move as blood seeped in a puddle around his head. A shadow passed through my peripheral vision. Dane seized one of the poor bastards by the crotch and neck and gorilla pressed him overhead. I'd not seen anything like that in my entire life, but there it was, Dane raising him up in a Frazetta pose from the cover of a Conan novel. Dane tossed him against the side of the truck. The frat boy bounced and landed on his shoulder and neck and Dane methodically lined up and drop-kicked him in the ribs. Like me, Dane wore heavy-duty boots, although his didn't have any metal reinforcement. It sounded like an axe whacking into a log. Magnificent.

The bartender stood in the doorway of the tavern. I waved at her and the kid whose jaw I'd certainly broken chucked a loose piece of concrete at me and it caromed off my temple. I was still flattened on the ground trying to shake free of the red haze as Cougars-cap wrapped himself around Dane's leg and bit him in the thigh. Somebody's boot thumped my left butt cheek. Victor came swooping in and snatched up the concrete chunk and hurled it, chasing away whomever was trying to punt my ass up around my shoulders. He helped me to my feet, and in the nick of time—Glenn went to the Land Rover and rummaged around under the front seat. He came around with a shiny, tiny automatic. Me and Victor got hold of him and I took the pistol away and stuck it in my pocket. Meanwhile, Dane elbowed poor Cougars-cap (the cap had flown off long since) on the crown of his skull until the frat boy stopped gnawing his leg and curled into a fetal position. The rest—the ones still ambulatory— had fled at the appearance of the gun.

"Jesus jumping Christ!" Victor said. "We gotta bail before the heat gets here and guns us down like dogs!"

"Shit, where'd you get the piece? Do you even have a permit?" I said to Glenn. His eyes were wild. "That time those gang-bangers cornered us in Rainier," he said. "I went to a pawn shop the next day." I said, "Oh, for the love of…nothing happened. They were just screwing with us." It scared and hurt me he'd gone to such an extreme and then successfully kept a secret for this long. The bus incident was two years gone and I'd not suspected it affected him so deeply. This trip was proving to be painfully educational. He looked away. "Not going to ever take chances again. Say what you like." I wanted to grab his collar and shake some sense into him. Things were moving too fast, my emotional equilibrium, my sense of security in our private little world together, was sliding from under my feet.

"So long, fuckers!" Dane said, vaunting as Achilles had after wreaking havoc among his foes before the walls of Troy. He stomped Cougars-cap's splayed hand. We piled into the truck. I shouldn't have been driving with what was a probable concussion and all the blood dripping into my eyes, but nobody else volunteered. I smoked rubber.

9.

I pulled into a Rite Aid and killed the engine. Victor was the only one of us who didn't look as if somebody had dumped a bucket of pig's blood over his head. He ran in and bought bandages, dental floss, cotton balls, Ibuprofen, medicinal alcohol, and two cases of Natty Ice.

Dane draped a towel over his face and it turned red. "Now this takes me back to the good ol' days," he said. His voice sounded nasally because his nose was smashed to a pulp. "We should get to an emergency room," Glenn said. His eye was blackened and he'd ruined his shirt on the asphalt. Otherwise, he'd escaped the battle relatively unscathed. He checked my scalp. The bleeding had mostly stopped. My left arm was swollen and purple from where the golf club had caught me. Sharp pains radiated from my foot. I figured it got stepped on in the confusion. "No hospital," I said. "If the cops are looking for us, we'll get nailed. Dane, I hope to God you didn't pay with a credit card back there."

"What? No, man, I paid cash. I always pay cash if I think there's gonna be a rumble."

"You thought there was going to be a fight?"

"Actually, I *knew* there'd be one. I decided to beat the hell out of those punks the minute we walked in. They rubbed me the wrong way."

"That lady bartender probably got our plates anyhow," Victor said. He cracked beers and handed them around. "Oh, man. Warm Natty sucks. Might as well gimme a can of watery cream corn," Dane said. "Guess if you're going to keep tangling with gangs of frat boys half your age you'd best cultivate a taste for creamed food in general, eh?" I said. Dane hissed in pain. "Yep, yep. Busted tooth. One of those assholes knocked it loose and I just swallowed the damn thing. Ha, Glenn tell you about the bikers we thrashed at a Willie Nelson concert? That's why I've got so much gold in my grill."

"Willie Nelson?"

"Everybody loves Willie," Glenn said. "Vicky, are you serious? You going to stitch the Danester's scalp with dental floss?"

Victor poured a capful of alcohol across a needle. "I can do it. Willem says no hospital. I am confident Hagar the Horrible is with Willem on this one—right sweetie?"

"Right," Dane said in his rusty, honking voice. "Besides, we still got some camping to do. That park is what, an hour from here? Let's make ourselves scarce in case Johnny Law comes round." Glenn said, "Look, boys. I'm not exactly high on roughing it in the boonies at the moment. I think we should get back to Seattle and soak away our misery in the hot tub. Willem?"

The adrenaline hadn't completely worn off, nor the rush from the sense of admiration I'd received from my comrades. I wasn't about to let Dane out-tough me. "I'm game for the park. Another case of beer and some ice for the cooler and we're good to go." Glenn took my face in his hands. He said in a whisper, "You look like you got hit in the head with a rock, my dear."

"Is that what it was?" I said. He kissed my nose. "You are such a Billy badass."

"Yee-haw!" I cheered sotto voce. Victor finished stitching Dane's lacerated scalp. He washed his hands in the alcohol, then returned to the store for bags of ice and more beer. I drove east from Sequim along the Old Mystery Mountain Highway, a two-lane blacktop in major decline. It carried us up from the valley floor into big timber along the flank of Mystery Mountain. I dodged potholes while keeping an eye on the rearview mirror for police flashers. Occasionally, deer froze in the sweep of the headlights, eyes glittering from the brush and ferns at the road's edge. I'd expected heavy July traffic, but there weren't any other cars in sight. Glenn said, "Jeepers, kinda creepy through here, isn't it?"

"Yeah, Fred," Victor said. "You should paint the pimp-mobile green and slap a flower on the door."

"Don't forget to recruit a hot, clueless Catholic school dropout and a not so hot dyke," Dane said. But Glenn was right—the woods were spooky. Mist thickened and clung to the bushes. Cold air rushed across my feet. I turned on the heater. Glenn explained that this road once served as the main access for several towns. A railroad line ran parallel, lost somewhere in the dark. A lot of timber was hacked down in the days of yore, although from my vantage the wilderness had recovered and then some.

Glenn unfolded a road atlas and studied it by flashlight. Victor told the story about the couple driving through woods—*just like these!*—while a radio broadcast reports the escape of inmates from a local asylum. Of course the car breaks down and the boyfriend leaves his girl locked up while he goes for help and all through the night she hears noises. She cowers on the floorboard as someone tries the door handles. The wind rises and branches scrape the roof. She wakes in broad daylight to the police rapping on the window. Upon exiting the car she glances back and witnesses her boyfriend hanging upside down from a tree limb, his bloody fingernails scratching the roof as his corpse sways in the breeze…

"No asylums in these parts," I said. "On the other hand, there might be ghouls and goblins. The Klallam peoples spoke of demons that dwelt among the trees and in the earth. The white pioneers sure came to believe some of the tales." I'd read about this and other eerie factoids in the guide. Victor pressed another beer into my hand. Even though I didn't dare lift my gaze from the twisting road, I felt my companions' attention focused on me. This convinced me Victor wasn't kidding when he said they were all way into the supernatural during college. Were circumstances otherwise I would've changed the subject, but I felt like a piece of meat tenderized by a mallet; the fight had drained from me, replaced by the fatalistic urge to confess or pontificate, which was an indicator I'd breached my alcohol threshold.

To distract myself from the excruciating pain in my foot, arm, and skull, I dredged up my research from the pages of the *Black Guide* and explained how according to local legends, diabolical spirits lurked in fissures and caverns of the mountains and the rivers and lakes and assumed the guise of loved ones, or beautiful strangers, and lured hunters and fishermen to their doom. There was even a tale of the Slango logging camp that vanished during the 1920s. The spirits seized unwary men and dragged them into the depths and feasted upon them, or worse. Victor wondered what "worse" meant. I assumed worse meant torture or transformation. The demons might lobotomize their victims and change them into something inhuman. As it was a cautionary branch of native mythology, it was doubtless left vague as storytellers couldn't hope to match whatever horrors were conjured by the imaginations of their audiences. "Maybe the monsters enslave the ones they don't eat," he said in a half-serious manner. I flashed to dead Tom lying in an unmarked tomb and wondered if Victor was sharing that unwholesome thought. I drained my beer and gestured for another.

"Now I really, really want to go camping," Glenn said. "The turn should be on the right. Another three miles or so." Victor screamed and I almost swerved the Land Rover into the ditch. Considering the size of the trees, we would've likely been squashed like a can of soup under a steamroller. Glenn and Dane yelled at Victor for almost making them pee their pants. I didn't say anything; I glimpsed his expression in the rearview. His eyes were shiny as quarters in Glenn's flashlight beam.

"Dude, what was that?" Dane said. "Willem almost hit a deer? Spider climb into your shorts? What?"

"Sorry, guys. I looked back to the storage compartment and something moved."

"WTF? One of those Native American bogeymen of Willem's? It have red eyes?"

"Yeah. Bright red as the Devil. That's why I yelled."

"You didn't yell, you screamed."

"Because a black form moved in the back of the truck and its eyes glowed. Course I screamed. Diabolical Disney cartoon shit going down, I'm giving a shout out. Just Glenn's coat, though. Headlight's reflected off the mile marker must've lit up the tape on the sleeves."

"Glad that's solved and we aren't parked inside one of these ginormous cedars."

I almost pulled over and asked Glenn to drive. Victor's cry had shaken me and the mist was screwing with my vision, because as I considered Victor's explanation, shadows slipped among the shrubbery a few yards ahead. Smaller than deer, and lower to the ground. I counted three of these jittery, fast-moving shapes before they melted into the greater darkness. Coyotes? Dogs? My febrile imagination powered by dopamine, a fistful of Ibuprofen, and God knew how many beers? The heavy, ponderous vehicle seemed fragile now, and I imagined how it must appear from above—a lonely speck trundling through an immense forest. Mild vertigo hit me and the vehicle swayed just enough to cause an intake of breath from Glenn. I clamped my jaw and rallied.

Thick branches obscured the Mystery Mountain Campground signpost, but I saw it in time and braked hard and swung into a gravel lane. I proceeded a hundred yards to the darkened ranger shack. A carved wooden sign read CAMPGROUND FULL. A few lights glimmered through the trees. A Winnebago was the closest vehicle. Its occupants, a family of four dressed in identical bright orange shirts, clustered around a meager fire roasting hotdogs. "Argh—we forgot the bloody marshmallows," Victor said.

"Maybe it's for the best there's no room at the inn," Glenn said. "The rangers might be on the lookout for us too." Victor said, "Aw, who cares. What now?"

The road forked: the paved section veered to the right and into the campground. The leftward path was unpaved and led into the boonies. If the *Black Guide* was accurate, this was the southern terminus of a logging road network that crisscrossed the mountains. The Kalamov Dolmen lay at the end of a footpath a few miles ahead. I said, "Two-thirds of a tank. I say we cruise up the trail and find a place to bivouac." The others agreed and I eased the rig along the washboard lane. It climbed and climbed. Brush closed in tight and lashed the windows.

A hillside rose steeply to my left. The hillside was covered in uprooted trees and rocks and boulders. A few of the rocks had tumbled loose and lay scattered in the path. I picked my way through them; some were the size of bowling balls. Victor and Glenn warned me to hug the left-hand side of the road as they were looking at a precipitous drop. I glanced over at the tops of trees below us, a phantom picket floating in an abyss. Erosion and debris narrowed the lane until the Land Rover had perhaps a foot to spare between its wheels and the cliff. I halted and shut off the engine and engaged the parking brake. I asked Victor to get my rucksack from behind his seat and hand me the humidor in the belly pouch.

"Oh, snap," Victor said. "Honduran?"

"Nicaraguan," I said. "Be a love and snip one for me. Glenn, that bottle of scotch still in the glove box?" He knew better than to say a word. He rummaged through the compartment, retrieved the quarter bottle of Laphroaig and popped the cap. I had a slug of whiskey, then accepted the cigar from Victor and got it burning with Victor's lighter. The sweet, harsh taste filled my mouth and lungs, sent a rush of energy through me. I exhaled and watched the smoke curl against the windshield. Nobody spoke. The only sound was the tick of cooling metal and Dane's wet breathing. "I saved these for a special occasion. A wedding, a funeral, a conjugal visit. But, hell…no better time for scotch and cigars than right before you roll your rusted-out Land Rover over a two-hundred-foot cliff. You boys help yourselves." Glenn and Victor lighted cigars. Dane said no thanks and held the towel to his face again. He said, "You up to this, Willem?" Glenn said, "He's got it handled. He drove transports in the Army."

"Oh. I didn't realize you'd been in the military," Dane said. "Thanks a lot, Glenn." Glenn shrugged. "He doesn't like to spread it around. So I don't."

"Hell, man. Thanks for all you guys do." Dane roused himself and leaned over and patted my shoulder. "Were you in Iraq?"

"Yeah. They stationed me in Baghdad for a year. And no, I didn't shoot anybody. I drove transports." We sat like that for a while. Finally, I drained the scotch and threw the bottle on the floorboard at Glenn's feet. I turned the key and pegged it.

10.

Eventually the grade leveled and swung away from the cliff. I parked in the middle of the road near a stand of fir trees. We pitched the tent by headlight beam, unrolled our sleeping bags, and collapsed. "Wait," Glenn said. "We need to make a bargain." He sounded strange, but it'd been a strange day. My heart beat faster. Dane and Victor kept quiet and that chilled me somehow, lending weight to the word *bargain*. These guys knew from bargains, didn't they? Glenn said, "Look, after what happened in town…maybe we'll get lucky and nobody will press charges. But, wow, Dane. You might've ruined a couple of those guys."

"I hope I smashed their guts out."

"Be serious." The edge in Glenn's voice surprised me. I wished I could see his face. "I'm not asking for anything heavy. Let's just promise to see this through, okay? Will, I'm so proud of you. We were going to tuck our tales and go yipping home. Thanks for showing grit. The plan was to camp out a couple of nights and see the dolmen. That's what we should do. Tommy would approve." The mention of dead Tom gave me the creeps and it reminded me how hurt I was that Glenn still hadn't confided the truth to me. Mostly, though, it gave me the creeps. Dane and Victor muttered acquiescence to Glenn's rather nebulous charge and we did the hand over hand thing, like a sports team. It was all awkward and phony, yet deadly serious in a Boy Scout way, and I squirmed and went along. Right before we fell asleep, I pulled him close and murmured, "We're going to talk about the gun when we get home." He kissed me, and put his cheek against my chest.

I dreamt horror-show dreams and woke panicked, Glenn mumbling into my ear, sunlight blazing through the mesh of the tent flap. I crawled outside and vomited. My skull felt as if a football team had taken turns stomping it with cleats. I couldn't make a fist with my left hand. From wrist to elbow, my arm was puffed like a black and purple sausage. The possibility I might have a hairline fracture further soured my mood.

"Man alive, I thought a bear was ralphing in the blueberry bushes,"

Dane said. His face resembled a bowl of mashed potatoes with the skins still on. He hunched on a log near the cold fire pit. The end of the log was charred to a point. I started to laugh and puked again. I worried my nausea might be due to a cerebral hematoma rather than a hangover, but it was pointless to follow that line of thought. Until I could find a loop, intersection, or wide spot in the road, we were committed to this rustic interlude of the vacation. No way was I man enough to back the truck down to the campground.

Glenn and Victor emerged from the lair. Glenn didn't look nearly as bad as Dane, but his black eye was impressive and he limped and complained about pissing blood. Dane told him pissing blood was a rite of passage (then corrected it as "pissage" to some effect). I broke out the propane camp stove and boiled water for coffee and instant oatmeal. Dane poured two fingers of Schnapps from his hip flask over his oatmeal and I almost barfed again. He grinned at us, and I saw that yes, indeed, he'd lost a tooth during the skirmish. His lip was fat and blistered and Victor tenderly dabbed it with a napkin as they huddled together and shared a mug of coffee.

Glenn spread the Triple-A roadmap of Washington State on the ground and weighed down the corners with rocks. "We're in *this* general vicinity." He poked the map with a dead stick. "Unfortunately, the area is represented as a green blob. No roads, nothing. Green blobbiness, and more green blobbiness. Willem?"

I fetched the *Black Guide* and opened it to the relevant entry which was accompanied by a rude sketch not unlike the Hollywood-popularized treasure maps, and cryptic directions such as—*Left at ravine* and *Keep north of Devil Tower. 'Ware crevasse. Leech.* "The dolmen is about twelve miles yonder. I propose we pull stakes and ease along a bit. Got to find a spot to turn this beast around." I indicated the Land Rover. "Good grief," Glenn said. "I didn't realize how far seventeen miles was when we were sitting around the bar back in Seattle." Dane said, "I'm with Willem—let's see what's over the next hill, so to speak. As for that dolmen, the more I think on it, the more I think we've been had. There aren't any goddamned dolmens in this part of the world. I ought a know, Eric The Red being kin and such."

"This whole expedition is your idea!" Victor swatted his shoulder. "There better be a 'dolmen' or I'm kicking your ass back down this mountain."

"Yo, man. Don't get so excited. I said dolmen, not Dolemite."

Breaking camp proved twice the job as setting it up because everyone was hurting from the previous evening's brutality—we hobbled like old men and it was noon before we got packed and moving. Glenn took over at the wheel while I navigated. With my arm injury, I couldn't be trusted to keep the rig out of the ditch. The road continued along the mountainside, wending its way through a series of valleys. Our path intersected a handful of decrepit logging roads. There were occasional fields where forest had been leveled to stumps and roots, but nothing more recent than a decade or two. "Who comes out here if not loggers?" Victor said. I said, "Mountain bikers. Hikers. Dope growers. Game wardens and surveyors. The state keeps tabs, I'm sure. The timber companies will be back with chainsaws buzzing sooner or later."

"Think anybody owns land, a house? Y'know, regular people."

The Land Rover hit a pothole and I almost flew through the windshield. "Nah," I said. "Imagine what this will be like when it rains in September. A man would need mules to get around." The ravines were steep and rugged with exposed rock and descended into cool, fuzzy shadows that never quite melted even during this, the hottest span of summer. Ridgelines hemmed the winding road, topped by evergreens and redwoods. Rabbits shot across our path. Far below in the vast crease of the landscape was the highway and civilization, obscured by a shifting blue haze. A hawk glided in the breeze.

As the afternoon light reddened near the horizon, we arrived at a T-intersection. There was a convenient site bracketed by several trees and a picturesque scatter of boulders, a couple the approximate height and girth of the Land Rover, and it reminded me of a scene from a western film where the cowboys sit around a cozy fire in the badlands, eating beans and drinking coffee from tin cups. If the guide was to be trusted, a semi-hidden footpath to the dolmen lay about a quarter of a mile down the southerly wending road. From there the anonymous author claimed it to be an hour's hike to the dolmen.

Once the tent was pitched we took stock of our supplies and determined that between trail mix, canned hash, chili, and fruit cocktail, three five-gallon Jerry cans of water, and a case of beer, the situation was golden for another night, and possibly two should the next day's expedition prove too exhausting. Dane and Glenn took a hatchet into the woods and chopped several armloads of firewood while Victor dug a shallow pit and lined it with stones. I munched aspirin and supervised. Glenn had made me sling from a shirt. I wore it to be on the safe side, and because it reduced the pain in my arm to the category of a toothache.

Night crept over the wilderness and the temperature cooled rapidly. Dane lighted a roaring bonfire and boiled a pot of chili and we washed that down with the better part of the case of beer. After supper, Glenn unpacked a teapot and mugs and fixed us instant cocoa. We sipped cocoa while Victor played a harmonica he'd bought in Seattle for the occasion.

"Dear God, not the harmonica," Dane said, and spat a gob of blood into the fire. His nose was definitely broken. He'd crunched it back into joint himself, much to my horror—at which Glenn and Victor snickered and mocked my squeamishness. Evidently, they'd seen this show many a time during their debauched college adventures.

Glenn fiddled with the transistor radio until he dialed in a grainy, but reasonably clear signal—a canned programming station playing big band music from the 1930s and '40s. Victor rolled his eyes and tossed the harmonica through the open window of the truck. He rolled a couple of joints and we passed them around. Talk turned to the macabre and I entertained them with Baba Yaga legends I'd heard around similar campfires while stationed in the Middle East; then Glenn and Dane discussed their favorite horror movies, most of which I knew by heart, and I nodded off, lulled by their easy laughter, the warmth of the fire.

Victor said something about "doorways" and I snapped awake, but missed the rest as he and the others were speaking softly. He said, "It's only a coincidence." Dane said, "Come on, dude. Don't even start down that road—" I cleared my throat. "What road?" Victor said, "The road not taken, of course. I need to shake hands with the Governor—ta, ta, my lovelies!" He rose and walked into the shadows. "That's a wrap—I'm for bed," Glenn said, and he kissed me and headed for the tent. Dane stared into the flames and the red light bathed his ravaged face, and he glanced at me as if about to speak. He smiled, a sad, pained smile, and followed Glenn.

Victor returned, zipping his fly. "C'mere, pull up a rock." I patted the log I was sitting on. He settled next to me, his posture stiff as a plank. Soon, Dane's snores drifted from the tent and Victor's shoulders relaxed. He tossed some dead leaves and twigs onto the fire, and said quietly, "What's on your mind, Will, old bean?" He was high as a kite.

"Not much. The book. Weird, weird thing happened to me before we left on the trip." I told him, as I had Glenn, about Tom's visitation, except I didn't pull any punches. As I spoke, Victor's expression became increasingly unhappy. He fumbled in his pocket for a pack of cigarettes and lighted one with apparent difficulty. He offered me a drag. I declined and said, "Glenn didn't tell you, huh? I sort of figured he would've."

"This explains a lot. No wonder he's treated me like I'm loony tunes for… He prefers to pretend we weren't a pack of superstitious nerds in college. Dane follows his lead. It's a survival tool. The front office in Denver sucks—they don't even know Dane is gay. And the hoodoo aspect—that shit ain't cool now that we're *grownups*. Getting your face punched like a speed bag is trendy; crystal meditation and *The Golden Bough* reading circle is for wackos. I mention anything along those lines, Dane gives me the stink eye and Glenn changes subjects like he's a senator putting the moves on the press corps. Why are we talking about it?"

"Because I can tell you want to. You aren't the kind of guy to keep deep, dark secrets."

"The thing with Tommy isn't really a deep, dark secret. A minor scandal. I had a bed-wetter type dream about him the other night. Neither of the other bozos dream about him, which seems unfair. But whatever, man. I couldn't stand him and you didn't even know him, yet we're the schleps who've got him on the brain."

"Seems rather simple to me," I said. "He's obviously haunting you from beyond the grave. You stole Dane away, then he got killed in a tragic manner that trapped his soul on the material plane."

"Oh, yeah? He didn't care for Dane like that. Well, fuck, maybe he did. Tommy loved to hump and he didn't seem too picky regarding with whom. What's he messing with you for?"

"He's not messing with either of us. I was checking your credulity."

"You got me, Tex. I'm a credulous motherfucker these days. Our boys are goddamned credulous too, if you could get them to cop to it. You're a devious one. Funny, you and Glenn getting together. He's such a rube." I chuckled. "Yeah, yeah, Glenn is as pure as the driven snow. Plus, unlike us his family was damned progressive. A well-adjusted man's one of my turn-ons."

"That's the attraction?"

"He reads. He can be a devil. I like that a whole lot."

"He's hot and makes a heap of money."

"Goodness, Vicky, you're a real bitch when you want." I didn't mean anything by that, however. His bluntness was sweet in its own way.

The fire burned low. Victor stood and stretched. "I was raised Pentecostal. Got any idea what that's like? I saw a few things you wouldn't believe. My daddy was a snake-handlin', babblin' in tongues psycho-sonofabitch, let me tell you what. I've no problem with the plausibility of the fundamentally implausible after witnessing my daddy and two uncles cast 'demons' from my cousin one sultry, backwoods night. I can't say I'm religious, but I surely do believe we aren't alone on this mortal coil. There are frightful things lurking in the shadows."

I remembered the woman's voice whispering in the dark—*There are frightful things.* I got goose bumps. He said, "Something else I didn't mention when I told you about the dreams I had of Tommy. I think I pushed it down into my subconscious. Whenever I first see him, for a split second he's somebody else. He covers his face with his hands, as if he's rubbing his eyes, or sobbing, and when he looks up, it's him, smiling this evil little smile. Once in a while, he ducks his head and pantomimes pulling on a ski mask. Same thing—it's him again. The act bothers the fuck outta me. Anyway. Goodnight."

Shadows from the dying fire capered against the trunks of the trees and the boulders nearby. The goose bumps returned and I recognized the nauseated thrill in my stomach as a reaction to being watched. This sense of being observed was powerful and I became conscious again of our frailty, the dim sliver of firelight, the flimsy shelter of the tent, our insignificance. I massaged my aching forearm. Farther out, branches crashed and grew still.

A few minutes passed as I listened to the night. Weariness overcame my nerves. I decided to make for the tent and as I rose, a large, dark shape emerged from the brush and moved onto the road about seventy feet away. There was sufficient starlight to discern its bulky outline, a patch of thicker blackness against the blurry backdrop, but not enough to identify individual features. It had to be a bear, and so I'm sure my brain gave it a bearlike shape. Bears didn't particularly frighten me—I'd gone hunting on occasion as a teen and hiked plenty since. Bears, cougars, moose; critters could be reliably expected to live and let live. This encounter, however, alarmed me. Had the cooking smells drawn it in? Glenn's gun lay snug in my pocket since the brawl, but that didn't comfort me—it was a .25 automatic with no stopping power; more likely to infuriate a bear than kill it.

The animal stood in the center of the road and there was no mistaking it was staring at me. Then another shape appeared near the first and that caused my balls to tighten. The second animal rose directly from the road, as if the shadows had coalesced into solid form, and as it materialized I noted that even obscured by darkness, it didn't resemble any bear I'd ever seen. The beast was too lean, too angular; the neck and forelegs were abnormally long, and its skull lopsided and cumbersome. I pulled the automatic and chambered a round. I considered calling to my companions, but hesitated because of the impression this entire situation was balanced on the edge of some terrible consequence and any precipitous action on my part would initiate the chain reaction.

There are terrible things.

A cloud rolled across the stars and as the darkness thickened, the animals moved in an unnatural, sideways fashion, an undulation at odds with their bulk, and vanished. Symbols of warning conjured from night mist and shadows; ill omens dispensed, they drained back into the earth.

I half-crouched, gun in my fist, until my legs cramped. A scream echoed far off from one of the hidden gulches, and I almost blew a hole in my foot. It took me a long while to convince myself it had been the cry of a bear or a wildcat and not a human.

By then it was dawn.

11.

During breakfast I relayed my encounter with the mystery animals, floating the idea that perhaps we should skip the hike. "Wow, a couple of bears outside? Why didn't you get us up? I would've loved to see that." Victor seemed truly disappointed while Dane and Glenn dismissed my concerns that we might run afoul of them during the day. Dane said, "We'll just let Vicky run his yapper while we walk. Bears will hear that a mile away and beat it for the hills."

"Gonna be hotter than the hobs of Hades," Glenn said after shrugging on his backpack. "What the hell are hobs?" Dane said. "Hubs, farm boy," Glenn said. "Don't neglect your canteens, fellow campers. Put on some sunscreen. Bring extra socks."

"How far we going? The Andes?"

"It's a surprise. Let's move out."

I took the lead, *Moderor de Caliginis* in hand. The sky shone a hard, brilliant blue and I already sweated from the rising heat. Fortunately, half the road lay in shadow and we kept to that. I felt rather absurd trudging along like a pith-helmeted explorer in a black and white pulp film, novelty almanac map clutched in a death grip—Dane and Glenn even carried the requisite hatchets and machetes.

Despite my morbid curiosity, it would've relieved me if the book had proved inaccurate, if we'd tromped for an hour or two until my comrades grew hot and irritable and voted to call it a trip and bolt for civilization. The beating I'd received in Sequim had taken its toll and I just wanted to face the music, to deal with any legal repercussions of the battle royal and then soak in the hot tub for a month.

But, there it was behind a screen of bushes and rocks—the path, little more than a deer trail, angled away from the road and climbed through a ravine overgrown with brush and ferns. There weren't any trail markers, nor recent footprints. We picked our way over mossy stones and deadfalls, pausing frequently to sip from our canteens and for Dane and Victor to share a cigarette. Victor unlimbered his camera and snapped numerous pictures. Walking was slightly difficult with the sling throwing off my balance. Glenn stayed close, taking my elbow whenever I stumbled.

We pressed onward and upward, past a dozen points where the game trail forked and I would've lost the way if not for the landmarks detailed in the guide entry and by the subtle blazes the author had slashed into the bark of trees along the way. I whistled under my breath. My companions were silent but for the occasional grunt or curse. A similar hush had fallen over the woods.

We rounded a bend and came to a spot where the trail forked yet again, except this time both paths were wider and recently trod by boots. Glenn spotted the ruins a second before I did and just after Dane wondered aloud if we'd gotten lost and pegged me in the back with a pinecone. "Everybody, hold on!" Glenn kept his voice low and pointed along the secondary path where it passed through a notch in the trees. I swept the area with binoculars. There was a clearing beyond the screen of trees, and piles of burned logs, like a palisade had ignited into an inferno. Further in, discrete piles of charcoal debris glittered with bits of melted glass. This appeared to be the old ruins of an encampment, or a village. I could imagine a mob of men in tri-corner hats loitering about, priming their muskets.

"This is weird," Victor said. "You guys think this is weird?" I said, "In my opinion this qualifies as weird. Also highly unsettling."

"Unsettling?" Dane said. Victor said, "Well duh. Don't know about you, but I'm picking up a creepy vibe. I dare you to walk down there and see if anybody's around."

"There's nothing left," Dane said. Victor said, "That path didn't make itself. *Somebody* uses it. Like I said, walk your sweet little butt down there and take a gander."

"Not a chance," Dane said, and briefly mimed plucking strings as he hummed "Dueling Banjos."

Glenn took the binoculars and walked uphill to get a better vantage. He slowly lowered the glasses and held them toward me. "Will..." I joined him and scanned where he pointed. Offset from the main ruins, a canted stone tower rose four or so stories. The tower was scorched and blackened and draped in moss and creepers, on a slight rise and surrounded by the remnants of a fieldstone wall. Window slots were bricked over and it was surmounted by a crenellated parapet. "Anything about this in the guide?" he said. I told him about the *Devil Tower* notation. "I thought the entry referred to a rock formation, or a dead tree. Not a real live fucking tower."

"Something strange about that thing," Dane said. "Besides the fact it's the completely wrong continent and time period for a medieval piece of architecture, and that said architecture is sitting on the side of a mountain in the Pacific Northwest, miles from any human habitation?" Victor said. Dane said, "Yeah, besides that. I've seen it before—in a book or a movie. Fucked if I remember, though. I mean, it looks like it should be on the moor, Boris Karloff working the front door when the dumbass travelers stop for the night."

"How much farther?" Glenn said. I consulted the book. "Close." He said, "Unless you guys want to hunt for souvenirs in the burn piles, let's mosey." None of us liked the ruins enough to hang around and we continued walking.

Fifteen minutes later, we arrived at our destination. The trail wound under the arch of a toppled dead log, and ended in a large hollow partially ringed by firs and hemlocks. The hollow was a shadowy-green amphitheatre that smelled of moist, decayed leaves and musty earth. Directly ahead, reared the dolmen—two squat pillars of rock supporting a third, enormous slab. I was amazed by its cyclopean dimensions. The dolmen was seated near the slope of the hill and blanketed with moss, and at its base: ferns and patches of devil's club. It woke in me a profound unease that was momentarily overshadowed by my awe that the structure actually existed.

None of us spoke at first; we stood close together and took in our surroundings. Glenn squeezed my wrist and pressed his hip against mine. Victor hadn't taken a single picture, demonstrably cowed upon encountering something so far beyond his reckoning, and Dane's mouth actually hung open. I whispered into Glenn's ear, "The History Channel isn't quite the same, is it?" He smiled and pecked my cheek. That broke the tension and, after shucking their packs, the others began exploring the hollow. My uneasiness remained, a burr that I couldn't work loose. I checked the book again—the author hadn't written much about the site proper, nor documented any revelations about its history or importance besides the astronomical diagrams in the appendix. I stowed the guide and tried to set aside my misgivings as well.

The moss that bearded the dolmen was also thick upon the ground and it sucked at my boots as it sucked at the voices of my friends and the daylight itself. I thought of lying in a sticky web, of drowsing in the heart of a cocoon. The pain in my arm spiked and I shook off the sudden lassitude. We approached within a few feet of the tomb and stared into the opening. This made me queasy, like peering over the lip of a pit. This was a stylized maw, the mossy path its unfurled tongue.

"This isn't right," Glenn said. Victor and Dane flanked us, so our group stood before the structure in a semicircle. "A hoax?" I said without conviction, thinking of the artificial Stonehenge modern entrepreneurs had erected in Eastern Washington as a tourist attraction. "I don't think so," Glenn said. "But, I've seen a few of these in France. They don't look like this at all. The pile of rocks is close. That other stuff, I dunno." The stones were covered in runes and glyphs. Time had eroded deep grooves and incisions into shallow, blurred lines of demarcation. Lichen and horrid white fungi filled the crevices and spread in festering keloids.

Dane forged ahead and boldly slashed at some of the creepers, revealing more carvings. Fat, misshapen puffball mushrooms nested in beds among the creepers and his machete hacked across some and they disintegrated in clouds of red smoke. I joined him at the threshold and shined the beam of my flashlight through the swirling motes of mushroom dust, illuminating a chamber eight feet wide and twenty feet deep. Stray fingers of reddish sunlight came through small gaps. Vines had penetrated inside and lay in slimy, rotten loops and wallows along the edges of the foundation. My hair brushed against the slick threshold and beetles and pill bugs recoiled from our intrusion. Just inside, the chamber vaulted to a height of fifteen feet and was decorated with multitudes of fantastical carvings of symbols and creatures and stylized visages of the kind likely dreamt by Neanderthals. The far end of the chamber dug into the mountain; a wall of shale and granite sundered by long past seismic violence into a vertical crack, its plates and ridges splattered rust orange by alkaline water oozing from rock.

The floor was composed of dirt and sunken flagstones, and at its center, a low mound of crumbling granite that was an oblong basin, the opposite rim worked into the likeness of a massive, bloated humanoid. The statue was worn smooth and darkened by grime with only vague hollows for its eyes and mouth in a skull too proportionally small for its torso.

I clicked off the flashlight and allowed my eyes to adjust to the crimson gloom. "Okay, I'm thunderstruck," Glenn said. "Gob smacked!" Victor said, his jovial tone strained. He shot a rapid series of pictures that promptly ruined my night vision with the succession of strobe flashes. The glyphs crawled and the primeval visages yawned and leered. Dane must've seen it as well. "Stash that goddamned camera or I'm going to ram it where the sun don't shine!"

Victor frowned and snapped the lens cap in place and in the midst of my visceral reaction to our circumstances, I wondered if this exchange was a window into their souls, and how much did Glenn know about *that*. I watched Glenn as he examined the idol and the pool. I felt a brief, searing contempt for his gawky frame, his mincing steps and too-skinny ass. I hung my head, ashamed, and also confused that something so petty and domestic would impinge upon the bizarre scene. For the hundredth time I considered the possibility my meninges were filling with blood like plastic sacks.

Up close, the basin was larger than I'd estimated, and rudely chiseled, as if it were simply a hollowed-out rock. Small squarish recesses were spaced at intervals around the rim, each encrusted with lichen and moss so they resembled mouths. Cold, green water dripped from the ceiling and filled the basin, its surface webbed with algae scum and fir needles and leaves. The attendant figurehead loomed, imposing bulk precariously inclined forward, giving the illusion that it gazed at us. I glanced at my companions, their faces eerily lighted by the reflection of the water.

…A horrible idea took root—that these men masked in blood, eyes gleaming with febrile intensity, had conned me, maneuvered me to this remote and profane location. They were magicians, descendants of the Salamanca Seven, necromancers of the secret grotto, Satan's disciples, who planned to slice my throat and conduct a black magic ritual to commune with their dear dead Tom, perhaps to raise him like Lazarus. Everything Glenn ever told me was a half truth, a mockery—Tom hadn't been the black sheep sidekick, oh no!, but rather the darksome leader, a sorcerer who'd initiated each of them into the foul cabal. Any moment now, Dane or my sweet beloved Glenn would reach into his pocket and draw the hunting knife sharpened just for my jugular, Victor's coil of rope would truss me, and then… Glenn touched my arm and I choked back a cry and everybody flinched. Their fear and concern appeared genuine. I allowed Glenn to comfort me, smiled weakly at his solicitous questions.

Victor said, "Boys, what now? I feel like calling CNN, the secretary of the interior. Somebody." Glenn rubbed his jaw. "Vicky, it's in the book, so apparently people are aware of this place. There's a burned-down village back thataway. That explorer, Pavlov, Magalov, whoever, named it after himself. People surely know."

"Just because it's in the book doesn't mean jack shit. How come there's no public record? I bet you my left nut this site isn't even on the government radar. Question is, why? How is that possible?"

I said, "An even better question is, do we want to screw around with the ineffable?" Victor sighed. "Oh, come on. You got the heebie-jeebies over some primitive art?"

"Take a closer look at the demon faces," Dane said. "This is forces of darkness shit. Hardcore Iron Maiden album cover material." He snorted and spat a lump of gory snot into the water. For a moment, we stood in shocked silence.

"If you want to flee, dears, say the word." Victor laid the sarcasm on too thick to fool anybody. "Let's march back to the land of beer, pizza, and long, hot showers." He drew a cigarette and leaned against the basin to steady himself. The snick of his lighter, the bloom of flame, shifted the universe off its axis. He shuddered and dropped the lighter and stepped back far enough that I glimpsed a shivering cord the diameter of a blue ribbon leech extended from beneath the lip of the basin and plunge into the junction of his inner thigh and groin.

Greasy bubbles surfaced from the depths of the stagnant water and burst, their odor more foul than the effluvium of the dead vines liquefying along the walls, and the scum dissolved to reveal a surface as clear as glass. The trough was a divining pool and the water a lens magnifying the slothful splay of the farthest cosmos where its gases and storms of dust lay like a veil upon the Outer Dark. A thumbnail-sized alabaster planetoid blazed beneath the ruptured skein of leaves and algae, a membranous cloud rising.

The cloud seethed and darkened, became black as a thunderhead. It keened—chains dragging against iron, a theremin dialed to eleven, a hypersonic shriek that somehow originated and emanated from inside my brain rather than an external source. Whispers drifted from the abyss, unsynchronized, unintelligible, yet conveying malevolent and obscene lust that radiated across the vast wastes of deep space. The cloud peeled, bloomed, and a hundred-thousand-miles-long tendril uncoiled, a proboscis telescoping from the central mass, and the whispers amplified in a burst of static. I went cold, warmth and energy drained from my body with such abruptness and violence, I staggered.

Glenn shouted and jerked my shoulder, and we tripped over each other. I saw Dane scrambling toward the entrance, and Victor frozen before the idol, face illuminated in the lurid radiance. His expression contorted and he gripped his skull in both hands, fingernails digging. The slimy cord drew taut and released from the muscle of his leg with a wet pop, left a bleeding circle in the fabric of his pants. Another of these appendages partially spooled from the niche nearest me, writhing blindly as it sought to connect with warm meat.

The howl intensified. My vision distorted into streaks of white, resolving to the flickering vacuum of space where I floated near the rim of the Earth, and the moon slid as a black disk across the face of the sun.

12.

Glenn cuffed and shook me awake. His cheeks were wet with tears. "You weren't moving," he said. I sat up and looked around. The unearthly light had faded to a dull glow, but I could make out some details of the chamber. Victor stood beside the idol, his back to us. He caressed the statue's rotund belly, palm flat the way a man touches his wife's stomach, feeling for the baby's kick. Dane was nowhere to be seen.

I said, "Vicky? Vicky, you okay?" It required great effort to form the words. Victor slowly turned. Something was wrong with his face. Dried gore caked his forehead and temples. He grinned ghoulishly. "You should've seen what I saw. This isn't a tomb…it's…" He laughed and it gurgled in his throat. "They'll be here soon, my sweets."

Victor's certitude, the lunacy in his expression, his tone, frightened me. "Glenn, we've got to get out of here." I pushed away his arm and rose. "Vicky, come on. Let's find your husband."

"Where's Dane going? He won't leave me here, nor you, his best buddies. However, if he doesn't come to his senses, if he's run screaming for the hills, I'll visit him soon enough. I'll drag him home to the dark."

"Vicky—" Glenn said. Victor mocked him. "Glenn! Be still, be at peace. They love you. You'll see, you'll see. Everything will change; you'll be re-made, turned inside out. We won't need our skin, our teeth, our bones." He licked his thumb and casually gouged his chest an inch above the nipple. Blood flowed, coursed over his rooting thumb and across the knuckles of his fist.

Glenn screamed. I glanced at the ground near my feet, hoping for a loose rock with which to brain Victor. Victor ripped loose a flap of skin and let it hang, revealing muscle. "We won't need this, friends. Every quivering nerve, every sinew will be laid bare." He leaned over and reached for the switchblade taped to his ankle. "Oh, shit," I said.

Glenn said shrilly, "What's that?" There was movement in the fissure. A figure manifested as a pale smudge against the background. It was naked and its skin glistened a pallid white like the soft meat of a grub. Its features were hidden by the gloom, and I was glad of that. Victor raised his arms and uttered a glottal exclamation.

The Man (it *was* a man, wasn't it?) crept forward to the very edge of the crevice, and hesitated there, apparently loath to emerge into the feeble light despite its palpable yearning to do so. Whether man or woman I couldn't actually determine as its wattles and pleats disguised its sex, but the figure's size and proportions were so large I couldn't imagine it being a woman. The weight of its hunger and lust echoed the empathic blast I'd received from the black cloud, and my mind itched as this damp, corpulent apparition whispered to me, tried to insinuate its thoughts into mine via a psychic frequency.

I beheld again the cloud, a dank cosmic mold seeping from galaxy to galaxy, a system of hollow planets and a brown dwarf star nested within its coils and cockles. Sunless seas of warm ichor sloshed with the gravitational spin of those hollow, lightless worlds, spoiled yolks within eggshells. Hosts of darksome inhabitants squirmed and joined in terrible communion. I felt unclean, violated in bearing witness to their coupling.

Beyond the entrance of the dolmen and the encircling trees, the sun burned cool and red. Soon it would be dusk…and then, and then… "Vicky! For the love of God, get over here." Victor ignored me and shuffled toward the figure, and the figure's luminous flesh darkened with a spreading, cancerous stain, like a piece of paper charring in a flame, or a sheet soaked in blood, and it reached, extending a hideously long arm. Its spindly fingers tapered to filthy, sharp points. Those fingers crooked, beckoning languidly. What did it promise Victor, with its whispers and wheedles?

I moved without thinking, for if I'd stopped to think I would've sprinted after Dane, who'd obviously exercised common sense in beating a retreat. I tackled Victor and slung him to the ground. The impact sent shocks through my wounded arm and I almost fainted again, but I hung tough and pinned him. Stunned, he resisted ineffectually, flopped like a worm until I freed the pistol from my pocket and smacked him in the forehead with the butt. That worked just like the movies—his eyes rolled back and he went limp. Glenn came running and we grabbed Victor beneath the arms and dragged him from the chamber. The figure in the crevice laughed, a hyena drowning or a lunatic with a sliced throat.

The flight down the trail toward camp was harrowing. We bound Victor's hands with his own belt, and made a tourniquet to staunch the bleeding from his leg as it refused to clot, and half-carried him as he raved and shrieked—I finally pistol-whipped him again and he was quiet after that. The entire way, I glanced over my shoulder fully expecting the dreadful presence to overtake us. Hysteria galvanized me into forty minutes of superhuman exertion—had Glenn not been there, I'm sure I could've easily hoisted Victor onto my shoulders and made like a track star.

Dane jumped from the bushes near the main road and Glenn nearly lopped his head with a hatchet. Dane had run to the camp before his panic subsided and he'd mustered the courage to double back and find us. His shame was soon replaced by horror at Victor's condition, which neither I nor Glenn could fully explain. I convinced Dane there wasn't time to talk lest someone or something had followed us from the dolmen. So, the three of us lugged Victor to camp, loaded the Land Rover and got the hell off Mystery Mountain.

13.

I put the pedal to the metal and Glenn made the calls as we hurtled down the logging road in the dark. The authorities were waiting at the campgrounds. Victor recovered from his stupor as they strapped him to a gurney. He cursed and snarled and thrashed until the paramedics tranquilized him. Dane, Glenn, and I were escorted to the local sheriff's office where the uniforms asked a lot of questions.

The smartest move would've been to fudge the details. That's the movies, though. None of us were coherent enough to concoct a cover story to logically explain the hole in Victor's leg, or the monster, or the bad acid trip phantasmagoria of the pool. We just spilled the tale, drew an X on a topographical map and invited the sheriff and his boys to go see for themselves. It didn't help our credibility that the cops found Victor's weed stash and several hundred empty beer cans in the truck.

Ultimately, they let us walk. The fight at the tavern wasn't mentioned, despite our mashed faces and missing teeth, which surprised the hell out of me. Victor's wound was presumed an accident; the investigators decided he harpooned himself on a branch while drunkenly wandering the mountainside. Personally, I preferred that version as well—the reality was too horrible. Victor's deranged state was obviously a hysterical reaction to the near-death incident. Our statements were taken and we were shown the door. Once the cops put two and two together that the four of us were queer, they couldn't end the conversation fast enough. Someone would be in touch, thank you for your cooperation, etcetera, etcetera.

Dane went to stay with Victor at Harborview Hospital while Glenn and I returned home. Neither of us was in any shape to linger by Victor's bedside. I'd tried to talk Dane into crashing at the house, to no avail—he hadn't even acknowledged the offer. His face was blank and prematurely lined. I'd seen refugees from shelled villages wearing the exact same look. In his own way, he was as removed from reality as Victor.

Glenn fared a little better—he was a wreck too, but we had each other. I dreaded his reaction when the shock dissipated and the magnitude of the tragedy sank in. He'd lost one friend, possibly forever, and the jury was out on the other. God help me, a bit of my heart savored the notion I finally had him all to myself. Another, even more bitter and shriveled bit slightly gloated over the fact it was finally his turn to suffer. I'd done all the crying in our relationship.

Daulton meowed when we came in and turned on the lights. The house, our comfy furniture and family pictures, all of it, seemed artificial, props from someone else's life. I showered for the first time in several days, spent an hour with my forehead pressed against the stall tiles. I saw the wound in Victor's leg, his mouth chanting soundlessly, saw the stars thicken into a stream that poured into that black hole. The black hole, the black cloud, was limned in red and it made me think of the broken circle on the cover of *Moderor de Caliginis*. These images were not exact, not perfectly symmetrical, and the hot water cascading over my back no longer thawed me. My teeth chattered.

I wrapped myself in one of the luxuriously thick towels we'd gotten for a mutual anniversary gift and limped into the hall and found Glenn on hands and knees, his ear pressed to the vent. "What the hell?" I said. He gestured awkwardly over his shoulder for quiet. After a few moments he rose and dusted his pajamas with a half-dozen brisk pats. "I thought the TV was on downstairs. It's not. Must've been sound traveling along the pipes from the neighbors, or I dunno. Let's hit the rack, huh?"

I lay in bed, chilled and shaking, Glenn a dead lump next to me. The accent lamp in the hall gave a warm, albeit fragile yellow light. Without shifting to face me like he normally would've, Glenn said, "Tommy fell into a hole in the woods. That's how he really died." I said, "Yeah. Vicky told me. You fucker." Glenn still didn't move. I couldn't recall him ever being so still. He said, "I figured that's why you've been so bent. Then you know why we kept quiet."

"No, I don't."

The light flickered and now Glenn's head turned. "True. You don't. I apologize. I should've come clean long ago. Tommy was so deep into black magic it blew my mind when I finally caught on. He always sneered at the lightweight stuff me and Dane fooled with. I really believed he was just a redneck who made good. Then we hit some extra heavy-duty acid one night and he bared his soul. We were on spring break and spending a weekend in the Mojave with some of the guys and he got to rambling. His parents were basically illiterate, but he had well-to-do relatives on his mom's side. Scholars. He lived a few summers with them and they turned him on to very, very dark occultism. Tommy intimated he'd taken part in a human sacrifice. He lied to impress me, I'm sure."

I wasn't sure. "What did they do? The relatives."

"His uncle was a professor. World traveler who went native. Hear Tommy tell it, the old dude was a connoisseur of the black arts, but specialized in blood rituals and necromancy. Tommy said the man could… conjure things. Dr. Faustus style."

"I might've laughed at that the other day," I said. The lamp flickered again and shadows raced across the wall. Glenn said, "Tommy showed me some moldy manuscript pages he carried in his pocket. They were wrinkled and obviously torn from a book. The words were written in Latin—he actually read Latin! He wouldn't say what they meant, but he consulted them later when we went on our trip into the Black Hills near Olympia. Looking back, I get the feeling maybe he had his own *Black Guide.*"

"It could've been a possum stew recipe from his grandma's cookbook," I said. "The motherfucker didn't come visit me in the night. I dreamed that when I was rocked off my ass. The guide, well there's a coincidence. I'm not going to buy a conspiracy theory about how dead Tom made sure we found it at ye old knickknack shop. I sure as fuck ain't going to worry my pretty head over what we saw on the mountain. I'm sorry for Vicky and Dane. We're okay, though and I say let sleeping dogs lie." I breathed heavily and stared at the hall lamp so hard my eyes hurt.

"Ignoring those sleeping dogs is what got us here. Tommy talked and talked that enchanted evening, had a scary expression as he watched me. His eyes were so strange. I got paranoid thinking he wasn't really high, that this was a test. Or a trap. I remember him saying there was 'sure as God made little green apples' life out there. He pointed at the stars. Cold night in the desert and those stars were right on top of us in their billions. He wanted to meet *them,* except he was afraid. His uncle warned him the only thing an advanced species would want from us would be our meat and bones."

Glenn didn't say anything for a while. He rubbed my arm, which still ached fiercely. Finally, he said, "Everything returned to normal after the Mojave trip—he didn't mention our chat, didn't seem to recall letting me in on his secret life. A few months later it was summer vacation and we were knocking around Seattle. I came home to visit my folks and the others tagged along. Tommy put together an overnight hike and away we went. I saw him fall into the hole as we were walking way up in the hills along a well-beaten path. Mountain bikers used it a lot, even though it's a remote spot. Dane and Victor were joking around and I glanced over my shoulder exactly as Tommy fell. I didn't tell those two what I saw. I made a show of yelling for him until Dane found the sinkhole. Course we called in the troops. I'm sure Vicky told you what happened next. Cops, Fish and Wildlife, everybody we could think of. No luck. That pit just dropped into the center of the Earth and it was impossible to help him. To this day nobody but me is completely sure that's where Tommy disappeared—it just makes the most sense. Him tripping into a bottomless pit is awful, yeah. Not as awful as other possibilities, though."

The lamp clicked off and on three times and I raised myself against the headboard and clutched the coverlet to my chin. I lost interest in finally getting to the bottom of Tommy's death and the weird conspiracy to sanitize its circumstances. "Holy shit— Glenn, please stop. I've got a bad feeling." I had a sense of impending doom, in fact. I could easily envision a colossal meteor descending from on high and smashing the house to bits. Daulton fluffed into a ball of bristling fur and scooted under the bed where he hissed and growled.

Glenn kept rubbing my arm and the light flickered again and again, and the filament ticked like a rattler. "I never told the guys what I really saw that day. Tommy didn't fall. He was snatched by a hand…not a hand that belonged to any regular person I've seen. An arm, fish belly white, shot up and caught his belt and yanked him in…and the hand had…claws. He didn't even scream. He didn't make a peep. It happened so fast I thought it couldn't be real. I dreamed it like you dreamed Tommy was in the living room after the party."

"I can't believe this shit," I said. What had Tommy expected to find in the Black Hills? Another ancient ruin hidden from all but the initiated and the doomed? I was getting colder. I wanted to ask Glenn if he still loved Tommy. Nothing he said would've mattered and so I comforted myself with smoldering resentment.

"When we were in the dolmen, did you get a look at that guy's face?" he said.

"The dude in the crevice? That freaky inbred motherfucker who got separated from all his Ozarks kin? No."

"I did," Glenn said. "It was *him*."

The light went off and stayed off.

14.

I woke with a dry mouth. Glenn's covers were thrown back and his side of the sheets were cool. I listened to the creaks of the house. The power was out. Glenn laughed, downstairs. He said something unintelligible. In my semiconscious state, I assumed he'd called the power company and was sharing a joke with the poor sap manning the phone center.

Fuzzy-headed, I put on my robe and negotiated the hall and the stairs. A bit of starlight and the tip of the crescent moon gleamed through the windows. Glenn had lighted a candle in the kitchen and it led me through the haunted woods to the doorway. It was only a single candle, a fat one I'd bought at a bookstore for my office but stuck in a kitchen drawer for emergencies instead, and so the room remained mostly in gloom.

She slouched at the opposite end of the dining table. She was naked and lush and repellently white. Her hair was long and thick and black. Her hands rested on the table, and her fingers and cracked, sharp nails were far too long and thin. *Moderor de Caliginis* lay open before her. She lazily riffled pages and smiled at me. I couldn't see her teeth.

Glenn stood to her left in the breakfast nook, the toes of his slippers in the light, his shape otherwise indistinct. He waited mutely. "Who are you?" I said to her, although I already knew. The covetous way she handled the guide made it clear. "Three guesses," she said in a perfectly normal, good-humored tone. "Rose, I presume," I said, voice cracking and ruining my attempt at bravado. "How kind of you to drop in." The gun was in my coat in the living room. I thought I might make it if I ran and if I didn't trip over anything.

"How kind of *you* to open your home. Thank you for the lovely note. Yes, I had a fabulous visit to the Peninsula—and points beyond. That saying, *a nice place to visit…* Well, I liked it so much, I decided to naturalize."

"Glenn," I said. I was exhausted. It came over me in a wave—the seasick feeling of giving way too much blood at the nurse's station. I resisted a sudden compulsion to collapse into a chair and lay my head on the table. My fingers and toes tingled. I gripped the doorframe for balance. "Glenn," I tried again, weak, hopeless. Glenn said nothing.

"He's not for you. He belongs to Tommy," Rose said. "He belongs to us. We love him. You were never part of their inner circle, were you Willem? Second best for Glenn. His vanilla life after graduation into the real world of jobs, bills, routine sex. No thrills, not like college." She closed the book and traced the broken ring on its cover. "Alas, nice guys do indeed finish last. I, however, believe in second chances and do-overs. Would you like a do-over, Willem? You'll need to decide whether to come along with us and see the sights. Or not. You are more than welcome to join the fun. Goodness knows, I hope you do. Tommy does too."

The cellar door had swung open while I was distracted. Rose stood and took Glenn's hand. They passed over the threshold. He turned and stared at me. Behind him was infinite blackness. Her arms, pale as death, emerged from that blackness and draped his shoulders. She caressed him. She whispered in his ear, and in mine.

The pull was ineluctable; I released the doorframe and crossed the room in slow, tottering steps like a man wading into high tide. The universe whirled and roared. I came within kissing distance of my love and looked deep into his dull, wet eyes, gazed into the bottomless pit. His face was inert but for the eyes. Maybe that was really him waiting somewhere down there in the dark.

"Oh, honey," I said, and stepped back and shut the door.

15.

I sold the house and moved across the country. For nearly a decade, I've lived on a farm in Kingston, New York, with an artist who welds bed frames and puts them on display in galleries. We share the property with a couple of nanny goats, some chickens, two dogs and Daulton. I write my culture essays, although Burt makes enough neither of us needs a real job. Repairing the fences in the field, patching the shed roof and making the odd repairs around the house keep me occupied, keep me from chewing my nails. Nothing can help me as I lie awake at night, unfortunately. That's when I do the real damage to myself. Against my better judgment I mailed the *Black Guide* to Professor Berman, though I cursed him for a fool during our last email exchange.

Victor's confined to an asylum and his doctor contacts me on occasion, hoping I'll reveal what "massive trauma" befell his patient to precipitate his catastrophic break from reality. From what I gather, Victor keeps journals—dozens of them. He's got a yen for astronomy and physics and at least one scientist thinks he's a savant. Dane disappeared three years after our fateful trip and hasn't resurfaced. His credit cards and bank accounts remain untouched. The cops asked me about this, too. I really don't know, and I don't want to, either.

Burt raised his eyebrows when I bought the .12 gauge shotgun a few months back and parked it by my side of the bed. I told him it was for varmints and he accepted that. There are cougars and bears and coyotes lurking in the nearby forest. He hasn't a clue that when he's away on his infrequent art show trips, I sit in our homey kitchen by the light of a kerosene lamp with the gun on the table and watch the small door leading into the cellar. The door is bolted, not that I'm convinced it matters. It began a few weeks ago and only happens when Burt's out of town. He's not a part of this, thank God for small favors. The dogs used to lie at my feet and whine. Lately, the normally loyal pair won't come into the room after dark, and I don't blame them.

Burt's in the city for the weekend. He's mixing with the royalty and pining for home, has said as much in no less than a half-dozen phone messages. I sit here in the gathered gloom, with a bottle of scotch, a glass, and a loaded gun. Really, it's pointless. I sip scotch and wait for the soft, insistent knocks against the cellar door, for Glenn to whisper that he loves me. Guilt and loneliness have worked like acid on my insides. God help me, but more and more, I'm tempted to rack the slide and eject the shells, send them spinning across the floor. I'm tempted to leave the deadbolt unlocked. Then see what happens next.

CATCH HELL

1.

For years she awakened in the darkest hours to a baby crying. She finally accepted the nursery they'd sealed like a tomb was really and truly empty, that the crib was empty. She learned to cover her ears until the crying stopped. It never stopped.

2.

Olde Towne lay forty miles east of Seattle in hill country, a depressed region populated by poor rural folk who worked the ranches, dairies, and farms. Forests, deep and forbidding, swept along the hem of tilled land. Farther on, the terrain rose into a line of mountains that divided the state.

The town's streets were bracketed by houses with peaked roofs. The houses were made of brick or stone with tall brick chimneys. People had settled here long ago; many homes bore bronze plates designating them as historic landmarks. Shops squeezed tight, fronted by wooden awnings and boardwalks; signs were done in gilt script over double-paned glass, or etched into antique shingles. Ancient magnolias and chestnuts reared at intervals to shade the sidewalks and the lanes. The police station, fire-house, and city hall occupied the far end of Main Street; art deco structures bordered by lawns, hedgerows, and picket fences. One could imagine the police gunning down the McCoys on the courthouse steps.

Sonny and Katherine Reynolds waited for the light to change at the intersection of Main Street and Wright. Options at the airport had been limited, so they rented a sedan—a blocky gas guzzler that swallowed most of its lane, but, happily enough, possessed far more than sufficient trunk space to accommodate their luggage and Sonny's carton of research texts and notes. He told her several times during the drive it was like steering a boat. Katherine wanted a chance behind the wheel. Sonny laughed and said he'd let her drive it on the return leg of their journey. She called him a liar, but the ease of his humor, so removed from his usual melancholy, surprised her into a smile and she reached across and clasped his hand. Their hands on the wheel caught fire and burned orange, then red, as if they'd renewed an unspoken blood compact.

"Wow, a real live soda shop," she said. The sign outside of town claimed a population of three thousand. She estimated two or three times that number seeded throughout the surrounding countryside. Such a small, insular community—no wonder it clung to its heyday.

"Stuck in the '50s," he said. "Cripes—is that a wooden Indian in front of the barber shop?

"Yes indeedy."

"You gotta be kidding."

"I've never seen so many weathervanes in one place," she said. This was true; she spied one on nearly every roof, lazily revolving in the westerly breeze. Most were iron roosters.

"Wisconsin, it's cheese, he said. "Here, the fascination seems to be with cock. Gotta watch out for them cock fetishists."

"It's a left. Up ahead past that pink building." She shook her road map open.

"Looks like the set of a modern gothic. I read there's a big institution just down the road with the lights still on and everything. Guess they weren't *all* closed in the '80s."

Katherine immediately withdrew from him, embittered by his indifference, his callous disregard for her aversion to such places. "You fuck," she said and turned away and rested her forehead against the window.

"Yeah, I'm a fuck," he said cheerfully, and played with the radio dial. The local station crackled in. Apparently the afternoon DJ was a transcendentalist; she spoke in the monotone of an amateur hypnotist and played recordings of wind chimes and the periodic rattle of what might've been gravel shaken in a jar.

The street narrowed to a bumpy stretch of country road, and climbed a series of bluffs that gave them a view of the entire valley. Sonny turned onto a blacktop drive that made a shallow, quarter-mile curve through a field of wild flowers and blackberry thickets and overgrown wooden fences, until it ended in a lot before the Black Ram Lodge. The building sat at the edge of a forest: brick and mortar and half-timber; three floors with a long, sloping tile roof flanked by hedges and a stand of enormous magnolia trees. The windows were dark and impenetrable.

"Nothing looks the same in real life," he said.

"It seemed way smaller in the pictures," Katherine said, even though she'd suspected otherwise all along. She'd taken the brochure from her purse, comparing black and white photographs against the real artifact. "God, I hope this place isn't as empty as it looks." *Why'd I have to say that? Another excuse for him to think of me as a needy little bitch? Being alone isn't so bad. Not like I'm alone, anyway. I got you babe, ha.* She glanced sidelong at her husband, checking for the oblique signs of contempt. *Maybe* I am *a needy little bitch. I'll say something stupid just to get a reaction. Some attention.*

There was no denying her dread of aloneness. She'd made peace with loneliness and sorrow, become accustomed to her own bleak thoughts, her recriminations and regrets. True isolation was a different proposition entirely. It seemed as if she'd dozed off during the drive from shiny, metropolitan Seattle and woken to find herself lost in a green wasteland. The town wasn't even comfortably picturesque anymore. Far below in the deepening gulf, lamps blinked on like the running lights of a seagoing vessel in fog. Sunset wasn't for another hour, yet a soft curtain of twilight had settled over the land. This was nowhere. *I hate you, Sonny. Selfish asshole.*

"I hope it is," Sonny said.

"Huh? Hope it's what?"

"Empty."

A wooden garage lay a hundred yards or so off in what had once likely been a cow pasture. Perhaps the garage was built from the bones of a massive barn, the place where they'd milked the cows, or slaughtered them. According to the pamphlet, more buildings were hidden beyond the central structure: a series of bungalows, a walled garden, a small distillery.

Two men stood in conversation on the cement steps of the main building. One was tall and lean, an older gentleman whose snowy hair touched the shoulders of his gray suit. The other man was a bit younger and heavier and dressed in slacks and a dark polo shirt.

"Welcome to Fantasy Island," Sonny said, and laughed. He put on his sunglasses and climbed out of the car. Katherine watched him approach the men on the steps. Exhaustion had stolen her will, melted her into the seat. She chafed at his ability to adopt a genial demeanor with such casual efficacy, like a chameleon brightening to match the foliage.

"Mr. Reynolds," the taller man said as he shook hands with Sonny. His voice was dampened by glass. "I'm Kent Prettyman, humble steward of the Black Ram. This is my accomplice, Derek Lang." As a group, they glanced at the car as Katherine emerged, a badger driven from her burrow. "Ah, Mrs. Reynolds! I'm Kent Prettyman. Call me Kent, please. And this is—"

Her sunglasses were the oversized variety worn by actresses and battered wives. "Kat. Just Kat."

"Meow," Mr. Lang said. His face was almost as dark as his shirt and he was brutishly muscular beneath the softness of his shoulders and belly.

Mr. Prettyman explained that Mr. Lang managed the grounds. There was a significant measure of yearly upkeep on the buildings and environs, a monetary burden divided between the state, the county, and the owners of the estate. When Katherine inquired who these owners were, he said the landlords, a family of hereditary nobility, resided in Europe. The family possessed numerous holdings and cared little for the lodge, leaving its management to intermediaries, most lately (as of 1995) a nonprofit foundation for the preservation of historical sites. All rather boring, he assured them. Did they have many bags? One of the boys would fetch their luggage and park the car.

The lodge predated Olde Towne and the very weight of its history settled upon Katherine's shoulders when she followed Mr. Prettyman through the double doors of age-blackened oak into the grand foyer. The Black Ram had been established as a trading post in the 1860s, doing a brisk business with settlers from Seattle and tribes from neighboring Snohomish Valley. The post was expanded and refurbished as the manse of the Welloc family, the very same who carried the deed to this day, until it finally became an inn directly following the Great Depression, and thus remained. Slabbed beams crisscrossed the upper vault and glowed gold-black from the light passing through leaded glass. Katherine squinted to discern the shadowed forms of suits of armor and weapons on display, moldering tapestries of medieval hunts, and large potted plants of obscure genus' that thrived in gloom. The flavor was certainly far more Western European than Colonial America, or America of any other era, for that matter.

She stood in the semicircle of men, oversized shades dangling from her fingers. Her arm brushed Sonny's and each of them instinctively flinched. She opened her mouth to mutter an apology and saw the gesture would be fruitless; he'd already forgotten her. His white shirt shone in the encroaching darkness and it illuminated his inscrutable, olive face, lent it the illusion of life. Mr. Prettyman said something to Mr. Lang, and Mr. Lang slunk away.

"No phones?" Sonny said, incredulous enough to drop his fake smile for a moment.

"There is a house phone," Mr. Prettyman said. He pointed to a wooden-paneled booth across from the front desk. Another bit of bric-a-brac from a dusty period in European history. Doubtless the lodge sported a billiards room, a smoking den, tables for baccarat and canasta. "And another in my office. No wireless internet, I'm afraid. We make every attempt to foster an atmosphere of seclusion and relaxation here at the

Black Ram. Guests needn't trouble themselves with intrusions from the city while in our care."

"A *house* phone…."

"It's all in the brochure," Katherine said. "Didn't you read the brochure, honey? It'll be an adventure, like the hotel we stayed at in Croatia, or the other one in Mexico." Remote, decrepit half-star hotels, the pair of them. It rained torrentially during their stay in Mexico and the roof leaked in a half dozen places, water fairly poured in, truth be told, and sent cockroaches skittering across the bed sheets in search of high ground. "Who cares. I'm sure we've got plenty of bars on this hill." She flipped open her cell phone and checked.

"Are we the only guests?" Sonny asked.

"Oh, well, there are several others. Fewer than a dozen, at the moment. Midsummer doldrums," Mr. Prettyman said. He rubbed his hands together when he spoke, absently polishing the malachite ring on the third finger of his left hand—Katherine couldn't make out the symbol embossed upon onyx; a star, perhaps. "At our peak we can host on the order of eighty or so guests. I'll give you a tour of the property—tomorrow morning, say? Allow me to introduce the staff." Even as he spoke, a pair of strapping boys laboriously rolled a baggage cart overstuffed with the Reynoldses' belongings through the lobby and onto the elevator at the opposite end of the room. The elevator was flanked by a pair of marble rams and appeared as ancient as everything else, a wide platform caged in wrought iron. It lifted almost silently, except for the soft ding of a bell and the hum and slide of well-oiled gears.

As promised, Mr. Prettyman walked them through the lodge, and Katherine smugly noted there was indeed a den containing card and billiard tables, an abundance of big game trophies, and the largest stone fireplace she'd ever seen—larger than the ones found in the proud old rustic ski lodges in Italy they'd frequented before Sonny broke his knee and gave up skiing altogether.

"Naturally it gets rather soggy during the winter, but summer storms are also fierce in these parts," Mr. Prettyman said. "A front will roll down out of the mountains and positively deck us with thunder and lightning. Nothing like a roaring fire and hot cocoa to steel a soul against the weather…."

The proprietor oversaw a chef and bartender and their requisite assistants, a handful of maids and custodial personnel, two porters (Billy and Zack, the burly farm boys), a maintenance man, and the concierge, a gaunt, clerkish gentleman named Kristoff. Kristoff had jaundiced eyes and old-fashioned false teeth that didn't quite fit his mouth. He smelled sharply of alcohol. Katherine thought the dour fellow probably kept a flask of something strong under the desk. As Mr. Prettyman swept them along to the upper floors, he mentioned Mr. Lang was responsible for nearly a dozen carpenters, laborers, and gardeners. In addition, Mr. Lang stood in as the de facto chief of security—he handled the infrequent trespasser; hunters, mainly. Poachers who slipped into the wooded preserve beyond the lodge in hopes of bagging a deer or one of the wild boars or black bears that roamed the hills. The land had once doubled as a private wildlife preserve.

"Wild boar? Bears?" Katherine wasn't happy with this revelation. "Is that even...well, legal?"

"I don't think the family concerned itself with the niceties back then," Mr. Prettyman said. "They stocked their game in the '20s, I believe. Possibly earlier. Money talks, as the saying goes. Local law enforcement was frequently invited to hunt with the, ah, royalty, as it were. Oh, and there's a small cougar population. Indigenous."

"So much for nature walks."

"Nonsense, Mrs. Reynolds! Don't bother them, they won't bother you. Very few of the big animals venture close to the lodge proper. Besides, if you'd care to explore the region, sightsee the ruins and whatnot, I'm sure Mr. Lang would be happy to organize a daytrip. He's a dead shot. Small likelihood of your being eaten by bears, I promise."

She pictured Mr. Lang's sadistic grin, his sweaty hands caressing a hunting rifle. "I think I'd like to lie down now."

Their suite occupied the second floor of the southern wing. It consisted of a living room, kitchenette, bedroom, and one and a half baths. The pine bureaus and armoire were antiques. A tapestry depicting a stag hunt hung over the bed, some pastoral oil paintings were scattered elsewhere, and in the living area a Philco radio that must've been popular in the 1940s, but no television. The living room window commanded a view of the forested hills.

Katherine eyed the stag hunt. The vision of the stag, rearing before frothing mastiffs and men on horses, all eyes black and wild, the horns and the spears—this visceral image looming over the bed was a disquieting prospect.

"First no phones, now no television." Sonny rummaged through the drawers of a small writing desk. A kerosene lamp perched atop the hutch of the desk, bookending a handful of clothbound volumes so decrepit, humidity had sloughed the titles from their spines. He sniffed the sooty glass. "Makes you wonder how often they lose power. Prettyman says there's a coal furnace in the boiler room."

"Maybe it's part of the ambience. Lamps, rose petals—"

"Yep, and a romantic game of cribbage. Or dominos." He rattled a velvet bag and she laughed.

A few minutes later they argued, an indication things were back to normal, or what passed for normalcy here in the lucky thirteenth year of their union. She'd made reference to Mr. Prettyman's offhand comment regarding ruins and Sonny immediately clammed up. He leaped to his feet and began pacing the bedroom. Then he grabbed his coat. Katherine asked where he was going, alarmed at the prospect of being deserted in this place, surrounded by strangers, one of whom gave her the serious creeps. "Out," he said.

"But where?" By an act of supreme will she kept her voice level.

"Don't worry about it. Take a nap. Whatever." He was on his way, face set, a man in action.

Jesus, and I thought the alpha male routine was sexy, once. "We're in this together. This leaky ol' rowboat. Right?"

"I'll see you for supper." His demeanor was that of a man announcing to his family he was running to the corner store for cigarettes. *I'll be right back!* He turned away, snuffing the conversation.

"Yeah, sure." She wanted to stick her nail file in his ass cheek.

"Kitchen's open till ten. Put on something nice. You look good in the taffeta." He walked out, shutting the door carefully behind him.

Katherine flipped him the bird with both hands and slumped on the bed and seethed. She hated him, not because he'd dismissed her as one dismisses an inferior, a child, although certainly that was a portion. Her rage sprang from the simple fact that he always seemed to know so much more than she did.

She went to the window and stared out at a landscape growing soft and shapeless as light slipped away. Toward the horizon and closing fast, came a towering storm cloud, a death's-head lit by internal fires. Her eyes grew heavy. She swallowed a couple of pills from one of multiple bottles that comprised her daily regimen of behavioral equalization, and fell asleep. Wind clattered the shutters and the last bit of evening sun faded and died.

3.

Katherine had spent six years dwelling on the accident, yet she seldom pictured Janie. Baby clothes, the odor of formula and spittle, but not the baby herself. In retrospect, the pregnancy, the seven months that had followed, were dreamlike; they left an impression that she'd engaged in a protracted struggle with some indefinable illness or injury. Yes, it seemed the stuff of dreams. There *were* scars: her vertigo persisted, and too, her phobia of bridges and overpasses. Sometimes the cry of an infant caused her to lactate. Sometimes it elicited a flood of tears and inconsolable sobbing. She'd screamed at a hapless mother in a coffee shop; told her to *shut up her squalling brat* and was instantly mortified at the lady's expression of shock and fear. Thankfully, the fits of lunacy had ebbed.

Sonny had wanted another child right away. A few months after the dust of the tragedy settled, he insisted they try again. His desire developed into an unequivocal force, an implacable usurper of their life-aspirations, of all they'd planned during their days as romantic conspirators.

Katherine's mother pulled her aside at the family Christmas dinner—she recalled her father and Sonny's laughter echoing from the living room, how it transcended the boom and roar of a football game on TV. Sonny hated football, sneered at the preening athletes, their "bling" and arrogance; he pretended to enjoy sports to bond with her father who'd been a devout booster of his own hometown high school team since forever.

Are you sure you're ready? Mom said. *Is it what you want?* And what Mom meant was, *Are you still the kind of bitch who eats her own puppies?* Katherine smiled brightly and bore down on the potato peeler. She said, *Yes, yes, of course we're ready. I want this.* Mom's eyes hinted at a profound unhappiness born of doubt that abruptly submerged to be replaced by her songbird cheer. Mom was a survivor, too. Everyone had a nice, fattening dinner and far too many Irish coffees. While they watched one of Pop's moldy old VCR tapes of a Bob Hope special, Katherine thought, *What I really want is to be punished. That's why I can't get well. Why I stay married to the sonofabitch.*

When a year passed without a positive result, they, or Sonny, to be specific, grew concerned. It developed his sperm count was merely adequate. The specialists were at a loss in her case; she tested fertile, nonetheless, her insides had lapsed into a peculiar dormancy. Adoption was out of the question; Sonny would accept no less than his own image in miniature. This went on and on. Then the desperate act—the surrogacy. They borrowed money, they recruited a volunteer, and the volunteer miscarried. Their marriage plunged into the Dark Ages.

It wasn't the end, though. There's no end to hell.

4.

Katherine and Sonny arrived in time for a late supper in the dining room. Sonny had apparently stopped off at the hotel bar and made the acquaintance of three fellow guests whom he invited to join Katherine and himself for supper. She instantly recognized that her husband had indulged in several drinks from his slightly disheveled hair, the width of his smile, the shine of his eyes. As he flushed, the old patina of acne scars became fiercely evident and roughened his cheeks, lending his expression a coarseness one might glimpse in a mug shot. Not good—Sonny's wit became caustic when he drank overmuch. Luckily, he didn't indulge frequently, preferring to focus upon less hedonistic pursuits. Katherine wondered if she might prefer an alcoholic husband to a morbidly obsessive one.

Gary Woodruff was a retired investment banker on vacation from Manhattan. He wore a suit out of place in their rustic surroundings. Lyle Cockrum neglected to divulge his occupation. Katherine pegged him for a playboy. His hands were fragile, his black hair expensively styled, his boredom complete and genuine. His designer clothes were loose and a compellingly tasteless shade of lime. He'd arrived with a frail blonde woman who'd immediately professed awful allergies and retreated to her room. The third guest, Melvin Ting, served as assistant curator of Olde Towne's most venerable repository of historical artifacts, the Welloc-Devlin Museum. Of evident Eurasian lineage, he struck Katherine as much too young for such a post: thirty years old at most, and clad in a turtleneck and slacks, a gold hoop in his left ear. He would've fit right in at a trendy coffeehouse slinging lattes or reciting the poetry of the disaffected. He also smiled too much for her taste. This, of course, was the very individual they'd traveled from California to meet. However, since the rendezvous was intended to be clandestine, neither she nor Sonny gave any hint.

The chef personally introduced the courses, which included salmon and truffles, and sorbet for dessert. Afterward, they ordered drinks and lounged near the softly crackling hearth, their conclave presided over by an enormous black ram's head on the mantle. Buzzed from several glasses of red wine and somewhat disarmed by her cozy surroundings, Katherine nonetheless wished they'd chosen to call it a night. The lights flickered and died to a chorus of gasps and mild curses. The group sat in tense silence, listening to grand old beams shift and creak, and rain slash against the windows while hotel staff bustled about lighting lanterns and refreshing drinks.

"So, what's your line?" Mr. Cockrum said. He studied Sonny over the rim of a brandy snifter.

"Until recently I taught cultural anthropology at a little college in Pasadena. Folklore. I've dabbled in archeology. Now I write for travel journals." And, in a perfunctory gesture to his wife, "Kat is vice president of communications for the Blessingham Agency. They design colors."

"For marketing strategies, I presume," Woodruff said.

"If you've ever wondered where Super Burger restaurants got that color scheme, or why Tuffenup Buddy pain reliever comes in a Day-Glo pink box, I'm the one to ask." She smiled faintly.

There was a long, dead pause.

"How does one become an expert in folklore?" Woodruff's tone suggested vast condescension. He exaggerated the syllables of "expert."

"His father was a famous primatologist," she said in automatic defense of her husband's pride. Whether it would bolster his confidence or annoy him was a gamble. She couldn't help herself.

"Ah, not really famous," Sonny said. "He read traditional fairy tales to us kids every night. The unvarnished ones where Cinderella's sisters cut off pieces of their feet to fit the glass slipper. Sex and cannibalism—all the good stuff modern publishers whitewash. It stuck."

"He researched ape languages at Kyoto University." Katherine tried her wine, determined to slug it out now that she'd gone this far. It had grown unpleasantly warm. "Sonny won't tell you this, but his father, Quentin, did a lot of important work for the Primate Research Group in the 1950s. A very prestigious organization. The Japanese thought so highly of him they bought him a house."

"He left the University long ago," Sonny said. "I'm sure you've never heard of him—"

"What kind of folklore do you study?" Mr. Ting asked. He'd remained silent during dinner while chain smoking and sipping espresso.

"Japanese mythology. I've some facility with Chinese and Indian oral traditions, a smattering of others." This was exceptionally modest of Sonny. He'd acquired extensive knowledge of several dozen mythological traditions.

"You get into the scary shit, I see," Mr. Cockrum said. Katherine wondered how much the man knew about the subject. *Cliff Notes* and *Penguin Abridged Classics* most likely. He hardly seemed the type to pore over scholarly treatises.

"Eh, the *really scary shit* would be the Slavic mythos. Or Catholicism, ha-ha," Sonny said.

"He's written books." Katherine stared at her glass. The vein in her temple began to pulse.

"Oh, more than magazine features? You mean real books?" Mr. Woodruff said.

"Ah, of course he has," Mr. Cockrum said. "Publish or perish; is this not the academic way, Mr. Reynolds?"

What the fuck do you know about academia, Cock-ring?

"Damned right it is." Sonny swallowed a half glass of whiskey and signaled the cocktail waitress for another. His ruddy flush deepened and crept beneath his open collar. He was growing bellicose and reckless and Katherine decided she'd best figure a graceful way to maneuver them away from the dinner party before things got truly ugly.

"Well, if you want spooky, get Prettyman or Lang to tell you about the local legends," Cockrum said. "An associate of mine spent his honeymoon here a couple of years ago. They sat right here in this den and swapped ghost stories. Prettyman and Lang had some doozies about the Old Man of the Wood."

"Oooh! The Old Goat!" Mr. Woodruff chortled at his own wit.

"I read about that," Sonny said. "The locals used to think he stole their livestock and seduced their womenfolk—"

"—and granted wishes," Mr. Ting said.

"For a price, no doubt." Mr. Cockrum had lighted a cigarette. Its cherry illuminated the panes of his face.

"He has colorful appellations—Wild Bill, Splayfoot Bill, Billy the Black—"

"—Mr. Bill," said Mr. Cockrum to Mr. Ting's pained smile.

"Hear, hear!" Woodruff said. "Seducer of women? A satyr."

Cockrum winked at Sonny. "Not a satyr. Not a randy flautist, not Pan incarnate. The legends around here are darker than that."

"The Old Man of the Wood is a devil," Sonny said. "One of Lucifer's circle."

"Or Satan Hisownself. Isn't that right, Mr. Ting?" Mr. Cockrum exhaled toward the curator.

Mr. Ting shrugged. "Admittedly, in the olden days many an unfortunate event was laid at the feet, erm, hooves, of the Old Man."

"I'd say rape, murder, mutilation, the kidnapping of wee children qualifies as *unfortunate*, all right." Mr. Cockrum leaned toward Katherine. "You wanna see what I mean, there's a painting of the old boy down the hall on the way to the stairs. Curl your toes." Then, he lowered his voice to a stage whisper, "Prettyman says the Goat Lord still blunders through the darkest woods, that occasionally he meets up with a lost hiker, or a kid, pardon the pun…. On nights such as these it almost seems plausible."

On her way to dinner, Katherine had stopped to view the painting of the so called Old Man of the Wood. The oils were old and blurry, yet the depiction of the naked figure in a grove was oddly disquieting. One could discern massive horns, obscured by shadow, a sinister smile, a beckoning hand, elongated and strange. The painting possessed a quality of tainted eroticism, the fanciful and unnerving impression of a piece of ancient history leaked into the present. It gleamed darkly from its alcove, insinuating the permanence of lust and wickedness and the mortal fascination with such corruption.

"Let us not forget, our esteemed proprietor was once a man of the cloth," Mr. Ting said. "A good Lutheran minister descended from the Olde Towne tradition of such men. Understandably his conjecture would veer to the ecclesiastical."

"Really?" Sonny said. "He appears a bit, I dunno, wild, to be a minister."

"*Former* minister," Mr. Ting said.

"I say, whoever named this lodge certainly possessed a fiendish sense of humor," Mr. Woodruff said. "*Black Ram* is a tad obvious, though."

"Placation," Sonny said. "One must give the Devil his due."

"Puhleeze!" Katherine reached over and smacked his arm to the accompaniment of groans and chuckles.

Lights sputtered and fizzed in their sockets and power was restored to a round of tipsy applause. There came a brief lull, and when people began yawning, she seized the opportunity to proclaim road exhaustion and soon the party drifted to their respective quarters.

5.

Mr. Ting knocked on the door after a discreet period. Sonny poured nightcaps from a complimentary bottle of vodka management had stored in the icebox. Ting drew a leather packet from his valise and set it on the table and clicked on the lamp. The leather had paled to yellow and was bound with rawhide strings. The curator undid the knots and delicately spread several sheets of ancient, curling parchment. The papers were written in Latin, and decorated with alchemical annotations and cryptic diagrams. Ting explained that the materials had once been the property of the Welloc-Devlin Museum via the estate of Johansen Welloc, one of Olde Towne's self-styled nobles during the early 1900s. Welloc was a trained archeologist and noted collector of antiquities, the latter including a preoccupation with manuscripts and art objects certain to have gotten him burned at the stake during quainter times.

"Olde Towne is a rather fascinating case," Mr. Ting said. "Reading between the lines one might surmise its founding fathers were predominately occultists. Witchcraft, hermetic magic, geomancy…the gentry pursued knowledge of all manners of superstitious methodology. A veritable goldmine for an anthropologist."

"A wet dream," Katherine said. Clearly the town hadn't escaped the eccentricities of its founders—a flock of Golden Dawn-style crackpots who'd transmitted their kookiness down through the generations.

While Sonny studied the papers, Ting made himself another drink. "You realize, I assume, this is all rubbish." He produced a battered geophysical map of Olde Towne and environs. Red X's marked several locations.

"Yes, yes. Rubbish." Sonny didn't bother to glance up. His eyes were slits twinkling with lamplight. He licked his lips.

Mr. Ting smiled dryly. "Nor should I need to warn you about the legality of traipsing across sites of cultural import...much less tampering with anything you might find. The locals frown upon tourists pocketing arrowheads and such as souvenirs. Mr. Lang keeps a sharp eye on the grounds, I might add."

"Not to worry, Ting. That's a contemptible sport." Sonny's grin wasn't his most convincing.

Mr. Ting nodded and dragged on his cigarette. He exhaled and his shrewd expression was partially screened by the blue cloud, the back of his hand. "You have to be cautious," he said. He gestured at the discarded leather case, the survey map. "A word to the wise, my friends: there are those in Olde Towne who enjoy meeting nice people such as yourselves. These parties I mention are possessed of selfish interests and curious appetites. That's all I'll say."

"Um, thanks," Sonny said.

"Forgive my crassness, but the fee... Regrettable, however, my acquisition of your papers was not without some jeopardy to my position."

"Forgive you?" Sonny scribbled a check for a sum that made him wince, and sent the fellow on his way.

"Finally," Katherine said. She thought of the rotting grimoires with titles in Latin, German, and Greek, the mandrake roots and moon dust, and the other items stowed among their suitcases and bags. What would the unflappable Mr. Ting think of those? *He'd probably think we're just two more loons in a long line.*

Sonny locked the door. He went to the bed and dragged it about eighteen inches away from the wall. He'd purchased crimson chalk from a witch in Salem, Massachusetts. The witch was the real deal, he said, and he only tracked her down after many weeks of legwork. The crone dwelt in a shack in a bog, like all authentic witches did. She sold him the chalk, a dirty nub allegedly preserved from the collection of a Renaissance sorcerer who dabbled in the summoning of various entities best not mentioned, and candles made from the tears of freshly hanged men and babies' fat. Katherine refused to ask what the so-called witch wanted in exchange for her services. The possibilities induced a shudder.

He drew a pentagram around the bed, and another on the ceiling directly above, all the while muttering a Latin incantation. When he'd finished, he dusted off his hands and surveyed his work. The pentagrams were protective circles designed to repel negative forces that crept upon hapless sleepers: the night hags, the succubae and incubi, whatever unnamed demons that made feasts of a dreamer's spirit. "Be sure to step carefully when you get into bed. Smudge the line and it's useless."

"The maid is gonna love this," she said. Probably Sonny had arranged for them to be left undisturbed, however. He thought of everything. "Maybe we should sacrifice a goat. Yeah, ram's blood. And a virgin."

"You're drunk. Go to sleep," he said.

6.

Katherine lay sleep-drugged and passive while Sonny fucked her. His face always changed during sex. His eyes narrowed, his teeth shone like tarnished gemstones; he seemed dangerous and she occasionally fantasized he was a criminal, maybe a gangster who'd decided to have his way with her.

She turned her cheek against the coolness of her pillow while he grunted in her ear. The room was dark, but by the glow of the guttering candles she slowly realized Mr. Lang stood in the doorway, watching. She groaned, and Sonny put his hand over her mouth as he'd gotten in the habit of doing back when they were young and lusty and dwelt in an apartment with paper-thin walls. She struggled and that excited him and he moved faster, pressed her so hard the mattress formed a cave around them. Mr. Lang sidled from the doorway and toward the bed and slipped from her field of view. All she could hear was Sonny panting, her own muffled moans and cries. She panicked and thrashed against him and then she came and moments later he finished and collapsed upon her like a dead man.

Gasping and sobbing, Katherine shoved him until he rolled over. She frantically looked around, but Mr. Lang was nowhere to be seen. Her chest squeezed so tight her vision twinkled with motes and stars. Then, the urge to pee came over her. She was terrified to walk across the floor and into the pit of darkness that was the bathroom.

She lay awake, curled tight as a spring until morning light slowly pushed the shadows away and into the corners of the room. By then she'd half convinced herself Mr. Lang's appearance was that of an apparition. She chuckled wryly: What if Sonny's pentagram had kept them safe?

7.

Good as his word, following breakfast Mr. Prettyman gathered a party, which included Mr. Cockrum and his girlfriend Evelyn Fabini, and squired his guests around the expansive property on foot. The morning was damp. Golden light fell over the leaves and grass. It was a hushed and sacred moment before reaping-time. The world was balanced on the edge of a scythe.

Mr. Lang, accompanied by a scruffy field hand type, shadowed them. Katherine's flesh crawled and she endeavored to walk so one or more of her companions blocked Mr. Lang's view of her backside. On several instances she'd begun to broach the subject of the man's intrusion into their bedroom, but Sonny ignored her this morning, submerged in one of his moods. He wouldn't have believed her anyway. She took her fair share of pills and that wasn't something he let her forget. The accident had destroyed his trust in her judgment, perhaps her rationality.

Their tour skirted the outlying forest. Katherine, a veteran hiker, was nonetheless impressed with the girth of the trees, the brooding darkness that lurked within their confines. Periodically, well-beaten paths diverged and disappeared into the dripping trees. Mr. Prettyman led them past a tract of stone bungalows and into a cluster of decrepit outbuildings. The distillery was in the middle stages of collapse, its equipment quietly rusting amidst the rye and blackberry brambles. A stream clogged with brush gurgled nearby. He claimed that one of the state's only functioning windmills, a stone and timber replica of the famous Dutch models, had long dominated the rolling fields. Storms destroyed it decades prior, but its foundation could probably still be located should an intrepid soul assay chopping back mountains of scotch broom and weedy sycamore.

It had grown hot. She stared into the distance where the tall grass had begun to turn yellow and brown, and felt an urge to fly pell-mell into the field and roll in the grass, to burrow and hide in the soft, damp earth, to stare at the sky through a secret lattice.

"What's that?" asked Ms. Fabini, Mr. Cockrum's pale young mistress. "Over there."

Katherine had previously noted a copse of rather deformed oak trees that crowned a low rise in the otherwise flat field. She counted five trees, each heavily entwined in hawthorn bushes to roughly waist height. The thorn bushes made a sort of arched entrance to the hollow interior. Shadows and foliage obscured what appeared to be large pieces of statuary.

Mr. Prettyman said, "Ah, that would be one of several pagan shrines scattered across this region. They're no secret, but we keep mention of them to a minimum. The edification of our esteemed guests is one thing. Wouldn't do to stir up a swarm of crass tourists, on the other hand."

"Of course, of course, my good man," Mr. Cockrum said, to which the rest of the party members added their semi-articulate concurrence.

"Indian totems?" Mr. Woodruff asked, shading his eyes. "Shall we nip over and take a closer look?"

"Celtic," Sonny said.

"Quite right," Mr. Prettyman said. "You've done your homework. The details are sketchy, but Mr. Welloc and those of his inner circle imported various art objects from Western Europe and installed them in various places—some obvious, others not so. Allegedly, this piece was recovered in Wales."

"In other words, robbed from the peasants," Mr. Cockrum said to his girlfriend from behind his hand.

They filed into the copse where it was cool and dim.

"My word," Mr. Woodruff said.

The stone effigy of a muscular humanoid with ram horns reared some eight or so feet and canted sharply to one side. It radiated an aura of unspeakable antiquity, its features eroded, its form shaggy with moss that issued from countless fissures. Pieces of broken masonry jutted from the bed of dead leaves at the statue's foot—the remnants of a marble basin lay shattered and corroded. Even in its ruin, Katherine recognized the sacrificial altar for what it was. Heat and chill cycled through her. Blue sky peeped through a notch in the canopy and it seemed alien.

"Exactly like the painting," Sonny said, his voice hushed.

"It's…ghastly," Ms. Fabini said, white-gloved hand fluttering near her mouth as she stared in awe and horror at the statue's prodigious endowment.

"Oh, honey, control yourself." Cockrum squatted to examine the base of the statue, which had sunk to its calves in the dark earth. Sonny joined him, dusting here and there in a fruitless search for an inscription. From Kat's vantage, their heads obscured the Goat Lord's genitals. It struck her as a disquieting tableaux and without thinking, she raised her camera and snapped a picture an instant before they rose, dusting off their hands.

Katherine toed the ashes of a small fire pit, stirred sand and charred bits of bone. She said to Mr. Prettyman, "Who comes here? Besides your guests."

"Only guests. No one else is permitted access to the property." Mr. Prettyman stood beside her. He'd tied his long, white hair in a ponytail. It matched the severity of his expression. "There are those who pay for the privilege of borrowing the shrine. They hold services, observe vigils."

"You find it distasteful," she said.

He laughed coldly. "I understand the will to madness that is faith."

"You say they imported this from Wales."

"Yes, from a ruined temple."

"But, isn't this a pagan god. It resembles—"

"Old Nick. Of course. Don't you suppose The Prince of Darkness transcends religion? The true Man of a Thousand Faces. He's everywhere, no matter what one may call him."

"Or nowhere," she said.

"Ah. You have a scientific mind."

"What's left of it. Not much room for superstition."

"He doesn't require much," Mr. Prettyman said. "A fly will lay eggs on the smallest morsel."

8.

They lay in bed in the darkness of their small Pasadena home. He spooned her, his arm across her shoulder. The weight of his arm used to be a comfort; now it frightened her somehow. She knew he was awake because he wasn't snoring. A fan revolved somewhere above them. The room broiled. Her skin was cold and slick. She trembled.

Katherine?

She held her breath, waiting for his hand to slide from her breast to her belly, to push her legs apart and begin stroking her pussy. This was how it started, if it started at all. The hairs on her neck stood and she felt sick, flush with precognition that sent a wave of queasiness through her.

Did you do it on purpose? His whisper came low and harsh. It might've been the voice of a perfect stranger.

She cried then. Her entire body shook, wracked with shame and grief and guilty terror. His hand fell from her and he began to snore.

9.

It wasn't a bad week. Sonny drank more than usual, which worried her at first. This seemed to improve his mood, however. Between his daylong excursions into the countryside and midnight sessions poring over the archaic tomes by candlelight in the far corner of the suite, he was utterly preoccupied. He acted euphoric, which was his custom when approaching the solution to some particularly thorny problem. He kissed her gently in the morning before his departure, and when they shared dinners on the deck overlooking the valley, he was absentminded, yet sweet. She warmed to her independence, lounging with a book in the shade of the yard trees, walking the grounds as she pleased, hopping rides with Mr. Cockrum and Ms. Fabini for daytrips into town.

One late morning, she and Ms. Fabini contrived to ditch Mr. Cockrum when he nipped into the Haymaker Tavern to slum with the plebeians. The women explored, although there wasn't much to see after one had taken in the Main Street shops and the museum. The abbreviated center of town lay cupped by gently rising hillsides. Industry was relegated to the eastern edge, beyond the deep, quick waters of Belson creek, where dwelt the junkyards, auto shops, tattoo parlors, taverns, and the brewery, a monument which had been installed shortly after the end of Prohibition. Most everything else had withered on the vine over the years, leaving a series of darkened warehouses, the shuttered bulk of an old mill, and a defunct textile factory. These last loomed in steadfast isolation like headstones.

Ms. Fabini spotted a decent antique shop and they spent an hour browsing through Depression-era furniture and bric-a-brac. Katherine had wandered into a cluttered aisle in a gloomy corner of the shop when she came across several framed photographs taken in the late 1800s. Most were bubbled and faded, but one stood in stark contrast, albeit yellow at the edges. A group of men in greatcoats and dusters stood around a wagon freighted with hay. The farmers were stoic as per the custom of pioneer America; even the youngest of them wore a thick, handlebar mustache. A blot of discoloration caught her glance. A person lay in the shadows beneath the wagon axle and leered between wheel spokes at the photographer, at her. She recognized the face.

10.

Katherine went for a stroll along the grounds in the afternoon. She reached the second gate and kept walking, kept treading the path until she'd come to the bungalows, all of them locked, drapes drawn tight; a cluster of family tombs.

Mr. Lang reclined in a wicker chair on the grass. He set a bottle of beer on the table near his elbow. "Hello," he said. His smile was insolent.

She hesitated, then walked directly to his chair and stood nearly looming over him, fists set into her hips. "What do you want?"

"I live here."

"This one?" She gestured.

"The Goat's Head Bungalow," he said. His face was a dark moon. "Thinking of dropping in for a beer later?"

"No, Mr. Leng—"

"Lang. Call me Derek."

"I want you to stay far away from us, Mr. Lang. I don't like you."

Mr. Lang raised an eyebrow and took a pull from his beer. "Yesterday your husband went into the country to a farm I told him about. He bought himself a cute little nanny goat. Pure, virginal white. Paid me a hundred bucks to help him smuggle the critter onto the property. We took the goat to that shrine in the field. Man, that's one nasty dagger your husband's got. Said he picked it up in India from some real live cultist types. Some screws rattling around in there, you ask me."

She stared, dumbfounded. *He's not lying. Sweet baby Jesus, he's not lying.*

"I charged him an extra c-note to dump the goat in the woods. I've done it before for a few other wackos—usually cats and rabbits, but hey."

"Screw you. Jesus, you're insane. You'd best stay clear of us." She hoped she sounded brave. She wanted to vomit. *Goddamn you, Sonny.*

"If you say so. I'm not the one slaughtering farm animals to get his kicks."

"I should march right into Mr. Prettyman's office and tell him what kind of psycho he's turned loose on the public."

"Should you?"

"Yeah. We'll see how smug you are when you're sent packing."

"And I should be reporting your husband."

That stopped her in her tracks. "About what? The goat? Go to hell. We're leaving on Monday. Frankly, it suits me if we blow this freak circus a couple of days early."

Mr. Lang's smile faded. He said with mock gravity, "Interesting hobby he's got, hiking in the hills, digging up things that don't belong to him. Probably thinks he hit the mother lode. I could just shoot him. The sheriff would thank me."

"What? No. Sonny doesn't… He takes notes for his articles. Sketches, sometimes. That's it." Her guts felt like they were sliding toward her shoes.

"That's it? That's all?"

"Yeah. Just sketches." She bit her lip until sparks shot through her vision and her eyes watered.

"Oh." He nodded as if her explanation was eminently reasonable. "You're a funny one, Mrs. Reynolds. Give me these come-hither looks all week, and now you get coy."

"You're deluded. Frankly, I can't believe you dare to threaten my husband. Mr. Prettyman will—"

"I know you," Mr. Lang said. "I check all the guests. That's *my* hobby."

She breathed heavily, her lungs thick as wet cotton. "You're a peeping Tom, too."

"You were in the papers. The Associated Press. You're kind of famous, Mrs. R."

"What's wrong with you?"

"With me? With me, you ask." He chuckled, a soft wheeze that originated from the depths of him. "They let you walk. We're so sympathetic these days. Throw your baby off a bridge and everybody gives you a hug and sends get well cards. So, Kat. Are you well? Those doctors fix your poor brain? Do those plainclothes detectives still follow you around, watching to see what 'that crazy Reynolds woman' is going to do next?"

She gagged on her tongue, choked when she tried to speak.

"Okay, darling. I'm not completely heartless. A cool grand, I forget to mention your hubby's hijinks to the good sheriff. Hell, bring it over personally and I'll take half in trade."

Her arm swung wide, as if connected to someone else, and her fist crashed into his mouth. He slumped, arms hanging slack, as she stumbled backward. Blood dribbled over his chin. His sides shook and that wheezing laughter followed her as she lifted her skirt and fled.

Katherine made it to the suite. She leaned over the toilet and dry heaved. Her knuckles bled where she'd sliced them against Mr. Lang's teeth. Numbly, she washed her hand and pressed a washcloth against the cuts until the bleeding stopped. *Christ, what now? What am I going to tell Sonny?* Who knew what Sonny would do. He'd probably accuse her of leading the bastard on. Not that he'd say it aloud. His disgusted expression would do the talking. She was the millstone around his neck. *Why, oh why don't you just leave? Why not fuck your secretary, why not run away with one of those nubile coeds who are eager to throw themselves at you? Surely you could knock up one of those bitches and solve all of our problems.*

A better question might be: If she must stay, why not have an affair of her own? Mr. Lang's bloody grin flickered in her mind and she realized her left hand had drifted to her inner thigh, that her fingers stroked softly, almost imperceptibly. "Oh, my God," she said, and jerked her hand away. Her face burned.

She collapsed into a chair near the window. The light shifted to orange. A breeze swirled the leaves of the magnolias. What she saw then, with pitiless clarity, was an overpass, a woman carrying a pink bundle above a stream of headlights. The woman's face was blank and cold as plaster. The woman opened her arms. "Yes. I think I did it on purpose," she said to the empty room, and wished she had a gun to put against her head.

11.

Sonny stumbled in well after dark. He'd been clambering through hill and dale by the look of him—his hair was mussed, pine needles and leaves clung to his jacket, gathered in the cuffs of his muddy pants. He said hello and began to undress. Katherine still sat in the oversized chair in the gloom. She turned on the lamp so they could see one another. He glanced at her hand without comment and tossed his clothes in a pile near the foot of the bed.

"Sonny?"

"Yeah?" He regarded himself in the mirror. "Did you do anything today?"

"I walked around. Read a bit." They'd been sharing a couple of the amusing potboilers from the reading shelves in the lodge's den. Sonny *had* been pleased to discover titles by Machen and Le Fanu among the dreck.

"That's nice."

"Find anything?"

He shook his head. He rubbed his arm where a bruise flowered, dark and angry. "It's like a jungle. Thorns everywhere. I could spend a whole summer in there with a chainsaw and not find anything. Sheesh."

"Oh?"

He smiled briefly and took off his watch and set it on the dresser.

"Sonny."

"Hmm?"

"You're being careful." When he didn't answer, she cleared her throat. "No one's following you, or anything. You'd know, wouldn't you?"

"I'm just taking pictures."

"Okay," she said.

He walked into the bathroom and the shower started.

12.

Sonny had tried to summon the Devil once. He'd drawn a complicated pentagram in the basement, lit some candles and slaughtered a stray cat with a ceremonial dagger. Satan was lord of all flesh; pay Him some blood and maybe He'd give them the means to make a child. It was the kind of stunt dumb, oversexed teenagers pulled to impress their friends and scare themselves. Sonny admitted such rituals were essentially powerless; on the other hand, mind over matter—spiritual placebo—was another beast entirely. She'd almost left him then. Only her numb guilt, her essential apathy kept her yoked to him. Later, she stayed because at its worst, their relationship made her a flagellant, made her a worthy penitent.

It all started innocently enough.

In high school and college Katherine had played with tarot cards and Ouija boards—the weird roommate with the weirder off-campus-friends syndrome. Drink a bit of wine, take a few hits and the next thing she knew she'd be having an unexpected quasi-lesbian experience, or would find herself smack in the middle of an amateur thaumaturgy session, or, on one infamous Halloween night, a botched séance. When she'd first dated Sonny it came as no surprise he dabbled in native rituals; this *was* his area of expertise. One didn't keep a stack of books on the nightstand such as the ubiquitous *The Golden Bough*, *The Key of Solomon*, and treatises by Agrippa, Bruno, and Mathers among a host of others, without dipping one's toe in on occasion. They practiced feng shui after a half-assed

142 · LAIRD BARRON

fashion; it was all the rage with their post-college associates like so many Westerners' fleeting dalliances with Buddhism and Kabala. Nothing serious; more a casual pastime akin to some couples' weekend canasta games. And if Sonny happened to study what he called "hoodoo" to a great degree, that was because his job depended on the research.

Then the accident. Matters had become bizarre. Kafka and William Burroughs type bizarre. At least Sonny hadn't tried to blast a glass off her head. He'd done other things, however. A quiet, festering resentment bubbled to the surface in a glance, a smile, the subtle tightening of his grip on her wrist, the way he hurt her in bed, though never beyond the pale, just enough to let her feel his animosity. She feared that's what they'd gradually become—a pair of mated animals who snapped and snarled at one another, who remained together due to instinct, to pure expediency.

His sophomoric attempt to raise hell, as it were, signaled a sharp descent.

Mind over matter, he said when first introducing her to the ebon figurine of some dead tribe's fertility god, a trinket he acquired during his travels abroad; he clutched the fetish in his left hand whenever they fucked—and, oh, hadn't sex become a choreographed event. He tried to put the fetish in her until she slapped him hard enough to leave a mark. *Mind over matter,* he said the next time from behind a Celtic mask while painting her with red ochre, and the time after that when feeding her peyote buttons while shaking voodoo rattles in her face. Once, they'd visited the wreckage of a church sunk beneath the projects in Detroit, and a priest in black robes killed a chicken and anointed her in blood as a circle of bare-breasted acolytes howled. The unholy congregation melted away and Sonny mounted her, his expression twisted, a mirror of her own insides, and after, neither could look the other in the eye. Riding the empty late-night bus back to their hotel, they huddled near the rear, she wrapped in a blanket, staring at her reflection, staring into and past her own dead eyes at block after block of urban blight; there were no streetlights, no blue flickering television screens or reading lamps, only the blackness.

No baby was forthcoming, either.

13.

The next morning, after Sonny slipped away, she took a long hot shower and was drying her hair when she heard a door shut in the other room.

Someone left an envelope addressed to her on the table. Her name was printed in a loose, sloppy hand. The envelope contained two dozen photographs. Several were shots of Sonny digging up artifacts. Ten or so were close-ups of arrowheads, pottery, figurines and the like. All were quite damning in their clarity. An itemized list documented various pieces, where they'd been acquired and who purchased them. Some of the photos were fifteen or more years old, dating back to Sonny's graduate days. Katherine knew about his compulsive theft, but she'd not allowed herself to dwell upon how long he'd engaged in his habits.

The list was signed: *Meet me, tonight. Witching Hour.* Mr. Lang was indeed wily, leaving her to infer his identity and where to rendezvous. Her hands shook as she tossed the envelope and its contents into the fireplace. She hugged herself and watched the packet curl and burn. Only much later, after she'd called Ms. Fabini to cancel their luncheon plans and burrowed under the covers to hibernate, did she recall that there were no ashes from the impromptu fire, only a fine tracing of soot that swirled and disappeared into the chimney.

In her dreams, Sonny called from the recesses of the chimney while she started a fire from his papers and books and a pile of his muddy clothes. She'd collected a sack of his clipped hair and threw it on for kindling. He screamed at her, but she didn't stop. She ripped off her wedding dress and added it to the blaze. A baby shrieked as it cooked and sizzled. She tossed on pieces of the old crib and watched them burn.

14.

At first, she tried to convince herself this would be about rescuing Sonny from the clutches of crazy, vindictive Mr. Lang. Except, that didn't fly—there was no way to avoid the reality that Sonny getting caught and jailed for a few years would be a relief from tension and satisfying to boot. Truthfully, his getting nailed for a career of misdeeds appealed to her on several levels.

Regardless of Sonny's legal hassles or potential financial ruin, it was really his problem alone. Her face hadn't been photographed. Her name hadn't appeared on any lists. In any event, no matter how dire the circumstances, she could run home to mama; a girl could always do that. No, there were other deeper, less rational motives for keeping the rendezvous. She just refused to face them directly.

Katherine crumbled sleeping pills and Valium into two consecutive glasses of vodka and watched Sonny gulp them down. He was already a bit drunk, so it was almost like the movies, almost frighteningly easy. For all she knew she'd dealt him an elephant's dose that might stop his heart. He fell asleep in his chair, snoring gently into his scattered notes. She blew out the candles.

The hour was late.

The moon hung cold and yellow behind a gossamer scrim. Her shoes crunched against the path that wound from the lodge and its attendant structures. Katherine arrived on the doorstep of the Goat's Head Bungalow at the appointed time and was slightly surprised to find it dark. She rapped on the door and waited. Her left hand dug into her jacket pocket and tightened around the can of mace attached to her keychain. In her right pocket was an envelope stuffed with twenty dollar bills she'd withdrawn from an ATM in Olde Towne earlier that day. The mace was a decade old: Sonny bought it for her after a guy mugged them in Venice. The thug gave her a shiner and a sprained neck in the process of yanking away her camera. Stunned, Sonny had stood there while it happened. That evening in the hotel, he berated her for carrying the camera, for attracting trouble. Later, he apologized by handing her the mace and some flowers. When they returned to the states he enrolled in karate lessons and attended classes religiously until he quietly dropped them in a few weeks.

No one stirred within the bungalow; it squatted dead and cold as a husk, tenanted by silence so palpable it throbbed in her ears. Clouds slid across the face of the moon, and its yellow light curdled, reddened into the eye of a drunk. The temperature had dipped and her breath streamed from her mouth. She stepped off the porch and surveyed the empty field. Fire briefly shone within the distant oak grove.

She walked the path to the very shadow of the grove, hesitated before the briar arch. A figure barred the way, a black form silhouetted by the dim illumination from coals dying in the pit. "Mr. Lang," she said, knowing in that instant her mistake, experiencing the sweet, horrific bloom of understanding that accompanies waking to a nightmare within a nightmare.

He laughed. His laugh was similar to Mr. Lang's, but deeper, darker. Hearing it was like hearing blood rush over pebbles. Red shadows crawled from the fire pit and enlarged him. His outline flickered, suggestive of manifold possibilities.

"I'm here," she said.

"Yes, you are," he said in a voice that whispered as from a distance. A familiar voice, but clotted with an excess of saliva and eagerness. She thought if some ancient creature of the wood could form words this would be their shape. "Bravery born of damnation isn't courageous, is it, lovely one?"

"You're Bill," she said.

"If you'd like."

"I brought money."

"But I don't want that."

"Four hundred and sixty dollars. That's all I could get. Take it… I'll write you a check when we get back home. I'll be wanting the negatives."

"Negatives? Negatives for pictures that never were? I wouldn't worry about them."

"Take the money—let's not play games, okay?"

"Yes, yes. It's time to quit pretending," he said.

"I don't understand."

He laughed again. The coals hissed and his silhouette became a lump of utter darkness. "These woods are very old."

"And dark; I know," she said. She could no longer see him. His presence magnified in her mind, it obliterated everything else.

"These woods are dear to me."

"It's right here. Please." She brandished the envelope in defiant supplication. The envelope absorbed the starlight, gleamed like a tooth. "Here. I swear, my husband won't trespass into the woods again."

"Yet, he's the fool who called me," he said. "What of you, sweet?"

Her arm shook from extending the envelope, so she folded her hands at her waist. "I've never gone into the forest."

"Pity, pity." He laughed again and now she imagined a hyena with an overdeveloped skull regarding her from the darkness, a stag crowned by tiers of crooked and decaying antlers. There was a terrible sickness in that laughter. "What of you? Tell me what *you* need."

"Nothing."

"Best wish for something," he said. "I could lie with you until you shrieked fair to drive the pheasants from their nests. Then I could split you open on the altar and have you to the fullest."

"Oh." The stars began to flash and she allowed her jelly legs to fold. She bowed her head, aware of the obscenity of this pseudo genuflection. "Not that."

"Then speak your desire."

Her mouth opened and she blurted, "You fucking well know, don't you?" Tears dripped from the end of her nose. She dared to raise her gaze, lips curled to bare her teeth in an expression of abject self-loathing. "Give me that. It's what I deserve, isn't it."

"I think you are both richly deserving."

"What…what must I do?"

"Why, pet, it's done. All these years I've been waiting to hold up my end of the bargain."

He emerged from the curtain of darkness and it stretched to limn him, to halo him in a writhing, black nimbus. She looked upon him and gave forth an involuntary moan of terror. For a moment, it was who she expected, the huntsman, florid and smug in triumph. The moonlight brightened and his face waxed ordinary—the face of a lover, the man who reads the meter, a blank-eyed passenger sharing a bus seat; a face mundane in its capacity for cruelty or avarice. Then he smiled and fulfilled every dreadful image conceived in a thousand plates in a thousand hallowed tomes, and woodblock illustrations and overwrought cinema. Corrupt heat pulsed from his flesh; his breath stunned her with its foul humidity. Yet, the impulse to clutch his lank beard, to twine her tongue in his, consumed her will. Her thighs trembled and she moistened. She wept as she pressed her lips against his muscular thigh and inhaled the reek of sulfur, bestial sweat, and rank, overripe sex.

His fingers tangled in her hair, long nails like hooks pricking at her scalp. He whispered, "Ask and ye shall receive."

15.

The sulfurous moon had almost dissolved into the horizon.

Katherine returned to the suite and stood for a while as a shadow among shadows, watching Sonny. He groaned in his sleep and called a name she couldn't recognize for his slurring. She erased a section of the ridiculous chalk pentagram with her bare foot, then went to him and murmured in his ear and coaxed him to bed. They fell across it and she undressed him. She sweated. The fierceness of her need was an agony, a pressure of such magnitude it eclipsed reason, caused the room to spin around her. The painting of the stag hunt caught her glance for a moment, its detail obscured and grainy, but—the mastiffs sat on their haunches and the stag towered on its hind legs, and the entire dark company gazed down upon the couple on the bed.

She caressed him, licked his ear and kissed his neck until he stirred and woke. It didn't take much more. Her heat was contagious and he made a sound in his chest and rolled atop her. She closed her eyes and arched, hooked her calves over his hips, pinned him to her with all her strength.

Motes and sparks behind her eyelids stuttered with her pulse. Pleasure shot through her brain and unfolded a kaleidoscope. She saw the white nanny goat bound at the foot of the statue. It bleated, then the knife and a fan of blood, her husband, his face one of legion, exultant and savage.

He drove into her without love, merciless; and in her skull, rockets. *Sonny, what did you wish?* She knew, oh, yes, but the question lingered, bored into her just as he did, and she trembled violently. *What did you wish?* The nanny goat rolled its head on the altar and its eyes flared red to a surge of panpipes, an offstage Gregorian litany, thunderous laughter.

She came, and, simultaneously, he rocked with a powerful spasm and bellowed. Her eyes snapped open. His face was a white mask, flesh stretched so tight his mouth pulled sharply upward at the corners. He vibrated as if he'd grabbed a high-voltage wire. Something cracked, a tendon, a bone, and he shoved away from her, flew from the bed and crashed to the floor. She managed to right herself. Her belly felt overfull. It was the strangest sensation, this ballooning inside, the sudden rush of nausea.

Sonny thrashed against the floorboards and continued to ejaculate. In the near darkness, she became confused by what she saw—the short, quick spurts that arced across his body were neither ropes nor strands, but thick and segmented. She'd seen a dead bird in the garbage and what had feasted upon it in oozing carpets, and her mental equilibrium wobbled mightily. He squealed as his rigid muscles softened and sloughed. He rapidly diminished and became physically incomprehensible, emptied of substance. What remained of him continued to flow in seeping tributaries toward the bed, and her. It happened very fast; a time lapse photo of an animal decomposing in the forest.

Sticky things squirmed upon her thighs and loins, and when she registered the flatworm torsos and embryonic faces, she screamed, was still screaming long after people finally battered through the door and everything was over.

They couldn't find a trace of Sonny anywhere.

16.

The pregnancy wasn't complicated. The hospital staff (they called it a "home") gave her a single occupancy room with a lovely view of the grounds. A squirrel lived in the chestnut tree near the window, and the nurses let her feed him breadcrumbs over the sill. Nurse Jennifer gave her medicine in the morning. Nurse Margaret tucked her in at night. Dr. Green visited daily and gave her peppermint candies, which she'd loved since childhood.

She slept a lot. She ate Jell-O cups whenever she liked, and watched *The 700 Club* on the television hanging in the corner. Occasionally, after dark, it'd be something nasty with bare tits and gouts of gore, children with withered faces who glared hatefully, and priests walking with their heads on backwards, but she didn't panic, the screen always went blank then returned to regularly scheduled programming when a nurse came in to check on her. Sometimes she watched the Reverend Jerry Falwell or Benny Hinn. She followed their sermons from a new King James Bible her father brought after an incident he'd jokingly referred to as an "exorcism" when she first came to the home. Admittedly, she'd had issues in the beginning, some outbursts. There hadn't been an incident in months and she'd practically blacked out entire sections of the Old Testament by underlining. She knew what to expect. She was ready. Things had gone so smoothly, so dreamily, it had scarcely felt like being pregnant at all.

It happened in the middle of the night and she didn't feel anything after the epidural except sweet, bright oblivion. They removed the baby before she revived. Nurse Jennifer told her she'd given birth to a healthy boy and they'd bring him around soon. Several days later they wheeled her into the sunshine and parked her on the patio by the fountain. She loved this spot. The grounds were decorated with manicured hedges and plum trees, and obscured by the trees, a high stone wall topped with wrought iron spikes.

Dr. Green, Nurse Jennifer, and one of the big male attendants brought the baby wrapped in a yellow blanket. The doctor and the nurse seemed reserved, disquieted despite their friendly greetings, and they exchanged looks. She'd heard them whispering about progeria while they thought she was asleep. They probably weren't sure what to tell her, were doubtless loath to upset her at this delicate juncture.

Dr. Green cleared his throat. "So, have you decided what you're going to call him?" He watched carefully as the attendant put the boy in her arms.

"Baby *has* a name," she said, staring with wonder and terror at her child's face. *You'll be talking in a few months. Oh, sweet Lord, won't that be interesting?* His smooth, olive skin was pitted by a faint scatter of acne scars. His eyes were alive with a dreadful knowingness. He already resembled his driver license photo.

STRAPPADO

Kenshi Suzuki and Swayne Harris had a chance reunion at a bathhouse in an Indian tourist town. It had been five or six years since their previous Malta liaison, a cocktail party at the British consulate that segued into a branding iron-hot-affair. They'd spent a long weekend of day cruises to the cyclopean ruins on Gozo, nightclubbing at the elite hotels and casinos, and booze-drenched marathon sex before the dissolution of their respective junkets swept them back to New York and London in a storm of tears and bitter farewells. For Kenshi, the emotional hangover lasted through desolate summer and into a melancholy autumn. And even now, when elegant, thunderously handsome Swayne materialized from the crowd on the balcony like the Ghost of Christmas Past—!

Kenshi wore a black suit; sleek and polished as a seal or a banker. He swept his single lock of gelled black hair to the left, like a gothic teardrop. His skin was sallow and dewlapped at his neck, and soft at his belly and beneath his Italian leather belt. He'd been a swimmer once, earnestly meant to return to his collegiate form, but hadn't yet braced for the exhaustion of such an endeavor. He preferred to float in hotel pools whilst dreaming of his supple youth, once so exotic in the suburbs of white-bread Connecticut. Everyone but his grandparents (who never fully acclimated to their transplantation to the West) called him Ken. A naturalized U.S. citizen, he spoke meager Japanese, knew next to zero about the history or the culture and had visited Tokyo a grand total of three times. In short, he privately acknowledged his unworthiness to lay claim to his blood heritage and thus lived a life of minor, yet persistent regret.

Swayne wore a cream-colored suit of a cut most popular with the royalty of South American plantations. *It's in style anywhere I go,* he explained later as they undressed one another in Kenshi's suite at the Golden Scale.

Swayne's complexion was dark, like fired clay. His slightly sinister brows and waxed imperial lent him the appearance of a Christian devil.

In the seam between the electric shock of their reunion and resultant delirium fugue of violent coupling, Kenshi had an instant to doubt the old magic before the question was utterly obliterated. And if he'd forgotten Swayne's sly, wry demeanor, his faith was restored when the dark man rolled to face the ceiling, dragged on their shared cigarette, and said, "Of all the bathhouses in all the cities of the world...."

Kenshi cheerfully declared him a bastard and snatched back the cigarette. The room was strewn with their clothes. A vase of lilies lay capsized and water funneled from severed stems over the edge of the table. He caught droplets in his free hand and rubbed them and the semen into the slick flesh of his chest and belly. He breathed heavily.

"How'd you swing this place all to yourself?" Swayne said. "Big promotion?

"A couple of my colleagues got pulled off the project and didn't make the trip. You?"

"Business, with unexpected pleasure, thank you. The museum sent me to look at a collection—estate sale. Paintings and whatnot. I fly back on Friday, unless I find something extraordinary, which is doubtful. Mostly rubbish, I'm afraid." Swayne rose and stretched. Rich, gold-red light dappled the curtains, banded and bronzed him with tiger stripes.

The suite's western exposure gave them a last look at the sun as it faded to black. Below their lofty vantage, slums and crooked dirt streets and the labyrinthine wharfs in the shallow, blood-warm harbor were mercifully obscured by thickening tropical darkness. Farther along the main avenue and atop the ancient terraced hillsides was a huge, baroque seventeenth-century monastery, much photographed for feature films, and farther still, the scattered manors and villas of the lime nabobs, their walled estates demarcated by kliegs and floodlights. Tourism pumped the lifeblood of the settlement. They came for the monastery, of course, and only a few kilometers off was a wildlife preserve. Tour buses ran daily and guides entertained foreigners with local folklore and promises of tigers, a number of which roamed the high grass plains. Kenshi had gone on his first day, hated the ripe, florid smell of the jungle, the heat, and the sullen men with rifles who patrolled the electrified perimeter fence in halftracks. The locals wore knives in their belts, even the urbane guide with the Oxford accent, and it left Kenshi feeling shriveled and helpless, at the mercy of the hatefully smiling multitudes.

Here, in the dusty, grimy heart of town, some eighty kilometers down the coast from grand old Mumbai, when the oil lamps and electric lamps fizzed alight, link by link in a vast, convoluted chain, it was only bright enough to help the muggers and cutthroats see what they were doing.

"City of romance," Swayne said with eminent sarcasm. He opened the door to the terrace and stood naked at the rail. There were a few tourists on their verandas and at their windows. Laughter and pop music and the stench of the sea carried on the lethargic breeze as it snaked through the room. The hotel occupied the exact center of a semicircle of relatively modernized blocks—the chamber of commerce's concession to appeasing Westerners' paranoia of marauding gangs and vicious muggers. Still, three streets over was the Third World, as Kenshi's colleagues referred to it whilst they swilled whiskey and goggled at turbans and sarongs and at the Buddhists in their orange robes. It was enough to make him ashamed of his continent, to pine for his father's homeland, until he realized the Japanese were scarcely any more civilized as guests.

"The only hotel with air conditioning and you go out there. You'll be arrested if you don't put something on!" Kenshi finally dragged himself upright and collected his pants. "Let's go to the discothèque."

"The American place? I'd rather not. Asshole tourists swarm there like bees to honey. I was in the cantina a bit earlier and got stuck near a bunch of Hollywood types whooping it up at the bar. Probably come to scout the area or shoot the monastery. All they could talk about is picking up on 'European broads.'"

Kenshi laughed. "Those are the guys I'm traveling with. Yeah, they're scouting locations. And they're all married, too."

"Wankers. Hell with the disco."

"No, there's another spot—a hole in the wall I heard about from a friend. A local."

"Eh, probably a seedy little bucket of blood. I'm in, then!"

Kenshi rang his contact, one Rashid Obi, an assistant to an executive producer at a local firm that cranked out several dozen Bollywood films every year. Rashid gave directions and promised to meet them at the club in forty-five minutes. Or, if they were nervous to travel the streets alone, he could escort them…. Kenshi laughed, somewhat halfheartedly, and assured his acquaintance there was no need for such coddling. He would've preferred Rashid's company, but knew Swayne was belligerently fearless regarding forays into foreign environments. His lover was an adventurer and hard-bitten in his own charming fashion. Certainly Swayne would mock him for his timidity and charge ahead regardless. So, Kenshi stifled his misgivings and led the way.

The discothèque was a quarter-mile from the hotel and buried in a misshapen block of stone houses and empty shops. They found it mostly by accident after stumbling around several narrow alleys that reeked of urine and the powerful miasma of curry that seeped from open apartment windows. The entry arch was low and narrow and blackened from soot and antiquity. The name of the club had been painted into the worn plaster, but illegible now from erosion and neglect. Kerosene lamps guttered in inset sconces and shadows gathered in droves. A speaker dangled from a cornice and projected scratchy sitar music. Two Indian men sat on a stone bench. They wore baggy, lemon shirts and disco slacks likely purchased from the black market outlets in a local bazaar. They shared the stem of the hookah at their sandaled feet. Neither appeared interested in the arrival of the Westerners.

"Oh my God! It's an opium den!" Swayne said, and squeezed Kenshi's buttock. "Going native, are we, dear?"

Kenshi blushed and knocked his hand aside. He'd smoked half a joint with a dorm mate in college and that was the extent of his experimentation with recreational drugs. He favored a nice, dry white wine and the occasional import beer, preferably Sapporo.

The darkness of the alley followed them inside. The interior lay in shadow, except for the bar, which glowed from a strip along its edge like the bioluminescent tentacle of a deep-sea creature, and motes of gold and red and purple passing across the bottles from a rotating glitter ball above the tiny square of dance floor wedged in the corner. The sitar music issued from a beat box and was much louder than it had been outside. Patrons were jammed into the little rickety tables and along the bar. The air was sharp with sweat and exhaled liquor fumes.

Rashid emerged from the shadows and caught Kenshi's arm above the elbow in the overly familiar manner of his countrymen. He was shorter than Kenshi and slender to the point of well-heeled emaciation. He stood so close Kenshi breathed deeply of his cologne, the styling gel in his short, tightly coiled hair. He introduced the small man from Delhi to a mildly bemused Swayne. Soon Rashid vigorously shepherded them into an alcove where a group of Europeans crowded together around three circular tables laden with beer bottles and shot glasses and fuming ashtrays heaped with the butts of cigarettes.

Rashid presented Swayne and Kenshi to the evening's co-host, one Luis Guzman, an elderly Argentinean who'd lived abroad for nearly three decades in quasi-political exile. Guzman was the public relations guru for a profoundly large international advertising conglomerate, which in turn influenced, or owned outright, the companies represented by the various guests he'd assembled at the discothèque.

Kenshi's feet ached, so he wedged in next to a reedy blonde Netherlander, a weather reporter for some big market, he gathered as sporadic introductions were made. Her hands bled ink from a mosaic of nightclub stamps, the kind that didn't easily wash off, so like rings in a tree, it was possible to estimate she'd been partying hard for several nights. This impression was confirmed when she confided that she'd gone a bit wild during her group's whirlwind tour of Bangkok, Mumbai, and now this "village" in the space of days. She laughed at him from the side of her mouth, gaped fishily with her left eye, a Picasso girl, and pressed her bony thigh against him. She'd been drinking boleros, and lots of them, he noted. *What goes down must come up,* he thought and was sorry for whomever she eventually leeched onto tonight.

The Viking gentleman looming across from them certainly vied for her attention, what with his lascivious grimaces and bellowing jocularity, but she appeared content to ignore him while trading glances with the small, hirsute Slav to the Viking's left and occasionally brushing Kenshi's forearm as they shared an ashtray. He soon discovered Hendrika the weathergirl worked for the Viking, Andersen, chief comptroller and inveterate buffoon. The Slav was actually a native of Minsk named Fedor; Fedor managed distribution for a major vodka label and possessed some mysterious bit of history with Hendrika. Kenshi idly wondered if he'd been her pimp while she toiled through college. A job was a job was a job (until she found the job of her dreams) to a certain subset of European woman, and men too, as he'd been pleased to discover during his many travels. In turn, Hendrika briefly introduced Kenshi to the French contingent of software designers—Françoise, Jean Michelle and Claude; the German photographer Victor and his assistant Nina, and Raul, a Spanish advertising consultant. They extended lukewarm handshakes and one of them bought him a glass of bourbon, which he didn't want but politely accepted. Then, everyone resumed roaring, disjointed conversations and ignored him completely.

Good old Swayne got along swimmingly, of course. He'd discarded his white suit for an orange blazer, black shirt and slacks, and Kenshi noted with equal measures of satisfaction and jealousy that all heads swiveled to follow the boisterous Englishman. Within moments he'd shaken hands with all and sundry and been inducted by the club of international debauchers as a member in good standing. That the man didn't even speak a second language was no impediment—he vaulted such barriers by shamelessly enlisting necessary translations from whoever happened to be within earshot. Kenshi glumly thought his friend would've made one hell of an American.

Presently Swayne returned from his confab with Rashid and Guzman and exclaimed, "We've been invited to the exhibition. A *Van Iblis!*" Swayne seemed genuinely enthused, his meticulously cultivated cynicism blasted to smithereens in an instant. Kenshi barely made him out over the cross-fire between Andersen and Hendrika and the other American, Walther. Walther was fat and bellicose, a colonial barbarian dressed for civilized company. His shirt was untucked, his tie an open noose. Kenshi hadn't caught what the fellow did for a living, however Walther put whiskey after whiskey away with the vigor of a man accustomed to lavish expense accounts. He sneered at Kenshi on the occasions their eyes met.

Kenshi told Swayne he'd never heard of Van Iblis.

"It's a pseudonym," Swayne said. "Like Kilroy, Or Alan Smithee. He, or she, is a guerilla. Not welcome in the U.K.; *persona non grata* in the free world you might say." When Kenshi asked why Van Iblis wasn't wel-come in Britain, Swayne grinned. "Because the shit he pulls off violates a few laws here and there. Unauthorized installations, libelous materials, health code violations. Explosions!" Industry insiders suspected Van Iblis was actually comprised of a significant number of member artists and exceedingly wealthy patrons. Such an infrastructure seemed the only logical explanation for the success of these brazen exhibitions and their participant's elusiveness.

It developed that Guzman had brought his eclectic coterie to this part of the country after sniffing a rumor of an impending Van Iblis show and, as luck would have it, tonight was the night. Guzman's contacts had provided him with a hand-scrawled map to the rendezvous, and a password. A password! It was all extraordinarily titillating.

Swayne dialed up a slideshow on his cell and handed it over. Kenshi remembered the news stories once he saw the image of the three homeless men who'd volunteered to be crucified on faux satellite dishes. Yes, that had caused a sensation, although the winos survived relatively intact. None of them knew enough to expose the identity of his temporary employer. Another series of slides displayed the infamous pigs' blood carpet bomb-ing of the Viet Nam War Memorial from a blimp that then exploded in midair like a Roman candle. Then the so called "corpse art" in Mexico, Amsterdam and elsewhere. Similar to the other guerilla installations, these exhibits popped up in random venues in any of a dozen countries after the mildest and most surreptitious of advance rumors and retreated underground within hours. Of small comfort to scandalized authorities was the fact the corpse sculptures, while utterly macabre, were allegedly comprised of volunteers with terminal illnesses who'd donated their bodies to science, or rather, art. Nonetheless, at the sight of grimly posed seniors in antiquated bathing suits, a bloated, eyeless Santa in a coonskin cap, the tri-headed ice cream vendor and his chalk-faced Siamese children, Kenshi wrinkled his lip and pushed the phone at Swayne. "No, I think I'll skip this one, whatever it is, thank you very much."

"You are such a wet blanket, Swayne said. "Come on, love. I've been dying to witness a Van Iblis show since, well forever. I'll be the envy of every art dilettante from Birmingham to Timbuktu!"

Kenshi made polite yet firm noises of denial. Swayne leaned very close; his hot breath tickled Kenshi's ear. He stroked Kenshi's cock through the tight fabric of his designer pants. Congruently, albeit obliviously, Hendrika continued to rub his thigh. Kenshi choked on his drink and finally consented to accompany Swayne on his stupid side trek, would've promised anything to spare himself this agonizing embarrassment. A lifetime in the suburbs had taught him to eschew public displays of affection, much less submit to a drunken mauling by another man in a foreign country not particularly noted for its tolerance.

He finished his drink in miserable silence and awaited the inevitable.

They crowded aboard Guzman's two Day-Glo rental vans and drove inland. There were no signs to point the way and the road was narrow and deserted. Kenshi's head grew thick and heavy on his neck and he closed his eyes and didn't open them until the tires made new sounds as they left paved road for a dirt track and his companions gently bumped their legs and arms against his own.

It wasn't much farther.

Daylight peeled back the layers of night and deposited them near a collection of prefabricated warehouse modules and storage sheds. The modules were relatively modern, yet already cloaked in moss and threaded with coils of vine. Each was enormous and had been adjoined to its siblings via additions and corrugated tin walkways. The property sat near the water, a dreary, fog-shrouded expanse surrounded by drainage ditches and marshes and a jungle of creepers and banyan trees.

Six or seven dilapidated panel trucks were parked on the outskirts; 1970s Fords imported from distant USA, their white frames scorched and shot with rust. Battered insignia on the door panels marked them as one-time property of the ministry of the interior. Alongside the trucks, an equally antiquated, although apparently functional, bulldozer squatted in the high grass; a dull red model one would expect to see abandoned in a rural American pasture. To the left of the bulldozer was a deep, freshly ploughed trench surmounted by plastic barrels, unsealed fifty-five-gallon drums and various wooden boxes, much of this half-concealed by canvas tarps. Guzman commented that the owners of the land were in the embryonic stage of prepping for large-scale development—perhaps a hotel. Power lines and septic systems were in the offing.

Kenshi couldn't imagine who in the hell could possibly think building a hotel in a swamp represented a wise business investment.

Guzman and Rashid's group climbed from the vans and congregated, faces slack and bruised by hangovers, jet lag, and burgeoning unease. What had seemed a lark in the cozy confines of the disco became a more ominous prospect as each took stock and realized he or she hadn't a bloody clue as to north or south, or up and down, for that matter. Gnats came at them in quick, sniping swarms, and several people cursed when they lost shoes to the soft, wet earth. Black and white chickens scratched in the weedy ruts.

A handful of Indians dressed in formal wear grimly waited under a pavilion to serve a buffet. None of them smiled or offered any greeting. They mumbled amongst themselves and loaded plates of honeydew slices and crepes and poured glasses of champagne with disconsolate expressions. A Victrola played an eerie Hindu-flavored melody. The scene reminded Kenshi of a funeral reception. Someone, perhaps Walther, muttered nervously, and the sentiment of general misgiving palpably intensified.

"Hey, this is kinda spooky," Hendrika stage-whispered to her friend Fedor. Oddly enough, that cracked everybody up and tensions loosened.

Guzman and Rashid approached a couple of young, drably attired Indian men who were scattering corn from gunny sacks to the chickens, and started a conversation. After they'd talked for a few minutes, Guzman announced the exhibition would open in about half an hour and all present were welcome to enjoy the buffet and stretch their legs. Andersen, Swayne and the French software team headed for the pavilion and mosquito netting.

Meanwhile, Fedor fetched sampler bottles of vodka supplied by his company and passed them around. Kenshi surprised himself by accepting one. His throat had parched during the drive and he welcomed the excuse to slip away from Hendrika whose orbit had yet again swung her all too close to him.

He strolled off a bit from the others, swiping at the relentless bugs and wishing he'd thought to wear that rather dashing panama hat he'd "borrowed" from a lover on location in the Everglades during a sweltering July shoot. His stroll carried him behind a metal shed overgrown with banyan vines. A rotting wooden addition abutted the sloppy edge of a pond or lagoon; it was impossible to know because of the cloying mist. He lighted a cigarette. The porch was cluttered with disintegrating crates and rudimentary gardening tools. Gingerly lifting the edge of a tarp slimy with moss, he discovered a quantity of new plastic barrels. HYDROCHLORIC ACID, CORROSIVE! and a red skull and crossbones warned of hazardous contents. He quickly snatched back his hand and moved away lest his cigarette trigger a calamity worthy of a Darwin Award.

"Uh, yeah—good idea, Sulu. Splash that crap on you and your face will melt like glue." Walther had sneaked up behind him. The man drained his mini vodka bottle and tossed it into the bushes. He drew another bottle from the pocket of his sweat-stained dress shirt and had a pull. The humidity was awful here; it pressed down in a smothering blanket. His hair lay in sticky clumps and his face was shiny and red. He breathed heavily, laboring as if the brief walk from the van had led up several flights of stairs.

Kenshi stared at him, considering and discarding a series of snappy retorts. "Asshole," he said under his breath. He flicked his cigarette butt toward the scummy water and edged around Walther and made for the vans.

Walther laughed. "Jap fag," he said. The fat man unzipped and began pissing off the end of the porch.

"I'm not even fucking Japanese, you idiot," Kenshi said over his shoulder. No good, he realized; the tremor in his voice, the quickening of his shuffle betrayed his cowardice in the face of adversity. This instinctive recoil from trouble, the resultant wave of self-loathing and bitter recriminations was as it ever had been with Kenshi. Swayne would've smashed the jerk's face.

Plucking the thought from the air, Walther called, "Don't go tell your Limey boyfriend on me!"

Guzman gathered everyone into a huddle as Kenshi approached. He stood on the running board of a van and explained the three rules regarding their impending tour of the exhibition: no touching, no souvenirs, no pictures. "Mr. Vasilov will come around and secure all cell phones, cameras and recorders. Don't worry, your personal effects will be returned as soon as the tour concludes. Thank you for your cooperation."

Fedor dumped the remaining limes and pears from a hotel gift basket and came around and confiscated the proscribed items. Beyond a few exaggerated sighs, no one really protested; the prohibition of cameras and recording devices at galleries and exclusive viewings was commonplace. Certainly, this being Van Iblis and the epitome of scofflaw art, there could be no surprise regarding such rules.

At the appointed time the warehouse doors rattled and slid aside and a blond man in a paper suit emerged and beckoned them to ascend the ramp. He was large, nearly the girth of Andersen the Viking, and wore elbow-length rubber gloves and black galoshes. A black balaclava covered the lower half of his face. The party filed up the gangway in pairs, Guzman and Fedor at the fore. Kenshi and Swayne were the next to last. Kenshi watched the others become swiftly dissolving shadows backlit as they were by a bank of humming fluorescent lamps. He thought of cattle and slaughter pens and fingered his passport in its wallet on a string around his neck. Swayne squeezed his arm.

Once the group had entered, five more men, also clothed in paper suits and balaclavas, shut the heavy doors behind them with a clang that caused Kenshi's flesh to twitch. He sickly noted these five wore machetes on their belts. Blood rushed to his head in a breaker of dizziness and nausea. The reek of alcohol sweat and body odor tickled his gorge. The flickering light washed over his companions, reflected in their black eyes, made their faces pale and strange and curiously lifeless, as if he'd been suddenly trapped with brilliantly sculpted automatons. He understood then that they too had spotted the machetes. Mouths hung open in moist exclamations of apprehension and dread and the inevitable thrill derived from the alchemy of these emotions. Yet another man, similarly garbed as his compatriots, wheeled forth a tripod-mounted Panaflex motion picture camera and began shooting the scene.

The floor creaked under their gathered weight. Insulating foam paneled the walls. Every window was covered in black plastic. There were two narrow openings at the far end of the entry area; red paint outlined the first opening, blue paint the second. The openings let into what appeared to be darkened spaces, their gloom reinforced by translucent curtains of thick plastic similar to the kind that compartmentalized meat lockers.

"You will strip," the blond man said in flat, accented English.

Kenshi's testicles retracted, although a calmness settled over his mind. He dimly acknowledged this as the animal recognition of its confinement in a trap, the inevitability of what must ultimately occur. Yet, one of this fractious group would argue, surely Walther the boor, or obstreperous Andersen, definitely and assuredly Swayne. But none protested, none resisted the command, all were docile. One of the anonymous men near the entrance took out his machete and held it casually at his waist. Wordlessly, avoiding eye contact with each other, Kenshi's fellow travelers began to remove their clothes and arrange them neatly, or not so much, as the case might've been, in piles on the floor. The blond instructed them to form columns and face the opposite wall. The entire affair possessed the quality of a lucid dream, a not-happening in the real world sequence of events. Hendrika was crying, he noted before she turned away and presented him with her thin backside: a bony ridge of spine, spare haunches. She'd drained white.

Kenshi stood between oddly subdued Swayne and one of the Frenchmen. He was acutely anxious regarding his sagging breasts, the immensity of his scarred and stretched belly, his general flaccidity, and almost chuckled at the absurdity of it all.

When the group had assembled with their backs to him, the blond man briskly explained the guests would be randomly approached and tapped on the shoulder. The designated guests would turn and proceed into the exhibit chambers by twos. Questions? None were forthcoming. After a lengthy pause it commenced. Beginning with Guzman and Fedor, each of them was gradually and steadily ushered out of sight with perhaps a minute between pairings. The plastic curtains swished and crackled with their passage. Kenshi waited his turn and stared at the curdled yellow foam on the walls.

The tap on the shoulder came and he had sunk so far into himself it was only then he registered everyone else had gone. The group comprised an uneven number, so he was odd man out. Abruptly, techno music blared and snarled from hidden speakers, and beneath the eardrum-shattering syncopation, a shrill, screeching like the keening of a beast or the howl of a circular saw chewing wood.

"Well, friend," said the blond, raising his voice to overcome the music, "you may choose."

Kenshi found it difficult to walk a straight line. He staggered and pushed through the curtain of the blue door, into darkness. There was a long corridor and at its end another sheet of plastic that let in pale light. He shoved aside the curtain and had a moment of sick vertigo upon realizing there were no stairs. He cried out and toppled, arms waving, and flopped the eight or so feet into a pit of gravel. His leg broke on impact, but he didn't notice until later. The sun filled his vision with white. He thrashed in the gravel, dug furrows with elbows and heels and screamed soundlessly because the air had been driven from his lungs. A shadow leaned over him and brutally gripped his hair and clamped his face with what felt like a wet cloth. The cloth went into his nose, his mouth, choked him.

The cloth tasted of death.

Thanks to a series of tips, authorities found him three weeks later in the closet of an abandoned house on the fringes of Bangalore. Re-creating events, and comparing these to the experiences of those others who were discovered at different locations but in similar circumstances, it was determined he'd been pacified with drugs unto a stupor. His leg was infected and he'd lost a terrible amount of weight. The doctors predicted scars, physical and otherwise.

There'd been police interviews; FBI, CIA, INTERPOL. Kenshi answered and answered and they eventually let him go, let him get to work blocking it, erasing it to the extent erasing it was possible. He avoided news reports, refused the sporadic interviews, made a concentrated effort to learn nothing of the aftermath, although he suspected scant evidence remained, anyway. He took a leave of absence and cocooned himself.

Kenshi remembered nothing after the blue door and he was thankful.

Months after their second and last reunion, Swayne rang him at home and asked if he wanted to meet for cocktails. Swayne was in New York for an auction, would be around over the weekend, and wondered if Kenshi was doing all right, if he was surviving. This was before Kenshi began to lie awake in the dark of each new evening, disconnected from the cold pulse of the world outside the womb of his apartment, his hotel room, the cabs of his endless stream of rental cars. He dreamed the same dream; a recurring nightmare of acid-filled barrels knocked like dominoes into a trench, the grumbling exertions of a red bulldozer pushing in the dirt.

I've seen the tape, Swayne said through a blizzard of static.

Kenshi said nothing. He breathed, in and out. Starless, the black ceiling swung above him, it rushed to and fro, in and out like the heartbeat of the black Atlantic tapping and slapping at old crumbling seawalls, not far from his own four thin walls.

I've seen it, Swayne said. After another long pause, he said, *Say something, Ken.*

What?

It does exist. Van Iblis made sure copies were circulated to the press, but naturally the story was killed. Too awful, you know? I got one by post a few weeks ago. A reporter friend smuggled it out of a precinct in Canada. The goddamned obscenity is everywhere. And I didn't have the balls to look. Yesterday, finally.

That's why you called. Kenshi trembled. He suddenly wanted to know. Dread nearly overwhelmed him. He considered hanging up, chopping off Swayne's distorted voice. He thought he might vomit there, supine in bed, and drown.

Yeah. We were the show. The red door people were the real show, I guess. God help us, Ken. Ever heard of a Palestinian hanging? Dangled from your wrists, cinder blocks tied to your ankles? That's what the bastards started with. When they were done, while the people were still alive.... Swayne stopped there, or his next words were swallowed by the static surf.

Of course, Van Iblis made a film. No need for Swayne to illuminate him on that score, to open him up again. Kenshi thought about the empty barrels near the trench. He thought about what Walther said to him behind the shed that day. He thought about how in his recurring dream he always chose the red door, instead.

I don't even know why I picked blue, mate, Swayne said.

He said to Swayne, *Don't ever fucking call me again.* He disconnected and dropped the phone on the floor and waited for it to ring again. When it didn't, he slipped into unconsciousness.

One day his copy arrived in a plain envelope via anonymous sender. He put the disk on the sidewalk outside of his building and methodically crushed it under the heel of his wingtip. The doorman watched the whole episode and smiled indulgently, exactly as one does to placate the insane.

Kenshi smiled in return and went into his apartment and ran a bath. He slashed his wrists with the broken edge of a credit card. Not deep enough; he bled everywhere and was forced to hire a service to steam the carpets. He never again wore short sleeve shirts.

Nonetheless, he'd tried. There was comfort in trying.

Kenshi returned to the Indian port town on company business a few years later. Models were being flown in from Mumbai and Kolkata for a photo shoot near the old monastery. The ladies wouldn't arrive for another day and he had time to burn. He hired a taxi and went looking for the Van Iblis site.

The field wasn't difficult to find. Developers had drained the swamp and built a hotel on the site, as advertised. They'd hacked away nearby wilderness and plopped down high-rise condos, two restaurants and a casino. The driver dropped him at the Ivory Tiger, a glitzy, towering edifice. The lobby was marble and brass and the staff a pleasant chocolate mahogany, all of whom dressed smartly, smiled perfectly white smiles and spoke flawless English.

He stayed in a tenth-floor suite, kept the blinds drawn, the phone unplugged, the lights off. Lying naked across crisp, snow-cool sheets was to float disembodied through a great silent darkness. A handsome businessman, a fellow American, in fact, had bought him a white wine in the lounge; a sweet talker, that one, but Kenshi retired alone. He didn't get many erections these days and those that came ended in humiliating fashion. Drifting through insoluble night was safer.

In the morning, he ate breakfast and smoked a few cigarettes and had his first drink of the day. He was amazed how much he drank anymore and how little effect it had on him. After breakfast he walked around the hotel grounds, which were very much a garden, and stopped at the tennis courts. No one was playing; thunderclouds massed and the air smelled of rain. By his estimation, the tennis courts were near to, if not directly atop, the old field. Drainage grates were embedded at regular intervals and he went to his knees and pressed the side of his head against one until the cold metal flattened his ear. He listened to water rushing through subterranean depths. Water fell through deep, hollow spaces and echoed, ever more faintly. And, perhaps, borne through yards of pipe and clay and gravel that hold, some say, fragments and frequencies of the past, drifted whispery strains of laughter, Victrola music.

He caught himself speculating about who else went through the blue door, the exit to the world of the living, and smothered this line of conjecture with the bribe of more drinks at the bar, more sex from this day on, more whatever it might take to stifle such thoughts forever. He was happier thinking Hendrika went back to her weather reporter job once the emotional trauma subsided, that Andersen the Viking was ever in pursuit of her dubious virtue, that the Frenchmen and the German photographer had returned to their busy, busy lives. And Rashid.... Blue door. Red door. They might be anywhere.

The sky cracked and rain poured forth.

Kenshi curled into a tight ball, chin to chest, and closed his eyes. Swayne kissed his mouth and they were crushingly intertwined. Acid sluiced over them in a wave, then the lid clanged home over the rim of the barrel and closed them in.

THE BROADSWORD

Lately, Pershing dreamed of his long lost friend Terry Walker. Terry himself was seldom actually present; the dreams were soundless and gray as surveillance videos, and devoid of actors. There were trees and fog, and moving shapes like shadow puppets against a wall. On several occasions he'd surfaced from these fitful dreams to muted whispering—he momentarily formed the odd notion a dark figure stood in the doorway. And in that moment his addled brain gave the form substance: his father, his brother, his dead wife, but none of them, of course, for as the fog cleared from his mind, the shadows were erased by morning light, and the whispers receded into the rush and hum of the laboring fan. He wondered if these visions were a sign of impending heat stroke, or worse.

August, and now these first days of September, had proved killingly hot. The air conditioning went offline and would remain so for God knew how long. This was announced by Superintendent Frame after a small mob of irate tenants finally cornered him as he was sneaking from his office, hat in hand. He claimed ignorance of the root cause of their misery. "I've men working on it!" he said as he made his escape; for that day, at least. By the more sour observers' best estimates, "men working on it" meant Hopkins the sole custodian. Hopkins was even better than Superintendent Frame at finding a dark hole and pulling it in after himself. Nobody had seen him in days.

Pershing Dennard did what all veteran tenants of the Broadsword Hotel had done over the years to survive these too-frequent travails: he effected emergency adaptations to his habitat. Out came the made-in-China box fan across which he draped damp wash cloths. He shuttered the windows and snugged heavy drapes to keep his apartment dim. Of course he maintained a ready supply of vodka in the freezer. The sweltering hours of daylight were for hibernation; dozing on the sofa, a chilled pitcher of

lemonade and booze at his elbow. These maneuvers rendered the insuf-
ferable slightly bearable, but only by inches.

He wilted in his recliner and stared at the blades of the ceiling fan cutting through the blue-streaked shadows while television static beamed
between the toes of his propped-up feet. He listened. Mice scratched
behind plaster. Water knocked through the pipes with deep-sea groans
and soundings. Vents whistled, transferring dim clangs and screeches from
the lower floors, the basement, and lower still, the subterranean depths
beneath the building itself.

The hissing ducts occasionally lulled him into a state of semi-hyp-
nosis. He imagined lost caverns and inverted forests of roosting bats, a
primordial river that tumbled through midnight grottos until it plunged
so deep the stygian black acquired a red nimbus, a vast throbbing heart
of brimstone and magma. Beyond the falls, abyssal winds howled and
shrieked and called his name. Such images inevitably gave him more of
a chill than he preferred and he shook them off, concentrated on baseball
scores, the creak and grind of his joints. He'd shoveled plenty of dirt and
jogged over many a hill in his career as a state surveyor. Every swing of
the spade, every machete chop through temperate jungle had left its mark
on muscle and bone.

Mostly, and with an intensity of grief he'd not felt in thirty-six years,
more than half his lifetime, he thought about Terry Walker. It probably
wasn't healthy to brood. That's what the grief counselor had said. The
books said that, too. Yet how could a man *not* gnaw on that bone sometimes?

Anyone who's lived beyond the walls of a cloister has had at least one
bad moment, an experience that becomes the proverbial dark secret. In
this Pershing was the same as everyone. His own dark moment had occurred many years prior; a tragic event he'd dwelled upon for weeks and
months with manic obsession, until he learned to let go, to acknowledge
his survivor's guilt and move on with his life. He'd done well to box the
memory, to shove it in a dusty corner of his subconscious. He distanced
himself from the event until it seemed like a cautionary tale based on a
stranger's experiences.

He was an aging agnostic and it occurred to him that, as he marched
ever closer to his personal gloaming, the ghosts of Christmases Past had
queued up to take him to task, that this heat wave had fostered a delirium
appropriate to second-guessing his dismissal of ecclesiastical concerns,
and penitence.

In 1973 he and Walker got lost during a remote surveying operation
and wound up spending thirty-six hours wandering the wilderness. He'd

been doing field work for six or seven years and should have known better than to hike away from the base camp that morning.

At first they'd only gone far enough to relieve themselves. Then, he'd seen something—someone—watching him from the shadow of a tree and thought it was one of the guys screwing around. This was an isolated stretch of high country in the wilds of the Olympic Peninsula. There were homesteads and ranches along its fringes, but not within ten miles. The person, apparently a man, judging from his build, was half-crouched, studying the ground. He waved to Pershing; a casual, friendly gesture. The man's features were indistinct, but at that moment Pershing convinced himself it was Morris Miller or Pete Cabellos, both of whom were rabid outdoorsmen and constantly nattering on about the ecological wonderland in which the crew currently labored. The man straightened and beckoned, sweeping his hand in a come-on gesture. He walked into the trees.

Terry zipped up, shook his head and trudged that direction. Pershing thought nothing of it and tagged along. They went to where the man had stood and discovered what he'd been staring at—an expensive backpack of the variety popular with suburbanite campers. The pack was battered, its shiny yellow and green material shredded. Pershing got the bad feeling it was brand new.

Oh, shit, Terry said. *Maybe a bear nailed somebody. We better get back to camp and tell Higgins.* Higgins was the crew leader; surely he'd put together a search and rescue operation to find the missing owner of the pack. That would have been the sensible course, except, exactly as they turned to go, Pete Cabellos called to them from the woods. His voice echoed and bounced from the cliffs and boulders. Immediately, the men headed in the direction of the yell.

They soon got thoroughly lost. Every tree is the same tree in a forest. Clouds rolled in and it became impossible to navigate by sun or stars. Pershing's compass was back at camp with the rest of his gear, and Terry's was malfunctioning—condensation clouded the glass internally, rendered the needle useless. After a few hours of stumbling around yelling for their colleagues, they decided to follow the downhill slope of the land and promptly found themselves in mysterious hollows and thickets. It was a grave situation, although, that evening as the two camped in a steady downpour, embarrassment figured more prominently than fear of imminent peril.

Terry brought out some jerky and Pershing always carried waterproof matches in his vest pocket, so they got a fire going from the dried moss and dead twigs beneath the boughs of a massive old fir, munched on jerky, and lamented their predicament. The two argued halfheartedly about whether they'd actually heard Pete or Morris calling that morning, or a mysterious third party.

Pershing fell asleep with his back against the mossy bole and was plunged into nightmares of stumbling through the foggy woods. A malevolent presence lurked in the mist and shadows. Figures emerged from behind trees and stood silently. Their wickedness and malice were palpable. He knew with the inexplicable logic of dreams that these phantoms delighted in his terror, that they were eager to inflict unimaginable torments upon him.

Terry woke him and said he'd seen someone moving around just beyond the light of the dying fire. Rain pattering on the leaves made it impossible to hear if anyone was moving around in the bushes, so Terry threw more branches on the fire and they warmed their hands and theorized that the person who'd beckoned them into the woods was the owner of the pack. Terry, ever the pragmatist, suspected the man had struck his head and was now in a raving delirium, possibly even circling their camp.

Meanwhile, Pershing was preoccupied with more unpleasant possibilities. Suppose the person they'd seen had actually killed a hiker and successfully lured them into the wild? Another thought insinuated itself; his grandmother had belonged to a long line of superstitious Appalachian folk. She'd told him and his brother ghost stories and of legends such as the Manitou, and lesser-known tales about creatures who haunted the woods and spied on men and disappeared when a person spun to catch them. He'd thrilled to her stories while snug before the family hearth with a mug of cocoa and the company of loved ones. The stories took on a different note here in the tall trees.

It rained hard all the next day and the clouds descended into the forest. Emergency protocol dictated staying put and awaiting the inevitable rescue, rather than blindly groping in circles through the fog. About midday, Terry went to get a drink from a spring roughly fifty feet from their campsite. Pershing never saw him again. Well, not quite true: he saw him twice more.

2.

Pershing moved into the Broadsword Hotel in 1979, a few months after his first wife, Ethel, unexpectedly passed away. He met second wife, Constance, at a hotel mixer. They were married in 1983, had Lisa Anne and Jimmy within two years, and were divorced by 1989. She said the relationship was doomed from the start because he'd never really finished mourning Ethel. Connie grew impatient of his mooning over dusty photo albums and playing old moldy tunes on the antique record player he stashed in the closet along with several ill-concealed bottles of scotch. Despite his fondness for liquor, Pershing didn't consider himself a heavy drinker, but rather a steady one.

During their courtship, Pershing talked often of leaving the Broadsword. Oh, she was queenly in her time, a seven-floor art deco complex on the West Side of Olympia on a wooded hill with a view of the water, the marina, and downtown. No one living knew how she'd acquired her bellicose name. She was built in 1918 as a posh hotel, complete with a four-star restaurant, swanky nightclub-cum-gambling hall, and a grand ballroom; the kind of place that attracted not only the local gentry, but visiting Hollywood celebrities, sports figures, and politicians. After passing through the hands of several owners, the Broadsword was purchased by a Midwest corporation and converted to a middle-income apartment complex in 1958. The old girl suffered a number of renovations to wedge in more rooms, but she maintained a fair bit of charm and historical gravitas even five decades and several facelifts later.

Nonetheless, Pershing and Connie had always agreed the cramped quarters were no substitute for a real house with a yard and a fence. Definitely a tough place to raise children—unfortunately, the recession had killed the geophysical company he'd worked for in those days and money was tight.

Connie was the one who eventually got out—she moved to Cleveland and married a banker. The last Pershing heard, she lived in a mansion and had metamorphosed into a white-gloved, garden-party-throwing socialite who routinely got her name in the lifestyle section of the papers. He was happy for her and the kids, and a little relieved for himself. That tiny single-bedroom flat had been crowded!

He moved up as well. Up to the sixth floor into 119; what the old superintendent (in those days it was Anderson Heck) sardonically referred to as an executive suite. According to the super, only two other people had ever occupied the apartment—the so-called executive suites were spacious enough that tenants held onto them until they died. The previous resident was a bibliophile who'd retired from a post at the Smithsonian. The fellow left many books and photographs when he died and his heirs hadn't seen fit to come around and pack up his estate. As it happened, the freight elevator was usually on the fritz in those days and the regular elevator wasn't particularly reliable either. So the superintendent offered Pershing three months' free rent if he personally dealt with the daunting task of organizing and then lugging crates of books and assorted memorabilia down six steep flights to the curb.

Pershing put his muscles to good use. It took him three days' hard labor to clear out the apartment and roughly three hours to move his embarrassingly meager belongings in. The rest, as they say, was history.

3.

Pershing would turn sixty-seven in October. Wanda Blankenship, his current girlfriend of nine months and counting, was forty-something—she played it coy, careful not to say, and he hadn't managed a peek at her driver license. He guessed she was pushing fifty, although she took care of herself, hit the Pilates circuit with her chums, and thus passed for a few years on the uphill side. "Grave robber!" he said when she goosed him, or made a half-hearted swipe at his testicles, which was often, and usually in public. She was a librarian too; a fantasy cliché ironically fulfilled during this, his second or third boyhood when he needed regular doses of the little blue pill to do either of them any justice.

Nine months meant their relationship had slid from the danger zone and come perilously near the edge of no return. He'd gotten comfortable with her sleeping over a couple of nights a week, like a lobster getting cozy in a kettle of warm water. He'd casually mentioned her to Lisa Anne and Jimmy during one of their monthly phone conferences, which was information he usually kept close to his vest. More danger signals: she installed a toothbrush in the medicine cabinet and shampoo in the bath. He couldn't find his extra key one night after coming home late from the Red Room and realized he'd given it to her weeks before in a moment of weakness. As the robot used to say, *Danger, Will Robinson! Danger! Danger!* He was cooked, all right, which was apropos, considering the weather.

"Oh, ye gods! Like hell I'm coming up there!" she said during their latest phone conversation. "My air conditioner is tip top. *You* come over here." She paused to snicker. "Where I can get my hands on you!"

He wanted to argue, to resist, but was too busy melting into the couch, and knew if he refused she'd come flying on her broom to chivvy him away most unceremoniously. Defeated, he put on one of his classier ties, all of which Constance had chosen, and made the pilgrimage—on foot in the savage glare of late afternoon because he walked everywhere, hadn't owned a car since he sold his El Camino in 1982. Walking generally suited him; he'd acquired a taste for it during his years of toil in the wilderness. He took a meager bit of pride in noting that his comfortable "traveling" pace left most men a quarter his age gasping and winded after a short distance.

He disliked visiting her place, a small cottage-style house in a quiet neighborhood near downtown. Not that there was anything wrong with the house itself, aside from the fact it was too tidy, too orderly, and she insisted on china dishes for breakfast, lunch, supper, and tea. He lived in constant fear of dropping something, spilling something, breaking something with his large, clumsy hands. She cheerily dismissed such concerns, remarking that her cups and dishes were relics passed down through the generations—"They gotta go sometime. Don't be so uptight." Obviously, this served to heighten his paranoia.

Wanda made dinner; fried chicken and honeydew, and wine for dessert. Wine disagreed with his insides and gave him a headache. When she broke out the after-dinner merlot, he smiled and drank up like a good soldier. It was the gentlemanly course—also, he was loath to give her any inkling regarding his penchant for the hard stuff. Her husband had drunk himself to death. Pershing figured he could save his own incipient alcoholism as an escape route. If things got too heavy, he could simply crack a bottle of Absolut and guzzle it like soda pop, which would doubtless give him a heart attack. Freedom either way! Meanwhile, the deceit must perforce continue.

They were snuggling on the loveseat, buzzed by wine and luxuriating in the blessed coolness of her living room, when she casually said, "So, who's the girl?"

Pershing's heart fluttered, his skin went clammy. Such questions never boded well. He affected nonchalance. "Ah, sweetie, I'm a dashing fellow. Which girl are you talking about?" That heart attack he sometimes dreamt of seemed a real possibility.

Wanda smiled. "The girl I saw leaving your apartment the other morning, silly."

The fact he didn't know any girls besides a few cocktail waitresses didn't make him feel any better. He certainly was guilty of *looking* at lots of girls and couldn't help but wonder if that was enough to bury him. Then, instead of reassuring her that no such person existed, or that there must be some innocent mistake, he idiotically said, "Oh. What were you doing coming over in the morning?" In short order, he found himself on the porch. The sky was purple and orange with sunset. It was a long, sticky walk back to the hotel.

4.

The next day he asked around the Broadsword. Nobody had seen a girl and nobody cared. Nobody had seen Hopkins either. *Him* they cared about. Even Bobby Silver—Sly to his friends—didn't seem interested in the girl, and Sly was the worst lecher Pershing had ever met. Sly managed a dry cackle and a nudge to the ribs when Pershing described the mystery girl who'd allegedly come from his apartment. Young (relatively speaking), dark-haired, voluptuous, short black dress, lipstick.

"Heard anything about when they're gonna fix the cooling system? It's hotter than the hobs of Hell in here!" Sly sprawled on a bench just off the columned hotel entrance. He fanned himself with a crinkled Panama hat.

Mark Ordbecker, a high school math teacher who lived in the apartment directly below Pershing's with his wife Harriet and two children, suggested a call to the police. "Maybe one of them should come over and look around." They made this exchange at Ordbecker's door. The teacher leaned against the doorframe, trying in vain to feed the shrieking baby a bottle of milk. His face was red and sweaty. He remarked that the start of the school year would actually be a relief from acting as a househusband. His wife had gone east for a funeral. "The wife flies out and all hell breaks loose. She's going to come home to *my* funeral if the weather doesn't change."

Ordbecker's other child, a five-year-old boy named Eric, stood behind his father. His hair was matted with sweat and his face gleamed, but it was too pale.

"Hi, Eric," Pershing said. "I didn't see you there. How you doing, kiddo?"

Little Eric was normally rambunctious or, as Wanda put it, obstreperous, as in *an obstreperous hellion.* Today he shrank farther back and wrapped an arm around his father's leg.

"Don't mind him. Misses his mom." Mark leaned closer and murmured, "Separation anxiety. He won't sleep by himself while she's gone. You know how kids are." He reached down awkwardly and ruffled the boy's hair. "About your weirdo visitor—call the cops. At least file a report so if this woman's crazy and she comes at you with a pair of shears in the middle of the night and you clock her with a golf club, there's a prior record."

Pershing thanked him. He remained unconvinced this was anything other than a coincidence or possibly Wanda's imagination, spurred by a sudden attack of jealousy. He almost knocked on Phil Wary's door across the hall. The fellow moved in a few years back; a former stage magician, or so went the tales, and a decade Pershing's senior. Well-dressed and amiable, Wary nonetheless possessed a certain aloofness; also, he conducted a psychic medium service out of his apartment. Tarot readings, hypnosis, séances, all kinds of crackpot business. They said hello in passing, had waited together outside Superintendent Frame's office, and that was the extent of their relationship. Pershing preferred the status quo in this case.

"Cripes, this is all nonsense anyway." He always locked his apartment with a deadbolt; he'd become security-conscious in his advancing years, not at all sure he could handle a robber, what with his bad knees and weak back. Thankfully, there'd been no sign of forced entry, no one other than his girlfriend had seen anything, thus he suspected his time schlepping about the hotel in this beastly heat playing amateur investigator was a colossal waste of energy.

Wanda didn't call, which wasn't surprising considering her stubbornness. Dignity prohibited *him* ringing her. Nonetheless, her silence rankled; his constant clock watching annoyed him, too. It wasn't like him to fret over a woman, which meant he missed her more than he'd have guessed.

As the sun became an orange blob in the west, the temperature peaked. The apartment was suffocating. He dragged himself to the refrigerator and stood before its open door, straddle-legged in his boxers, bathed in the stark white glow. Tepid relief was better than nothing.

Someone whispered behind him and giggled. He turned quickly. The laughter originated in the living area, between the coffee table and a bookshelf. Because the curtains were tightly closed the room lay in a blue-tinged gloom that played tricks on his eyes. He sidled to the sink and swept his arm around until he flicked the switch for the overhead light. This illuminated a sufficient area that he felt confident to venture forth. Frankie Walton's suite abutted his own—and old Frankie's hearing was shot. He had to crank the volume on his radio for the ballgames. Once in a while Pershing heard the tinny exclamations of the play-by-play guys, the roar of the crowd. This, however, sounded like a person was almost on top of him, sneering behind his back.

Closer inspection revealed the sounds had emanated from a vent near the window. He chuckled ruefully as his muscles relaxed. Ordbecker was talking to the baby and the sound carried upstairs. Not unusual; the hotel's acoustics were peculiar, as he well knew. He knelt and cocked his head toward the vent, slightly guilty at eavesdropping, yet in the full grip of curiosity. People were definitely in conversation, yet, he gradually realized, not the Ordbeckers. These voices were strange and breathy, and came from farther off, fading in and out with a static susurration.

Intestines. Kidneys.

Ohh, either is delectable.

And sweetbreads. As long as they're from a young one.

Ganglia, for me. Or brain. Scoop it out quivering.

Enough! Let's start tonight. We'll take one from—

They tittered and their words degenerated into garble, then stopped.

Shh, shh! Wait!… Someone's listening.
Don't be foolish.
They are. There's a spy hanging on our every word.
How can you tell?
I can hear them breathing.
He clapped his hand over his mouth. His hair stood on end.
I hear you, spy. Which room could you be in? First floor? No, no. The fifth or the sixth.
His heart labored. What was this?
We'll figure it out where you are, dear listener. Pay you a visit. While you sleep. Whoever it was laughed like a child, or someone pretending to be one. *You could always come down here where the mome raths outgrabe….* Deep in the bowels of the building, the furnace rumbled to life as it did every four hours to push air circulation through the vents. The hiss muffled the crooning threats, which had ceased altogether a few minutes later when the system shut down.

Pershing was stunned and nauseated. Kidneys? Sweetbreads? He picked up the phone to punch in 911 before he got hold of his senses. What on earth would he say to the dispatcher? He could guess what they'd tell him: *Stop watching so many late night thrillers, Mr. Dennard.* He waited, eyeing the vent as if a snake might slither forth, but nothing happened. First the phantom girl, now this. Pretty soon he'd be jumping at his own shadow. *First stage dementia, just like dear old Dad.* Mom and Uncle Mike put Ernest Dennard in a home for his seventieth birthday. He'd become paranoid and delusional prior to that step. At the home Pop's faculties degenerated until he didn't know if he was coming or going. He hallucinated his sons were the ghosts of war buddies and screamed and tried to leap through his window when they visited. Thankfully, long before this turn of events Mom had the foresight to hide the forty-five caliber pistol he kept in the dresser drawer. Allegedly Grandma went through a similar experience with Gramps. Pershing didn't find his own prospects very cheery.

But you don't have dementia yet, and you don't knock back enough booze to be hallucinating. You heard them, clear as day. Jeezus C., who are they?
Pershing walked around the apartment and flicked on some lights; he checked his watch and decided getting the hell out for a few hours might be the best remedy for his jangled nerves. He put on a suit—nothing fancy, just a habit he'd acquired from his uncle who'd worked as a professor—and felt hat and left. He managed to catch the last bus going downtown. The bus was an oven; empty except for himself, a pair of teens, and the driver. Even so, it reeked from the day's accumulation; a miasma of sweat and armpit stench.

The depot had attracted its customary throng of weary seniors and the younger working poor, and a smattering of fancifully coiffed, tattooed, and pierced students from Evergreen; the former headed home or to the late shift, the latter off to house parties, or bonfires along the inlet beaches. Then there were the human barnacles—a half-dozen toughs decked out in parkas and baggy sports warmup suits despite the crushing heat; the hard, edgy kind who watched everyone else, who appraised the herd. Olympia was by no means a big town, but it hosted more than its share of beatings and stabbings, especially in the northerly quarter inward from the marina and docks. One didn't hang around the old cannery district at night unless one wanted to get mugged.

Tonight none of the ruffians paid him any heed. From the depot he quickly walked through several blocks of semi-deserted industrial buildings and warehouses, made a right and continued past darkened sporting goods stores, bookshops, and tattoo parlors until he hooked onto a narrow side lane and reached the subtly lighted wooden shingle of the Manticore Lounge. The Manticore was a hole in the wall that catered to a slightly more reserved set of clientele than was typical of the nightclubs and sports bars on the main thoroughfares. Inside was an oasis of coolness, scents of lemon and beer.

Weeknights were slow—two young couples occupied tables near the darkened dais that served as a stage for the four-piece band that played on weekends; two beefy gentlemen in tailored suits sat at the bar. Lobbyists in town to siege the legislature; one could tell by their Rolexes and how the soft lighting from the bar made their power haircuts glisten.

Mel Clayton and Elgin Bane waved him over to their window booth. Mel, an engineering consultant who favored blue button-up shirts, heavy on the starch, and Elgin, a social worker who dressed in black turtlenecks and wore Buddy Holly-style glasses and sometimes lied to women at parties by pretending to be a beat poet; he even stashed a ratty pack of cloves in his pocket for such occasions. He quoted Kerouac and Ginsberg chapter and verse regardless how many rounds of Johnny Walker he'd put away. Pershing figured his friend's jaded posturing, his affected cynicism, was influenced by the depressing nature of his job: he dealt with emotional basket cases, battered wives, and abused children sixty to seventy hours a week. What did they say? At the heart of every cynic lurked an idealist. That fit Elgin quite neatly.

Elgin owned a house in Yelm, and Mel lived on the second floor of the Broadsword—they and Pershing and three or four other guys from the neighborhood got together for drinks at the Manticore or The Red Room at least once a month; more frequently now as the others slipped closer to retirement and as their kids graduated college. Truth be told, he was much closer to these two than he was to his younger brother Carl, who lived in Denver and whom he hadn't spoken with in several months.

Every autumn, the three of them, sometimes with their significant others, drove up into the Black Hills outside Olympia to a hunting cabin Elgin's grandfather owned. None of them hunted; they enjoyed lounging on the rustic porch, roasting marshmallows, and sipping hot rum around the campfire. Pershing relished these excursions—no one ever wanted to go hiking or wander far from the cabin, and thus his suppressed dread of wilderness perils remained quiescent, except for the occasional stab of nervousness when the coyotes barked, or the wind crashed in the trees, or his unease at how perfectly dark the woods became at night.

Mel bought him a whiskey sour—Mel invariably insisted on covering the tab. *It's you boys or my ex-wife, so drink up!* Pershing had never met the infamous Nancy Clayton; she was the inimitable force behind Mel's unceremonious arrival at the Broadsword fifteen years back, although judging from his flirtatious behavior with the ladies, his ouster was doubtless warranted. Nancy lived in Seattle with her new husband in the Lake Washington townhouse Mel toiled through many a late night and weekend to secure. He'd done better with Regina, his second wife. Regina owned a bakery in Tumwater and she routinely made cookies for Pershing and company. A kindly woman and large-hearted; she'd immediately adopted Mel's cast of misfit friends and associates.

After the trio had chatted for a few minutes, griping about the "damnable" weather, mainly, Elgin said, "What's eating you? You haven't touched your drink."

Pershing winced at *eating*. He hesitated, then chided himself. What sense to play coy? Obviously he wished to talk about what happened. Why else had he come scuttling in from the dark, tail between his legs? "I…heard something at home earlier tonight. People whispering in the vent. Weird, I know. But it really scared me. The stuff they said…"

Mel and Elgin exchanged glances. Elgin said, "Like what?"

Pershing told them. Then he briefly described what Wanda said about the mystery girl. "The other thing that bothers me is…this isn't the first time. The last couple of weeks I've been hearing stuff. Whispers. I wrote those off. Now, I'm not so sure."

Mel stared into his glass. Elgin frowned and set his palm against his chin in apparently unconscious imitation of *The Thinker*. He said, "Hmm. That's bizarre. Kinda screwed up, in fact. It almost makes me wonder—"

"—if your place is bugged," Mel said.

"Bugged?"

"This from the man with a lifetime subscription to the *Fortean Times*," Elgin said. "Damn, but sometimes I think you and Freeman would make a great couple." Randy Freeman being an old school radical who'd done too much Purple Haze in the '60s and dialed into the diatribes of a few too many Che Guevara-loving hippie chicks for his own good. He was another of The Red Room set.

Mel took Elgin's needling in stride. "Hey, I'm dead serious. Two and two, baby. I'll lay odds somebody miked Percy's apartment."

"For the love of—" Elgin waved him off, settling into his mode of dismissive impatience. "Who on God's green earth would do something crazy like that? *No-freaking-body*, that's who."

"It is a bit farfetched," Pershing said. "On the other hand, if you'd heard this crap. I dunno."

"Oh, hell." Elgin took a sip of his drink, patently incredulous.

"Jeez, guys—I'm not saying Homeland Security wired it for sound… maybe another tenant is playing games. People do wacko things."

"No forced entry." Pershing pointed at Mel. "And don't even say it might be Wanda. I'll have to slug you."

"Nah, Wanda's not sneaky. Who else has got a key?"

Elgin said, "The super would have one. I mean, if you're determined to go there, then that's the most reasonable suspect. Gotta tell you, though—you're going to feel like how Mel looks when it turns out to be television noise—which is to say, an idiot."

"Ha, ha. Question is, what to do?"

"Elgin's right. Let's not make a bigger deal of this than it is… I got spooked."

"And the light of reason shines through. I'm going to the head." Elgin stood and made his way across the room and disappeared around a big potted fern.

Pershing said, "Do you mind if I sleep on your couch? If I'm not intruding, that is."

Mel smiled. "No problem. Gina doesn't care. Just be warned she goes to work at four in the morning, so she'll be stumbling around the apartment." He glanced over to make certain Elgin was still safely out of sight. "Tomorrow I'll come up and help you scope your pad. A while back Freeman introduced me to a guy in Tacoma who runs one of those spy shops with the mini-cameras and microphones. I'll get some tools and we'll see what's what."

After another round Elgin drove them back to the Broadsword. Just before he pulled away, he stuck his head out the window and called, "Don't do anything crazy."

"Which one of us is he talking to?" Mel said, glaring over his shoulder.

"I'm talking to both of you," Elgin said. He gunned the engine and zipped into the night.

5.

Regina had already gone to bed. Mel tiptoed around his darkened apartment getting a blanket and a pillow for Pershing, cursing softly as he bumped into furniture. Two box fans blasted, but the room was muggy as a greenhouse. Once the sleeping arrangements were made, he got a six-pack of Heineken from the refrigerator and handed one to Pershing. They kicked back and watched a repeat of the Mariners game with the volume turned most of the way down. The seventh-inning stretch did Mel in. His face had a droopy, hangdog quality that meant he was loaded and ready to crash. He said goodnight and sneaked unsteadily toward the bedroom.

Pershing watched the rest of the game, too lethargic to reach for the remote. Eventually he killed the television and lay on the couch, sweat molding his clothes to him like a second skin. His heart felt sluggish. A night light in the kitchen cast ghostly radiance upon the wall, illuminating bits of Regina's Ansel Adams prints, the glittery mica eyes of her menagerie of animal figurines on the mantel. Despite his misery, he fell asleep right away.

A woman gasped in pleasure. That brought him up from the depths. The cry repeated, muffled by the wall of Mel and Gina's bedroom. He stared at the ceiling, mortified, thinking that Mel certainly was one hell of a randy bastard after he got a few drinks under his belt. Then someone whispered, perhaps five feet to his left where the light didn't penetrate. The voice chanted: *This old man, this old man...*

The syrupy tone wicked away the heat as if he'd fallen into a cold, black lake. He sat upright so quickly pains sparked in his neck and back. His only consolation lay in the recognition of the slight echoing quality, which suggested the person was elsewhere. Whistling emanated from the shadows, its falsetto muted by the background noise. He clumsily sprang from the couch, his fear transformed to a more useful sense of anger, and crab-walked until he reached the proper vent. "Hey, jerk!" he said, placing his face within kissing distance of the grill. "I'm gonna break your knees with my baseball bat if you don't shut your damn mouth!" His bravado was thin—he did keep a Louisville slugger, signed by Ken Griffey Jr., no less, in the bedroom closet in case a burglar broke in at night. Whether he'd be able to break anyone's knees was open to question.

The whistling broke off mid-tune. Silence followed. Pershing listened so hard his skull ached. He said to himself with grudging satisfaction, "That's right, creepos, you *better* stuff a sock in it." His sense of accomplishment was marred by the creeping dread that the reason his tormentors (or was it Mel's since this was his place?) had desisted was because they even now prowled the stairwells and halls of the old building, patiently searching for him.

He finally went and poured a glass of water and huddled at the kitchen table until dawn lighted the windows and Gina stumbled in to make coffee.

6.

The temperature spiked to one hundred and three degrees by two P.M. the following afternoon. He bought Wanda two dozen roses with a card and arranged to have them delivered to her house. Mission accomplished, he went directly to an air-conditioned coffee shop, found a dark corner, and ordered half a dozen consecutive frozen drinks. That killed time until his rendezvous with Mel at the Broadsword.

Mel grinned like a mischievous schoolboy when he showed off his fiber-optic snooper cable, a meter for measuring electromagnetic fluctuations, and his battered steel toolbox. Pershing asked if he'd done this before and Mel replied that he'd learned a trick or two in the Navy.

"Just don't destroy anything," Pershing said. At least a dozen times he'd started to tell Mel about the previous night's visitation, the laughter; after all, if this was occurring in different apartments on separate floors, the scope of such a prank would be improbable. He couldn't devise a way to break it to his friend and still remain credible, and so kept his peace, miserably observing the operation unfold.

After lugging the equipment upstairs, Mel spread a dropcloth to protect the hardwood floor and arrayed his various tools with the affected studiousness of a surgeon preparing to perform open-heart surgery. Within five minutes he'd unscrewed the antique brass grillwork plate and was rooting around inside the guts of the duct with a flashlight and a big screwdriver. Next, he took a reading with the voltmeter, then, finding nothing suspicious, made a laborious circuit of the entire apartment, running the meter over the other vents, the molding, and outlets. Pershing supplied him with glasses of lemonade to diffuse his own sense of helplessness.

Mel switched off the meter, wiped his face and neck with a damp cloth. He gulped the remainder of the pitcher of lemonade and shook his head with disappointment. "Damn. Place is clean. Well, except for some roaches."

"I'll make Frame gas them later. So, nothing, eh? It's funny acoustics. Or my imagination."

"Yeah, could be. Ask your neighbors if they heard anything odd lately."

"I dunno. They already gave me the fishy eye after I made the rounds checking on Wanda's girl. Maybe I should leave it alone for now. See what happens."

"That's fine as long as whatever happens isn't bad." Mel packed his tools with a disconsolate expression.

The phone rang. "I love you, baby," Wanda said on the other end.

"Me too," Pershing said. "I hope you liked the flowers." Meanwhile, Mel gave him a thumbs up and let himself out. Wanda asked if he wanted to come over and it was all Pershing could do to sound composed. "It's a date. I'll stop and grab a bottle of vino."

"No way, Jose; you don't know Jack about wine. I'll take care of that— you just bring yourself on over."

After they disconnected he said, "Thank God." Partly because a peace treaty with Wanda was a relief. The other portion, the much larger portion, frankly, was that he could spend the night well away from the Broadsword. *Yeah, that's fine, girly man. How about tomorrow night? How about the one after that?*

For twenty years he'd chewed on the idea of moving; every time the furnace broke in the winter, the cooling system died in the summer, or when the elevators went offline sans explanation from management for weeks on end, he'd joined the crowd of malcontents who wrote letters to the absentee landlord, threatened to call the state, to sue, to breach the rental contract and disappear. Maybe the moment had come to make good on that. Yet in his heart he despaired of escaping; he was a part of the hotel now. It surrounded him like a living tomb.

7.

He dreamed that he woke and dressed and returned to the Broadsword. In this dream he was a passenger inside his own body, an automaton following its clockwork track. The apartment smelled stale from days of neglect. Something was wrong, however; off kilter, almost as if it wasn't his home at all, but a clever re-creation, a stage set. Certain objects assumed hyper-reality, while others submerged into a murky background.

The sugar in the glass bowl glowed and dimmed and brightened, like a pulse. Through the window, leaden clouds scraped the tops of buildings and radio antennas vibrated, transmitting a signal that he felt in his skull, his teeth fillings, as a squeal of metal on metal. His nose bled.

He opened the bathroom door and stopped, confronted by a cavern. The darkness roiled humid and rank, as if the cave was an abscess in the heart of some organic mass. Waves of purple radiation undulated at a distance of feet, or miles, and from those depths resonated the metallic clash of titanic ice flows colliding.

"It's not a cave," Bobby Silver said. He stood inside the door, surrounded by shadows so that his wrinkled face shone like the sugar bowl. His face was suspended in the blackness. "This is the surface. And it's around noon, local time. We do, however, spend most of our lives underground. We like the dark."

"Where?" He couldn't manage more than a dry whisper.

"Oh, you *know*," Sly said, and laughed. "C'mon, bucko—we've been beaming this into your brain for months—"

"No. Not possible. I've worn my tinfoil hat every day."

"—our system orbits a brown star, and it's cold, so we nestle in heaps and mounds that rise in ziggurats and pyramids. We swim in blood to stay warm, wring it from the weak the way you might squeeze juice from an orange."

Pershing recognized the voice from the vent. "You're a fake. Why are you pretending to be Bobby Silver?"

"Oh. If I didn't wear this, you wouldn't comprehend me. Should I remove it?" Sly grinned, seized his own cheek, and pulled. His flesh stretched like taffy accompanied by a squelching sound. He winked and allowed it to deform to a human shape. "It's what's underneath that counts. You'll see. When we come to stay with you."

Pershing said, "I don't want to see anything." He tried to flee, to run shrieking, but this being a dream, he was rooted, trapped, unable to do more than mumble protestations.

"Yes, Percy, you do," Ethel said from behind him. "We love you." As he twisted his head to gape at her, she gave him the soft, tender smile he remembered, the one that haunted his waking dreams, and then put her hand against his face and shoved him into the dark.

8.

He stayed over at Wanda's place for a week—hid out, like a criminal seeking sanctuary with the Church. Unhappily, this doubtless gave Wanda the wrong impression (although at this point even Pershing wasn't certain what impression she *should* have), but at all costs he needed a vacation from his suddenly creep-infested heat trap of an apartment. Prior to this he'd stayed overnight fewer than a dozen times. His encampment at her house was noted without comment.

Jimmy's twenty-sixth birthday fell on a Sunday. After morning services at Wanda's Lutheran church, a handsome brick building only five minutes from the Broadsword, Pershing went outside to the quiet employee parking lot and called him. Jimmy had wanted to be an architect since elementary school. He went into construction, which Pershing thought was close enough despite the nagging suspicion his son wouldn't agree. Jimmy lived in California at the moment—he migrated seasonally along the West Coast, chasing jobs. Pershing wished him a happy birthday and explained a card was in the mail. He hoped the kid wouldn't check the postmark as he'd only remembered yesterday and rushed to get it sent before the post office closed.

Normally he was on top of the family things: the cards, the phone calls, the occasional visit to Lisa Anne when she attended Berkeley. Her stepfather, Barton Ingles III, funded college, which simultaneously indebted and infuriated Pershing, whose fixed income allowed little more than his periodic visits and a small check here and there. Now graduated, she worked for a temp agency in San Francisco and, embarrassingly, her meager base salary surpassed his retirement.

Toward the end of their conversation, after Pershing's best wishes and obligatory questions about the fine California weather and the job, Jimmy said, "Well, Pop, I hate to ask this…"

"Uh, oh. What have I done now? Don't tell me you need money."

Jimmy chuckled uneasily. "Nah, if I needed cash I'd ask Bart. He's a tightwad, but he'll do anything to impress Mom, you know? No, it's… how do I put this? Are you, um, drinking? Or smoking the ganja, or something? I hate to be rude, but I gotta ask."

"Are you kidding?"

There was a long, long pause. "Okay. Maybe I'm… Pop, you called me at like two in the morning. Wednesday. You tried to disguise your voice—"

"*Wha-a-t?*" Pershing couldn't wrap his mind around what he was hearing. "I did no such thing, James." He breathed heavily, perspiring more than even the weather called for.

"Pop, calm down, you're hyperventilating. Look, I'm not pissed—I just figured you got hammered and hit the speed dial. It would've been kinda funny if it hadn't been so creepy. Singing, no less."

"But it wasn't me! I've been with Wanda all week. She sure as hell would've noticed if I got drunk and started prank calling my family. I'll get her on the phone—"

"Really? Then is somebody sharing your pad? This is the twenty-first century, Pop. I got star sixty-nine. Your number."

"Oh." Pershing's blood drained into his belly. He covered his eyes with his free hand because the glare from the sidewalk made him dizzy. "What did I—this person—sing, exactly?"

"'This Old Man,' or whatever it's called. Although you, or they, added some unpleasant lyrics. They slurred... falsetto. When I called back, whoever it was answered. I asked what gave and they laughed. Pretty nasty laugh, too. I admit, I can't recall you ever making that kinda sound."

"It wasn't me. Sober, drunk, whatever. Better believe I'm going to find the bastard. There's been an incident or three around here. Wanda saw a prowler."

"All right, all right. If that's true, then maybe you should get the cops involved."

"Yeah."

"And Pop—let me explain it to Mom and Lisa before you get on the horn with them. Better yet, don't even bother with Mom. She's pretty much freaked outta her mind."

"They were called."

"Yeah. Same night. A real spree."

Pershing could only stammer and mumble when his son said he had to run, and then the line was dead. Wanda appeared from nowhere and touched his arm and he nearly swung on her. She looked shocked and her gaze fastened on his fist. He said, "Jesus, honey, you scared me."

"I noticed," she said. She remained stiff when he hugged her. The tension was purely reflexive, or so he hoped. His batting average with her just kept sinking. He couldn't do a much better job of damaging their relationship if he tried.

"I am so, so sorry," he said, and it was true. He hadn't told her about the trouble at the Broadsword. It was one thing to confide in his male friends, and quite another to reveal the source of his anxiety to a girlfriend, or any vulnerability for that matter. He'd inherited his secretiveness from Pop who in turn had hidden his own fears behind a mask of stoicism; this personality trait was simply a fact of life for Dennard men.

She relented and kissed his cheek. "You're jumpy. Is everything all right?"

"Sure, sure. I saw a couple of the choir kids flashing gang signs and thought one of the little jerks was sneaking up on me to go for my wallet."

Thankfully, she accepted this and held his hand as they walked to her car.

9.

A storm rolled in. He and Wanda sat on her back porch, which commanded a view of the distant Black Hills. Clouds swallowed the mountains. A damp breeze fluttered the cocktail napkins under their half-empty Corona bottles, rattled the burnt yellow leaves of the maple tree branches overhead.

"Oh, my," Wanda said. "There goes the drought."

"We better hurry and clear the table." Pershing estimated at the rate the front was coming they'd be slammed inside of five minutes. He helped her grab the dishes and table settings. Between trips the breeze stiffened dramatically. Leaves tore from the maple, from trees in neighboring yards, went swirling in small technicolor cyclones. He dashed in with the salad bowl as the vanguard of rain pelted the deck. Lightning flared somewhere over the Waddel Valley; the boom came eight seconds later. The next thunderclap was much closer. They stood in her window, watching the show until he snapped out of his daze and suggested they retreat to the middle of the living room to be safe.

They cuddled on the sofa, half watching the news while the lights flickered. Wind roared around the house and shook its frame as if a freight train slammed along tracks within spitting distance of the window, or a passenger jet winding its turbines for takeoff. The weather signaled a change in their static routine of the past week. Each knew without saying it that Pershing would return to the Broadsword in the morning, and their relationship would revert to its more nebulous aspect. Pershing also understood from her melancholy glance, the measured casualness in her acceptance, that while matters between them would remain undefined, a line had been crossed.

He thought about this in the deepest, blackest hours of night while they lay in bed, she gently snoring, her arm draped across his chest. How much easier his life would be if his mock comment to Elgin and Mel proved true—that Wanda was a lunatic; a split personality type who was behind the stalking incidents. *God, I miss you, Ethel.*

10.

"Houston, we have a problem," Mel said. He'd brought ham sandwiches and coffee to Pershing's apartment for an early supper. He was rattled. "I checked around. Not just you hearing things. Odd, odd stuff going on, man."

Pershing didn't want to hear, not after the normalcy of staying with Wanda. And the dreams…. "You don't say." He really wished Mel wouldn't.

"The cops have been by a couple of times. Turns out other tenants have seen that chick prowling the halls, trying doorknobs. There's a strange dude, as well—dresses in a robe, like a priest. Betsy Tremblay says the pair knocked on her door one night. The man asked if he could borrow a cup of sugar. Betsy was watching them through the peephole—she says the lady snickered and the man grinned and shushed her by putting his finger over his lips. Scared the hell out of Betsy; she told them to scram and called the cops."

"A cup of sugar," Pershing said. He glanced out at the clouds. It was raining.

"Yeah, the old meet-your-cute-neighbor standby. Then I was talking to Fred Nilson; he's pissed because somebody below him is talking all night. 'Whispering,' he said. Only problem is, the apartment below his belongs to a guy named Brad Cox. Cox is overseas. His kids come by every few days to water the plants and feed the guppies. Anyway, no matter how you slice it, something peculiar is going on around here. Doncha feel better?"

"I never thought I was insane."

Mel chuckled uneasily. "I was chatting with Gina about the whole thing, and she said she'd heard someone singing while she was in the bath. It came up through the vent. Another time, somebody giggled in the closet while she dressed. She screamed and threw her shoe. This was broad daylight, mind you—no one in there, of course."

"Why would there be?"

"Right. Gina thought she was imagining things; she didn't want to tell me in case I decided she was a nut. Makes me wonder how many other people are having these…experiences and just keeping it to themselves."

The thought should have given Pershing comfort, but it didn't. His feelings of dread only intensified. *I'm almost seventy, damn it. I've lived in the woods, surrounded by grizzlies and wolves; spent months hiking the ass end of nowhere with a compass and an entrenchment spade. What the hell do I have to be scared of after all that?* And the little voice in the back of his mind was quick to supply Sly's answer from the nightmare, *Oh, you know.* He said, "Food for thought. I guess the police will sort through it."

"Sure they will. Maybe if somebody gets their throat slashed, or is beaten to death in a home invasion. Otherwise, I bet they just write us off as a bunch of kooks and go back to staking out the doughnut shop. Looks like a police convention some mornings at Gina's store."

"Wanda wants me to move in with her. I mean, I think she does."

"That's a sign. You should get while the getting's good."

They finished the sandwiches and the beer. Mel left to meet Gina when she got home from work. Pershing shut the door and slipped the bolt. The story about the strange couple had gotten to him. He needed a stiff drink.

The lights blinked rapidly and failed. The room darkened to a cloudy twilight and the windows became opaque smudges. Sounds of rain and wind dwindled and ceased. "Gracious, I thought he'd *never* leave." Terry Walker peeked at him from the upper jamb of the bedroom door. He was attached to the ceiling by unknown means, neck extended with a contortionist's ease so his body remained obscured. His face was very white. He slurred as if he hadn't used his vocal chords in a while, as if he spoke through a mouthful of mush. Then Pershing saw why. Black yolks of blood spooled from his lips in strands and splattered on the carpet. "Hello, Percy."

"You're alive," Pershing said, amazed at the calmness of his own voice. Meanwhile, his brain churned with full-blown panic, reminding him he was talking to an apparition or an imposter.

"So it seems." Terry was unchanged from youth—clean-shaven, red hair curling below his ears, and impressive mutton chop sideburns in the style that had been vogue during the '70s.

"It was you in the vents?" Then, as an afterthought, "How could you terrorize my family?"

"I got bored waiting all week for you to come back. Don't be mad— none of them ever cared for you anyway. Who knows—perhaps we'll get a chance to visit each and every one, make them understand what a special person you are." Terry grinned an unpleasant, puckered grin and dropped to the floor, limber as an eel. He dressed in a cassock the color of blackened rust.

"Holy crap. You look like you've come from a black mass." Pershing chuckled nervously, skating along the fine line of hysteria. There was something wrong with his friend's appearance—his fingers and wrists had too many joints and his neck was slightly overlong by a vertebra or two. This wasn't quite the Terry Walker he knew, and yet, to some degree it *was,* and thus intensified his fear, his sense of utter dislocation from reality. "Why *are* you here? Why have you come back?" he said, and regretted it when Terry's smile bloomed with satanic joy.

"Surveying."

"Surveying?" Pershing felt a new appreciation for the depths of meaning in that word, the inherent coldness. Surveying preceded the destruction of one order to make way for another, stronger, more adaptable order.

"What else would I do? A man's got to have a niche in the universe."

"Who are you working for?" *Oh Lord, let it be the FBI, Homeland Security, anybody.* Still trying for levity, he said, "Fairly sure I paid my taxes, and I don't subscribe to *American Jihadist.* You're not here to ship me to Guantánamo, or wherever, are you? Trust me, I don't know jack squat about anything."

"There's a migration in progress. A Diaspora, if you will. It's been going on... Well, when numbers grow to a certain proportion, they lose relevance. We creep like mold." Terry's grin showed that the inside of his mouth was composed of blackened ridges, and indeed toothless. His tongue pulsed; a sundew expanding and contracting in its puddle of gore. "Don't worry, though, Earthman. We come in peace." He laughed and his timbre ascended to the sickly sweet tones of a demented child. "Besides, we're happy to live in the cracks; your sun is too bright for now. Maybe after it burns down a bit..."

The bathroom door creaked open and the woman in the black dress emerged. She said, "Hullo there, love. I'm Gloria. A pleasure to meet you." Her flesh glowed like milk in a glass, like the sugar bowl in his visions. To Terry, she said, "He's older than I thought."

"But younger than he appears." Terry studied Pershing, his eyes inscrutable. "City life hasn't softened you, has it, pal?" He nodded at the woman. "I'm going to take him. It's my turn to choose."

"Okay, dear." The woman leaned her hip against the counter. She appeared exquisitely bored. "At least there'll be screaming."

"Isn't there always?"

Pershing said, "Terry... I'm sorry. There was a massive search. I spent two weeks scouring the hills. Two hundred men and dogs. You should've seen it." The secret wound opened in him and all the buried guilt and shame spilled forth. "Man, I wanted to save you. It destroyed me."

"You think I'm a ghost? That's depressingly provincial of you, friend."

"I don't know what to think. Maybe I'm not even awake." Pershing was nearly in tears.

"Rest assured, you will soon make amazing discoveries," Terry said. "Your mind will shatter if we aren't careful. In any event, I haven't come to exact vengeance upon you for abandoning me in the mountains."

The woman smirked. "He'll wish you were here for that, won't he?"

"Damn you, you're not my friend," Pershing said. "And lady, you aren't Gloria, whoever she was—poor girl's probably on a milk carton. You wear faces so we will understand your language, so you can blend in, isn't that right? Who are you people, really?"

"*Who are you people?*" Gloria mimicked. "The Children of Old Leech. Your betters."

"Us?" Terry said. "Why, we're kin. Older and wiser, of course. Our tastes are more refined. We prefer the dark, but you will too. I promise." He moved to a shelf of Pershing's keepsakes—snapshots from the field, family photos in silver frames, and odd pieces of bric-a-brac—and picked up Ethel's rosary and rattled it. "As I recall, you weren't a man of any particular faith. I don't blame you, really. The New Testament God is so nebulous, so much of the ether. You'll find my civilization's gods to be quite tangible. One of them, a minor deity, dwells in this very system in the caverns of an outer moon. Spiritual life is infinitely more satisfying when you can meet the great ones, touch them, and, if you're fortunate, be indulged…."

Pershing decided to go through the woman and get a knife from the butcher block. He didn't relish the notion of punching a girl, but Terry was bigger than him, had played safety for his high school football team. He gathered himself to move—

Gloria said, "Percy, want me to show you something? You should see what Terry saw…when you left him alone with us." She bowed her neck and cupped her face. There came the cracking as of an eggshell; blood oozed through her fingers as she lifted the hemisphere of her face away from its bed. It made a viscid, sucking sound; the sound of bones scraping together through jelly. Something writhed in the hollow. While Pershing was transfixed in sublime horror, Terry slid over and patted his shoulder.

"She's got a cruel sense of humor. Maybe you better not watch the rest." He smiled paternally and raised what appeared to be a bouquet of mushrooms, except these were crystalline and twinkled like Christmas lights.

Violet fire lashed Pershing.

11.

In UFO abduction stories, hapless victims are usually paralyzed and then sucked up in a beam of bright light. Pershing was taken through a hole in the sub-basement foundation into darkness so thick and sticky it flowed across his skin. They *did* use tools on him, and, as the woman predicted, he screamed, although not much came through his lips, which had been sealed with epoxy.

An eternal purple-black night ruled the fleshy coomb of an alien realm. Gargantuan tendrils slithered in the dark, coiling and uncoiling, and the denizens of the underworld arrived in an interminable procession through vermiculate tubes and tunnels, and gathered, chuckling and sighing, in appreciation of his agonies. In the great and abiding darkness, a sea of dead white faces brightened and glimmered like porcelain masks at a grotesque ball. He couldn't discern their forms, only the luminescent faces, their plastic, drooling joy.

We love you, Percy, the Terry-creature whispered before it rammed a needle into Pershing's left eye.

12.

His captors dug in his brain for memories and made him relive them. The one they enjoyed best was the day of Pershing's greatest anguish:

When Terry hadn't returned to their impromptu campsite after ten minutes, Pershing went looking for him. The rain slashed through the woods, accompanied by gusts that snapped the foliage, caused treetops to clash. He tramped around the spring and saw Terry's hat pinned and flapping in some bushes. Pershing began to panic. Night came early in the mountains, and if sundown found him alone and isolated… Now he was drenched as well. Hypothermia was a real danger.

He caught movement from the corner of his eye. A figure walked across a small clearing a few yards away and vanished into the underbrush. Pershing's heart thrilled and he shouted Terry's name, actually took several steps toward the clearing, then stopped. What if it wasn't his friend? The gait had seemed wrong. Cripes, what if, what if? What if someone truly was stalking them? Farfetched; the stuff of late-night fright movies. But the primeval ruled in this place. His senses were tuned to a much older frequency than he'd ever encountered. The ape in him, the lizard, hissed warnings until his hackles rose. He lifted a stone from the muck and hefted it, and moved forward.

He tracked a set of muddy footprints into a narrow ravine. Rock outcroppings and brush interlaced to give the ravine a roof. Toadstools and fungi grew in clusters among beds of moss and mold. Water dripped steadily and formed shallow pools of primordial slime. There was Terry's jacket in a wad; and ten yards further in, his pants and shirt hanging from a dead tree that had uprooted and tumbled down into the gulley. A left hiking shoe had been dropped nearby. The trail ended in a jumble of rocks piled some four or five yards high. A stream, orange and alkaline, dribbled over shale and granite. There was something about this wall of stone that accentuated his fear; this was a timeless grotto, and it radiated an ineffable aura of wickedness, of malign sentience. Pershing stood in its presence, feeling like a Neanderthal with a torch in hand, trembling at the threshold of the lair of a nameless beast.

Two figures in filthy robes stood over a third, mostly naked man, his body caked in mud and leaves. The moment elongated, stretched from its bloom in September 1973 across three and a half decades, embedded like a cyst in Pershing's brain. The strangers grasped Terry's ankles with hands so pale they shone in the gloom. They wore deep cowls that hid their faces…yet, in Pershing's nightmares, that inner darkness squirmed with vile intent.

The robed figures regarded him; one crooked a long, oddly jointed finger. Then the strangers laughed—that sickening, diabolic laughter of a man mimicking a child—and dragged Terry away. Terry lay supine, eyes open, mouth slack, head softly bumping over the slimy rocks, arms trailing, limp, an inverted Jesus hauled toward his gruesome fate. They walked into the shadows, through a sudden fissure in the rocks, and were gone forever.

13.

The one that imitated Terry released him from the rack and towed him, drifting with the ungainly coordination of a punctured float, through a stygian wasteland. This one murmured to him in the fashion of a physician, a historian, a tour guide, the histories and customs of its race. His captor tittered, hideously amused at Pershing's perception of having been cast into a subterranean hell.

Not hell or any of its pits. You have crossed the axis of time and space by means of technologies that were old when your kind yet oozed in brine. You, sweet man, are in the black forest of cosmic night.

Pershing imagined passing over a colossal reef of flesh and bone, its coils and ridges populated by incalculable numbers of horridly intelligent beings that had flown from their original planets, long since gone cold and dead, and spread implacably across the infinite cosmos. This people traveled in a cloud of seeping darkness. Their living darkness was a cancerous thing, a mindless, organic suspension fluid that protected them from the noxious light of foreign stars and magnified their psychic screams of murder and lust. It was their oxygen and their blood. They suckled upon it, and in turn, it fed upon them.

We eat our children, Terry had said. *Immortals have no need for offspring. We're gourmands, you see; and we do love our sport. We devour the children of every sentient race we metastasize to…we've quite enjoyed our visit here. The amenities are exquisite.*

He also learned their true forms, while humanoid, were soft and wet and squirming. The human physiognomies they preferred for brief field excursions were organic shells grown in vats, exoskeletons that served as temporary camouflage and insulation from the hostile environments of terrestrial worlds. In their own starless demesne they hopped and crawled and slithered as was traditional.

Without warning, he was dropped from a great height into a body of water that bore him to its surface and buoyed him with its density, its syrupy thickness. He was overcome with the searing stench of rot and sewage. From above, someone grasped his hair and dragged him to an invisible shore.

There came a long, blind crawl through what felt like a tunnel of raw meat, an endless loop of intestine that squeezed him along its tract. He went forward, chivvied by unseen devils who whispered obscenities in his ear and caressed him with pincers and stinging tendrils, who dripped acid on the back of his neck and laughed as he screamed and thrashed in the amniotic soup, the quaking entrails. Eventually, a light appeared and he wormed his way to it, gibbering mindless prayers to whatever gods might be interested.

"It is always hot as hell down here," Hopkins the custodian said. He perched on a tall box, his grimy coveralls and grimy face lighted by the red glow that flared from the furnace window. "There's a metaphor for ya. Me stoking the boiler in Hell."

Pershing realized the custodian had been chatting at him for a while. He was wedged in the corner of the concrete wall. His clothes stuck to him with sweat, the drying juices of a slaughterhouse. He smelled his own rank ammonia odor. Hopkins grinned and struck a match and lighted a cigarette. The brief illumination revealed a nearly done-in bottle of Wild Turkey leaning against his thigh. Pershing croaked and held out his hand. Hopkins chuckled. He jumped down and gave Pershing the bottle.

"Finish it off. I've got three more hid in my crib, yonder." He gestured into the gloom. "Mr. 119, isn't it? Yeah, Mr. 119. You been to hell, now ain't you? You're hurtin' for certain."

Pershing drank, choking as the liquor burned away the rust and foulness. He gasped and managed to ask, "What day is it?"

Hopkins held his arm near the furnace grate and checked his watch. "Thursday, 2:15 P.M., and all is well. Not really, but nobody knows the trouble we see, do they?"

Thursday afternoon? He'd been with *them* for seventy-two hours, give or take. Had anyone noticed? He dropped the bottle and it clinked and rolled away. He gained his feet and followed the sooty wall toward the stairs. Behind him, Hopkins started singing "Black Hole Sun."

14.

As it happened, he spent the rest of the afternoon and much of the evening in an interrogation room at the police station on Perry Street. When he reached his apartment, he found Superintendent Frame had left a note on the door saying he was to contact the authorities immediately. There were frantic messages from Mel and Wanda on the answering machine wondering where he'd gone, and one from a Detective Klecko politely asking that he report to the precinct as soon as possible.

He stripped his ruined clothes and stared at his soft, wrinkled body in the mirror. There were no marks, but the memory of unspeakable indignities caused his hands to shake, his gorge to rise. Recalling the savagery and pain visited upon him, it was inconceivable his skin, albeit soiled with dirt and unidentifiable stains, showed no bruises or blemishes. He showered in water so hot it nearly scalded him. Finally, he dressed in a fresh suit and fixed a drink. Halfway through the glass he dialed the police and told his name to the lady who answered and that he'd be coming in shortly. He called Wanda's house and left a message informing her of his situation.

The station was largely deserted. An officer on the opposite side of bulletproof glass recorded his information and asked him to take a seat. Pershing slumped in a plastic chair near a pair of soda machines. There were a few empty desks and cubicles in a large room to his left. Periodically a uniformed officer passed by and gave him an uninterested glance.

Eventually, Detective Klecko appeared and shook his hand and ushered him into a small office. The office was papered with memos and photographs of wanted criminals. Brown water stains marred the ceiling tiles and the room smelled moldy. Detective Klecko poured orange soda into a Styrofoam cup and gave it to Pershing and left the can on the edge of the desk. The detective was a large man, with a bushy mustache and powerful hands. He dressed in a white shirt and black suspenders, and his bulk caused the swivel chair to wobble precariously. He smiled broadly and asked if it was all right to turn on a tape recorder—Pershing wasn't being charged, wasn't a suspect, this was just department policy.

They exchanged pleasantries regarding the cooler weather, the Seattle Mariners' disappointing season, and how the city police department was woefully understaffed due to the recession, and segued right into questions about Pershing's tenancy at the Broadsword. How long had he lived there? Who did he know? Who were his friends? Was he friendly with the Ordbeckers, their children? Especially little Eric. Eric was missing, and Mr. Dennard could you please tell me where you've been the last three days?

Pershing couldn't. He sat across from the detective and stared at the recorder and sweated. At last he said, "I drink. I blacked out."

Detective Klecko said, "Really? That might come as a surprise to your friends. They described you as a moderate drinker."

"I'm not saying I'm a lush, only that I down a bit more in private than anybody knows. I hit it pretty hard Monday night and sort of recovered this afternoon."

"That happen often?"

"No."

Detective Klecko nodded and scribbled on a notepad. "Did you happen to see Eric Ordbecker on Monday…before you became inebriated?"

"No, sir. I spent the day in my apartment. You can talk to Melvin Clayton. He lives in 23. We had dinner about five P.M. or so."

The phone on the desk rang. Detective Klecko shut off the recorder and listened, then told whoever was on the other end the interview was almost concluded. "Your wife, Wanda. She's waiting outside. We'll be done in a minute."

"Oh, she's not my wife—"

Detective Klecko started the recorder again. "Continuing interview with Mr. Pershing Dennard…. So, Mr. Dennard, you claim not to have seen Eric Ordbecker on Monday, September 24? When was the last time you did see Eric?"

"I'm not claiming anything. I didn't see the kid that day. Last time I saw him? I don't know—three weeks ago, maybe. I was talking to his dad. Let me tell you, you're questioning the wrong person. Don't you have the reports we've made about weirdoes sneaking around the building? You should be chatting them up. The weirdoes, I mean."

"Well, let's not worry about them. Let's talk about you a bit more, shall we?"

And so it went for another two hours. Finally, the detective killed the recorder and thanked him for his cooperation. He didn't think there would be any more questions. Wanda met Pershing in the reception area. She wore one of her serious work dresses and no glasses; her eyes were puffy from crying. Wrestling with his irritation at seeing her before he'd prepared his explanations, he hugged her and inhaled the perfume in her hair. He noted how dark the station had become. Illumination came from the vending machines and a reading lamp at the desk sergeant's post. The sergeant himself was absent.

"Mr. Dennard?" Detective Klecko stood silhouetted in the office doorway, backlit by his flickering computer monitor.

"Yes, Detective?" *What now? Here come the cuffs, I bet.*

"Thank you again. Don't worry yourself over…what we discussed. We'll take care of everything." His face was hidden, but his eyes gleamed.

The detective's words didn't fully hit Pershing until he'd climbed into Wanda's car and they were driving to Anthony's, an expensive restaurant near the marina. She declared a couple of glasses of wine and a fancy lobster dinner were called for. Not to celebrate, but to restore some semblance of order, some measure of normalcy. She seemed equally, if not more, shaken than he was. That she hadn't summoned the courage to demand where he'd been for three days told him everything about her state of mind.

We'll take care of everything.

15.

Wanda parked in the side lot of a darkened bank and went to withdraw cash from the ATM. Pershing watched her from the car, keeping an eye out for lurking muggers. The thought of dinner made his stomach tighten. He didn't feel well. His head ached and chills knotted the muscles along his spine. Exhaustion caused his eyelids to droop.

"Know what I ask myself?" Terry whispered from the vent under the dash. "I ask myself why you never told the cops about the two 'men' who took me away. In all these years, you've not told the whole truth to anyone."

Pershing put his hand over his mouth. "Jesus!"

"Don't weasel. *Answer the question.*"

In a gesture he dimly acknowledged as absurd, he almost broke the lever in his haste to close the vent. "Because they didn't exist," he said, more to convince himself. "When the search parties got to me, I was half-dead from exposure, ranting and raving. You got lost. You just got lost and we couldn't find you." He wiped his eyes and breathed heavily.

"You think your visit with us was unpleasant? It was a gift. Pull yourself together. We kept the bad parts from you, Percy my boy. For now, at least. No sniveling; it's unbecoming in a man your age."

Pershing composed himself sufficiently to say, "That kid! What did you bastards do? Are you trying to hang me? Haven't I suffered enough to please you sickos?"

"Like I said; you don't know the first thing about suffering. Your little friend Eric does, though."

Wanda faced the car, folding money into her wallet. A shadow detached from the bushes at the edge of the building. Terry rose behind her, his bone-white hand spread like a catcher's mitt above her head. His fingers tapered to needles. He grinned evilly at Pershing, and made a shushing gesture. From the vent by some diabolical ventriloquism: "We'll be around. If you need us. Be good."

Wanda slung open the door and climbed in. She started the engine and kissed Pershing's cheek. He scarcely noticed; his attention was riveted upon Terry waving as he melted into the shrubbery.

He didn't touch a thing at dinner. His nerves were shot—a child cried, a couple bickered with a waiter, and boisterous laughter from a neighboring table set his teeth on edge. The dim lighting was provided by candles in bowls and lamps in sconces. He couldn't even see his own feet through the shadows when he glanced under the table while Wanda had her head turned. The bottle of wine came in handy. She watched in wordless amazement as he downed several consecutive glasses.

That night his dreams were smooth and black as the void.

16.

The calendar ticked over into October. Elgin proposed a long weekend at his grandfather's cabin. He'd bring his latest girlfriend, an Evergreen graduate student named Sarah. Mel and Gina, and Pershing and Wanda would round out the expedition. "We all could use a day or two away from the bright lights," Elgin said. "Drink some booze, play some cards, tell a few tales around the bonfire. It'll be a hoot."

Pershing would have happily begged off. He was irritable as a badger. More than ever he wanted to curl into a ball and make his apartment a den, no trespassers allowed. On the other hand, he'd grown twitchier by the day. Shadows spooked him. Being alone spooked him. There'd been no news about the missing child and he constantly waited for the other shoe to drop. The idea of running into Mark Ordbecker gave him acid. He prayed the Ordbeckers had focused their suspicion on the real culprits and would continue to leave him in peace.

Ultimately he consented to the getaway for Wanda's sake. She'd lit up at the mention of being included on this most sacred of annual events. It made her feel that she'd been accepted as a member of the inner circle.

Late Friday afternoon, the six of them loaded food, extra clothes, and sleeping bags into two cars and headed for the hills. It was an hour's drive that wound from Olympia through the nearby pastureland of the Waddell Valley toward the Black Hills. Elgin paced them as they climbed a series of gravel and dirt access roads into the high country. Even after all these years, Pershing was impressed by how quickly the trappings of civilization were erased as the forest closed in. Few people came this far—mainly hunters and hikers passing through. Several logging camps were located in the region, but none within earshot.

Elgin's cabin lay at the end of an overgrown track atop a ridge. Below, the valley spread in a misty gulf. At night, Olympia's skyline burned orange in the middle distance. No phone, no television, no electricity. Water came from a hand pump. There was an outhouse in the woods behind the cabin. While everyone else unpacked the cars, Pershing and Mel fetched wood from the shed and made a big fire in the pit near the porch, and a second fire in the massive stone hearth inside the cabin. By then it was dark.

Wanda and Gina turned the tables on the men and demonstrated their superior barbequing skills. Everyone ate hot dogs and drank Löwenbräu and avoided gloomy conversation until Sarah commented that Elgin's cabin would be "a great place to wait out the apocalypse" and received nervous chuckles in response.

Pershing smiled to cover the prickle along the back of his neck. He stared into the night and wondered what kind of apocalypse a kid like Sarah imagined when she used that word. Probably she visualized the polar icecaps melting, or the world as a desert. Pershing's generation had lived in fear of the Reds, nuclear holocaust, and being invaded by little green men from Mars.

Wind sighed in the trees and sent a swirl of sparks tumbling skyward. He trembled. *I hate the woods. Who thought the day would come?* Star fields twinkled across the millions of light years. He didn't like the looks of them either. Wanda patted his arm and laid her head against his shoulder while Elgin told an old story about the time he and his college dorm mates replaced the school flag with a pair of giant pink bloomers.

Pershing didn't find the story amusing this time. The laughter sounded canned and made him consider the artificiality of the entire situation, man's supposed mastery of nature and darkness. Beyond this feeble bubble of light yawned a chasm. He'd drunk more than his share these past few days; had helped himself to Wanda's Valium. None of these measures did the trick of allowing him to forget where he'd gone or what he'd seen; it hadn't convinced him that his worst memories were the products of nightmare. Wanda's touch repulsed him, confined him. He wanted nothing more than to crawl into bed and hide beneath the covers until everything bad went away.

It grew chilly and the bonfire died to coals. The others drifted off to sleep. The cabin had two bedrooms—Elgin claimed one, and as the married couple, Mel and Gina were awarded the second. Pershing and Wanda settled for an air mattress near the fireplace. When the last of the beer was gone, he extricated himself from her and rose to stretch. "I'm going inside," he said. She smiled and said she'd be along soon. She wanted to watch the stars a bit longer.

Pershing stripped to his boxers and lay on the air mattress. He pulled the blanket to his chin and stared at the rafters. His skin was clammy and it itched fiercely. Sharp, throbbing pains radiated from his knees and shoulders. Tears formed in the corners of his eyes. He remembered the day he'd talked to Mark Ordbecker, the incredible heat, young Eric's terrified expression as he skulked behind his father. Little pitchers and big ears. The boy heard the voices crooning from below, hadn't he?

A purple ring of light flickered on the rough-hewn beam directly overhead. It pulsed and blurred with each thud of his heart. The ring shivered like water and changed. His face was damp, but not from tears, not from sweat. He felt his knuckle joints split, the skin and meat popping and peeling like an overripe banana. What had Terry said about eating the young and immortality?

How does our species propagate, you may ask. Cultural assimilation, my friend. We chop out the things that make you lesser life forms weak and then pump you full of love. You'll be part of the family soon; you'll understand everything.

A mental switch clicked and he smiled at the memory of creeping into Eric's room and plucking him from his bed; later, the child's hands fluttering, nerveless, the approving croaks and cries of his new kin. He shuddered in ecstasy and burst crude seams in a dozen places. He threw off the blanket and stood, swaying, drunk with revelation. His flesh was a chrysalis, leaking gore.

Terry and Gloria watched him from the doorways of the bedrooms—naked and ghostly, and smiling like devils. Behind them, the rooms were silent. He looked at their bodies, contemptuous that anyone could be fooled for two seconds by these distorted forms, or by his own.

Then he was outside under the cold, cold stars.

Wanda huddled in her shawl, wan and small in the firelight. Finally she noticed him, tilting her head so she could meet his eyes. "Sweetie, are you waiting for me?" She gave him a concerned smile. The recent days of worry and doubt had deepened the lines of her brow. "Good Lord—are you naked?"

He regarded her from the shadows, speechless as his mouth filled with blood. He touched his face, probing a moist seam just beneath the hairline; a fissure, a fleshy zipper. Near his elbow, Terry said, "The first time, it's easier if you just snatch it off."

Pershing gripped the flap of skin. He swept his hand down and ripped away all the frailties of humanity.

--30--

You know how this is going to end.

—What? He woke, although it was only a slight shift between states of consciousness, an emergence from a lucid dream state. His eyes were already open and focused on a flickering panel. In his ears, rapidly ascending to inaudible decibels, Dracula's organ music, the wheedling peep of a theremin, now the gentle hiss of air through the vents.

—Yes? she said. She didn't look up from the exposed circuit board on her lap. She gripped a soldering gun like a real weapon. Her hatred wasn't fixed upon him at the moment.

—What did you say?

—I didn't say anything.

—I thought—

—Let's see. An hour ago I asked for a caliper. Had to get it myself.

—An hour?

She set aside the soldering gun and waved her hand to disperse the coils of rising smoke. —Forty-eight minutes and change. Sorry.

—You are not. He said this under his breath.

—Excuse me?

All six security feeds went dark. He toggled switches, then tapped the nearest screen with his ring, as if *that* made any sense.

—Problem? she said.

—I've lost all video.

—*Ooo-weee-ooo*, she said in a sinister voice. —Starring Keith David and Jessica Lange: *In a world gone mad, two scientists spend a month in the badlands, haunted by the Ghost of Christmas Past*—

—Laugh now. He smacked the screen again. —You're no Jessica Lange, honey-pie. Me, I'm Sidney Poitier. Except badass.

—Poitier was badass. You're more like Poitier if he were scary-looking.

Feed One remained down, but the others revived in sequence. Feed Two displayed a keyhole perspective of the southeastern quadrant—a sloping field of short, dry grass and scrub brush wavering in the breeze. Feed Three, a vista of pebbly ground and small boulders, Four through Six, a line of trees. Feed One would've revealed the module, their little habitat itself. But the monitor was still dead. It bothered him that Feed One wouldn't work and he kept flipping the switch. Slow-moving clouds passed over the translucent dome and reflected a diamond pattern of shadows on the control boards, the fabric of his coat sleeves.

—Funny thing, she said. —I dreamed this would happen. A couple of nights ago.

—Dreamed what? *Flip, flip, flip.*

—The video monitors went on the fritz. You screwed them up, somehow.

—Did I spill a glass of scotch into the works?

Now she *did* look at him. —Tell me you smuggled in a bottle of single malt.

—In fact, I did. We'll save it for a special occasion. Anyway, I meant that Tommy Billings and his love of booze might've been responsible for the Siberian debacle.

—You're kidding, she said.

—Listen, this is good. I'm surprised you haven't heard. The team was partying at three o'clock in the morning and TB got a little crazy and dumped a full glass of liquor into some circuitry. It started an electrical fire and *whoom!* The site went up like a torch.

—Color me dubious. That's too convenient.

—Less titillating than the espionage rumors, alas.

—Who told you?

—I don't recall. And I was sworn to secrecy.

—The jerk was probably drinking vodka. What with it being a joint project with the Russians. That adds a nice touch of verisimilitude, don't you think?

—Sure, why not? We'll never know. None of them are around anymore. They froze pretty quick.

—If there was no one left to tell the tale…. she said.

He said, —…then how come we have the legend of the Manitou? Boy follows stag up a mountain—

She said, —…boy discovers stag ain't no stag. That's easy—it's a *story.* As in a bedtime story. Just like TB killing everybody with a glass of hooch. Although.

—Yeah?

—Accepting the hearsay as true for a moment, if Tommy really did something like that, it might've been on purpose.

—Where do you get that?

—I met him once at a cocktail party. Doctor Toshi Ryoko and the boys had just gotten back from Japan—the Devil Sea thing, I think—and the department threw them a shindig.

—Oh. I wasn't invited.

—I'm shocked! You're such a people person!

—You think Tommy was working for another team?

—Sure, why not? He struck me as the type.

—The type?

—Yeah, you know, an asshole. He was a farm boy who made good.

—No call to hack on farm boys. They're the backbone of this great union.

— Give me a break. Those days are history. One driver on a machine does it all. It'll be robots in a few years. *Steelworkers* are where it's at.

—I'm sure, I'm sure. "Allentown" was a mighty sexy song. So why do you think ill of the late, lamented Tommy Billings? Did you catch him exchanging passwords with an FSB operative by the punch bowl?

—No, it was just subtle things. TB stumbled around all night with a bottle in his fist, dopey as a cow. He was too stupid to be true…he had a shifty glint in his eyes. Toshi loved him. Toshi collects guys like that. These days he's got this Aussie goon named Beasley to carry his spears. Ex-rugby star, or something. Ugly, but sort of beautiful too. I know a girl in the Denver office who balled him. She was pretty high on the whole experience.

—Toshi. You're on a first name basis with him? Cozy. Got a key to his chateau, do you? No wonder you're on the fast track.

—Don't be jealous. I don't think Toshi likes girls. He's married to the media frenzy, and busting the chops of all those academic enemies he's made.

—Jealous? I'm so far beyond all that, you don't even know. Since they'd broken it off after the job in the Sierras, he'd said this very thing to himself so many times it had become a fact.

—Getting your money's worth out of your therapist?

He laughed again. It was growing harder not to match her naked antipathy, and it had only been eighteen days. Twenty, if one counted the flight from Seattle to Yakima and the interminable briefing, then the ninety-minute chopper transport into the hills. He said, —She keeps the top two buttons of her blouse undone. I cannot complain.

—Liar. You've been watching those straight-to-video flicks starring Shannon Tweed. You poor lonely bastard.

—I'm going to retrieve the footage at B5 and B6. He stood and stretched, and opened the gun cabinet. He checked the action on the rifle, a sleek 7mm with a Leopold scope, and slung it over his shoulder. —Be back in a jiffy.

—Do try to return before dark, or I won't let you in.

—I'll hustle. Gonna be chilly tonight.

She wasn't listening.

The module was a hemisphere nestled in a clearing among sagebrush and junipers. It was constructed of composite plastic with viewports of thick, shatterproof glass, and segregated into several compartments. The module was designed to function as a self-sufficient habitat, sturdy enough to withstand vast temperature swings and powerful winds that howled out of the northwest from the high desert. Lights and surveillance equipment were powered by a pair of generators and, because this was an inordinately sunny part of the state, a battery of solar panels. Thus, all the comforts of home: TV, microwave dinners, solitaire on the sadly outdated computer, even very brief showers. A thousand gallons of water sat in storage. The chemical toilets were designed to separate solid and liquid waste. Garbage was incinerated, composted in the tiny hydroponics cubicle, or packaged to be shipped home during resupply. This was a minor, but long-term operation. The pair would stay for six months conducting field work, then rotate with the next team.

He shut the entry hatch. He wore a camouflage jumpsuit with a heavy belt. On the belt: canteen, knife, walkie-talkie, and a pouch containing waterproof matches, a screw-on flashlight, a compass, antivenin, and trail mix. In his left hand he carried a rucksack containing batteries and tapes for the remote cameras.

The Family's ranch sprawled for thousands of acres under skies that, come sunset, darkened like blood edged in molten gold. Homesteaders grabbed every parcel they could lay hands on during the 1880s when dirt was cheap. Not that it resembled a ranch—nor had it functioned as one since the 1960s when the Family took it over. Cowboys would refer to the vista as rough country, an expanse of rocky steppes, and canyons, and in the near distance, limestone ridges that gradually built into mountains. A coyote behind every bush, a rattlesnake under every rock. At night, the stars shone bright and cold, and he could count the pits and cracks in the moon, it hung so full and yellow.

Not far south, things were greener, softer; the original settlers raised cattle and horses, once upon a time. Headquarters provided him an assortment of area maps—according to these, a road cut the property in half and connected it to the nearest town, forty-five kilometers south. HQ told him not to worry about ground transportation. Supplies would be brought in by helicopter and, in the event of emergency, he and she would be airlifted to safety.

He adjusted the timer on his watch and headed northeast, toward the mountains. A horse would've been nice—a big, soft-eyed pinto to carry him through this Howard Hawks landscape. At least he'd the smarts to bring an appropriate hat instead of the god-awful baseball caps and sun visors the CSIs wore. The hat was of crumpled, sun-bleached leather and it once belonged to a vaquero who worked in Texas. The vaquero went home to Mexico to be with his wife when she gave birth, and bequeathed him the hat as a token of friendship. It chafed his ears because it was hard as an old leather football left to dry in the mud. He took it off and beat it against his knee, used it to sop the sweat streaming from his face. Once the oils of his flesh got in there, it would loosen and fit his head.

He walked.

The coyote den was located amid the root system of a copse of shaggy pines. Its size and elaborateness still surprised him. Generally, coyotes chose to lair among rocks if they couldn't co-opt the abandoned shelters of other animals. His work here proved a bit more intrusive than he preferred. He'd installed cameras to monitor den entrances. The cameras were encased in waterproof boxes and mounted on trees. After days of zero activity, despite his squirting synthetic musk on nearby bushes, he resorted to inserting a probe into the den—the probe was a flexible tube attached to a braincase. The case was affixed to a wooden stand. He spent hours manipulating the device, mapping the labyrinthine interior via the infrared eye ring. Ultimately, he positioned the eye in a central burrow and programmed the VCR to record at certain intervals throughout a twenty-four-hour cycle.

The company spared no expense for equipment, and he'd lain awake the past two and a half weeks turning that over in his mind. In his experience, corporations were loath to part with a penny more than circumstances absolutely required—the crappy computer in the module, and the lack of a jeep or four-wheeler, as exhibits A and B. The exception to this rule being the opportunity for great profit, or in the interest of mitigating some potential risk to their reputation. The government wanted people here, had selected his company of all the best North American subcontractors, to perform studies and collect data, but their motives remained unclear. Need to know, they said. It was enough for him to track and film and file the reports. The whole thing was likely on the level. What else could it be, anyway? Nonetheless, he found it simplest to distrust people until proven wrong, a product of spending most of his adulthood dwelling alone in shanties and shacks, of lying motionless in a thousand lonely coverts, spying upon the beasts of the woods.

He changed the batteries on all of the cameras and swapped out the cassettes. There was still time, so he withdrew the probe and spent an hour navigating it into an entrance on the opposite flank of the den. Then he sat in the shade and drank some water and chewed a handful of trail mix, and wondered why, despite the heat, a chill tightened the muscles in his shoulders and neck. He glanced around with affected casualness. The trees shifted in a mild breeze. A cloud partially occulted the sun.

Without question, spoor indicated several coyotes lurked in the vicinity. Bizarrely, the tracks didn't approach the den, but rather circled it, and he envisioned them creeping about the bushes, fearful, yet inexorably drawn and entrapped by simple fascination. This was beyond his twenty years of experience in the wild. Certainly one would expect an extended family to dwell inside such a massive den. He found its desertion, the haunted house quality, disquieting to say the least.

This disquiet, this aura of strangeness, permeated the entire northern sector of the range. The patterns were off, the behaviors of fauna unchar- acteristic. The other day a hawk fell from the sky, stone dead. He'd seen gophers curled up in the middle of a field, oblivious; a murder of crows had slipped from hidden roosts and followed him for several kilometers as he scouted the surroundings. The birds swooped and circled in utter silence. The preceding CSI team had witnessed even more disturbing things—a pack of coyotes sitting patiently beyond the campsite, and a black bear that watched from the cover of a juniper. After a couple of days stalking them, the bear walked right into camp, grabbed one of the techs by the arm, and tried to drag him away. They shot it and sent its head to the lab. The CSI team decided it must be rabid. No rabies, though. Just a fat and healthy five-year-old boar with devilry on its mind. And that's why he carried a rifle.

The canyon wasn't far. Its jagged walls averaged a height of ten meters. A stream trickled along its floor where squirrels and mice nested in the heavy clusters of brush; numerous bird species, including thrush, gray catbirds, and canyon wren, occupied the mossy crevices above. Red-tail hawks and great horned owls hunted the area.

He picked his way through the boulders and alder snags. Sunlight was blocked by the narrow walls and overhanging bushes. It was cold. The open range, its long sweeps of baked dirt, seemed a world removed as he traveled farther into the shadows. He carried the rifle in his right hand, against his hip. He would've been happier with a shotgun in the brush where matters could escalate in seconds. There was no bear sign—and he'd been most scrupulous in ascertaining that detail. Still, he couldn't shake his unease. He'd noted it from day one, put it down to heebie-jeebies from the stories in the paper, the briefings and the short film recovered from Site 3. After all that, he went to a bar and drank the better part of a bottle of Maker's Mark, as if that might obliterate what he'd seen. Site 3 lay a kilometer west where the foothills verged on mountainous. The forensics people referred to the area as The Killing Grounds. The excavation had dragged on for three weeks and the teams only verified the presence of half a dozen bodies. The forensics experts estimated more, probably *many* more, victims had decomposed beyond detection, much less retrieval. Eleven sites total, but the economy was crashing like the *Hindenburg* and the state was too broke to keep digging. He thought maybe *afraid* to keep digging was closer to the truth.

He'd left a pair of cameras trained on a small pool. There were significant animal signs in the immediate vicinity—they'd captured footage of mice and birds, and a bobcat on its nightly prowl. The bobcat sat there by the water, its eyes shiny and strange, and finally it zeroed in on the second camera, which was fairly well camouflaged, and stared—stared for exactly eleven minutes until the machine clicked off. He could only speculate how long the cat waited in the dark. Then he thought of the bear and tightened his grip on the rifle.

When he reached the covert, the cameras were missing.

He arrived home after dark, and she had indeed locked the hatch. He knocked and she let him in anyway. The central space, their work area, was lighted by the warm, mellow glow of three accent lamps she stowed in her luggage. Fluorescent lighting made her edgy—she claimed to have suffered a near breakdown during an expedition into a remote region of the Pyrenees.

He unpacked the cassettes and piled them on her desk for processing. Processing film was her main task, although as a geologist with specialties in zoology and insect ecology, it likely chafed. As the amount of data to sift was paltry thus far, she spent a portion of her days investigating the immediate environs. She showed him one of a series of jars she'd collected that afternoon.

—Even the insects are acting weird, she said. She slowly turned the jar, and the wasps slid across its killing floor, wings fluttering. The glass stifled their complaints, a ghostly buzzing.

—How weird are they?

—Completely, totally fucked up.

He considered mentioning the missing cameras. The idea dissolved even as it formed. —How so?

—Their hive is in the trees south of here. Huge sucker. *Cecidostiba semifascia* crawling everywhere. On the trees, the bushes, all over the ground. Thousands and thousands. Millions. It's like a nest of driver ants exploded. None of them fly. Scores were clumping together and dropping to the ground, like ripe apples. So creepy.

—What the hell is that about? he said.

—Beats me, man. It only gets screwier.

—Wonderful.

—When I first started watching, I was repulsed. Recalling them squirming over each other kind of sickens me too. Only thing is—for a few minutes, all that discomfort morphed into…well, fascination. I was—Christ, how do I explain. I was attracted to the scene. Being a passive observer wasn't enough. Suddenly, I had to participate in the, well, in the whatever thing these insects were doing. Goddamned orgy. I scooped a whole bunch of them into the specimen jars…and then….

He leaned into the counter. The rhythm of her voice enervated him. He said, —What did you do?

—Man, I sat down at the edge of their swarm. The fuckers started climbing on me. They found pant openings, cuffs, my collar, and crawled inside, got tangled in my hair. I had to pinch my nose to block them, close my mouth to keep them out.

—Hmm, he said.

—I should've been stung to death. She pressed her cheek to the jar and tilted it so the wasps seemed to spill over her eye. Her hand shook. —Then, it was getting dark. Cold. They peeled from me, crawled away to their tree, the hive. Some just burrowed into the pine needles. Pretty soon, every last one was gone. The enormity of the situation hit me. I ran the whole way back here.

He watched her play with the jar until she set it aside and stuck her hands into the pockets of her coat. He said, —I'm going to make myself a sandwich. Want me to open you a can of something?

—Peanut butter crackers, she said.

—We've Spam, and more Spam.

—We don't have peanut butter?

—You gobbled up the bucket. I don't think HQ could've anticipated your peanut butter fetish.

—Spam and crackers. There's another thing.

—The wasps aren't enough?

—I've heard knocking on the hatch. Two nights this week. Woke me from a dead sleep. Very soft, kind of tapping. Yeah, probably my imagination. Only problem with that is, I know what knuckles on metal sound like.

—Okay, he said, rolling his eyes.

—Oh, yeah? I'm not an idiot.

—I'll reserve judgment until we check the perimeter footage. Somebody's sneaking around, we'll see.

They didn't screw, which initially was a bit of a surprise to him until he heard her vibrator buzzing one night. Their sexual rift was acceptable —some of her kinks unnerved him. So he fiercely masturbated to images of early Playmate-era Shannon Tweed, and fell asleep.

He dreamed of his fellow scientist sitting lotus style among the torpid wasps. Her jumpsuit was dark with them. The sun hid behind the mountains and stained the sky a rich red that was almost black—the color that wells from a deep wound. The red light spattered her, dripped from her. She began stuffing handfuls of wasps into her mouth.

He awoke and lay on his cot, overcome by a sense of claustrophobia. Horrors skittered and scuttled at the fringes of his consciousness, feverish impressions that afflicted children with a fear of the dark. He listened to her working on the other side of the thin fabric wall. She clicked steadily at a keyboard and the dim, blue light from her monitor flickered on his ceiling.

She gasped, and said, —Holy shit. What the fuck.

He almost rose, almost went into the other room to ask what she'd seen. Another wave of weariness bore down upon him and his eyelids fluttered, and he was gone again, falling into a sea of red.

In the morning he made good on his promise to troll for suspicious activity on the tapes. There was nothing, of course.

He darted a mule deer and tagged it with a GPS chip. That was the most excitement he'd had since his arrival, and it was short lived. Within hours, the deer traveled deeper into the hills beyond his research radius. He waited three days and then moved the cameras at the den to sector C1, a prairie rife with rabbits and groundhogs. The backbreaking job left him caked in dirt and exhausted. He returned to the module and fixed a huge meal, chewed aspirin, and drank a quart of water. He sprawled on the floor, dressed in shorts, feet propped on a chair.

She said, —What's it called when you can't remember if you dreamed an event, or if it actually happened?

—Crazy?

—Yesterday I was lying in the hammock—

—I saw you'd strung one over there by that fir. Must be nice to have free time. I'll think of you whenever I'm travois-ing three hundred pounds of shit across the rocks.

—No, no, I'll be swinging in my hammock thinking of *you*, she said. —I made myself a pitcher of pink lemonade. Yummy.

—There you were, lying naked in your hammock—

—Sure, why not? There I was, sipping lemonade, watching the clouds, and someone called my name. I almost peed myself. Probably for the best I don't pack heat—I'd have blasted the living crap outta some bushes.

—If you thought the bushes were talking to you, I think we should analyze the lemonade.

—I'm telling you, somebody stage-whispered my name from behind a juniper. Heard it clear as can be. I sort of froze, not quite accepting the situation. Of course it occurred to me you were playing one of your practical jokes. I also knew in the next instant it wasn't. This was way different. It didn't sound friendly, either. Whoever it was snickered.

—Are you kidding? You thought it was me? I'm hurt.

—For a second or two. Who else? Don't get your nose out of joint.

—It's a common phenomenon, the phantom voice. That's your subconscious looking for attention. Happened to me a lot when I got rummy, scrunched into a blind or tree stand. Get tired enough, you see and hear things that aren't there.

—But, I'm not tired.

—Yeah, however, we *are* isolated. Like I said, the mind gets bored and plays games. Don't sweat it too much.

She said, —I had another dream last night.

—A wet one?

—Don't be nasty. Yeah, okay, maybe. The other one—not so nice. It was sunset. Just about the most hideous redness covered everything. Made my eyes hurt. The light seeped from the sky, cracks in the earth, until I couldn't see anything but shadows and blurry outlines of figures. People sort of appeared and gathered around me. Maybe they weren't human.

—It being a dream, he said.

—My God, you are a jerk. I hate smug guys.

—If you were a model you could file that under turnoffs: smug guys!

—I *was* a model.

—Really?

—No. My sister was, though. I'm way better looking than her.

—Meh, you're all right. Your teeth are too big.

—Jerk, jerk, jerk! Why did I say yes to this stupid assignment?

—The obvious answer would be…

—Grow up. We had a thing and so what? I bet you've humped a half-dozen sleazy little bitches since we called it quits.

—At least.

—At least?

—I lost count after ten.

—That's a hell of a lot of money to blow on whores, so to speak. Besides, you're a liar. I doubt half your stories come close to the dreary, mundane truth. The man, the myth. I call bullshit.

He laughed. —Tell me more about your dream, he said in a thick accent. —Vas your mudder involved?

—No. I didn't recognize anyone. I was terrified, so I ran. The red light blinded me and I tripped and fell into a pit. Kept falling and falling until the sky became a pinhole, and finally not even that.

—Is that when you woke?

—I don't think I ever did, she said. —Everything went black. Like the movies.

He limped across a plain that stretched beneath a wide, carnivorous sky. He'd run a great distance and was on his last legs; his breath was ragged, his boots crunched on gravel. Red light flooded the horizon. This was the light of a thin atmosphere, Martian light. He stumbled upon a cluster of low, earthen mounds. The mounds were brown and covered in fine, white dust. He thought this might be a native burial ground, a sacred place, and that had to be the cause of his fear. He'd trespassed and the spirits were furious, the spirits were going to punish him.

He realized his mistake soon enough when he came to a crater. Someone had stuck a shovel in the nearby pile of fresh dirt. At the bottom of the pit were arranged scores of plastic tarps, each wrapped around an object the size and shape of a human form. Among these forms were ruined bicycles, discarded coats, hats, and backpacks. Dresses, bits of costume jewelry, handbags, and wallets.

She said, —Psst! I wasn't being straight with you earlier.

The bloody light of the sky winked out of existence. His sleeping cubicle was pitch black. He shuddered at the sound of her breathing nearby. His chest hurt and he massaged his ribs, thinking, here came the heart attack that felled his father, and his father's father, and several uncles, hardy woodsmen all. Like them, he smoked and drank too much. Like them, he suffered night terrors.

—I *did* hear a voice, she said, her mouth centimeters from his own.

—Not a phantom voice, either. Whoever it was, whatever I heard, it whispered my name. Then it asked me where you were. *Where's your friend? Where's your friend? Where's your friend?*

His eyes watered. He put his hand over his mouth to stifle a sob, shocked at the power of his compulsion to scream. He couldn't remember if his dream was only a dream, or the reenactment of something he'd witnessed and immediately repressed. His father shot several people in Vietnam and said that he couldn't always separate his nightmares from things that really happened. She didn't say anything else and exhaustion descended like a club and smashed him into unconsciousness.

He climbed a ridge and stood in the shade of an oak. Its leaves were broad and dusty. Near the toe of his left boot was a snare of barb wire still attached to a post. Ants boiled from the rotten core of the wood. He removed his hat and hung it on a branch. Flies buzzed, drawn to the moisture. He sipped canteen water and scratched the deep itch at the center of his skull. The longer he watched the ants, the more intensely his brain itched.

He unsnapped the protective covers of his field glasses and used one hand to cup them to his eyes. Below the ridge, a basin spread for a half-kilometer to the foot of the mountains. Washboard ruts, decayed remnants of several abandoned roads, zigzagged through scrub and rocks. A stream ambled its crooked way toward the lowlands. His map designated this area as the infamous Site 3. The original ranchers lived to the extreme southern extents of the property—their homes nearest the city were converted to low-income housing, or bulldozed for school soccer fields and parks. After the last of the ranchers' lines died off in 1965, the cattle and horses were auctioned and the vast acreage returned swiftly to wilderness. The Family hadn't arrived until 1969 or 1970 and their presence wouldn't have altered much. The shacks they'd squatted in had long since fallen apart, and they'd moved from place to place, migrating like nomads across the property in a pair of antiquated school buses.

—Oh, the places we'll go, he said, lowering the glasses.

—Eh? What are you on about? she said.

He didn't recall dialing her on the cell, but there the phone was pressed to his ear, and her sounding belligerent on the other end. —I'm looking at Site 3. Nice place to build a house, raise some kids. A tad on the dry side.

—A tad on the creepy side, you mean. Seems like you're the one with idle hands now. Shouldn't you be staking out a coyote den, or sniffing deer droppings?

—I'm munching on some at this very moment, he said. —Did I mention my great-great-great grandfather rode with Kit Carson? Why'd you call? Everything okay?

—You called me, silly. Yeah, I'm going through the tapes. There's not much on them. Three, count 'em, three freakin' coyotes in B5 and B6. No further visuals on the bobcat, and not a single bear. Did you scare all the animals?

—You sure are ornery today.

—I'm ornery every day; you're too busy playing Boy Scout to notice, is all.

—Ri-i-ght—I'm tramping through the woods while you're barefoot and pregnant in the kitchen. How's supper coming?

—Spam and beans. You'll get it cold if you don't take a shower, buster.

He touched the post and a few ants scurried onto his fingers. —Don't get rid of the packing jelly.

—Ugh. You like the Spam afterbirth? I can't believe I let you kiss me on the mouth.

—Spam placenta, if you please. He raised the binoculars. A brown shape separated from the cover of sage and trotted across open ground. The coyote was a scrawny specimen. —Fuck. Maybe there *is* a rabies outbreak.

—The ones on tape are definitely off. You gotta take a look. My theory is rabies, or a man-made agent. Something toxic. Hunters might've poisoned the water. There's a bounty on coyote heads in this region.

—We've lived here, what, a month? You spot any hunters? Nobody's coming this far into the boonies to bag a few coyotes.

—There's another possibility. Government isn't above testing its latest bio weapons on animal populations. The risk to humans is low. The Army could've dosed the area five, ten years ago. Now we're here checking on their work, all unwitting like.

—Thanks for brightening my day, sunshine.

—My advice is, don't drink the water.

—Got it.

—Super. Back to the horrors. She broke the connection.

He slipped the phone into his pocket and shook his wrists, flinging ants into oblivion. His lips were cracked. Thick, coarse stubble covered his jaw. He kept forgetting to shave. Personal hygiene was the first thing to go when he settled into the bush. Animals could smell chemical products all too readily. Gun oil was trouble enough.

A half-hour later, he'd carefully picked his way down the hillside and walked across the basin to the former CSI team campsite. The team pulled

stakes months before. Signs of its presence were mostly erased by the
elements, the proliferation of weeds. He flipped an empty soda bottle with
the side of his foot. There was a fire pit, its ashes washed to gray mud and
baked hard, and nothing else. This was where the team of fourteen men,
women and dogs spent the better part of a month taking core samples
and ground X-rays, sniffing for elements of organic decay, and snapping a
thousand photographs. Yes, she was right—definitely creepy. He was glad
their own camp was at a good, safe distance. It was irrational, and that
didn't bother him. In the animal kingdom, paranoia equaled sanity.

Why had he come to Site 3? No reason except curiosity, an overwhelming
urge to reconcile his curiosity and fear. Fear was such a strong word, yet
an appropriate one. That he carried a weapon and was trained to survive
any conceivable scenario, that there was no visible threat, did nothing to
pacify his mounting anxiety.

He was alone in the wilderness, yet when he spied the set of human
tracks, he wasn't surprised. He followed for a while—the prints of a large
male in boots were made within the last seventy-two hours. The trail
eventually led into the hills. The Family's hideout lay in that direction:
long-gone tepees, tarpaper shacks, and caves. He looked at the sky. Sunset
creeping along, it would arrive within forty-five minutes. He told himself
discretion was the better part of valor and turned away.

Later that night a storm rolled in as he lay awake, listening to the wind
tear at the module. —You fool, he said. —There's not a damned thing
to be afraid of. He closed his eyes and slept. In his dreams, he stood in a
field and regarded the carcass of a black bear. The bear lay on its side in
several inches of jellified gore. Green rot wafted and a cloud of blowflies
orbited the remains. From his angle he couldn't tell if the head had been
chopped off. A woman laughed and her hand clamped upon his shoulder.
The hand was all rawhide and bone.

He spent the next day in a tree on the ridge overlooking Site 3. The
branches were steamy from rain, but the stony earth had already drunk
the puddles and pools. A hawk circled so far overhead it was a black grain
against the superheated blue sky. A couple of coyotes padded along the
basin floor. He contemplated shooting one, removing its blood and tissues
and shipping them to HQ for analysis. He replaced the bunting lens caps
on his rifle scope, and drowsed. When the light thickened and dimmed
he lowered himself to the ground and walked back to camp.

—There's no video of…of you know what, she said.

Stars cluttered the sky and the air was almost too crisp. They sat on lawn
chairs at the edge of a dying fire. They smoked cigarettes from her carton

of Pall Malls and drank many tumblers from his bottle of Laphroaig. A light wind swirled from the mountains and stirred the fire, occasionally scattering cinders upon their clothes. The wind tasted sweet, like ashes of a green tree.

—Of what happened at S3? A guy showed it to me, all right, he said. A third of the scotch was in his belly. He didn't care if she believed him. He thought about the two ragged coyotes, the circling hawk, the coyote den empty as a forgotten mausoleum. He thought about the lone set of boot prints winding among the rocks, impressions coagulated in the soft earth. He wondered what it all meant.

—A guy? What guy?

—I don't remember his name. He was with somebody. Oh, yeah, Bleeker, or Blecher. One of the CSIs. I think.

—Bleeker showed you a video.

—Not Bleeker. The guy with Bleeker. Lab rat type. Pasty, soft.

—Bleeker's pal showed you a video.

—The Site 3 home video that those freaks shot in '72.

She puffed on her cigarette. The light from the fire glowed red in her eyes.

—When did this happen? We were sitting together at the briefing.

—During the lunch break. He took me to an empty conference room and played it against one of those pull-down screens.

—The dude was walking around with the tape in his pocket?

—Maybe he's stalking Michael Moore. Gotta be ready to demo at the drop of a hat, right?

—*The Religious Freaks and Me*. But, the lunch break was like only fifteen minutes.

—The film was a short-short.

—Well, hell. Now I know where you went to smoke a cigarette. Wish I'd followed you.

—No, you don't.

—The Family didn't film anything. That's an urban legend. No photographs, either. Buncha dirt-munching, tree-hugging druids. I hear one of 'em worked in the Army motor pool before he got a Section Eight. Crazy fucker kept the school buses running. Otherwise, homeboys didn't have a pot to piss in, much less a camcorder. If you actually watched anything, it was a fake. Guy was yanking your chain.

—It looked authentic. Really horrible.

—Um-hm. She extended her glass and he poured. —I take it there was some Dario Argento-style mayhem going on.

He filled his own tumbler until whiskey quivered at the rim, and closed his eyes and considered her voice, how it lately came to him deep in the darkness when he was alone on his cot. Her voice was breathy and harsh, like a breeze combing through dry leaves, a raspy lullaby. He said, —You're right. It was a hoax. Hamburger and catsup in papier-mâché dummies. Smack that shit with a sledgehammer, watch it splat against a wall. Fooled the hell out of me.

—Catsup?

—Corn syrup and chocolate, he said. —I was a baby when the Family made the scene. Rabbits and wolves are more my thing. Starvation, predator/prey dynamics, I understand. Rabies, I understand. This psychobabble, religious bullshit, not a damned bit.

—Not me. I loooved my psych classes. People, bugs. Step back far enough, it's all the same. I did a midterm paper on the cult. Honestly, I was kinda sweet on the D.A. He came to the university and lectured us about the case. Real sexy older guy. I wasn't paying much attention to what he said, but luckily my dorm mate was pathological about taking notes. Anyhow, what they did was lure kids from parks and concerts. The Old Man sent his followers to train stations and bus depots on the lookout for runaways, war vets, anybody down and out and desperate for a meal, a place to crash. The Family brought 'em here, to the ranch.

—And then?

—And then? She smiled and threw back her head so her hair fanned over one shoulder. —I dunno. Mostly sat around eating peyote buttons and reading those anti-establishment pamphlets Father wrote by the bushel. Fucking and dancing to wild flute music. Some of the visitors converted, joined the cause. The shit that went down in Portland—

—At the retirement home.

—The Pleasant View Massacre. Yeah. Three of the four killers had joined the Family the preceding year. Probational members. A lot of the indigents stayed awhile and then moved on. How many wound up getting tortured and murdered? A few. Gets a mite boring in these parts, I reckon.

He watched her closely, drawn to the way she rubbed the glass against her collarbone, how perspiration gleamed there. The whiskey in his own glass lay black as blood. He gritted his teeth and took it all in a gulp.

—You figure, the Family had a following in the hundreds during the late '60s. At least double *that* left or disappeared. I think, in my heart of hearts, you can take all the death scores by Dahmer, Bundy, Gacy, that crowd—and add 'em together. What's buried on this range is probably way worse. Plain old math.

—But why?

—Thrills. The core group were anarchists, the kind who want to watch the world burn. I bet a lot of unpleasant talk occurred around the campfire.

Those who heard the gospel and acted squeamish got the ax, literally. I also think the Family was paranoid about Fed narks infiltrating the ranks. Motive enough to bury a few.

—Could be another reason. You called them anarchists. They weren't anarchists, they were a cult. Satanists.

She finished her whiskey and regarded the glass. —Damn, you had to go and do that, didn't you? Here we are, miles from civilization and you gotta suggest those freaks were sacrificing people to the Devil.

—Would it have been more acceptable if they were splitting people open to satisfy Jehovah? Wasn't thrill-killing scary enough for you?

—I hadn't thought of it like that. Satanism freaks me the fuck out.

—No need to be scared, baby. We've the computer, a radio, cell phones. We're wired.

—Lot of help that shit will be if cultists sneak in and cut our throats in the dead of night. I don't need any more nightmares.

—Wanna cuddle? I'll protect you from the bogeymen.

—Thanks anyway. Sadist.

The coals faded and after a while, the two sat hunched, separated by a gulf of darkness. She began to reminisce about the good old days in college, how her parents disapproved of her career in biology; lawyers both, they'd expected her to attend an Ivy League school and carry on the family tradition. Her mother had died last year of complications from diabetes and her father remarried a drunken witch who really, really enjoyed money. Stepmom was evil incarnate, of course.

—I always hated my real mom, she said. —Worse than evil stepmom, even. You haven't asked about the puppy you gave me. Rex. I named him Rex.

He wasn't listening.

—Look at this, she said. Neither had dressed after breakfast; just a plain white t-shirt and shorts for him; an Army gray sports bra and faded green panties for her. Rain spackled the dome and the humidity didn't do much to soothe his hangover. —I meant to play this for you earlier.

—Well, why didn't you?

She frowned at the blurry image on her computer monitor. —I dunno. This is footage from the probe at B5. Watch closely, 'cause it happens fast.

His temples throbbed. The image shot by the infrared eye ring was static, taken long after he'd positioned the device. The picture stuttered, revealed a ghostly vista of roots and rock of the den interior. Five or six seconds in, a shape in the frame. A mud-encrusted human face. The person grinned or snarled, perhaps aware of the lens, perhaps not. Either way, he was worming along on his belly. Then the recording ended. —Don't try telling me that's a man, he said.

—Here it comes again. And…freeze.

—No way, he said. —No way. The lighting is so poor. It's a coyote.

—I don't think so, she said.

—Fuck that noise. He leaned over her and killed the recording. —You're going stir crazy. Hit the trail with me today. We'll have a picnic.

—That's a person.

He stroked his beard, mastering the impulse to smash the monitor. He said, —I've spent many precious hours of my life wiring that den. If a human being came within a hundred meters, I would've seen their tracks. I would've seen evidence at one of the entrances. There's nobody hiding in that den.

—For Chrissake, run it again. You'll see.

—Oh, we're gonna run it again.

She flipped her chair and paced to the opposite end of the enclosure. —Somebody's crazy, and it's you.

He started the recording and set it to loop. —Say it with me: It's a coyote.

—I know how to process film and I know what that is.

—Come here.

—Kiss my ass I'm coming over there.

—Come on.

Her eyes brightened. She went through the hatch and let it slam behind her. He unclenched his fingers and whistled. The creature in the den sneered at him, then vanished, over and over. After a while he decided it actually resembled a feral woman, her lank hair obscuring vulpine features, a mouth twisted in rage. He couldn't tear his gaze away.

She returned a few minutes later and dressed. She stood next to him and stared at the monitor. Her jaw twitched. —You're right. It's a coyote.

—Exactly.

Her face was dark with sunburn and this magnified the shine of her eyes. Her pupils were black holes eating the whites. She said, —Where do you go all day?

The supply helicopter landed in the field at daybreak. The pilot, a wiry man who wore yellow-tinted aviator glasses, briskly unloaded three crates of supplies and handed over a manifest list. The pilot glanced around, nervous as a dog accustomed to dodging rocks. —Cripes, this place is spooky. Good luck. He jumped into the helicopter and zoomed away.

He watched the helicopter make a broad arc. He could grab a rock and chuck it at a rotor. What would happen? In the movies, there'd be a fireball. Shrapnel would sizzle past and shred the module, leaving him unscathed. In the real world? Probably nothing, even in the unlikely event he could actually throw a rock that far. He wondered if he ran inside and got the rifle how many rounds he could fire before the helicopter escaped. It was a bolt action. The magazine held five rounds.

He sighed and hefted his crowbar and began levering apart the crates. She stared after the helicopter until it vanished into the horizon.

Today he changed the tapes in his remote cameras. He carried the tranquilizer gun. He'd decided to zap the first coyote he saw. Unfortunately, none ventured from their lairs by early afternoon, so he enjoyed a long siesta under his favorite tree above the killing grounds. Ants scuttled across his legs. None of them bit him.

He walked into camp a few minutes before sunset and saw it there, leaning against a boulder. He removed his hat and fanned his face, and stared. —I don't understand, he said.

—It's my revenge, she said.

—Revenge about what? he said.

—You're treating me with disrespect. Your asshole-ishness. I'm sick of your eccentricity. Up to here. She made a slashing motion under her chin.

—That's good. Let it all spew out. I really think we're making progress.

She laughed and strode to her trophy. She braced her foot next to it on the boulder and said, —Look at this freakin' thing. I stumbled upon a footpath that leads to a gulch, a bit west of here. A secret path, beaten hard like pavement and screened in juniper and thorn bushes. The trail ended at a cave. Not so much a cave as a deep, vertical crevice. They held ceremonies there. Fuckers left kerosene lanterns hanging from branches and in niches. Wrote a bunch of crazy occult symbols on the walls in chalk and paint. Foul, foul shit, too. I went inside. This was lying, broken, near a big, ugly rock with a groove chiseled into it.

—Must have been a bitch dragging it all the way here, he said. The horn appeared petrified; yellow and gray with streaks of black, like a rotten tooth. Balanced on end it reached his breastbone, and at its thickest, he estimated a circumference equal to his own muscular thigh. —Gotta weigh fifty kilos, easy.

—You aren't the only one who knows how to make a travois, she said.

—I assume you took photographs.

Her mouth ticked in a smile, or a grimace. —Once I saw it, I lost my head... Everything is a blur.

The weird horn, her inconceivable lapse of protocol, stymied his inclination to argue. —So, what else?

—They'd hacked this free from the wall of the cave. There's a glaciated curtain of stone farther back. I didn't bring a flashlight and it was dim...man, there's something huge fossilized in that wall. Maybe ten feet tall. A statue. Has to be. This horn came from whatever's in there.

He brushed his fingers across the horn. His cock stiffened. Saliva poured down his throat. He stepped away from the horn fast. —Good fucking God....

—Yeah, exactly, she said.

He studied the sky, the emerging stars. —Let's grab a lamp and mosey over to this cave of yours.

—No chance in hell, buddy. I won't go back there. Not in the dark.

—Why not?

—Take a good look at that thing. It's obscene.

—Fine. In the morning.

—Okay.

She unzipped his sleeping bag and crawled inside. They fucked. She howled into the pillow, hands locked on the frame of the cot. He rode her in a haze, arm around her hips, lifting her into each slow, savage thrust. It was so good he spent a few dizzy moments in the afterglow confused as to why he'd let the relationship die, and fell asleep while still puzzling. His eyes popped open a bit later when she nuzzled his ear and stuck her finger into his asshole, exactly as she'd done one too many times during their previous affair. He smacked her hand away. She snored, occasionally mumbling. He lay uncomfortably wedged against her, his heart thudding, useless anger kindling in the pit of his gut.

The first knock was faint and he didn't realize what it was until the second one came, slightly louder; a distinct rap against the hatch. He stopped breathing, mouth wide, his entire body an antenna tuned to this most unwelcome vibration at the entrance of the habitat. Then, three sharp knocks. He was on his feet and fumbling for the hunting knife he kept hanging in its sheath. She didn't stir, although her muttering became querulous.

Conscious of his nakedness, he crept through the module, navigating the obstacle course of chairs, benches, and crates by the ethereal glow from the monitors. He quickly toggled the security feeds, but they crackled with snowy interference, revealing nothing of the perimeter. He ventured to the

mud room, a cramped chamber inside the entrance, designed for removing outdoor gear prior to entering the central compartment. His tongue
was thick as leather, and his hands shook, yet a sense of grim exultance
drove him forward. Of all the biologists a creep, or creeps, might choose
to pick on, he was likely to be the most hostile, if not the most capable
of retaliating in a vicious manner.

He crouched against the hatch, pressing his ear to the metal while testing the bar with his free hand. Locked tight. He waited, ticking off the
seconds as they built into minutes, and his legs started to cramp. Something scratched against the steel door—nails, a stick. He scuttled on his
haunches from the door, knife held reflexively before his eyes. The rifle
was nearby in its cabinet and he decided now was an appropriate instance
to consider deadly force. Someone laughed and he froze. The scratching
came again, then the laughter, farther away. It sounded like two voices.
He couldn't be sure and the darkness became thick and suffocating.

After a while, he gathered the courage to unlimber the rifle and slip
outdoors. He padded in a stealthy circuit of the module, stalking from
shadow to shadow, finger heavy on the trigger. Wind scuffed up little puffs
of dust. When he began to crash from the adrenaline high, he went inside,
locked the hatch, and settled in to keep watch until daylight.

She found him sleeping in the fetal position under the table, the rifle
clasped to his breast. —Get laid and go back to the Stone Age. Why the
hell are you letting all the bugs inside?

The hatch hung ajar. Gnats swarmed in the cold white light of the
opening. —The world is large and unknowable, he said.

She stepped into the threshold, her form rendered a black shadow
limned by fire. —I lied about the horn, she said. —I made up that stuff
to scare you, piss you off. I like telling tales. Whatever. It was lying in the
bushes near an ant nest I've been studying. Been there so long it looked
like petrified wood. Animals dug it up, probably. Freaky as fuck no matter how you slice it. She closed the hatch and its clang reminded him of
a cage locking.

The only tracks around the module belonged to him and her. As expected, the surveillance footage went offline in conjunction with the
nocturnal visitation and the recordings were useless. He waited until she'd
gone into the field to check on her ants, or wasps, or what-the-hell-ever
she did instead of analyzing tape, and dialed his supervisor in Seattle to
deliver the weekly report.

His supervisor was intrigued by the theory that the aberrant wildlife
behavior could be linked to poison, although he dismissed the idea of

military testing. Hunter activity, on the other hand, was sexy. —I'll send a chopper in next week. Have some water samples ready.

He cleared his throat and said, —My partner may not be handling the stress.

—How so? Are you two having problems?

—She's cracking. He was grateful they weren't speaking via satellite video, acutely aware of his wild, matted hair and beard. —Nothing serious, yet.

—If it's not serious, than what?

—Look, it's difficult to describe. Her work hasn't been stellar. Make a note, is all I'm saying. We get back to civilization, I don't want the blame for shoddy data.

His supervisor sighed. —The Sierras rumor is true, huh? I'm not much of a marriage counselor, but my best advice is if you ever get another opportunity to spend sixty days stranded in the wilds with an ex, pass.

—Thanks. Never mind. An insidious thought surfaced: What if hooking him up with his ex-lover and stranding them in the wilds *was* the whole point of the exercise?

His supervisor said goodbye and good luck.

He sat for a while, observing her on Feed One. She was insubstantial, wandering across the foreground with a stick, flipping over rocks. Looking for bugs. Innocently or not, erasing clues. He thought about the scratching against the hatch, the faint unearthly lullaby his mother sang when he was a baby and before she left forever. He switched the camera off. He took his rifle and left, muttering about checking his traps as he passed her.

He didn't go far, perhaps two hundred meters into a copse of alder on a nearby hill with a clear view of the camp. Burrowed like a tick deep into the leaves and the dirt, he tenderly wiped moisture from the scope and snugged it to his eye. There she was. A blurred patch of shadow. When he looked through the scope it was as if the largest part of him dissolved and what remained was the kernel everything sprang from. The cathode stole everything, rendered him nameless, a seed floating on a vast cosmic tidal current.

—Where's your friend? he said. Sweat poured into his eyes until the world doubled and distorted like a kaleidoscope. —Where's your friend? Where's your friend?

—You believe in God? She was snapping pictures of the cryptic horn, working it from multiple angles.

He remembered with clear and explicit detail his father walking with him through the reeds where the buck had dropped in its tracks. The buck was alive, its eyes warm with a last, candescent surge of vitality. The marsh was cold and dim. Their collective breath rose like smoke into the black sky. His father handed him the knife.

—Which one? I can get behind the idea of one of those evil cocksuckers the ancients kowtowed to. A few years ago a lost temple was discovered beneath some rainforest. There were caverns with altars to a hideous anthropomorphic beast. Researchers documented dozens of enormous slabs with sluices, for what was literally rivers of blood. There was a primitive sewage system built to handle the gore. Could be they gathered up slaves and enemies and sacrificed thousands at a time during festivals. There's the real deal. That's how a real super being would roll.

—I mean the our Father who art in Heaven.

—Oh, that guy. The Old Testament dude, sure. He'd slept the entire day and dreamed of fleeing through a barren, red-lit landscape. He wore the form of the buck and his father was the hunter.

The afternoon had been brutally hot, and stars undulated as though through warped glass. He felt mentally and spiritually torpid, helpless to make meaningful decisions. It was as if a low-grade sedative pumped through his veins, robbing him of volition; it was the sensation of being trapped in quicksand, or paralyzed in a permanent nightmare. Everything around him was television, and he was acting from a script. He should call HQ and tell them the project had gone off the rails in a major way. He *would* make that call. In a few minutes, once he gathered the ambition to rise from the lawn chair and stumble inside.

She half-straddled the prodigious horn. Her sinewy back gleamed. She'd worn only his hat and a pair of panties the last two days. The sun had scorched her bronze, except for slashes of ivory at her hips and the creases of her buttocks. He too went shirtless since that morning. She chuckled and called him a Nubian stud and flirted with unbuckling his belt until he pushed her away and retreated into his sleeping berth. He didn't think either of them had bathed in several days. Her cheeks were smudged with grime. She appeared wild as an ancient Celt, naked, her hair lank and stiff as if limed for battle. His nails were black and he smelled the ripe sourness of his own body.

—Did you hear the knocking? I bet you did.

He wished for another bottle of scotch. —Yeah.

—Someone wants in.

—I know, he said. —Who?

She grinned at him over her shoulder. She stroked the horn's ridges, dug the inside of her thigh against them until blood welled and ran in a thin rail toward her ankle.

His head felt light and empty. Static hissed like windblown sand somewhere in the depths. —We should bag this job and head home. I'm getting a bad feeling. He turned his gaze from her legs, regarded the stars.

—A bad feeling? You're so primal, so in touch with your roots. I can see you and your homies with spears and loincloths on the savanna.

—Go on, let your hair down, he said. —You're among friends.

—Don't be touchy. It's a fucking compliment.

—Shut up.

She chuckled.

—It's not as if every single nut case that followed the cult went to the slammer, he said. —What if some of those crazy bastards have come home to the ol' stomping grounds? Makes me very uncomfortable.

—We're alone, she said.

—Are we?

—You've said so at least a hundred times. Don't change your story now.

—Only fools and the dead never change their mind.

She turned and walked over and sat beside him. —I haven't even heard a plane since we got here. Might as well be on the moon. There's a certain aura, something in the fabric of the land. Feels like an acid trip. Whatever happened to the farmers who settled these parts?

—Ranchers.

—Right, ranchers.

—The original parcel got split and sold to a bunch of local interests. The hardcore folks dwindled, moved away. The grandkids weren't eager to carry on with the Old West lifestyle. I'm sure they'll put in a mall or a parking lot. Haha, condos and a retirement center.

—No, she said. —Nothing will be built. They'll be sorry if they do. I think you're wrong about the ranchers, by the way. Did you research it, or just accept what we got spoon fed at the briefing?

—I was a baby bird. Cheep, cheep.

—Me too, buddy-boy. Me too. I've been pondering it more lately. I bet anything, if you were to dredge up a hundred and twenty years' worth of newspaper articles, county documents, federal reports and local folklore, you'd get a completely different perspective. Murder, lynching, rape....

—Which would be typical of much of rural, agricultural America, he said.

—Oh, sure. Except here, you'll find it was epidemic. The cowpokes and their kin were probably crazy as shithouse rats by the time the second generation outgrew diapers. Society kept its mouth shut, of course. Glossed over the frequency, downplayed all but the most sensational atrocities.

I've seen it in more genteel settings. This shit's happened since when. I think the Family came because like attracts like. They were drawn by lunatic music only the Devil's own can hear. Yeah, man, no way to ever be sure, but I'd put money that the sickos were nothing more than the latest victims of Hell Range.

—Pretty insane, he said.

—That's how this would go if it was a horror flick, she said.

—Scripting one?

—There's this producer in L.A. who says I'm talented.

—Him fucking you and you actually being able to write are two different things.

—Nah, he's ugly as sin. My sister, the model, he did fuck her. Got her a gig doing hand lotion spots. Silly bitch's face only appears for like two milliseconds. I believe in God.

—Yeah?

—Because I know who that horn belongs to. Can't have one without the other.

He didn't say anything.

—C'mon, can't you feel it? she said.

—Can't *you* feel it when something should remain unspoken? Most cultures consider that a survival trait.

—Beware of Things Man Is Not Meant to Know? I don't fear the immensity of the universe. Some things are too big to worry about. I'm highly credulous.

Once, when he was much younger, he'd walked across an ice-locked expanse of the Bering Sea and comprehended his insignificance. —Chickens have a twenty-minute memory. We primates cope through booze and denial. Dial up more of that denial part, you'll last longer.

—We all end up in the fire, anyway. This friend of mine told me a story. He was raised in Kansas on a farm. He told me his older brother met Satan. Billy Bob was riding his tractor one miserably hot afternoon and the Devil was sitting on a stump at the end of a row. Fire engine red, horns, tail, pitchfork stuck in the ground. The Devil said, *Hi, Billy Bob.*

—And? I'm on the edge of my seat here.

—I dunno. My pal couldn't get anything else from his brother. His bro was one of those sullen, salt o' the earth types. You, know, the kind I despise. He only mentioned it when he was drunk as a skunk and preached the Rapture.

—Probably didn't know what came next because he'd cooked his brains sitting on the tractor one too many summers. Now full darkness was upon them and they were two lumps of shadow, side by side.

—When I saw the horn, kinda peeking out of the dirt, ants swarming over it, this feeling, a shock, hit me. A moving picture, a sick, sick black and white movie, clicked on in my mind. I wanted to sit in the dirt and keep replaying it. This morning I watched you sleeping and the movie started again. For a few seconds I got why our cult friends went to the nursing home and went wild. I really, really understood.

He couldn't see her face. He didn't know what to do with her, so he pretended not to hear. —My father was a woodsman, he said. —After Mom died, he disappeared into the Olympic National Forest with a backpack and his dog. He made a ramshackle camp in the heart of the forest and lived there about eighteen months. He had cancer and he didn't want to go on without his wife, so he did what the mountain men used to do. He went into the wilderness to die. Animals ate him. Only the bones were left.

—That's a beautiful story, she said. —My dad's fat as a cow and farts his way through CNN and tournament poker sixteen hours a day. I wish a wild animal would eat him.

The buck, the knife. Him trudging across the ice, in the distance a steel-gray wall closing fast. There wasn't anything left to say, so they sat as if shackled to their chairs until the full moon floated to the surface of the sky like a corpse buoyed and bloated by its decomposition. The moon was yellow as a skull. He imagined it resembled the skulls of any of the people who'd ended their days at the bottom of a hole on this ranch. The skull moon resembled their own future selves, he was certain.

It rained hard for two days and they cooped in the module, she entering reports into the computer, he descaling the live traps and foothold traps he'd left hanging outside from a rack. The climate was harsh and limescale built quickly. She didn't say much, didn't come into his compartment again. She'd gone cold. Her eyes were strange and she sat for hours staring into the monitor, hands motionless on the keyboard. He realized he'd become afraid of her. This paranoia was exacerbated by flu symptoms, the sense of terrible vulnerability. His muscles ached, the strength drained from them. He spent hours on the toilet, bowels convulsing. The damned pilot had obviously brought them the gift of plague from town.

On the third morning, the weather cleared and he slipped away and lit out for the hills without saying goodbye. Crows roosted in the trees, and they alighted on the wet earth as he passed. The birds hopped from bush to bush in dreadful silence, following him in a dark train. He plodded directly to the coyote den, tranquilizer gun in hand, his mind mostly blank. Coyotes had been in the vicinity; their sign was sparse, but recent. He leaned against a tree and concentrated on blending into the scenery, willing one of his furry friends to make an appearance. His brain itched for a cigarette and he bought himself time by promising to smoke at least two if he remained stoic for an hour, three should he strike gold and nail his quarry.

It wasn't like him to fidget, to chafe at the sweat on his neck, to twitch at every gnat bite and mosquito prick. Dad taught him better, taught him to sink into himself and leave the body an insensate shell, a blind within a blind. He was going to pieces. Inside of twenty minutes his nerve endings were on fire. A coyote appeared, moving unhurriedly, nose to the ground. He raised the gun without hesitation and fired. The coyote yelped, jaws snapping at its flank where the dart penetrated. He chambered another round and the little beastie was gone, fled like smoke into the shadows of the trees.

—Fuck! Fuck! Fuck! Fuck! Fuck! He leaped to pursue, charged into the underbrush, and this too was contrary to a lifetime of character. Branches gored his arms, drew blood from his cheek. He shouted more obscenities, roared like a bull. The coyote had vanished, and after half a kilometer, he stood on the edge of a prairie, lungs burning, sparks pin-wheeling across his vision. He bellowed at the sky, seized the gun by its stock and hurled it with all his might. The gun arced, end over end, like a tomahawk, and smashed to pieces against the hard ground.

He kept walking, tears stinging the scratches on his cheek, matting his beard. The chopper had crashed behind a hill in a shallow ravine. He recognized the vehicle instantly. There hadn't been a fire and it was largely intact. Crows perched on the bent tail rotor, and the mangled struts, pecked and preened among the glittering bed of shattered safety glass. The cockpit was empty. One of the flight seats lay a few meters from the wreck.

He uncapped his canteen and drank, then screwed the cap on again and dialed HQ. He reported the accident to an anonymous functionary who advised him law enforcement would be apprised and rescue personnel dispatched directly. He closed the phone and walked away from the crash site. The crows stayed.

He tracked his own footprints toward the mountains. The pilot's tinted glasses twinkled where they hung from a sage bush. He stuck the glasses into his shirt pocket and kept moving, hardly bothering to glance down now; instinct dragged him forward. He came to a low rise. The ground was trampled. A long, sloping slab of carved rock dominated. A strange misshapen skull was transfixed on a wooden pole; the skull of an impossibly large ram missing a horn.

Two men stood at either end of the rock. The pilot's flight suit was torn and grimy. —Give those back. The pilot pointed at the glasses. In the near distance, a column of deadly black storm clouds mounted vertically, its interior shot with brief flares of lightning.

The other man wore a toga open at the chest. His flesh glowed blue-white like the wings of a moth. The man looked at him and said, —Hello, Billy Bob.

He awakened, cross-legged, the bole of a pine digging into his back. Red, evening light filtered through a scrim of clouds. The coyote den remained silent, lifeless. His canteen lay beside him, open so that most of the water had leaked and made a small, mucky depression. He poured what remained over his cracked lips, then spat, stomach recoiling at the acrid taste; bitter grains he couldn't identify lingered on his tongue. A beam of light illuminated the canteen so that it fractured like a prism and continued along his optic nerve and into the recesses of his brain where something turned over. A crow's shadow flitted and fluttered, and danced away.

—You crazy bitch, he said, staring at the canteen with mounting horror. This couldn't be happening. He dropped the canteen, then with bleary resolve, retrieved it and hooked it on his belt. He'd need evidence.

The module glistened red and orange, then winked out, a blown match head, as he walked into the yard. Simon and Garfunkel sang about darkness, their old friend, on the intercom. She was in a far better mood. She hummed while industriously clacking away at the keyboard, occasionally stirring a spoon in her tin cup. He stowed the tranquilizer gun, undressed, then went to the toilet, pushed his fingers down his throat, and retched. He clutched the sides of the toilet and listened to her chuckle in the other room. She sounded like a witch, he thought. Cackling and rubbing her knuckles as she plotted his doom.

He eventually emerged from the stall and took a can of beans from the shelf and cleared a space at the table. He sat, head in his hands, gazing numbly at the can of beans, realizing he'd forgotten the can opener, a plate, or a spoon.

—Want me to fix you something? she said. —You look weak as a kitten.

He licked his lips and smiled until they cracked and bled. —Don't worry about me. I jogged three kilometers after a coyote. I'm winded, is all.

—Know what my favorite story is? *The Landlady*, by Roald Dahl. Great story. My sister read it to me when we were kids. Scared the shit outta me, but I loved it. It stuck with me. Do you know the story I'm talking about?

—Sounds familiar. He flicked his tongue over his lips, tasting the blood. —I feel as if I should recall because it's famous. Like Tyson and Holyfield.

—Hee, hee, that's so funny. You have a hell of a sense of humor, lover boy.

—There's a dog that doesn't move. A bird sitting in its cage. He closed his eyes, concentrating. Bitter almonds. The acrid silt at the bottom of his canteen, burning his throat.

—The old lady was into taxidermy. Once you figure that part out, you know what a train wreck is coming. Not one drop of blood is spilled and it's the creepiest, ickiest story ever. Dahl was the shit.

—Why are you angry? he said. —This is about what happened with us back when, isn't it? My God, girl, it wasn't a thing. He had difficulty enunciating. —Not worth this. Not worth this.

—I've spiked your water for two weeks. O mighty hunter that you are, it's pathetic. I thought it'd be so much harder. I almost feel guilty; it's like strangling a child.

—Not worth this, he said.

—Do you even know what this *is?* Her chair squeaked as she rose, and her bare feet scuffed on the floor as she crossed the space between them. —I wondered where you went all day. You've been doing some heavy thinking at long last, haven't you? But I'm sorry to say, it's too late, moth-erfucker. Too late for you.

He looked up and saw she was holding the tin cup. She pinched her nostrils between thumb and forefinger, smiled and twitched her wrist, and dashed the contents of the cup into his face. He knew it was muriatic acid from the smell. He blocked with his left arm and twisted partially away, lurching from the chair, but some went into his eye and reality was eclipsed by a sudden blizzard of white.

—Oh, honey, are you okay? she said. —Did you get any on you?

Meanwhile, his eye bubbled into its socket, cooked like an egg white. He punched her with the can in his fist, not aiming, not thinking, because the acid was searing him, eating him alive, flesh and thought alike. The can smashed edgewise into her temple, and the tremor reverberated through his arm as bone gave way. She stepped backward, then sat abruptly in one of the plastic chairs. He threw the can at her, but his remaining vision flickered wildly and he couldn't see whether he struck her or not. His lungs began to burn. Pain was a clothes hanger twisting into his soft gray matter. He shrieked and plowed through tables, chairs, a wooden partition; he tripped and sprawled on his belly. He curled into himself, writhing and retching, and slammed his head against the floor until he lost consciousness. The agony followed him down.

* * *

The Sierras team had camped near a hot spring and everyone leaped in naked and shouting. Someone brought booze, someone else a bag of grass, and it was a hell of a party beneath the full moon. After the others had drifted to their tents, drunken and singing, rough-housing and playing grab-ass, he took her on a flat white rock by the light of a dying fire, slick from the water, steam boiling from them as they clinched. An owl screamed as she screamed and dug her heels into his ribs. Two weeks of smoldering glances and glancing touches had led to this apocalyptic moment.

They took a vacation that began in Kenya and rambled south. He wanted to see the lions. Six weeks of safaris and relentless fucking in every hostel and two-star hotel along the Barbary Coast. She was recently divorced from a fellow geologist who worked in Washington D.C. as the head of a department in a small, but respectable museum. She described her ex-husband as a soft, lovely man. She was on top of him when she said this, hands flat on his chest, nude but for the thick belt she wore on her hiking breeches. The buckle scraped his belly as she fucked him. He wasn't listening. His head hung off the bed and he stared through a set of billowing curtains at the clouds.

He found the puppy, an orphaned mix, in an alley in Denver. He took the pup to the vet for shots and worming. While he stood at the counter, bemused by his impulsiveness, one of his long-lost contacts, a buddy from college days, called with a job offer; a nine-month gig in Alaska. He said yeah, and put the puppy in a box and took it to her apartment. She fell in love, as he expected. He asked to her to watch it for him during the Alaska trip. They had dinner at a French restaurant, stumbled home high on a bottle of Chablis, and made sweet, tearful love while the puppy whined and scratched at the door. The next day she drove him to the airport and told him to write. He didn't write, not once in nine months, didn't speak to her again, and a couple of years later he heard she was dating some guy who snuffed fires on oil rigs. The guy died in one of the fires, but whoever told him didn't know what she was doing or where she lived.

Sometimes, especially when he was very drunk, he'd awaken and smell her scent on the pillow. He'd think about her and the dog. Eventually, he didn't.

She was still sitting in the chair when he regained his senses. Her head lolled and her legs splayed crudely, the way men often sat, crotches exposed. She'd pissed herself. A fly preened on her thigh.

The module was full of red shadows, or his head was full of red shadows.

His left eye was gone, a crater leaking gelatin. He felt it sliding around. His forearm and hand were blistered; they resembled microwaved hamburger. The flesh of his cheek seemed to be sloughing, and when he touched his head, a hank of hair came free. The interior of his mouth was spongy, and his throat felt as if she'd dragged a rusty fork down his esophagus and then stabbed his lungs repeatedly. Pain broke over him in waves and when he coughed, blood and mucus shot forth. He gibbered and rocked with his head in his hands until finally he regained enough sense to find the first aid kit and take a half bottle of aspirin and a shot of morphine. Through it all, she watched him, one eye slightly higher than the other, the corner of her mouth downturned. He went to the radio, afraid to turn his back on her, but there wasn't much choice.

He keyed the mike and made the call. The answer, when it finally came, surfaced from dead static. The voice was garbled, made unintelligible by the white noise and gain distortion. It responded to his cries for help with bursts of vaguely menacing gobbledygook until a red light on the radio's console blinked and the machine shut down and went cold. His cell phone couldn't locate a signal. He slumped in the corner, gnawing his wrist bloody to quiet the ravening fire consuming his brain. He heard himself whimper and was vaguely ashamed and horrified at how abruptly a man could be reduced to an animal.

Sometime later the power died and the interior of the module went dark. Moonlight trickled in and illuminated her face. Had her neck twisted slightly so she might focus upon him with her glistening eyes? Had her hand shifted position? He summoned the courage to stir from his niche and crawl like a wounded beast to the next compartment. He locked the door and wedged a mop from the supply locker under the handle and propped himself against the wall.

He'd dozed for several minutes when the noises began in the main area. It was a stealthy sound, the scrape and scuffle of feet navigating wrecked furniture. The relentless throbbing in his eye dulled his senses, rendered him effectively inert as he listened to the floor squeak closer, ever closer. Why hadn't he grabbed the gun? Or his work belt with the big hunting knife? A thick, scummy layer of foam had curdled in a ring around his mouth. He scratched it, bit down hard on his fingers, trying in vain to shock himself into action. How many times had he watched a coyote or a cougar in a leg-hold trap, dying by inches until it caved in and lay there, impassive and docile, awaiting the end? It was too dim for him to see the door handle jiggle, but he heard it clearly enough and thought maybe this was his turn to skip from the face of the Earth.

—Honey, unlock the door.

He gibbered and chewed his fingers. It wasn't her voice and he didn't know how to assess that fact beyond the terror of the situation. The voice was soft and guttural, sexless and abominable in its alien timbre. The voice emanated pure malice, and it wanted him. Oh yes, it wanted him.

—Open the door. We can help you.

We, it said. What the fuck was *we*? Where had he heard that? From what trash book, from what horror flick? The Bible, the Old Testament. Almighty God had occasionally referred to Himself in the plural. Demons, too. But it wasn't an angel or a devil on the other side of the door. No way, and he nodded his head to reinforce the assertion. There was a fucking cultist standing there. He'd been correct to suspect one or more of those creeps lurked in the brush, spying and plotting, poised for the moment he could move in for the kill. Either that or his sweet ex-girlfriend could alter her voice, or her ability to form words was severely impaired from her fractured skull.

—Let us in. You aren't well. We can smell you. You're burned. Your flesh is suppurating. It's rotting. It's falling from the bone.

He covered his good eye, trying to make his pain and fear subside, the voice to leave him in peace. He was caught in his own kind of leg-hold trap, except he couldn't chew his leg off to escape.

—Come, open up. Let us help.

—Go to hell! he said, first in a mumble, then a hoarse shout. —Get the fuck away! He repeated this until his voice cracked to pieces and the only sound he could make was a dry, pathetic whine.

—Help me, she said. Not the guttural voice, but hers. She sounded afraid.

He wept.

Pale light filtered through the window. His cheek was pressed against the floor, gummed to the surface by its own juices. Light pooled around his limp hand. The skin was scorched and ruined and a dark scab covered his knuckles. The tendons had tightened like violin strings and he couldn't make a fist.

He peeled himself free, unlocked the door and surveyed his world. Deranged chimpanzees had redecorated the interior. Every bit of equipment was smashed. Dust leaked through a gash in the hull. The hatch was missing, in its place a ragged hole. She was gone too.

A bomb had detonated in the yard. Canned goods, wiring, bits of wood and silverware and crushed glass twinkled in the dirt. The hatch lay nearby, twisted and deformed. He wanted to call for her, but his throat was stripped. The air was hot and sickeningly bright. His good eye didn't seem reliable. Everything shimmered like a photograph negative. Everything glowed white or oozed darkness. There was no telling the time; the face of his watch was blank. He scrabbled about the yard, tears and pus rolling down his cheek.

He wrapped a sliver of glass in cotton and went forth on hands and knees with his nose to the earth like a dog. Her trail started at the edge of camp. It was easy to follow the broken twigs, the gore-splattered needles and leaves, and though it wound serpentine through brush and trees, he quickly guessed the destination. She'd been dragged by her hair, like a carcass.

It was a long, bloody crawl to the den.

He lay on his side, panting, fixated on her sandal. The sandal was caked in black grime and wedged between split halves of a stone. He'd seen the other shoe a ways back, dangling from a bush. The sun fell below the jagged rim of the mountains. Heat rapidly dissipated, sucked into the advancing red shadows. He mumbled and whined to himself, incoherent except for flashes of insight that urged him to slice his throat and be done, and he would've committed the act, except when the moment came, he realized he'd dropped the improvised blade, that it was lost. And so all was lost. The moon crept up from its lair and grinned its devil grin. She cried out, muffled and faint. Or a coyote yipped over the ridge. He trembled from head to toe, galvanized to pitiful life by the image of her screaming, buried alive.

He coughed and pulled himself, hand over hand, among the roots, smelling her blood mixed with the cool dust, husked leaves and dead needles. The entrance was narrow, but he forced his head through, then his shoulders. He wriggled like a snake and his flesh scraped raw, and his hips were past the threshold and he coiled in the rank, decaying warmth of the den. The mountain breeze tickled the soles of his feet in a lingering caress, then he squirmed fully inside.

For an eon he floated in perfect darkness, listening to insects burrowing through wood and bark. He wasn't surprised when something larger stirred. A cold, hard hand touched his cheek and clamped his mouth, stifling any sobs, or shrieks of terror or joyous exclamation. He relaxed, too weak for the struggle. He was home.

Her tongue went into his ear like the worm into the apple.

A coyote sneaked from the trees and crouched near the ancient den, the forbidden ground, sniffing at the fresh furrows in the earth, at the blood and the piss and the acrid stench of fear musk. The coyote had roved far from its normal haunts tonight. It was very young and didn't understand why none of the packs lived here, why the only scents were the scents of sickness and death.

The animal's ears pricked forward, and it froze, head cocked toward the mound. A cloud rippled across the face of the moon, and when it passed, the coyote bolted, racing from shadow to shadow, and vanished into the silvery gloom. Farther off, the pack howled, their cries echoing along hidden canyons in a damned chorus.

SIX SIX SIX

…Over the course of the long afternoon of thunderclaps and rain squalls they had unpacked most of the living room of the ancestral home.

He stared into a box at his feet for a long while.

She put on a Sinatra record.

The wind slackened and left in its stead a charged stillness that accentuated the remoteness of the house, the artificiality of the music.

Out of the blue he said, —Pop used to play this game with me and Karl when we were kids. He called it *Something Scary.* His voice was hushed like a soap actor emoting as he reveals a deep, dark secret to his love interest.

She set aside the silver and blue vase that contained some of her mother's ashes and watched him in the mirror over the fireplace. —Uh, oh, she said.

He chuckled, still regarding the contents of the box which was labeled "misc" in bold magic marker strokes. It was not one of the boxes unloaded by the movers, rather a venerable, dusty container he'd retrieved from the attic. —Yeah, uh-oh, but not in an inappropriate touch, danger zone, bathing suit area way, or anything.

—Am I relieved?

—Maybe, maybe not, he said.

She heard a noise, a cough or a growl, off to the left in the deeper shadows, but saw nothing unusual when she glanced that direction.

The house was a source of many unexplained noises.

What if there were rats in the walls? Thank God for the cat.

Pine floorboards gleamed in the light of the lamps near the arched door that let into a drawing room, then a library full of moldering books. She'd dusted a few off and found their foreign titles illegible, spines so withered and decayed she dared not handle them lest they disintegrate.

Everything else that had defined the house as the demesne of his parents was tidily stowed away. His brother and sister, aunts and uncles, had swept through and claimed everything that wasn't nailed down.

So, a blank slate for the happy couple.

There were several multi-paned windows along the far wall of the living room. Like the rest of the house the windows were old and quaint and to her mind, vaguely ominous; portals to a dimmer, less hospitable era.

It was well past sundown and the glass was dark as steel.

The forest across the country lane was far older than the house and it reinforced the darkness that pressed against the windows.

There were bears and deer in the woods; and coyotes and cougars and snakes.

Earlier that day she'd brushed a large black spider from its nest in the porch eave with a long-handled broom left in the pantry. The broom handle was worn smooth as glass and it bowed in the middle; its bristles were rocky nubs, blackened.

She thought about the woods and how someone or something could even now be lurking out there, spying on her, and imagined hoarse breathing, hot on her neck.

Drapes would certainly be the first order of business tomorrow.

An exterminator would soon follow.

She said, —I'm going to see what we have for dinner, and walked through a second arch into a hallway.

The hallway led her to the farm-style kitchen with low beams and dangling meat hooks that framed a long, scarred wooden table in shadow.

The table had seated farmers and patricians alike for the house's foundation predated the arrival of her husband's kin by a decade or more.

A gas range with double ovens squatted opposite a cold hearth.

A cast iron pot hung from a hook at the center of the hearth.

The pot was corroded with rust.

She heated a kettle of water for pasta and grabbed some shrimp from the stainless steel fridge, the only concession to modern convenience in the room.

He materialized in the doorway.

For a moment his features were occulted by the gloom. He could've been *anyone* standing there, and her skin prickled.

Then he emerged into the light and kissed her and fetched the cheese he'd bought in the township and poured the wine he'd also bought in the township.

They sat together at the table and ate pasta and drank wine while Sinatra continued to sing, his voice ethereal as it stretched across time and space and echoed through the empty rooms.

Something panted under her chair, near her ankle.

The vent shushed to life as the furnace powered on in the cellar and a cool draft swirled around her open toe sandals.

—Jesus Mary, she said, and gulped her wine.

Their black cat, Elvira, scuttled from between her ankles and bolted into the hall.

He whistled and tipped his chair back and studied the timbers above the table, the cold, iron hooks. —I know, he said. —I know. Let's get a dog to keep her company.

—Elvira probably doesn't want that kind of company.

—I'm thinking of you taking one of your leisurely nature strolls. The woods are full of vermin.

—The house is full of vermin.

The house didn't have a name although it was large enough to warrant one. Four generations of his family had dwelt here. His childhood bedroom was on the third floor, sealed tight as a drum.

Gone for twenty years, he wouldn't have returned, but his parents were suddenly dead, victims of a helicopter accident while on vacation in Colorado.

Now everything was his, whether he wanted it or not.

The will made it plain, much to the consternation of his immediate and extended family who'd thrived upon petty grievances and longstanding feuds, each secure in his or her place within the pecking order.

No more efficiency flat in the city.

The commute to the station was thirty-five minutes through somber pastoral vistas, then another hour by train to his uptown office. Meanwhile, she would work from home; she could work anywhere her computer plugged into a wall.

Yet, she disliked the place, loathed the idea of inhabiting its haunted rooms for days and weeks and months of the years to come.

And the encroaching wilderness…

Money was tight and it was for the best. Maybe there would be a tragic fire and an insurance settlement. Hope sprang eternal, indeed.

—We'll go look at puppies at the shelter on Saturday. How's that sound?

—Why would your father want to frighten you? she said, not wishing to discuss the ordeal of visiting a dog shelter. Animal shelters and hospitals depressed her. She couldn't watch the scene at the pound in *Lady and the Tramp* for fear of bawling.

—He was a card, he said.

She poured another glass of wine, leaving the dregs.

She'd met his father twice.

Once at an Easter dinner, again at the wedding.

A lean man with a lean face and hair as pale and thin as straw. He'd kissed her hand and said charming things. She feared him instantly.

—But why screw with your head? Kinda psychotic.

—Isn't that how fathers get their kicks? He rose and went to the cabinet and brought forth another bottle of wine she'd no idea was there. He popped the cork and filled his glass.

He didn't return to the table, but shoved his hip against the counter and held the glass tight to the breast of his jacket.

His tie hung loose and sloppy. —Pop was a big Ingmar Bergman fan. *Hour of the Wolf* was his favorite. A sucker for those austere, Baltic landscapes. The cruel beauty of it all. He romanticized isolation and eccentricity. He fantasized about doing in his enemies in the name of art.

—You too are a raging Bergman fan, she said.

—And so now you see I come by it honestly. Pop raised us to be good little Yanks, but he was always a Swede, through and through, just like Grandpa. And a film lover. He met Max Von Sydow in New York at a party. Before I was born.

—Weren't you four or five?

He frowned and ran the rim of the glass over his lip. —Was I?

—Yeah, because Karl was in first grade and the two of you were hiding out under the table with the punchbowl. You stayed up all night and everybody got drunk and nobody missed you. You've told it to me. If your father loved Sweden so much, why didn't he repatriate? She'd never asked before and he'd never volunteered a rationale. His strained familial ties were well documented and not a subject to broach lightly.

He smiled a smile that wasn't real. —What, and give up all of this? My great-great grandfather rowed us to America. You can never go home.

—Right. All this. She was sufficiently buzzed to ignore the warning in the fake smile and feel pleased in the doing.

Her husband was so insufferably unflappable, it was fun to needle him on occasion, and no better occasion than on the eve of their occupation of a rambling, patriarchal tomb he'd dragged her to, willy-nilly.

—My family is *persona non grata*. It is impossible for us to return, ever. He smiled again, a sharp, feral baring of his teeth. —Pop got Von Sydow's autograph on a cocktail napkin. Locked it in his writing desk. I hunted for it the other day... He trailed off, lips pursed, eyes narrowed.

She swallowed more wine and stared with morbid fascination at her reflection as it warped in the window.

Quite odd, his use of the word *hunted*. Not *looked* or *searched*, but *hunted*. How peculiarly specific of him.

She wondered if he could sense her thoughts and had decided to play *Something Scary*, whatever that might be, with *her*. —Were you planning to sell it on Ebay, or what?

—Baby doll is drunk. How can I tell? She's getting bitchy.

—Bitchier, you mean. I'm only half in the bag.

—No, sweet pea, I don't intend to hock Pop's effing keepsake. He played with his tie loop, snaring his fingers and twisting. —I was going through his stuff. Memories from when me and Karl were kids came rushing in. I haven't thought of that party for ages. Dunno why it hit me. Being here is stirring a lot of muck, I guess. He chuckled unhappily.

He resembled his father as his father had appeared a decade ago, except his hair was thick and his eyes were kind.

Perhaps not kind tonight, tonight they were mysterious.

He acted like he'd been drinking heavily when she knew that this wasn't the case. Her man could hold his liquor, and hers as well. —The time has come, I fear, to speak of cabbages and kings.

—You're so cute when you're earnest, she said.

—Don't you fucking mock me.

She said, —All right, I'm sorry. Tell me more about your faddah.

His neck reddened, flushing as dark as the wine in his glass.

The record skipped, making a garbled, demonic wreck of Old Blue Eyes' voice as if someone were dragging the needle back and forth across the vinyl.

Six times, then it abruptly stopped and the house was silent.

They remained very still, heads turned toward the doorway.

She felt sick, right on the edge of spontaneous diarrhea.

Finally, he set his glass on the counter and walked out of the kitchen. His footsteps faded.

She waited, not realizing she'd held her breath until her temples throbbed.

He called from the living room, —Damned cat. What do you want to listen to?

—Something upbeat.

—Like what?

She visualized the pile of records by the record player. —I don't know. Put on the Abba.

—Abba. I don't see it.

—It's there. Probably under The Village People.

He cursed. —Okay, looking. A minute later Billy Joel began to sing "Movin' Out." A minute after that, he reappeared and walked over to his wine and drank it all in a single steady draught, which was unlike him, he being a consummate wine snob. One didn't gulp wine unless one was a boor. He refilled his glass. —No Abba today. The defiance in his tone sounded playful, except she knew better.

—Why do you hate Abba so much?

—Truly, I hate Abba with a pure white hot passion. So did Pop.

—Shit, isn't that ironic. The drummer died a couple of years ago. Brunkert. He tripped into a glass door. The glass shattered and cut his neck. He wrapped a towel around his neck and went for a neighbor's house. Died in the yard. Tragic.

—Not tragic.

—That's cold, honeybunch.

—The drummer in the famous bands always gets offed. That's part of the pact with the Devil. Somebody's got to take one for the team.

—Tell it to Ringo. Down to him and Paul, unless Paul's dead for real.

—Ringo is a special case. Best got the hook, then Satan traded up for Lennon. Exception that proves the rule.

—I've got nothing, she said. —Even now, in the gloaming of our lives, every day I discover a new facet of your personality.

He rolled his eyes and poured more wine. He nodded toward the ceiling. —Did you notice the door to my old bedroom is nailed shut?

—I thought it was locked.

—Uh-uh. No latch on the door. Pop nailed it shut. With spikes. Who does that?

—He was hinting that you were dead to him.

—The bastard wouldn't let go that easily. He liked to think his claws were in deep, that me and Karl would come crawling back to him one day. He took the long view. This is something else.

—You don't mention your sister.

—Honey bunny, I don't mention my *family*, if you hadn't noticed. Thus the confessional.

—Yeah, but you don't mention her with a vengeance.

—Would you feel better if I did?

—She's nice. I like her. Elvira likes her.

—When the hell was Carling at our place? His eyes bulged slightly.

—Lots of times. She came over for tea or we'd go have lunch. I did her hair. She did mine. Billy Joel sang "Stranger," and the part about the masks made her shiver.

—She's not as nice as you think. I don't want her coming around here.

—What do you mean, not as nice as I think? I'm not simple. I didn't fly off a turnip truck.

—I mean she's good at fooling people. Better than Pop. She's all teeth. Beware, beware!

—Does she take after your mother?

—She takes after Pop. Mother wasn't anything like either of them. Too bad she was so beaten down when you met her. Mom used to argue with him like cats and dogs. He broke her eventually. By the time I graduated she just sat around knitting. His opinions were her opinions. Mom survived breast cancer. Too bad, really. What did Carling want, anyway?

—Company. You won't talk to her. Karl won't talk to her. Neither you nor Karl talk to one another. None of you talked to your parents. Carling is sad. I think she's holding out hope there'll be a family reunion of sorts.

—Ha! I hope she liked the funeral, because that's the last reunion she's gonna get for a while. Trust me when I say, don't trust her. She's a witch. She even collaborated with Pop when he played *Something Scary*. I'm convinced she helped him drive Mom over the edge. She was a daddy's girl, all right.

—What did she do?

—What do you mean, what did she do? She's a monster, a witch. Pulls the wings off flies, torments kittens. Worse than that.

—I did not notice these qualities. Does Karl feel the same?

—Hell yes. He hates her worse than I do. He tried to kill her when we were in middle school. Pushed her off the balcony on the second floor. She fell into the rose bushes and thus his assassination attempt was foiled by the gods.

—I'm sure Karl wasn't really trying to kill her.

—Oh, yes, yes he was. He put rat poison in her lemonade. She didn't drink it, though. Once, and I can't swear it's true, when they were on spring break, he slipped her a roofie and left her in Daytona with a local biker gang. There's real sex on the beach for you. I wouldn't leave them in a locked room.

—Remind me to spit on your brother the next time I see him. Unless he's on fire…unless you're lying.

—I'm lying about the poison and the bikers. Karl did shove her fat ass over the balcony. You wonder why none of us talk, now you know. Both of them suck in their own special way. Childhood was survival. I kept my head down and put one foot in front of another. I bled my folks for an education, then I beat feet and never looked back. I *did* find something weird in Pop's study, by the way.

—Oh?

—Yeah. A black robe hanging from a hook in the closet. Only thing in there.

—Like a magistrate's robe?

—You know that's not the kind. I guess it's not weird so much that he owned the robe, but that nobody packed it away or locked it up. Not a speck of dust on it either. Could've easily just been returned from the dry cleaner.

—I'm cold, she said. —Let's start a fire and knock the damp off this joint.

They adjourned to the living room. She arranged the plush pseudo-leather divan near the fireplace and fetched a quilt from their bedroom on the second floor—a very large guest room, actually. She wasn't ready to set up shop in the master bedroom. The bad vibes were overpowering. Surprisingly, he acceded to her decision without comment. Maybe he had the creeps too.

He brought wood in from the shed that abutted the fence at the far end of the yard, stamping a muddy trail across the floor. He got a fire cracking and spitting and she began to feel cozy. She slipped off her sandals and stretched across the divan and watched him clump around, fussing with the pokers and jostling the flaming logs, adjusting the screens, until he finally sat on the couch, one ankle braced on a settee. Red and gold and orange light flickered through the grate and made a shifting, crystalline pattern on the planks, raced along the wall and shimmered and swirled in the nearest window. The light-play reminded her of magic lanterns from the eighteenth century, casting fairytale monsters and vistas of haunted forests and mountains across the walls and ceilings of peasant cottages late, late in the lonesome night.

—Now, she said. —give on this *Something Scary*.

—Funny you should mention magic lanterns. My dearly departed father was obsessed with them and there is one in that box yonder, along with a handful of color plates he collected from antiquarians around the globe. A handful were made by Eadweard Muybridge, the guy who invented motion pictures. Crazy, murderous bastard who filmed horses and buffaloes and such. He also did a series with naked people performing menial tasks. But I've only seen the other plates, the ones with fake monsters and demons. There are frightful things on those plates.

—I didn't mention magic lanterns, she said, drawing the quilt closer to her chin.

He smiled. —You muse aloud, sugarplum. You also talk in your sleep. It's curious that you brought up Satan. Pop's obsession with the Prince of Darkness rivals his Bergman fetish. There's some outlawed tomes in the library and a case of knives and ritual masks and black candles around here somewhere. Carling might've taken them. Big sister knows what to do with sacrificial daggers. Yeah, I just bet she had her eye on poor Elvira. Word to the wise, she shows her face on our doorstep you better send her packing.

—But I didn't mention Satan, either. You did.

—You started in with the drummer business. One thing led to another. Know what Pop said to me one night when he crawled from under my bed? It was pitch black, but I recognized his breath as he crouched over me. He whispered, *Lucky you can't see me like this, kiddo. Me and your sister are out of our faces.* Carling grabbed my foot. Her hand was ice cold. I pissed myself.

—I…faces? She didn't quite grasp this shift in her reality and the buzz from the alcohol wasn't helping. His matter of fact revelation unnerved and confused her.

—You're shitting me, right? Your dad wasn't a satanist. Carling? How could you not tell me?

—I'm deadly serious, love. This isn't the kind of thing one brings up on first date…

—How about on the hundredth, the thousandth? How about before moving us to the Overlook Hotel?

—…and then I decided I was hot for you and the urge to spill my guts sort of faded away. You're a good thing, baby. I didn't want to lose you.

—The honeymoon is over. So here comes the dirty laundry.

—I didn't anticipate inheriting the house. I figured at best Pop would carve it to pieces and dole it out like that. We'd each get a check. But here we are and the lies will surely come to light. There's power here.

—So, let's sell. You should hate this house. I mean, I thought you loved it before you dropped the bombshell that your family is full of psychos. My God, I thought it was plain old garden variety sibling rivalry and resentment of being the youngest heir. My god, my god.

—Yes, I should hate it, and I do. Unfortunately, I can't sell.

—Why not? Far as I'm concerned, we can offload this pile of wood for below market value and lease a condo.

—You don't get it. I literally can't sell. Believe me, putting this on the market was on my to-do list. Every time I dial the realtor, a spike of pain stabs me between the eyes. I vomited in the office last week. Then comes these…I'd call them nightmares, except they're closer to prophetic visions. Somebody who resembles my dad tying me to the bed and cutting out my heart. I'm ten or eleven and he says I'm promised to the Devil, that I can never leave, and starts hacking. Baby, it's so real I wake shrieking.

—I haven't heard you shrieking. You don't even snore.

—That's because it doesn't make a sound, doesn't escape my mouth. My face is sort of paralyzed. Or I dunno what. I'm cursed. This place is mine and I can't leave…who knows what will happen if I really, really try.

—There's a condition. A night terror where you feel like someone is sitting on your chest. You can't move, can't scream.

—I think it's Pop's ghost. Turning the screws.

She thought about this for a while, or tried to. Her mind jumped from point to point, conjuring a panoply of bloody sacrifice, murderous relatives, and Satan laughing from a bed of fire. She didn't bother arguing that while his father might've been a lunatic, it would take an even bigger nut to entertain the notion of a family curse. Mind over matter. If his father had truly dominated him as a child, then that control might persist on a subconscious level. She pictured an EC Comics panel of a putrefying claw reaching for her husband from beyond the grave. She giggled, mildly embarrassed at the shrillness of her outburst.

—Sure, laugh.

—Forgive me. Carling should've inherited. She's the eldest. Why you?

—Excellent question and one that I put to Karl when we met with the executor. He still talked to Pop on the rare occasion and I hoped he might have some insight. Little brother was cagey. It's been two months since the reading of the will. I've called Karl every other day, left him a dozen messages. He's gone.

—Gone on vacation?

—Gone as in vapor. I filed a police report.

—And this is another thing you decided not to tell me?

—We're a secretive bunch, my clan. The cops say he's around, but won't say where. I think they're wrong. Or lying. Something happened when that helicopter crashed and my father got turned into hamburger. I feel strange. Physically, emotionally. Don't even try to suggest it's grief.

—The police aren't going to lie. That's tinfoil hat jibber-jabber, man. He skipped town after the funeral, probably to blow the wad he nabbed. Your parents left him fifty grand. Not too shabby. Coke and hookers would keep him busy for a while, especially if he went to someplace with a depressed economy. Mexico, Costa Rica, Haiti, one of those places where Main Street is all whitewashed facades and discos, and one block over everybody's living under corrugated tin roofs and pissing in buckets.

He didn't say anything. Firelight moved across his face and she had a bad moment where he resembled his father so much her stomach turned over. He rose and went to the "misc" box and rummaged and brought forth a selection of wooden sticks that telescoped into a tripod. Next, he unwrapped a bulky metal contraption with gears and lenses and a small hand crank. He set the metal gadget on the tripod and pointed its central aperture at a blank section of the wall, a pale block where a cabinet had rested until recently. —Behold my father's favorite toy in the whole wide world. He used this to put on phantasmagoria performances for the kids.

—Phantasmagoria?

—A horror show. Very popular with the Victorian set. You'll see. He switched off the lamp and shut the panels in the fireplace so the glow became dim. He made adjustments to the magic lantern and vigorously cranked the handle like he was winding a jack in the box. Lastly, he inserted the edge of an object that resembled a film reel into the side of the box. He said, —A rudimentary model appeared in Europe during the fifteen hundreds. This one was built by a Viennese clockmaker in 1930 and is exponentially more sophisticated than its predecessors. The clockmaker was an occultist who cherished Chivalric and Renaissance theatrical traditions. He built several dozen variations on this design and they were purchased by wealthy collectors such as Pop.

—Is this the game?

—The game has a lot of components. This worked on us when we were tykes, less so later. *Voila!* A switch snapped into place and a yellow light came on in the guts of the machine and magnified through the apertures into a series of ovals on the wall. The ovals gradually brightened and ran together with a jittery, liquid quality like cells combining under a microscope. Black-trunked trees unfolded from the shimmering edges of the imagery and spread talons. The canopy intertwined and creepers slithered forth in a primitive Claymation effect, off-kilter and mesmerizing, and bubbles of swamp gas floated and sputtered among the branches, and the light brightened and dimmed, surging, retreating as branches became snakes and knotholes glittered like eyeballs and slowly widening mouths, oozing sap and slime.

—Wow, she said. —That's amazing.

—Shh, he said.

Figures, distorted by the shuddering frames, skulked between the boles of the trees, capered as the light downshifted to red, then black, and when the panel brightened, beneath a conical hat a white, lunatic face with strips of flesh peeled to chipped bone leered at her, twisting a stork neck to get a better view. She screamed even as the ghoulish visage rippled and morphed into a hillock amidst a sea of long grass beneath a too-full moon. More figures loped and gamboled toward the foreground;

tall, yet stooped, garbed in cowls and robes, sinewy arms raised in an apish manner. The oval fractured and the pictures multiplied and flowed up the walls, rippled across the floor, warped as they passed through curtains and furniture. The room fell away, its wood and stone dissolving, leaving her on cushion floating in undefined space. Vertigo stunned her. A scabrous hand clawed at her and she screamed again and toppled backward. She covered her eyes and lay sobbing until he touched her arm and stroked her hair. He said, —I'd forgotten. I'm sorry. It's safe to look. She peeked through her fingers. The magic lantern still whirred and clicked and projected grainy, diffuse blob of light. The ghouls and specters had receded into the undulating murk. He kissed her forehead. —Pop would set that rig in my room and commence playing. If I shut my eyes, he'd slap me with his belt. If I screamed, I'd get the belt. I got the belt a lot. There are four hundred plates in that box. See what I mean? See what I was dealing with?

—Shut it off.

—It's off.

—All the way off. Do it, or I'm going to get a hammer and smash that Goddamned thing into a billion Goddamned pieces.

—Easy, the spring has to unwind. I put the dropcloth over it.

She wiped her eyes and sat on the couch. —What the hell was that?

—A phantasmagoria, like I said. It's called *Lepers of the Black Wood*. Made by a guy in Snoqualmie around 1890. He probably enjoyed scaring the bejeezus out of his kids, just like my old man. Damn, you're shaking like crazy.

—The face, the half skull…thing. That was Carling.

—Really. A keen light entered his eyes, less sympathetic than interested. —It's not a real picture. It's a drawing, a facsimile. The artists would gather a well-heeled crowd into a parlor and lay this on them. Then the girls would faint, the gents would scream, and everyone had hot toddies after and pretended it was all so very vulgar and it hadn't affected them in the slightest.

—That was your sister.

—No. It's an abstracted figure etched onto a plate over one hundred years ago.

She leaped to her feet, took three steps and grabbed the tripod and slung it across the room. The magic lantern crashed through the window and sailed on, shutters shuttering, frail beams of blue and red and yellow rotating, a satellite launched beyond the solar system and into deep space. A breeze ruffled the curtains, snagged them in the jagged hole in the window glass.

—Feel all better? The little fake smile was back, sharper than before. His arms were folded. He clicked the button on the foot of the lamp with his toe. Click, click, clickety-click, and no light. He tried the other lamp. More clicking and the living room remained in darkness but for a bit of light seeping through the hall from the distant kitchen. —Bloody ancient wiring, he said.

—I need a drink, she said. Her pleasant high had been snuffed in the rush of terror.

—Well, that's a shame, he said. —We're plumb dry. Dry as a dry county in Bible-thumping country.

—The hell we are, she said. She shrugged on her pea coat and tucked her hair under the collar and walked out the front door. The walkway was paved in irregular stones and bordered by a knee-high stone fence cluttered with roses and other thorny plants. The weak illumination from the kitchen window showed her the way to the car. Clouds hung low against the impenetrable mass of trees and the air was thick and damp and the wan light in the window gave the impression that the house floated atop a vast dark sea. She unlocked the car and considered sliding behind the wheel and making good her escape. The dome light flashed and died. Her gym bag lay on the back seat. She'd stuffed two bottles of whiskey and one of brandy inside. She wasn't much for hard liquor, save for special occasions. Tonight seemed a worthy exception and she popped the cork and had a slug of whiskey. It helped. A patch of sky brightened and the clouds thinned over the field that separated the lane from the forest. A beam of moonlight filtered down and shone upon the long wet grass, spread rapidly across the field. Mist steamed from the grass and hung like cobwebs in the branches of the trees. The trees shuddered, tops whipping together without wind to stir them, and the grass vibrated rapidly and clods of leaves and dirt drifted lazily into the air. The vista was a snow globe shaken until its innards separated. She swayed, realizing in that instant the phantasmagoria, like a bad acid trip, was still altering her perceptions, and with an act of will she forced the world to steady. Mist and the clouds reformed and the light reversed itself and the curtain of darkness dropped upon the field. Someone shrieked in the distance. She quickly returned to the house. She bolted the door. He came through the French doors that let into the back yard. He carried a flashlight in one hand and some tools wrapped in canvas under his arm.

—A terrible thought has occurred to me, he said. She stared at him, not wanting to know what form this terrible thought of his would assume. She didn't say anything. He said, —I'm gonna see why Pop spiked my bedroom door. Wanna help?

—After, maybe. She showed him the bottle. They went into the kitchen. There was a bag of crushed ice in the freezer and she put a handful of it into a pair of water glasses and filled them the rest of the way with whiskey. They drank the whiskey and then stood for a while, holding their empty glasses without speaking or glancing at one another. She thought he was looking worse for the wear. His face was pale and the flesh around his eyes was bruised. A bat smacked into the window and they both jumped. The bat scrabbled and fluttered against the panes and she thought it was trying to warn them.

—Bah. I'm going. He set his glass in the sink and collected his tools. His face was sweaty and pale. He shuffled with his head below his shoulders.

She said quickly, —Let's get a hotel. For tonight. We'll come back in the daylight and do whatever it is you've got to do. He shook his head and continued into the hall and toward the stairs at the far end. She followed, and again resisted the temptation to run to the car and burn rubber for the city. The hall was dark. His footsteps creaked on the landing just above her, but when she climbed to the third floor he was already kneeling before the door of his old bedroom, prying at it with a crowbar. He muttered and growled, his hair sticky and disheveled, his features contorted in the shine of the flashlight lying nearby. —What was the terrible thought? she said. He turned his head toward her. His mouth articulated, but made no sound. He stood, gripping a hatchet instead of the crowbar, and she took an unsteady step backward, grabbed the railing at the top of the stairs and narrowly avoided a tumble. —What is it? she said, trying not to sound desperate. At some point during the evening reality had reconstituted at the quantum level, had remade itself, was accelerating toward a final, apocalyptic transmogrification. He swung the hatchet in a ponderous overhand blow against the middle of the door. And again. And again until it cracked and splintered and became a toothy maw. He stopped to survey his work. She cautiously approached him and peeked over his shoulder at what he'd made. An angular hole bored into a space as stale and dry as a tomb. The flashlight was in his hand and its beam wavered across vague shapes, revealing piecemeal, a chair, a trunk, the brass footboard of a child's bed. The bed itself lay in the thicker darkness.

—Wait here, he said. He wriggled through the hole, head and shoulders first. His pants leg ripped. From her perspective she couldn't make sense of the proportions of the room, nor his movements. Suddenly his silhouette, seemed farther away than it should've, as if he'd descended into a cavern. A breath of air sighed from the hole in the door and fluttered her hair. She called his name. He said, —There's something on the...Oh, no. He gave a cry of anguish. The flashlight beam swept in erratic circles as he repeated *Oh no,oh no,oh no!* The light went out and his cries ceased. She peered into the void and said his name again. He didn't answer. Another faint puff of stale air stirred dust motes and burned her nose and throat. The dust stuck to her lips like pollen and tasted vaguely sweet. She briefly entertained the idea of clambering after him, but this notion filled her with overwhelming dread and sent a cascade of disjointed images through her mind. A sluice of blood poured from a split skull, a carrion bird ate a string of guts, a lake of maggots churned and she fell into it from a great height. Was this what he saw whenever he contemplated selling the house? She recoiled with a groan and after a few moments of shocked paralysis, regained her strength and screamed for him until her fear grew too strong and she backed away from the door and made her way down the stairs, leaning against the rail lest she collapse. The record player scratched at a low volume, back to Sinatra and that old black magic. There was a soft, flickering light at the bottom of the stairs. The light emanated from white and black candles arranged at the points of a pentagram scrawled in black wet paint on the living room floor. Her naked husband knelt inside the pentagram and beside a pair of bare feet. She could not see the owner of the feet as the couch partially blocked her view. Carling reclined on the couch. Carling wore a black robe; the robe was open, revealing the white curve of her hip and breast. The family patriarch stood, dressed in a black robe with the cowl thrown back. He was flushed and beaming with paternal joy. His left hand rested upon his son's head. Her husband made a labored sawing motion and the feet twitched and danced, slapping against the floorboards. The room blurred in and out of focus and began to slide toward the crimson edge of her vision. She made a small sound and the trio glanced toward the stairs. They seemed surprised to see her.